OUTSTANDING PRAISE FOR
BLOOD ON THE LEAVES

"In the tradition of the best contemporary commercial fiction . . . Stetson paints with broad strokes and bold polemic colors, raising provocative questions while keeping the plot on the move."
—*Kirkus Reviews*

"Razor-sharp dialogue . . . provocative . . . Examines justice, loyalties, and the tinderbox of racial tensions with . . . an unflinching eye toward history . . . Sure to spark debate."
—Tananarive Due, author of
The Living Blood and *The Good House*

"Powerful . . . as haunting as the song from which it takes its title . . . In taut suspense scenes and dramatic courtroom moments, the writing shines. In depth of characters and breadth of theme, this novel resonates long after its final words."
—*Mystery Scene*

"A high-octane legal thriller that puts the justice system on the stand . . . Will keep the reader hanging on until the very end."
—*Black Issues Book Review*

"Distinguished by passion . . . A meditation on love and hate, nonviolence and revenge, evil and justice . . . an anguished, agonizing debate over right or wrong."
—*Washington Post Book World*

more . . .

"Spurs on thought and excitement . . . Stetson looks at anger, frustration, fear and disappointment, self-pride and the self-love that has come full circle . . . since the turbulent and contentious civil rights era."
—*Rolling Out Atlanta*

"A seething novel of race, justice, and revenge that accelerates at a feverish pace . . . This one will stay with you long after the jury verdict is announced. Jeff Stetson is a startlingly original writer: funny, angry, incredibly smart, and able to create three-dimensional characters."
—William Lashner, author of *Hostile Witness* and *Fatal Flaw*

"Excellent . . . electrifying . . . will leave a lasting impression . . . Add this one to your reading list."
—BestsellersWorld.com

"Entertaining . . . exhilarating . . . an exciting crime thriller, a suspenseful courtroom drama and a provocative social commentary that will keep its grip on you until the very last page."
—Gary Hardwick, author of *Supreme Justice* and *Deuce and a Quarter*

"Excellent . . . shows two men, more alike than either will admit, on different sides of a moral divide. And it takes the stand that color (black or white) should never decide justice."
—BookLoons.com

more . . .

"A well-told story of passion and pain, vengeance and justice . . . A shocking yet cathartic journey from the old South to the new."
—Solomon Jones, author of *The Bridge* and *Pipe Dream*

"A great legal thriller . . . one helluva story . . . deals with intense issues and tackles the weighty concerns of ethics and morality . . . [and] the suspense lasts until the book's final word."
—Bookreporter.com

"A novel of cruel decisions. Moral choices have tremendous consequences as justice is relentlessly pursued in this **compelling first novel."**
—Jervey Tervalon, author of *Dead Above Ground* and *Lita*

"Totally engrossing . . . unputdownable. Stetson displays remarkable command of dialogue and character. His courtroom scenes are as accomplished as Scott Turow's, and his pacing rivals that of James Patterson. A thrilling debut!"
—Herb Boyd, editor of *The Harlem Reader* and *Brotherman*

"Highly recommended . . . amazingly assured . . . a very real examination of race relations, both past and present."
—TheRomanceReadersConnection.com

"A remarkably well-crafted debut with a perfect mix of elements. **The reader is hurled ever forward, page after page, on an intense ride."**
—Lolita Files, author of *Getting to the Good Part* and *Scenes from a Sistah*

"Thoroughly enjoyable . . . refreshingly honest . . . food for the mind and the soul."
—Robert Greer, author of *Heat Shock*

BLOOD
ON THE
LEAVES

———

JEFF
STETSON

WARNER BOOKS

NEW YORK   BOSTON

Copyright © 2004 by Elisia-Paul Productions, Inc.
All rights reserved. No part of this book may be reproduced in any form or by any electronic or mechanical means, including information storage and retrieval systems, without permission in writing from the publisher, except by a reviewer who may quote brief passages in a review.

Lyrics from (Inner City Blues) "Make Me Wanna Holler," words and music by Marvin Gaye and James Nyx (1971); "Search Me, Lord," words and music by Thomas A. Dorsey, (1948); "Strange Fruit," words and music by Lewis Allan, (1939); and "Come Sunday," from Black, Brown and Beige, included in the Concert of Sacred Music, words and music by Duke Ellington, (1943).

Lines from Address at March on Washington for Jobs and Freedom, August 28, 1963, "I Have a Dream," speech, by Dr. Martin Luther King, Jr; and *Native Son*, by Richard Wright; originally published by Harper & Brothers, (1940) and "Picture It," Mississippi Department of Economic and Community Development, Division of Tourism, (1991).

Cover design by Mimi Bark
Cover photo of fire by Photodisc/PictureQuest
Cover photo of trees by Creatas/PictureQuest

Warner Books

Time Warner Book Group
1271 Avenue of the Americas, New York, NY 10020
Visit our Web site at www.twbookmark.com

Printed in the United States of America

Originally published in hardcover by Warner Books
First Paperback Printing: August 2005

10 9 8 7 6 5 4 3 2 1

To Addie Mae, Carole, Cynthia, and Denise, as well as all other victims of ignorance and hate: Your blood is either in our veins or on our hands; may God save us if we can't tell the difference.

unconscious by the choir's whirling robes.

BLOOD
ON THE
LEAVES

PROLOGUE

The terror returned. Except this time the color of the flesh to be burned wasn't black. The moonlight guided the stranger as he worked among the shadows of a forest that bore witness to his crime. Soon the night would rescind its protection, leaving him to face the sunrise alone.

He marveled at the awesome power of the past. He'd never felt this alive, which terrified him, for he knew in his heart he'd lost the desire to seek forgiveness and, with it, his capacity to forgive. If that was the price to pay for justice, he'd accept his punishment. And now, at long last, so would the man bound against the fallen tree.

He studied the poorly drawn map of sweat, dirt, and blood intersecting the man's tormented face, then carefully tested the strips of sheet that bound his hands and feet. He poured liquid on the twisted body and could tell from the man's whimpering that it stung. The faded electrical tape over the man's mouth muffled his cries but couldn't conceal the pain in his eyes. In a different time and place that pain would have mattered—but not tonight, not ever again.

He understood that retribution made one simple demand: to travel at its own pace down the path paved by others. He wondered if he was fully prepared for the journey. Then he lit the match, and with a simple flick of his finger, the body erupted into flames. The smell of burning flesh sickened him. He wanted to scream almost as much as he needed to watch. He stepped back to get a better look at the future, and confirmed that the past was indeed powerful. It was never behind, as many wished, but rather always in front, always ahead, a haunting reminder of the relentlessness of memory.

He observed the man stretched out on his back, muscles melting violently into bone. He listened intently to the feeble cursing that escaped the burning hole once protected by human lips. For the first time he pitied white skin. But pity wouldn't save this man, nor would it rescue his companion, who hung lifelessly from a sagging branch just above his head.

He tried to remember the words to "America the Beautiful." He thought back to his childhood, when the rendition sung by Ray Charles had always made him cry. *"America! America! God shed His grace on thee. . . ."*

The flames, brighter now, engulfed the man pleading to become a corpse. And they cast a colorful yellow-orange glow on the grotesquely swaying second man, his neck broken and eyes frozen shut in unfinished prayer. His shredded shirt glistened with blood that had, until tonight, pumped for over six decades through an unrepentant heart. *". . . and crown Thy good with brotherhood . . ."*

The crackling sound of fire replaced the stranger's recollection of the music. He closed his eyes, but the images remained: one burned, one lynched; two condemned to hell—three if he included himself.

"They kill you before you die. . . ." He now knew with absolute certainty what those words meant. His eyes burned, but he refused to shed any tears. There'd be no freedom from the burden of history and no release from the sorrow.

"*. . . from sea to shining sea!*"

CHAPTER
1

THE DEFECTIVELY REPAIRED air conditioner murmured and moaned, harmonizing with Professor Martin Matheson, whose soothing voice hardly needed musical accompaniment. "Andrew Reid was on leave from his second tour in Vietnam when he stopped to have a drink in a local bar with his nineteen-year-old brother."

Dr. Matheson stuck a pushpin through the photo of a black man burned at the stake and attached it to a poster board. Some students let out audible gasps. Others turned away or diverted their eyes to the polished hardwood floor of the former dance hall where Matheson's class had been reassigned to accommodate greater than expected enrollment. Even in this larger space, many undergraduates were forced to stand alongside the mirrored walls. Their reflections made the room appear twice as crowded.

A number of students sat on the floor. Women who'd left their previous classes five minutes early to ensure they'd sit closest to the faculty member nicknamed "Mister Knowledge" and "Doctor Fine" filled front-row seats. They watched Matheson unbutton the top of his Armani linen-and-silk-blend shirt as he gracefully walked past.

"Waitress was white. They smiled at her. She smiled back." He retrieved an eight-by-ten photo of two grinning white men in their mid- to late twenties. He casually pinned it to a second poster board resting against an easel.

"Her husband, Robert Taylor, and her brother, Reginald Hopkins, followed the two young black men out of the bar and at gunpoint drove them to a deserted wooded area." Matheson returned to the first poster board and uncovered a photo of another black man, a thick-knotted noose around his fractured neck. He was hanging from a tree that had once borne less precious fruit.

The professor placed the photo next to the picture of the charred corpse, making it easier for his students to imagine the unimaginable. "They tied Reid to a log and burned him at the stake, but not until they tortured him and forced him to look at the lynched body of his younger brother."

Brandon Hamilton, a second-year graduate student, sat in the back row. He stared at the horrific remains of two black men who, in the words of Matheson, "once shared the same earth as us and perhaps the same dreams." His large right hand gripped the side of the desk, then slowly closed, making a powerful fist. At six feet four, carrying 235 pounds of solid muscle, he'd been the most sought-after athlete in the country. In his freshman year he set collegiate records in three sports and became captain of the football and basketball teams. As a sophomore he was giving serious consideration to turning pro until, by accident or destiny, he signed up for a class taught by Matheson. On the day he handed in his term paper to the professor, he also turned in all his uniforms and forfeited his scholarship. He vowed never again to serve a system content to exploit him as a commodity but never respect him as a man.

"In deliberations that lasted three minutes, a jury of their peers found Taylor and Hopkins not guilty." Matheson was reaching for a stack of photocopies when the oak door creaked open and two white policemen entered. Matheson smiled as he watched Dr. Henry Watkins, assistant vice president of administrative affairs, passively follow the police. The only black man in the university's central administration, Watkins had long ago grown accustomed to following behind quietly.

"It would've taken less time, but the foreman had difficulty filling out the verdict forms. I suppose some people are just naturally inept when it comes to carrying out instructions." Matheson directed this last remark to Watkins, who was meticulously adjusting his glasses.

The first officer waited quietly near the rear entrance, seeming reluctant to interrupt class proceedings any further. The second officer chose to be more conspicuous. He paced the area with his short, stocky arms folded across his police shield. Heavy footsteps beat rhythmically against the shining parquet floor, announcing his impatience.

Matheson, ignoring the officers, picked up the stack of papers, and handed it to Regina Davis, seated in the front, center row. She'd been voted the first black homecoming queen in the university's 168-year history. But to her the only honor that mattered was the privilege of serving as

Matheson's teaching assistant. She'd been chosen from among 112 eager applicants.

Matheson sensed her anxiety and touched her hand. She looked briefly at the policemen before dividing the large stack into smaller sections, placing a pile on each front-row desk for the students to distribute.

The impatient police officer stared at Watkins, which seemed to provide the prodding the timid administrator needed. "Professor Matheson, will you be long?"

"Not as long as justice takes in the great state of Mississippi," Matheson responded politely. "But, as they say, good things come to those who wait." The class erupted in laughter.

"Although they also say, 'Justice delayed is justice . . .'"

"'Denied'!" the students shouted out as they'd done many times before.

Matheson felt immensely proud of them. He'd become a teacher to make a difference, to hold up a mirror before the despised and dispossessed so they'd see just how beautiful they really were. If nothing else, he hoped he'd achieved that goal.

The students reviewed the material. Each page contained a recent photo of Taylor and Hopkins along with their home addresses, phone numbers, and other personal information.

"Remember your history. It can be painful, but it's all we have. I'll see you Friday. Until then . . . good hunting." Matheson nodded at the impatient policeman, who'd finally stopped pacing.

The students gathered their books and quickly filed past the uninvited visitors. Regina, the ever-vigilant witness, returned to her seat and opened her notebook. Brandon marched toward Matheson and stood silently by his side.

Matheson focused his attention on the two officers. "Did you come for these?" He removed the photos of the black victims. "Or those?" He pointed at the photo of the smiling white men, then leaned against the podium.

The policeman dropped his arms to his sides and studied Matheson curiously. "I need to read you your rights."

"That presumes they come from you. They don't." Matheson, displaying absolute conviction in his response, still delivered it with surprising congeniality.

The policeman removed a pair of handcuffs from his belt, clanking together the two sides.

Brandon approached him and stared at his name tag. The officer started to issue a command when Brandon turned toward Regina and announced, "Officer Macon, badge number three-seventeen."

Regina recorded the information, and Brandon directed his attention to the handcuffs. "You're not putting those on him," he warned.

Macon slowly placed his hand on his holster and unsnapped the thin restraining strap. Matheson stepped in front of the anxious officer. "It's all right, Brandon," he spoke softly. "Putting two fists together is always preferable to one."

Matheson held out his hands in a manner that suggested a challenge more than an offer to submit to arrest. He smiled disarmingly at Macon, then voluntarily extended his arms while shifting his attention to Watkins. "Don't look so worried, Dr. Watkins; the publicity will probably drive up enrollment." The professor winked, which obliged Watkins to smile in appreciation.

The annoyed officer placed the handcuffs on Matheson, making them fit as tightly as possible.

Matheson felt the cold steel binding his wrists and

recalled the first time he'd seen his father arrested. Television cameras were supposed to ensure safety but didn't. A deputy sheriff had unwittingly become part of recorded history by twisting the cuffs until they dug deep into his father's skin; a vein was cut, almost severed. The blood gushed onto a camera lens, which led a moment later to a baton striking glass, then flesh, then bone. He'd been five years old and had never seen violence or felt terror or imagined his father helpless. His first impulse had been to overcome the fear and place his small body in harm's way. Instead, he did as he'd been taught. He sang songs of protest and faith and love and watched his father bleed.

"Are you comfortable, Professor?" Macon's partner asked, genuinely concerned.

"Oh, yes, very. But I'm a teacher, so it's my job to make others uncomfortable. The search for truth is often unsettling. If acquiring knowledge were easy, everyone would have it." Regina and Brandon exchanged a smile while Macon remained stoic.

Matheson moved his fists as far apart as the cuffs allowed and examined his hands in front of Watkins. "The chains are more sophisticated now," he stated reflectively.

"So are the crimes," volunteered the quiet officer.

"Not the crimes—the criminals," Matheson corrected.

"You want to know why we're taking you in?"

Matheson looked kindly at Macon's partner, who had asked the question. "I was expecting you to arrive the first week of classes. Have you ever read *Pedagogy of the Oppressed*?" He didn't wait for a response. "There's a myth that the truth shall set you free. It won't, but it'll make you angry as hell. Making people angry by telling them the truth has been considered a crime in virtually every jurisdiction in this country." He looked at Watkins. "I believe it's called sedition."

For all the rhetoric, Matheson's tone remained non-confrontational. He delivered his words dispassionately, with a style that set others at ease.

Regina rose from her seat and joined Brandon. "If he's not released within twenty-four hours, you'd better expect half the university outside his cell."

"I'll keep that in mind, young lady," replied Macon.

"Keep this in mind, too," interjected Brandon. "We won't stop going after the people on Professor Matheson's list, no matter what you do or how many of us you arrest."

"Is that a fact?" Macon said with disdain.

"And here's another," Brandon said, his vehemence escalating. "If he's harmed in any way, the next person we're going to visit is you."

"You threatenin' a police officer, son?" Macon's chest expanded until Matheson's voice relieved the officer's tension.

"My students don't make threats, Officer Macon. As a general rule it's not advantageous to give your adversary any warning."

Macon grabbed Matheson's elbow. "I think it's time for you to go with us."

Regina studied Matheson. "Do you want me to come with you?"

"Just tell my father not to worry," Matheson said calmly. "And let the students know I don't intend on missing any classes, so I expect everyone to complete their assignments on time."

A group of black male students quietly entered the room and stationed themselves on either side of the door.

Macon released Matheson's arm with a trace of apprehension. "There's not gonna be any trouble, is there, Professor Matheson?" He'd been finally forced to use Matheson's name and the entitlement that went with it.

Matheson leaned in close to Macon. "I'd never allow that," he replied gently, carefully emphasizing the word "allow."

Matheson glanced at Regina and signaled his permission for her to leave. She and Brandon walked through the parallel rows of student guards, and Watkins followed seconds later. The loyal entourage remained attentive. The policemen led Matheson out of the room, although from his demeanor the professor appeared to be the person in command.

CHAPTER 2

TODD MILLER MIGHT have been the last native-born white liberal lawyer in Mississippi, perhaps in the whole South. Certainly, he had to be the only good ol' boy over sixty-five who wore a gray braided ponytail, although he preferred to call it silver—and call it was precisely what he did. Like the Lone Ranger summoning his white steed, Miller had been known to command his ponytail with a confident toss of his head, swinging it over his left shoulder and allowing his limp badge of honor to rest inches above his heart.

He once told a jury that his hair was an extension of his mind, and if the mind became "courageous enough to touch the heart, then true justice would be found." By the time the judge admonished the jury to disregard that definition, Miller had already flung the thing over his shoulder and endeared himself to the twelve men and women who would decide his client's fate.

He particularly enjoyed tossing his ponytail during

opening argument, when he'd rather the jurors remember his hair than any promises he hadn't kept. He never used the trick during his closing, when he preferred they recall his eloquence, along with the sincerity of his eyes. Those eyes had been credited with winning every close case, changing color with his passion, and intensity with his choice of shirts. Normally bluish gray, his eyes became solid blue with indignation, green with defiance—and, sometimes, humor—and on rare occasions, when he expended every ounce of energy and needed to draw from his legendary well of oratorical magic, they switched to gold. Jurors had sworn to it. A few even claimed that his eyes had actually displayed a hint of red, which Miller later declared was caused by a fire in his belly.

Actually, that fire hadn't blazed for some time. It had gone out shortly after the Movement was extinguished— the same Movement that had been the driving force of his life, and that had almost cost him his life on more evenings than he could possibly remember. Once he'd believed that the struggle for civil rights represented a battle for the soul of humanity. He'd committed himself to the axiom that if strangers were treated with dignity, neighbors would have no reason to fear each other.

But that platitude had shattered long ago. His neighbors had grown accustomed to living in fear, even though they owned twice as many guns as locks. And the Civil Rights Movement that had once moved a nation no longer moved him. Yet there still were moments when he saw nobility in his work. At such times his words rang with a majesty that inspired the blindfolded lady to balance the tears on her scales while clearing the lump in her throat.

Perhaps that explained why Miller was in the courtroom today instead of a retirement home. Why he was in it yesterday and would be here tomorrow, returning every morning until he found one more case, one more cause, that would make Justice weep in hope of forgiveness and, ultimately, redemption.

"Mr. Miller, do you wish to play the violin before sentencing?" asked Judge Louis "Fritz" Tanner. He gestured toward Miller's client, Darnel Williams, who at nineteen appeared angrier than most black convicts twice his age.

Miller lightly stroked the back of his head. He located his ponytail and glanced to the side, hoping to find inspiration. Instead, he discovered the smiling face of Deputy District Attorney James Reynolds.

Reynolds had entered the practice of law sixteen years ago with aspirations of one day being appointed to the Supreme Court. Somewhere along the line he'd settled for becoming the highest-ranking black prosecutor in the district attorney's office in a city that still flew the Confederate flag in its heart and would wave it proudly at the slightest provocation.

Handsome in a way unlikely to turn heads, and charming without being charismatic, Reynolds dedicated himself to being prepared but never overrehearsed. Jurors didn't always like him, although they implicitly trusted him, which contributed to his 95 percent conviction rate. The primary reason for his stellar record, however, was his natural abhorrence of losing on any level.

Miller took a deep breath and looked respectfully at the judge. By the way Tanner rubbed against the bottom of his chair, Miller knew the judge's hemorrhoids had flared up, a bad sign for any defense attorney.

"Your Honor, while I have great fondness and admiration for you, I——"

Tanner interrupted with a low groan and arched eyebrow. "No one can think more highly of me than myself, Mr. Miller, so if flattery's your goal, it's already been achieved if not surpassed." The judge squirmed a moment, endeavoring to find a spot that promised no pain. "If you have similar views on behalf of your client, share them now or return your retainer."

"My client, Darrell Williams—"

"Darnel, asshole." Miller's young client corrected the record and, at the same time, demonstrated his disgust for the proceedings.

Miller beamed with affection and attempted an explanation with as much sincerity as he could fake. "I have a nephew named Darrell, and in his innocence he reminds me of—"

The judge's gavel struck once. "I'm a patient man, but it's past lunchtime. I believe there's a direct correlation between late lunches and long prison terms. Wanna test my theory?"

Miller placed his hand on Darnel's shoulder and paused for greater effect. "Your Honor, I believe my client can more eloquently address the court's concerns." He took a ceremonial step back and gave Darnel an encouraging nod. Reynolds leaned forward to ensure an unobstructed view.

The judge folded his thick arms across his barrel chest and allowed the wide sleeves of his robe to rest gently on a stomach that benefited greatly from being covered. "Is there something you wish to state for the record before I impose sentencing?"

Darnel glared at the judge the way a mugger stares at his intended victim. "Yeah . . . Fuck you." Darnel reclaimed his seat with a renewed sense of power.

Reynolds wiped at his mouth in an attempt to conceal a smile.

Judge Tanner confronted a sheepish Miller. "Counselor, did your client seek your advice before addressing the court, or was his eloquence spontaneous?"

"I understood him to say 'Your Honor,' Your Honor."

"I hope your legal acumen hasn't diminished as quickly as your hearing." Tanner lifted his gavel. "Three years for possession, six for distribution. Sentences to run concurrently." The gavel came down hard. "Nice meeting you, Darrell."

"Darnel!" the defiant defendant responded in a last-ditch effort to showcase his manhood.

"You'll be a number by tonight." Tanner rose as gracefully as his "condition" permitted, and was proceeding from the bench toward his chambers when he suddenly stopped. "Oh, Attorney Reynolds?"

Reynolds deferentially came to attention, looking up from his paperwork.

"I saw that smile. It'll cost you fifty dollars. Next time I'm insulted, try to appear offended." Tanner waddled away like a wounded duck, with no further effort to conceal the discomfort of his ailment.

The deputies escorted Darnel past his emotionally devastated mother. Miller thought about turning away from the woman before she shared the one luxury he knew the poor would always be permitted to own: a steady flow of tears. Instead, he extended his hand and felt her trembling fingers.

"There are several solid grounds for appeal." He lied very easily when he genuinely liked someone.

She thanked him, then, overcome with grief, buried her face in her hands. He guided her head to his left shoulder, and she sobbed when he held her. In that intimate exchange he tried to remember what it had felt like back when he truly shared the agony and humiliation of the people who'd mortgaged their homes to invest their future in him. He touched the dampened spot over his heart and then said good-bye to the woman whose tears he now carried.

By the time his jacket dried, he'd already maneuvered his way through the most crowded sections of the parking lot and was intercepted by Reynolds.

"Don't you have any white clients?" Reynolds teased.

"I prefer representing the oppressed. It provides me with unlimited business."

The two men crossed the lot together, heading toward Miller's car. "Twenty-five years ago, I represented Darnel's father," Miller confided. "He wanted a career in law enforcement, but as we know, the sheriff's office didn't hire blacks back then. It only arrested them."

"Did you win the lawsuit?"

Miller nodded yes, with no sense of satisfaction. "A week after the verdict they planted drugs in his patrol car, then fired him."

"You're the one who keeps reminding me that justice is blind."

"Did I remember to add deaf and dumb?" Miller reached his vehicle, an ancient British Triumph sports car with a badly torn convertible top. He pried open the driver's door and crawled through the small rectangular crevice, narrowly missing scraping his forehead on a jagged piece of vent window. Noting a patch of ripped leather that hung loosely from the side of his bucket seat, he reattached it with transparent tape. He reached for the stubborn door and tried unsuccessfully to close it.

Undaunted, he raised his head toward the sun and pro-claimed, "Three more payments and it's all mine."

Reynolds applied maximum force against the dented metal frame. "Then you can get a new one." In exaspera-tion he slammed it shut.

Miller cranked down his window as far as it would go, an inch or two more than halfway. He used the partial opening to wax philosophical. "New isn't always desir-able. Take our great city, for example." He vigorously pumped the gas pedal several times. "We spend a fortune on ballet just to be seen as international." He tested the ignition. "Yet somewhere in Europe they're lusting for our Delta blues." The engine sputtered but clung to life.

"Tradition's a glorious thing," mused Reynolds.

"Only if you claim it as your own." The car backfired before finally kicking into full power. Miller's eyes gleamed with delight. He signaled thumbs-up and raced his sports car through a parking lot full of police heading for traffic court.

Reynolds hadn't yet taken a step when, in the distance, he heard his name called by a voice so unmistakable, his initial impulse was to reach for his wallet and wait for the collection plate to arrive. Legend had it the Reverend Samuel Matheson's whisper could calm children while frightening the wicked. But the Reverend Matheson wasn't whispering today; he was at full throttle. He made it easy to understand why God chose the human voice as His favorite instrument.

Reynolds turned to greet his pastor.

"James . . ." The preacher's voice remained unshak-able. "I need you to render a great service."

Reynolds felt his heart race and tried to conceal his alarm. The Reverend Samuel Matheson had become a southern institution. Every civil rights and community leader in the surrounding five states had at one time or another sought his advice or guidance. Reynolds couldn't believe the man who had ordered Martin Luther King Jr. to "keep walking forward and don't show any trace of fear" might actually require a mere mortal's help.

"Of course, Reverend, anything I can do."

Pastor Matheson closed his eyes and then, with the hand that had grown accustomed to carrying the full weight of the Scriptures, touched Reynolds on the shoulder. In a tone barely audible he asked, "Would you please find out what they've done to my son?"

CHAPTER
3

REYNOLDS ABRUPTLY ENTERED Melvin Vanzant's office and discovered a meeting in progress that should have included him. "Why didn't you tell me about Matheson?" he blurted out angrily.

Vanzant received a sympathetic sigh from his chief assistant, Woody Winslow, a lifelong bureaucrat who was eminently capable in matters of the law but perpetually handicapped by a limited vocabulary. Reynolds believed there existed no greater curse than having so many ideas and so few ways to express them; it rendered a man incomprehensible to all but himself.

"I was under the impression you worked for me, not the other way around," said Vanzant without bothering to look at Reynolds.

"What's he charged with?" Reynolds asked.

"Your information's as bad as your attitude. I extended an invitation for a friendly visit, and he graciously accepted."

"That's not what his father said."

"The reverend may represent God, but neither speaks for my office." Vanzant passed a file to Lauren Sinclair, who, when she wasn't prosecuting a case and causing hardened felons to tremble, appeared as mild as an elementary school teacher. If there'd been any justice in government, her thirty years of dedicated service would have made her Vanzant's boss just long enough to fire him.

"Is he being charged with anything?" Reynolds looked at Sinclair for a clue.

"If arrogance was a crime he'd be facing twenty-five to life," said Vanzant. He leaned back in his chair and looked accusingly at Reynolds. "But then, he'd have a lot of company in his cell, wouldn't he?"

Reynolds took a breath and silently counted to five. "Why was he taken away in cuffs?"

"I've already asked the chief to write up a letter of reprimand to cover everyone's ass. Last thing we need is a public relations problem with either the college or the community." Vanzant scratched the inside of his left thigh. "If you're so anxious to find out what's going on, just sit down and listen. I realize it'll be a new experience, but who knows? You may learn enough to challenge me for real one day." Vanzant had never forgiven Reynolds for running against him in the last election. That experience intensified his paranoia about losing his job and caused him to deny career advancement opportunities to his most talented staff members.

Reynolds sat at the small round conference table and poured himself a glass of water. He'd barely tasted it when Sinclair began her report.

"Two bodies were discovered in Greenville last night. Coroner identified them this morning as Robert Taylor, tied to a tree trunk and set on fire, and Reginald Hopkins, lynched just a few feet away. Both white, late fifties, give or take."

Reynolds surveyed the room. Its large L shape looked impressive but utilized space inefficiently and impeded communication, making it as dysfunctional as the man who occupied it. The arrangement of the windows provided minimal ventilation and admitted very little light from the outside—an apt metaphor for what was often lacking at work sessions conducted by Vanzant.

"What else do we know about them?" Reynolds asked, wondering how the answer might implicate Matheson.

Sinclair reviewed the file. "Arrested thirty years ago for allegedly burning to death a black soldier while they were lynching the man's brother. Jury found them not guilty, despite the defendants' bragging about the murders to a barroom full of patrons."

"There *is* a God. He's Negro and He's definitely pissed," said Winslow.

Reynolds decided to filter his response through a veil of sarcasm that Winslow probably would have difficulty penetrating. "Haven't you heard the news, Woody? We don't use the term 'Negro' anymore."

Winslow removed a carrot stick from a plastic sandwich bag and took a bite. He ran eight miles each day and snacked on raw carrots, celery sticks, apples—anything loud. Reynolds theorized that Winslow's eating habits had less to do with health and more to do with a desire to be noticed.

Sinclair handed Reynolds some paperwork from the folder, along with two photos of the victims. He'd just started reviewing the material when Vanzant reasserted control of the meeting.

"The professor's compiled an extensive set of biographies of unpunished civil rights 'war criminals.' That's his term, not mine." Vanzant placed an unlit pipe in his mouth. Cigars were actually his oral stimulant of choice. The stench from his habit permeated every piece of furniture and contaminated the floor-to-ceiling drapes. Vanzant lit the pipe, took a long puff, and turned on a tiny fan, which tried mightily to circulate the foul air more evenly.

"Each week he selects two new names from the list and shares them with his students along with their photos, home addresses, places of employment, phone and license plate numbers, church and civic memberships, favorite restaurants, and preferred method of committing murder. The reverend's son is very thorough. He supplies everything except the actual weapons he wants used."

Vanzant took a break from his pipe to spray decongestant up his right nostril. "By the time the deputies interrupted his schedule, he'd already taught several classes. Needless to say, we've got a couple of bodies in the morgue that were alive and well until they became the subject of one of his more popular and, undoubtedly, provocative lectures."

The information stunned Reynolds, but he didn't show it. "The fact that he teaches a controversial class doesn't mean he knows anything about the two murders." Reynolds's tautologically correct statement did little to ease his growing discomfort.

Vanzant inhaled deeply and tested his nasal passage. He pulled a second file from the pile on the table and shoved it in front of Reynolds. "If he can't help us with the deceased, perhaps he can shed some light on the whereabouts of the living."

Reynolds opened the new file and pulled out photos of two more white men. He laid the pictures side by side, then turned them so they faced Sinclair. "I'm afraid to ask this, but were these two gentlemen assigned as homework?"

"Required reading on the first day of class," she answered, then pointed to the photo on her left. "That one's Theo Crockett, accused in nineteen sixty-two of shooting Joseph Dean, a voter registration volunteer and single father of three, then dumping the body in the bayou. The bald, short guy with the pleasant smile and protruding midriff is former Deputy Sheriff Travis Mitchell, suspected of beating to death a fifteen-year-old, hacking the corpse to pieces, and concealing the remains in the marsh. They were both acquitted of all charges."

Reynolds studied the pictures without exhibiting a visible expression, a skill that had served him well throughout his career.

Winslow filled in the relevant information. "Mitchell's wife says he's been missing for two weeks, which coincides with the beginning of Matheson's course. The police haven't been able to locate Crockett's family." He took another bite of his carrot.

Reynolds stared at the wall behind Vanzant. Suddenly, the room felt claustrophobic. "Was Matheson cooperative?" he asked.

"Oh, yeah," said Vanzant. "He's been a marvelous help, just like the good church *boy* he is."

Something about the way Vanzant said "boy" pierced Reynolds and forced his eyelids to shut ever so briefly. Sinclair offered an apologetic glance, which he appreciated, but the damage was done.

It no longer mattered to Reynolds how the word "boy"

was delivered—it always had the same debilitating effect. It could be disguised as a smile, a look, a pat on the back, a demand, or it could be cloaked inside a phrase that sounded like homage. Whatever its permutations, it forced Reynolds to restrain himself from reacting in a way detrimental to his continued employment.

He'd never grown accustomed to paying the black tax: the penalty, imposed on him by the color of his skin, that made it impossible to be certain of someone's intent. If a stranger on the elevator ignored his greeting, he was forced to decide whether it was rudeness or racism. If at a meeting he made a suggestion to which no one responded, he wondered if he hadn't been heard or if no one wanted to acknowledge his existence. If someone told him with sincere amazement that he was very bright and articulate, he considered whether to accept it as a compliment or feel insulted that his intelligence generated such astonishment.

When he had started at the DA's office, he contended with a large number of white people who made him extremely uneasy by trying terribly hard to make him comfortable. He never realized basketball was so popular until everyone felt the need to discuss it with him. He suddenly became a connoisseur of soul food; he regularly was asked for recommendations when the staff ordered barbecue from the takeout menu. The thing that bothered him most, though, was when his advice was sought about the things that bothered him most.

He was expected to serve as official barometer for the thoughts, feelings, and behavior of all black people; to explain their hopes, aspirations, fears, achievements, shortcomings, and, most of all, what they really wanted. He was their ambassador for goodwill and good times, attending cocktail parties on their behalf and assuring white folks they were both forgiven for past indiscretions and loved for their present benevolence.

His position showcased him as the model for success; proof positive the system worked; a prime illustration of what could be achieved through hard work, fair play, and civility. He also functioned as an ongoing reminder to less fortunate blacks of their own personal inadequacies in failing to climb the ladder. After all, wasn't this ladder readily accessible to all those of fine character and high moral upbringing? To demonstrate it, the vast powers of the state were available and conveniently at his disposal to prosecute those who jeopardized his exemplary existence.

He played the role of gatekeeper, safeguarding those in power who needed a guarantee that the enemy had been infiltrated and thereby emasculated. In truth, he was little more than a boiler valve that could be used to ease pressure and prevent an explosion. Rather than serve as a catalyst for change, his dissenting voice validated the virtue and fair-mindedness of the system that now paid his salary.

Matheson promised to be a major threat to that system, a greater danger than all the inner-city gangbangers and hard-core gangsters who passed through life's revolving door as convict or parolee but were permanently unable to win entrance to the place where opportunity truly existed. Vanzant used the term "boy" to describe and define Matheson in an effort to minimize him. It was his method of expressing anger that someone given the keys to the kingdom had reverted to the streets, perhaps even preferred them to the carpeted suites provided to those who relinquished their rage, no matter how justified.

Reynolds believed all this as deeply as he'd ever believed anything. Yet he knew the people who sat around the table were incapable of accurately measuring how he felt about Matheson, because they'd never truly comprehended how he felt about *them*. Although, to be fair, he'd devised a virtual labyrinth of escape routes and secret passageways that saved him on countless occasions from the moral obligation ever to tell them.

"Is Matheson still being detained?" Reynolds asked.

"He was escorted home more than an hour ago," said Vanzant. "I'd hoped a casual visit might convince the professor to change the subject of his research before these folders got any thicker." Vanzant puffed meditatively on his pipe. "You don't agree with what he's doing, do you?"

Reynolds knew this question was calculated to test his allegiance, not to the law but to the cause. His answer would ultimately have to prove they had no reason to doubt his loyalty, because, after all, he was one of them.

"As a matter of fact, I don't. And—this might surprise you—I'm not even sure I like him." So far, Reynolds's response was satisfactory, even commendable. "He's still got the right to speak the truth—no matter how uncomfortable it makes us." He'd given his boss the gun but, for the moment, withheld the ammunition.

"The truth?" said Vanzant, scowling. "You wanna go tell the families of those butchered homicide victims exactly what your version of the truth is?"

"Matheson didn't invent the list. He just compiled it." Reynolds had found his way onto the slippery slope and couldn't stop himself from taking the next huge leap. "You can't blame him for wanting the same thing we're all sworn to uphold—real justice, regardless of color or creed or . . . You know the rest." He studied his colleagues but knew the traitorous damage had been done.

"Well, I guess that tells us whose side you're on," summarized Vanzant.

"That's unfair, Melvin," said Sinclair.

Reynolds rose to leave.

"The meeting's not over," pointed out Vanzant.

"I wasn't invited, so technically I'm not here," replied Reynolds, who'd reached the door.

"You got something better to do?" queried Vanzant.

"I'm gonna make sure Professor Matheson wasn't detained against his will." Reynolds left without closing the door.

Vanzant cleaned out his pipe. "Some folks would feel more at home practicing criminal defense," he remarked.

CHAPTER
4

REYNOLDS PLAYED NO role in facilitating Matheson's release. In the eyes of the church, that didn't matter. A request had been made, a prayer answered, and now someone had to share credit with the Almighty.

Reynolds decided to go to church without his family. He'd rather they not participate in a celebration he neither wanted nor fully deserved. That didn't prevent the congregation from offering their foot-stomping, hand-clapping, heart-thumping congratulations. A Baptist church didn't need much of an excuse to praise God, even less to bless his servants.

The church welcomed just about any opportunity to sing and dance for the Lord. But when the pastor's son circumvented imprisonment—a miracle due partly to divine intervention and partly to a courageous black deputy DA—well, then, there was little left to do but shout hallelujah while striving your best to avoid getting slapped unconscious by the choir's whirling robes.

As James Reynolds, the hero of the hour, sat two pews behind Professor Matheson, the organist shamelessly engaged in showcasing his talent. He received a signal from the Reverend Matheson that Jesus wasn't going to be impressed any further, so it might be best to stop now and remain in His good grace. The choir, not to be outdone, continued their harmony a cappella, repeatedly singing the verse *"I Just Wanna Praise Him . . ."* The Reverend Matheson didn't mind; in fact, he actively encouraged them with a rhythmic nodding of his head and a syncopated gesture of his left shoulder in coordination with his right leg. He even lifted his arms straight into the sanctified air—a sure sign the spirit had entered the building and planned on staying.

Professor Matheson turned and acknowledged Reynolds, but the deputy DA quickly shifted his attention to a large stained-glass window containing images of angels reaching for the sky. He studied the multicolored panes, hoping to find an escape hatch somewhere between the white clouds above and the red windowsill below.

The Reverend Matheson assumed the conductor's responsibility and led the choir to a rousing finale, alternately shifting focus from Jesus to Reynolds and back again. The song hadn't finished reverberating when his booming voice called the congregation to order. "There's a special feeling in this church today!" He elicited murmurs of agreement.

"We enjoy a newfound sense of power and strength!" Hands waved and eyes closed in search of a deeper message.

"We sing because we're happy!" He had them now.

"We sing because we're free!" Shouts of "Yes, Lord"

and "Speak the truth!" drew him to the front of the pulpit and caused him to abandon the electronic amplification.

"His eyes are on the sparrow, and I know He watches me!" Bodies were spiritually lifted from their pews. Hands came together in sustained applause. Laughter echoed throughout the sacred walls. Men and women stripped away their masks, revealing themselves to be children of God.

To Reynolds, the Reverend Matheson was living proof there was no greater theater than the church, no finer actor than the one who auditioned every Sunday before the Creator of all things. The Reverend Matheson extended his right arm toward Reynolds as if commanding the Red Sea to part and exalted his audience to rise. "I'd like to thank Brother James Reynolds." The congregation shouted their unbridled support.

"Used to be a time when people were taken from their homes in the middle of night, brought to a jail cell never to be seen alive again. But no more!"

Reynolds wanted to disappear but couldn't help being captivated by the younger Matheson's curious smile.

"Now we not only have pressure on the outside, but we also have pressure from the inside. Next election, I say we eliminate that word *deputy* from Brother Reynolds's title and just go ahead and make him district attorney!"

The congregation roared approval. Reynolds reluctantly rose and accepted their adulation. He sat back down and graciously smiled throughout the next half hour of praise and commendation. He listened to every other word, then every other sentence. After fifteen minutes, he filtered only bits and pieces of the pastor's speech, just enough to nod at the appropriate places. He nodded agreement at "the importance of character," again at "courage," and twice more at "the power of faith." Mercifully, the sermon ended before he sustained permanent neck damage.

At the rear of the church Reynolds continued to accept expressions of heartfelt gratitude from members of the congregation, all of whom promised to vote for him the next time. He thought he'd shaken his last hand and endured his final backslap when he felt the presence of his pastor.

The Reverend Matheson had taken off his robes but still walked with the air of royalty. "I meant what I said in there. You can count on me to support your candidacy next year. If we'd put together a better coalition the last election, we wouldn't be having this conversation."

"I appreciate that, Reverend, but I didn't deserve any special recognition today. The police just wanted to talk with Martin. He'd already been released before I got involved."

The two men approached the entryway and stood near the huge mahogany doors lavishly decorated with religiously inspired hand-carvings.

"Forty years as an activist has taught me to take victories wherever you find them." The pastor touched Reynolds on the shoulder in a secret pact. "If none exists, you better make up one. Just be damn sure it's useful and will attract a lot of attention."

Reynolds respected this man who'd never cashed in his moral authority by pimping for the camera. The Reverend Matheson fought for causes that stood no chance of being covered by the media or supported by the powers that be. He did so based solely on the principle that it was the right thing to do. His appreciation, even when it wasn't deserved, meant a great deal.

"James, I'm grateful to you. I know you and my son may not always see eye to eye on certain matters."

Before Reynolds could downplay any difficulties, real or perceived, the pastor motioned toward his son. "There he is now. I'm sure he'd like to thank you himself."

"That's not necessa—" Reynolds couldn't avoid this gracefully. Matheson joined them just as his father found a convenient reason to leave.

"I'll go tend to the new garden we're planting out back. I'd planned to have a little patch of cotton for old times' sake, but I'd forgotten how ugly a plant that was." He placed his arm around his son's shoulder. "Martin, I think you and James ought to share a moment of prayer—together." The Reverend Matheson descended the church steps, leaving the two men alone.

Reynolds twiddled his jacket and tried to do something useful with his hands.

"I hope you didn't ruin your standing in the DA's office on my account," said Matheson.

Reynolds squelched the urge to slap the smirk off the professor's face. "Your father asked me to help. It was the least I could do."

"My father does have a way of getting the most out of his congregation."

"I hope our fine police department treated you with the respect you deserved," replied Reynolds. "If you don't mind my asking, what did they want from you?"

"They wanted to know about my students. If I thought any might be capable of violence. I think what they really wanted was for me to cancel the course."

"Given the circumstances, that might not be a bad idea."

"*Bad* or *good* are ambiguous concepts in the secular world—not unlike *villain* or *hero*. It all depends on who pays the historians." The two men proceeded down the steps into the sunlight.

"This thing you're doing at the college . . ."

"By 'thing' I take it you mean *education*?" Matheson walked directly alongside Reynolds. They reached the bottom of the stairs. Reynolds searched for solid ground.

"Two men on your list are dead and two others are missing. How long are you going to keep this up?"

"Until justice rolls down like waters, and righteousness like a mighty stream." Matheson dropped the sarcasm, but it didn't fall too far. "I don't normally quote Dr. King or the Scriptures, but I've always liked that passage. It has a refreshing ring to it."

Reynolds felt a surge of animosity, but he kept it in check. "Your course may have contributed to murder. Doesn't that affect you?"

"Quite deeply. A teacher never knows how much he's inspired his students, or the positive difference he might've made in their lives. Changing people for the better is truly one of the more profoundly rewarding aspects of the profession."

"Even if you've inspired one of your students to become a murderer?" Reynolds was looking to coax from Matheson some acknowledgment of regret, no matter how grudging.

"I don't believe any of them are involved, but if I'm wrong, it might qualify for extra credit."

Reynolds was contemplating Matheson's apparent moral indifference when the professor suddenly changed his manner and tone.

"I'm sorry; I didn't mean to sound so cavalier." Matheson lightly touched his lower lip. "It's been a rather disturbing week, and I guess my defense mechanisms have kicked in." He cleared his throat. "Look, I'm sure you want to get back to your family, so thanks again for coming to my defense with your boss. If I can ever vouch for you, please let me know."

Before any trained reflex could force Reynolds to extend his hand, Matheson walked away. He'd completed a few strides when he suddenly turned back, allowing the sun to shine directly over his shoulders. It made him look taller than his impressive six-foot-two frame.

"Oh, James?" he said with remarkable warmth and sincerity. "Do give my love to Cheryl. I'm disappointed she wasn't here to share our celebration." He left with a smile too charming to be spontaneous.

CHAPTER
5

A HALF-CRAZED BLACK *man stumbled to the marsh, his face made numb from the slashing attacks of wild brush and thick branches. He flayed his arms at the darkness and searched for the five-year-old boy, who could no longer distinguish the night sounds attacking his ears. The confusion caused the child to hear more than one voice. He thought about pleading with the man to let him live, but what if the thing chasing him was a ghost who wouldn't listen to reason? The boy saw a cross, bright, dangling from the heavens. Surely this was a sign of deliverance. If he could pray before it, his life would be spared. The man's breathing grew louder than usual. His fingers were longer and covered in more blood, appearing to have a life of their own. If only those fingers could speak, history might be revealed. Instead, they silently grabbed the child, who released a scream, ensuring innocence would be forevermore lost.*

*　　　*　　　*

Reynolds awoke from the nightmare that had never before been so vivid. The room felt smaller and dangerous, every object a potential weapon. He sat up in the bed, wanting to know why the terrifying image invaded his thoughts again.

His mother used to blame it on the chocolate he ate. "Shouldn't eat candy before you go to bed," she'd warn. He'd stopped eating sweets for a whole year. He lost the desire for chocolate long before he relinquished the vision of bloody fingers and a sparkling cross.

The clock's red digital numbers flickered *3:15,* casting a mellow glow on the small wedding picture. He needed assurance of his safety and found it in the warmth of his wife's body. For seventeen years she'd provided him a permanent refuge, a place to escape the evil spirits that would have overtaken him by now if not for her protection.

He watched her breathe, touched her satin gown, and gently slid it down a few precious inches, exposing her shoulder then part of her breast. The sight of her bare skin used to drive him mad. Now it maintained his sanity. That was how he'd defined love: an anchor that kept you a proper distance from danger yet still provided the freedom to soar.

This anchor held him in place long enough to acquire a home, a son and daughter, a parakeet that chirped too much, a canary that sang too little, and a dog that barked at the wrong time—in other words, heaven. But the past threatened to ruin his happy world. He couldn't be completely certain if it was his past or someone else's. His grandfather used to say, "Once you sleep with ugly, there's no tellin' when or where it will show up in the genes. But you can bet your now-shared inheritance that

sooner or later it will arrive and speak your name."
Whatever the cause of the nightmare, it called out to him.
It would continue until he gave the response that would
send it away once and for all.

Somehow he managed to leave the security of his
wife's bedside and found himself rummaging through the
kitchen cabinet to locate the one bottle of bourbon he
vowed never to throw away. It represented his private
test, his poison elixir. He kept it out of sight but always
within reach. It served to challenge his internal fortitude
as well as the promise he'd made to himself. He would
never become his father and find courage at the bottom of
a bottle.

He unscrewed the top and poured some liquor into a
paper cup. He swirled it around and searched for any
residue that might cling to the side of the container, providing him with an alcohol-etched road map or sorcerer's
vision of the future. Unlike the tossing of chicken bones
or the reading of palms, this ancestral potion left behind
no clues. He ceased the experiment and creased the cup,
returning the useless liquid to its genie's prison. It would
have to wait for the time when its power could be called
upon by more accommodating, if not desperate, hands.

He walked quietly down the hallway, past two walls
filled with family pictures arranged and maintained by
his wife. He'd never believed in such sentimental displays, choosing instead to keep his treasures and important memories in his heart, where he'd visit without
notice or fear of interruption. He cracked open the door
of his daughter's bedroom and peeked inside, finding
Angela sound asleep, protected by her favorite dolls.
They were relaxing on a quilt blanket, which always
managed to stay in place no matter how restless her sleep.

At eleven going on thirty-four, she'd break some man's heart one day, he knew, because, as her mother constantly reminded her, she'd broken everything else.

He closed the door and took a few steps to Christopher's room. He walked immediately to the bed and picked up the blanket that had fallen to the floor. He untwisted his son's legs, which, as usual, had managed to become entwined in the sheets. He carefully straightened his child's left arm, half of which appeared mangled behind the headboard, then freed the other half, buried underneath the pillow. This was accomplished without either waking up the nine-year-old or dislocating the boy's shoulder.

He neatly placed the top sheet over his son, then followed with the blanket, which he folded back halfway. He crossed to the window and adjusted the drapes, allowing air and moonlight into the room. By the time he turned around, his son had once again knocked the blanket onto the floor. Reynolds left it there, believing some idiosyncrasies should be respected.

He'd tried to convince his wife of that notion to no avail. She also obstinately disagreed with him regarding theories of discipline; she believed in it, while he didn't. She subscribed to the primitive adage that saying no once in a while produced healthier children. Reynolds believed in giving them everything they wanted, whenever they wanted it. He saw no reason to deny their requests. They'd have plenty of occasions to be disappointed when they were adults.

It remained one of the few things they fought about. She called him a "pushover." He claimed she exercised control for the sake of exercising control. She felt moderation was good. He argued excess was better. She wanted to hold back. He sought to give his children what he never had: a father unafraid to say yes.

He kissed Christopher on the cheek and left wishing his son better dreams than the one that forced him to walk the corridors of his home at four A.M., chasing away ghosts. His mission took him to the back porch, where he walked past the chairs with the soft round cushions and sat on the wooden steps. There was something reassuring about resting on a surface that offered the option of moving up or down.

This was his absolutely favorite space in the house, maybe in the world. A porch epitomized the midpoint between home and everything else—the place where one step in either direction took you closer or farther away from the people you most loved. He'd made a pledge with each member of his family that no one ever violated: Never, under any circumstances, were arguments permissible on this patch of neutral territory. Conflicts could be resolved or continued inside the house or outside, near some mutually agreed-upon area of the yard. The porch, though, stayed off limits to any hostility. This part of their home they designated "the womb." You could enter or exit with impunity. And Reynolds made an interesting discovery: Once you created a free zone devoid of disagreement, differences didn't last very long anywhere else.

He listened to the sounds just beyond the darkness and inhaled the night air. The mingled scents of freshly mowed grass, bittersweet lilac, and vine-ripened tomatoes soothed him. He had once thought of himself as a city boy who would buy his vegetables wrapped in cellophane, from an all-night supermarket that served cappuccino and fresh croissants. Then he put his hands into the earth and gave birth to a garden. Shortly thereafter, he quit purchasing his drinks from an imported machine in exchange for watching his children compete for the right to make him hot cocoa. Well, usually hot, sometimes boiling, occasionally thick—but it always, always caused him to smile. Six heaping tablespoons of anything would do that, especially when the main ingredient was love.

He watched the moon disappear behind a cloud just as the porch light came on. "You usually do this when the jury's out." Cheryl had a comforting voice, but it didn't eliminate his need to be held. She took a seat next to him and stroked his arm.

He smiled. "Maybe I'm waiting for you to reach a verdict on Matheson."

"I don't see anything wrong in what's he doing," she said. "I think he should teach the course. It's the only way this place will ever heal."

"Murder's a strange method of curing a disease," he said.

"It's not his fault if some nutcase took the information and went off the deep end. It's like blaming violence on television."

"You blame violence on television all the time."

"We aren't having that discussion now, so I'm not obligated to be consistent." She avoided his look of disbelief.

"How much do you know about him?"

"What everybody else knows. He's handsome. Intelligent. Passionate. Successful. Did I say handsome?" she teased.

"He sent his regards."

"Really?" she said with interest.

"Actually, it was his love."

"How considerate." Her voice sounded overly pleased.

"Now I know why I've never liked him." He looked away from her and sulked.

She put her arm around his waist. "You don't get along because he's too much like you."

"I prosecute people who break the law. He encourages folks to commit murder."

"He couldn't possibly want that. His father's preached against violence his entire life."

"His father's not teaching the course." He studied her for a moment, then searched for the moon.

"Can he get into trouble for what he's doing?" she asked.

"Not as much as the people on his list." He hoped the moon wouldn't fade quite yet.

She lightly placed her hand on his knee. "What are you going to do?"

"He agreed to supply us with a complete list of the names he's going to reveal in the remainder of the course. We'll notify the people on it along with the local authorities."

"You don't think he's personally involved, do you? With the murders, I mean."

"Not even Vanzant thinks that. But Matheson's motivated *somebody* to take justice into their own hands." He watched the moon peek through one cloud, then hide behind another.

"You called it 'justice.'" She leaned against him and closed her eyes. "You may not be as different from Martin as you think."

CHAPTER
6

SHERMAN BANKS HAD sat in the same spot, under the same tree, in between the same bushes, every Tuesday and Friday since hunting season began. But after experiencing a series of intuitions that made the toes on both feet tingle then curl, he'd become absolutely convinced that this night his patience would be rewarded. When he returned home this evening, he'd celebrate his sixty-third year by eating a devil's-food birthday cake frosted with mocha icing, smoking a hand-rolled cigar with tobacco meticulously soaked in brandy and black licorice, and cooking fresh venison acquired through his unyielding belief in the power of duplicity.

He lifted his rifle with the same respect he'd give the Holy Grail filled with the blood of his Lord and Savior. He'd never been a deeply religious man, but he prayed on a few special occasions: when he gambled, or hunted, or needed money to buy a young girl's affection during those fortunate times when his wife trusted him enough to visit overnight at her sister's.

He peered down the long barrel of his weapon and felt his manhood stiffen. He gently maneuvered the scope against his eye socket with the precision of a surgeon. He carefully focused on the six-point buck in his crosshairs. Damn, what a beautiful animal, he thought, then decided out of respect to wait until it finished drinking from the stream.

Sherman had been baptized in that water. He caught his first trout there before he could spell *fish,* not that he'd necessarily won any spelling contests in the years to follow. He dropped out of school halfway through the sixth grade. That made him two years more educated than his daddy, the wisest man he'd ever known. He believed in education, just didn't see the need for it to take place in a single classroom over such an extended period of time.

His trigger finger shook mildly, a sign that age had affected his nerves. The sweat from his forehead dripped onto the stock of the rifle, near the spot where he'd carved his son's initials. He'd placed them there on the day the child was born, just below the date of the first deer he'd ever killed. His wife objected to the ritual, but he dismissed her with the question: "What does a woman know about the things that make a man proud?"

The deer quenched its thirst. Its head rose slowly until its face perfectly positioned itself within the center of the glass ring that would first magnify then obliterate its life. If the lens had belonged to a camera rather than a rifle scope, the shot about to be taken would preserve genuine beauty rather than destroy it. But Sherman wasn't a photographer in search of a memory to frame. He took pride in being a hunter and needed an event to brag about.

He'd exaggerate the deer's size and its weight and the angle of the shot. Most important, in the version he'd retell over drinks and a friendly card game, he'd swear the animal had galloped at full speed just before he cut it down, his expert marksmanship surmounting near-impossible odds. Only he and the deer would know the truth: that in an otherwise tranquil night, it had posed innocently for its own destruction.

The gunshot was louder than Sherman's rapidly beating heart. Louder than the deer's sickening thump or the noise of its hind legs kicking and thrashing in the dirt to no avail. Louder than the escaping flight of terrified birds. And louder than the footsteps that followed closely behind.

Sherman heard nothing as he arose from his hiding place and licked his lower lip. There'd never be a feeling greater than this: He'd killed again, taken yet another life. On a battlefield this made him a hero; out here in the wilderness, it made him a god. He stepped forward and allowed himself the satisfaction of a smile—but it quickly turned to a grimace when a strand of barbed wire sliced into his neck. Unable to breathe, he dropped his rifle and grasped furiously at the gloved hands that worked to tighten the metal noose. As his throat leaked thick blood, he struggled to catch a glimpse of the stranger but saw only the fallen deer, twitching horribly near the water's edge.

He thought of his baptism and how he'd been afraid he might drown. He thought of his youth and how it had deserted him without warning. He thought of the birthday cake and how he'd miss the celebration; the cigar and how it would remain unlit; the deer and how he'd never taste the fruit of his labor. He thought of the Scriptures and how you must reap what you sow. And then, as he'd done on other hunts, he thought of the black boy he'd choked to death on a night not unlike this one. How, he marveled, after all these years, had that boy managed to return from the grave to avenge his murder?

Sherman fought in vain to see the face he believed he'd buried in the abyss. He'd confront his attacker if it was the last thing he did. He fell to his knees and violently threw back his head, knowing full well the action would further expose his neck. This was his only hope of discovering the truth.

He looked at the sky overhead, dark and uninviting. He observed the trees standing in line, their branches reaching out anxiously, seemingly awaiting the chance to strangle him, too. He thrust his arms upward and searched for the face that would have ended the torment and solved the mystery. He managed to clutch it between his hands and, with his final bit of strength, forced the face inches from his own, as it had been on so many drunken, haunted nights before. He recognized the black skin and thought the eyes appeared familiar: unrepentant, unforgiving, but this time, unharmed. Without the blood and terror he'd vividly remembered, it was impossible to identify this face as that of the boy he'd condemned to death.

In the distance he saw the deer, now motionless, no longer suffering. The animal's death made him think once again about the black boy's quiet plea to live. He tried to envision what the boy might have become if fate hadn't intervened. Foolishly he searched his memory in an effort to recall the boy's name, then remembered he never knew it. He slumped to the ground. As death overtook Sherman's body, he realized too late that in his quest to discover who—or what—was exacting vengeance, he'd forgotten to pray.

The gloved hands relaxed their grip, and the coiled wire unraveled, leaving behind a ghastly red necklace deeply engraved around Sherman's swollen pink neck. His lifeless eyes remained open but would never see this or any future sunrise. Nor would he hear the twigs that crackled underneath the feet of the retreating stranger, who may not have been a ghost but had left one behind.

Thirsty, the stranger walked toward the stream and watched the moonlight distort his image shimmering across the water's surface. He took a drink and created a series of ever-expanding ripples, which allowed him to reevaluate his reflection. No. It wasn't the light that had distorted him but the journey he'd chosen—a journey where he hoped both saints and sinners would pass each other, judging not lest they be judged.

CHAPTER 7

V ANZANT ENGAGED IN one of his famous tirades, except this time Reynolds detected something different in his voice. Usually, his boss would sit in his large taxpayer-financed Brazilian leather chair with the rosewood frame and stale cigar smell and simply flail his arms. Everyone in the office had gotten used to his displays of outrage—usually ignited by a desire to blame others for his miscalculations. The more he knew he was wrong, the louder he yelled; the more pronounced his gyrations, the more certain he was that his colleagues knew it as well.

But this time, his unsteady voice and sweeping gestures exposed something much greater than the desire to conceal fault or redirect blame. His agitation couldn't be mistaken for anger. This wasn't indignation rising to the surface—far from it. *Fear* gripped Vanzant. His level of trepidation couldn't be camouflaged by any amount of profanity.

"The son of a bitch published the entire fuckin' list in

the state's largest black newspaper!" Vanzant waved the newspaper in front of Reynolds. "Why doesn't he just take out an ad and offer a bounty on every white man over the age of fifty?"

Reynolds suppressed his desire to smile.

Vanzant marched to the window and shoved it open. "Lauren, I want you to research recent case law. See if we can pursue an indictment against the paper."

"I already checked," Sinclair replied. "They're just reporting what Matheson's teaching and relying on public records to substantiate his claims."

"What about the university?" Vanzant asked. "Can't we maintain they're using public funds to incite violence?"

"The university protects academic freedom. The Constitution safeguards freedom of the press." She waited for the explosion.

"Freedom, my ass!" he snorted. "This is a death warrant! If he's not directly inciting violent reprisal, he's encouraging it."

"He's referring to the men on his list as 'unpunished alleged murderers and terrorists.'" Sinclair's voice softened. "That insulates him from civil lawsuits and, for the moment, criminal liability."

Vanzant tossed the paper on his desk and knocked over a framed picture of his wife and two daughters. The glass shattered onto the Oriental carpet. "I want an investigation of each and every student taking Matheson's class." He placed both hands on the edge of his desk and squeezed. "I want to know who they live with and who they visit overnight. If they've ever been in trouble, I want to be apprised of the date of the problem and the nature and extent of the offense." He pointed at Sinclair. "Get me a complete list of every organization they've ever belonged to." He rubbed his chin and worked his way toward the base of his neck. "If they've used computers at the campus, I want their E-mail confiscated and analyzed."

Reynolds wanted to bring this to a halt before any more civil liberties were threatened. "He teaches more than one hundred sixty registered students in four classes. There's another fifty or so who audit." He studied Vanzant but saw no indication he'd been dissuaded.

"It gets worse," added Sinclair. "He offers a class that meets in the community two nights a week and is open to anyone who wishes to attend. I'm told it's extremely popular."

"Does that fool really want to relive the sixties? 'Cause if he does, he just opened up a can of whoop-ass, and I'm just the man who can close it on him. I damn well promise you that!" Vanzant swiveled out of his chair and strutted across the room. "Let's put some pressure on the professor. Interview his colleagues, his friends, neighbors. Let's embarrass him. Hell, let's treat him like a damn suspect. See if that doesn't grab his attention!" Vanzant assumed a Napoleonic pose.

Winslow entered carrying a police report and chewing an apple. "Is there a Sherman Banks on the list?" His question caused Vanzant to rub his eyes.

Sinclair flipped through a file. When she stopped, Vanzant had worked his way to his temple, which he massaged deeply.

"Accused of strangling a black college student," she said.

Everyone looked at Winslow, waiting for his next question.

"With barbed wire?" he asked.

Sinclair reviewed her file one last time and, without ever glancing up from the paperwork, nodded yes.

Vanzant moved solemnly to his prized chair. He sat with his head bowed, unaware of the word that escaped his lips not once but twice: "Jesus . . . Jesus."

CHAPTER
8

FOR THE PAST twenty years Rachel had owned and operated the Red Bird Café. Her father had given it to her after he'd run off with one of his teenage part-time waitresses. Rachel's mother tried for several months to locate the employee who'd stolen her husband, in order to give the girl a handsome gratuity. After all, the poor girl would no doubt one day need the money to escape from her youthful dalliance.

Rachel had long ago given up the possibility of escaping the inheritance bequeathed to her by an adulterous father. She put much of her life and all of her resources into maintaining the small diner. She prided herself on the reasonably priced dinner specials. And unlike some other eateries, her diner offered food that patrons actually favored, such as roast duck in season and pot roast on Thursday.

She'd forgotten the number of big-name chain restaurants that had opened and closed in the past few years, all within quick traveling distance of her establishment. She'd outlasted them by attracting a loyal group of customers. Folks felt at home whether relaxing in one of her eight booths—tastefully decorated in light maroon vinyl upholstery—or spinning comfortably on extra-plush cushions balanced atop matching silver-and-blue metal stools.

Rachel, now a shade under fifty, had never been married, although she'd known her share of husbands. She often wondered what it might be like to have her own to worry about, but in the end decided she was better off remaining mildly amused at someone else's problem. There was, however, one frequent visitor who could have made her slip into an elaborately embroidered gown and stroll down a church center aisle to take a vow she fully believed they'd both violate. She had no way to explain her attraction other than to admit it had something to do with the way he drank her coffee, tasted her pies, and left her shop with his sparkling silver ponytail trailing behind, beckoning for her to climb his personal ladder to freedom.

"When you gonna finally let a woman take care of ya?" she asked Miller, who'd just sweetened his second cup of coffee.

"The law is my mistress, and I love her even when she's unfaithful." He took a sip and burned his upper lip.

"You ever want to get even with her, I'm off on Tuesday nights." She took an ice cube from his glass of water and ran it across his wounded mouth. She removed a cloth from just inside her freshly ironed apron and dried his chin. Rachel started to say something seductive, when he commented on the increased noise level just outside the café.

"What the hell's goin' on out there?" He turned toward the commotion.

She released a frustrated groan, then completed the pleasurable task of drying the moisture that had dripped to his neck. "Damn students been comin' down here every day for the last week accusin' Arnold Rankin of killin' some black girl thirty years ago. I've known that man half my life and he treats everybody decent, even the Coloreds."

" 'The Coloreds'?" he asked in mock surprise.

"Blacks. Afro-'mericans. Whatever they call themselves. Ought to let sleepin' dogs lie, that's all I know."

"Just be thankful they're not here protesting your coffee, because I'd march with them."

"Don't go bitin' the hand that feeds ya. My coffee saved your butt many a time."

"And my butt's eternally grateful." He withdrew his wallet from his rear pocket and placed on the counter some money, which he tantalizingly pushed toward her. "I look forward to the time when my lips are once again singed in the unending effort to taste and, indeed, savor your deliciously hot nectar."

Miller left the café and hurried down the street to observe a crowd mostly of college students blocking the entrance to Rankin & Son Hardware. They chanted slogans and carried signs that read *MURDERER* and *RACIST* along with a sprinkling of poorly scribbled threats.

Arnold Rankin stood in the middle of the crowd, blatantly defying their taunts. Miller remembered Rankin as one of the founding fathers of the movement to resist integration at all costs. He'd called any white man disagreeing with his ambition a "nigger lover." Miller had forgotten the language Rankin used against anyone brazenly advocating the rights of blacks to seek redress in a court of law; however, he was certain the phrase included a promise of bodily injury.

"You want a piece of me? I ain't hidin' and I sure as hell ain't runnin'!" Rankin challenged Brandon Hamilton, the leader of the demonstration. In his early seventies and with a fragile physique, Rankin appeared more ludicrous than dangerous.

"You still selling dynamite to the Klan?" Brandon shouted.

In his youth, Rankin had been nicknamed "Arnold the Mad Bomber," and from the way he acted, he seemed to cherish the memories that went with the name. "I don't need the Klan to rid myself of the likes of you!" Becoming more and more animated, Rankin's arthritic fingers pointed in all directions. Miller had the distinct impression Rankin actually enjoyed all this.

"Dad, go back inside." Rankin's son attempted to control his father and the crowd at the same time.

"This is *my* store and I'll decide when I want to go in it!" Rankin shoved his son hard in the chest.

Arnold Jr. appealed to the students. "Why don't you leave us alone? My father's never done anything to you."

"He's a murderer," said Brandon, confronting the two men. "We're not gonna let anyone in this town forget that." Brandon encouraged the crowd to become more vocal.

As the atmosphere became increasingly hostile, Miller decided it was time for calmer heads to prevail. He walked directly into the lions' den. "Mr. Rankin, why don't you listen to your son and go home?" Miller sweetened the logic. "It's the only way you're gonna get rid of them."

Rankin studied Miller curiously. Slowly a glimpse of recognition appeared on Rankin's face, followed immediately by an expression of absolute contempt. "I remember you," he said with revulsion, as though spitting out something foul. "This is what you and other white trash like you made possible. Look around; all this is your doin'!" Rankin grabbed Miller and forced him to assess the crowd. "You see? You see what you've done?"

Miller observed the faces of young black men and women exercising their constitutionally protected right to freedom of expression. So, why did his insides churn? Why was the sight of so many committed students actively participating in the time-tested political process of protest distressing? He was struggling for an answer when Rankin pushed him into the middle of the crowd.

"There! That's where you belong!" Rankin again lunged at Miller, pushing him farther into the crowd. "Go be with your goddamn nig—"

"Dad!" Rankin's son urgently intervened, taking his father's shoulders and holding on until the old man relented. "Dad, I'm not asking you anymore. I'm pleading with you to go home before you get yourself hurt or you rile these people into destroying our property. Please, Dad, just leave."

The elder Rankin's disgust changed to resignation. "I'm goin' home," he uttered. "But I'm comin' back tomorrow with my shotgun. We'll see how much protestin' they'll do with buckshot in their behinds."

Rankin approached Miller. "I oughta kill you now. But I owe a white man, even a poor excuse for one, a warning." A large vein protruded from his forehead. He moved closer. "If you're out here with 'em in the mornin', I'm aimin' the first shot at your stomach so you can die the slow death you deserve." Rankin entered his store and slammed the door. The small overhead bell crashed to the ground, ringing its final greeting.

The younger Rankin reasoned with Brandon. "Listen to me. Please listen! My father's gone. All we want is some peace. If you want to come inside and talk about this, then—"

"We've got nothing to say to you. Let your father talk to us and admit he's a murderer." Brandon signaled to his fellow students to continue their protests. They immediately returned to shouting slogans that, for Miller, failed to conjure up past images of righteous indignation. In his eyes, their protest resembled a fun-filled collegiate rally held to celebrate a football game against a hometown rival. Miller shook his head and accepted the judgment that youth was indeed wasted on the young.

The noise grew louder, the voices more determined; the demonstration was now unified. Thirty years ago Miller would have held one of the signs, even orchestrated the chants, but times had changed. It wasn't a matter of his being out of place. He simply felt unwanted. To these students he'd never be a comrade, for he was a white man, an outsider, the other.

People were more divided in this system of integration than they'd ever been under the institution of Jim Crow. The lines of separation were more deeply drawn, more permanently entrenched, and far more difficult to cross than any *For Whites Only* sign. He knew from personal experience that the very people who once had the passion to die for the rights of a stranger today lacked the wherewithal or moral fortitude to live next to that stranger as a neighbor, let alone a friend.

Miller's noble experiment had failed. The war he'd

waged as a young man had cost him his friends, his family, and for a long time his livelihood. But he'd kept the dream intact—a bit battered and bruised, to be sure, yet still recognizable even if it was for him no longer within reach.

He was thinking about seeing Rachel under the pretense of needing more coffee, when an explosion shattered metal and glass and moved the earth beneath his feet. He fell to the ground, either from impact or instinct, and watched Arnold Jr. race into his store. The students rushed through a narrow alley leading to the parking lot. Miller rose in time to see a frightened Rachel standing at her entrance. He motioned for her to stay, then hurried through the store, knowing full well what awaited him on the other side.

In the rear parking lot, under a large pine tree originally planted to provide shelter from the sun, an Oldsmobile sedan was being consumed by fire. The flames licked at the side door, swallowing the trapped figure behind the steering wheel.

Rankin's son dashed hysterically toward his father, whose mouth opened wide enough to scream for help but seemed to whisper good-bye. Miller tackled Arnold Jr. to the ground. The fire reached the gas tank and caused a second explosion, which lifted the sedan into the air and suspended Rankin's body within the inferno. His flesh melted, and his scorched remains merged with deteriorating red-hot metal.

Miller held on tightly to the man who'd been reduced to whimpering, "Dad . . . Dad . . . Dad." His pathetic voice gave way to the muted thumps of his fists pounding the pavement, intermittently interrupted by the sobbing of the word "No" over and over again. He pounded the earth so forcefully, his hands began to bleed, the droplets spraying on Miller's face.

Miller saw a group of students gleefully staring at the conflagration. He half expected them to exchange high fives or other congratulatory celebrations. Had it come to this? he wondered. Had the legacy of hate finally made a complete circle and confined everyone within it? He searched the faces in the crowd and found a young woman in tears. Two or three others appeared startled. Another displayed disbelief and fear. The vast majority, however—both men and women—were entertained, enthralled by the excitement of witnessing an old man's body being reduced to ash.

He'd seen these faces before, except they'd been white and gathered around a black corpse or freshly dug grave or charred torso or half-burned head. He'd viewed photos of white men invited to a "Negro barbecue, southern style" as it so fondly had been called. Those photos, keepsakes from his heritage, had always caused him to feel ill without ever allowing him the relief of vomiting up his pain and disgust. Now he felt the urge to regurgitate it all, to disgorge a lifetime of obscenities and prejudices and fears. Miller watched as the fiery corpse in the front seat of the smoldering automobile slumped forward and emerged as a skeleton that had escaped one closet only to perish in another.

Brandon Hamilton stood silently in the distance. He removed a small pocket camera from his leather waistband, placed it near his eye, and took several pictures. The automatic flash competed with the light from the flames. He turned and walked away, prompting Miller to wonder what burden, if any, this young black man carried on his broad shoulders. Miller wanted to leave this graveyard quickly. He needed to replace his feeling of despair with the impartial solace only a courtroom could provide, regardless of its final verdict.

Miller helped Arnold Jr. to his feet, then noticed, beyond the incinerated car, that the towering pine tree had caught fire. He listened to the branches crackle and heard the sirens blare. The fire trucks finally arrived. He studied the huge pine burning in the background, fully ablaze.

CHAPTER
9

LAUREN SINCLAIR STOOD in front of a large bulletin board that had a map of the state pinned against it. She used a red Magic Marker to add a final circle, then stepped back and studied all the multicolored markings. Three areas were circled in red, two others in blue, and two dozen more in green.

"I had no idea we had this many," she said to Reynolds, who moments earlier had completed highlighting sections of the map located in the northwest and central regions. "It's frightening."

"Ghosts usually are," said Reynolds.

"Let's ensure the ones circled in green don't enter the spirit world before their time." Sinclair double-checked her list and compared it to the markings on the map.

"That's a job for the police, not us," Reynolds pointed out.

"You don't seem terribly sympathetic."

"At least our office is giving them a warning. That's more than they gave their victims."

"They were all acquitted, remember?"

"I remember," was as far as he'd go.

Vanzant entered the office without knocking, a privilege he abused constantly. He reviewed his master list. "Two-thirds of the folks have been notified." He moved to the display. He absorbed it for a moment, then shook his head in disbelief. "What's the blue for?"

"Crockett and Mitchell, assuming they're still alive and missing," Sinclair responded.

Vanzant quickly exhaled. "If I were a betting man, I'd circle them red."

"Hopkins and Taylor were found a hundred twenty miles northwest, just outside Greenville," said Reynolds. He pointed to the locations on the map as he spoke. "Sherman Banks's body was recovered in Hattiesburg, ninety miles southeast. Rankin was local and the only one not murdered in the general locations where the original civil rights slayings occurred."

"Any theory as to why he was treated differently?" asked Vanzant.

"Rankin's alleged crimes consisted of a series of car bombings," answered Sinclair. "To that extent, the pattern may not have deviated."

Reynolds touched the display. "With all those green circles, I'd say whoever's doing this still has a lot of traveling left."

"Could be more than one person," Sinclair mentioned as an afterthought.

"After tonight, it just might be." Vanzant directed the remark to Reynolds and waited for a response.

"What's happening tonight?" Reynolds obliged.

"Your friend Professor Matheson has a worldwide audience on CNN."

Sinclair sighed at the revelation.

Vanzant approached Reynolds. "I want you to talk to him. See if he'll condemn the killings or at the very least tone down his rhetoric."

"What makes you think he'll listen to me?" Reynolds asked, knowing his boss would never give an honest answer.

"Just a hunch." Vanzant quickly headed for the exit and, without turning back, provided his parting directive: "Call me at home tonight after you've spoken with him." He was gone before Reynolds could respond.

Sinclair retrieved a used case of Magic Markers and separated them by color. "Guess we better order some more red."

Reynolds didn't know why September was his favorite month. Perhaps he liked the way it sounded: serene, a bit seductive. It marked the end of a frivolous summer and the beginning of something more serious. Flowers turned color. People changed jobs. For some, maybe it meant the chance to start over and recover from a romantic fling that had occurred halfway through vacation and terminated when they reentered the real world. It represented a thirty-day odyssey ideally suited for the young to write poetry and for the old to read it and, together, delight in the magic of the moment and the mystery of what endured. Whatever made September special, nothing underscored it better than a new academic year. You could stroll across the main grounds of a university campus, where the hunger for knowledge was never fully satisfied but always enthusiastically nurtured.

Reynolds savored every sun-drenched step down a magnolia-laced walkway, which wrapped around the library's Gothic structure. It turned out to be a gorgeous afternoon, but that couldn't compensate for the difficult task ahead. His leisurely walk through the campus was forcing him to rethink his job in the district attorney's office. He recalled how often he'd contemplated resigning to accept a teaching position at the law school.

He remembered the first time he'd considered becoming a lawyer. He was six years old. His father had taken a drink of cold water from the garden hose in their backyard and was wiping the side of his mouth with the sleeve from his red-and-brown checkered work shirt when he asked the all-important question: "Little Jimmie, what you gonna be when you grow up?"

The boy, who preferred to be called James, took the garden hose from his father and, without a second's hesitation, answered in a voice filled with childhood conviction. "Dad," he announced, "I'm gonna be a lawyer." He triumphantly placed the nozzle close to his lips to conceal his excitement.

In truth, the young Reynolds didn't know what a lawyer did. For some reason buried in the secret aspirations of youth, he hoped the answer might make his father proud. He turned off the flow of water and waited for a reply that never came. Instead, he watched his father's face go through a myriad of expressions. At first, he saw the normal display of pride, followed by a look of tenderness that took his breath away. Just as quickly it changed to doubt and pain and insecurity and fear. Although only a child, he instinctively knew there was something in his world his father couldn't protect him from—something about the lives of others like himself that made it impossible for grown men to believe they'd ever be able to help their children realize their dreams.

After that day, Reynolds never told his father what he intended to become. His father never again dared to ask, yet the memory of that original question, and the subsequent expression of pain it generated, would linger a lifetime. It would haunt Reynolds long after he earned his law degree, and way beyond the morning a coffin containing a diploma and the man who called his son "little Jimmie" was lowered into a darkened grave. It was a terrible thing to see a child's dream die on a father's face. That look, far more than any other, eventually drove Reynolds to leave his home in search of a place where grown men and the children who loved them were not destroyed by a single wish.

He'd left the South, intending never to revisit. But he'd forgotten about funerals and voices from the past and dreams that had a right to flourish and how good water tasted when shared from the same hose. Reynolds obtained his undergraduate and graduate degrees while living in Boston. The day he learned he'd passed the bar, he received notification his father had passed away. He returned home with his degrees and the results of his law exam. He neatly folded and placed them inside the pocket of a dark blue jacket, the first and last suit he'd ever seen his father wear. He buried the man who'd given him three precious things: life, a nickname he initially detested but grew to love, and the motivation to empower fathers to believe they could help their children obtain any goal.

He stopped for a moment and observed a young couple seated on a blanket in the shade of a dogwood. The woman read aloud to her male companion from a slender volume of poetry. He stroked her arm and fed her a strawberry. She closed the book, and they shared a kiss. Reynolds smiled and continued his journey. He thought of his wife and felt fortunate he'd been given another chance to rediscover the South and meet his one true love. After leaving home in an effort to find it, he'd settled down in the town he'd almost renounced.

He immediately found himself inundated with offers to join every major firm specializing in criminal law, international finance, corporate takeover, or any other endeavor that promised more money than anyone should ever need. He rejected them all in favor of putting away bad people so they'd never hurt the innocent. After a dozen years of success, measured by his conviction rate and by the number of overcrowded prisons, he wondered if he'd made the right choice. He still wanted to put away the bad and protect the innocent, yet no longer felt certain about who belonged in which category. More troubling, he worried whether innocents even existed anymore. He feared they might have become casualties of the war on drugs—a war that made criminals of the sick and destroyed families under the pretense of saving them. Even a rookie prosecutor knew he could convert one drug conviction into a dozen. From there he'd multiply that dozen into a pyramid scheme. The result would be a series of career advancements built upon the broken lives and contaminated needles of junkies who would gladly set up their neighborhood minister for the promise of a lighter sentence.

Was it any wonder he'd be thinking of giving up that life for the chance to walk across a campus that began anew each September? His musings had taken him to the entrance of the humanities building. Inside, the cooled air from an efficient machine replaced the purity of a fresh breeze. Reynolds took the staircase to the second floor and walked down a long corridor filled with the distinctive scent of learning. He saw a small group of highly animated black students leaving an office, which suggested he'd found the right place. To make certain, he read the name inscribed in gold lettering on the lightly smoked surface of beveled glass: *Dr. Martin S. Matheson, Chair, Department of History.*

He didn't have to wait long to be ushered into Matheson's private quarters, but it took a while for the professor to acknowledge his presence. Reynolds used the time to study the many plaques and awards neatly arranged on each wall, evidence of Matheson's scholarly achievements and community service. There were also a significant number of certificates and honors presented by appreciative students and alumni. The citations hung alongside smiling photos of Matheson with dignitaries, celebrities, and business and civic leaders.

Reynolds studied a large framed picture of the professor at the helm of a small boat. Beside him, his father, the Reverend Matheson, proudly beamed over a batch of freshly caught bluegill, speckled trout, and king mackerel. Reynolds browsed through the collection of leather-bound books—probably rare first editions, from the way they were showcased. He admired the distinctive display of original paintings and sculptures adorning the room. Everything about Matheson's resplendent office shouted perfection, which made Reynolds feel both envious and uncomfortable.

"James, what a pleasant surprise. All my classes are overbooked, but if you're sincere about wanting to register, I can make an exception." Matheson motioned for Reynolds to sit, then finished going through some statewide tourist catalogs and brochures. He reviewed a road map and jotted down some notes.

"You handing out directions on how to find the people on your list?" Reynolds asked.

"If you don't know where you're going, it's easy to get lost," Matheson responded.

Reynolds couldn't resist the temptation to spar. He picked up a travel brochure and flipped through it. "Taking a vacation?" he asked.

"I'm sure your colleagues in the DA's office would pay for the ticket, but I'm afraid I'll have to disappoint them. These are part of a lecture for tomorrow night. You're welcome to attend." Matheson smiled pleasantly.

"I appreciate the offer, but it doesn't look that interesting." Reynolds tried to match the professor's smile.

Matheson took the brochure from Reynolds and referred to it as he spoke. "It's important to know how your history is defined, James, even in something as seemingly innocuous as a tourist brochure." The professor turned to the second page and began reading: "'Almost every area of Mississippi boasts a battle site or antebellum home, timeless testimonies to the elegance and majesty of the Old South, and the tragedy and sorrow of the American Civil War.'" He looked at Reynolds with the charm that had influenced so many students.

"The South's glorious past is nostalgically described as 'elegant' and 'majestic' until it was shattered by that evil insurrection which resulted in freeing the slaves. But fear not, the South has risen again, and as is so eloquently stated on page three of our tax-supported propaganda"— he retrieved the brochure and continued reading— "'Mississippi represents the best of yesterday and the promise of tomorrow.'" Matheson tossed the pamphlet onto his desk and studied Reynolds. "Makes you wonder, doesn't it?"

"About the past?"

Matheson leaned forward the way a medical doctor might to issue a warning to a recalcitrant patient. "About the future."

"Speaking of the unknown, I hear you're about to embark on a show biz career."

Matheson looked disappointed. "So that's why you came by." He studied Reynolds for a moment. "I'm sure CNN's colorful news anchor Thomas Jackson is being coached as we speak. He was selected to play the role of the indignant and outraged citizen. It's fascinating how they use us when it serves their purpose."

"'They'?" echoed a mildly amused Reynolds. "Isn't the frequent use of that pronoun the first sign of paranoia?" He gave a trace of a smile, which Matheson seized on.

"You ever notice how so many black professionals always smile whenever they're around white folks? I imagine it's a desperate attempt to make their bosses feel comfortable."

"Maybe they wear the mask," Reynolds countered, less in an effort to defend himself than to stand up for the rights of his fellow accused black professionals.

"I've actually seen the contours of a face change as a result of such frequent grinning, almost as if it's become rubberized by necessity; should it get angry by mistake, it can be quickly reshaped to a smile before anyone notices." Matheson rose from his seat and moved to the front of his desk. He leaned close to Reynolds. "The ones who can't convincingly smile anymore suffer from severe stomach discomfort, but rather than take an antacid, they conceal their pain in the hope it'll go away." He studied Reynolds, then added secretively, "But it never does." He bent over slightly and assumed the posture of a priest hearing a confession. "Tell me, James, do you smile a lot?"

Reynolds looked directly into Matheson's face. "No. Just in case you're wondering, my stomach doesn't hurt, either."

"Then I'll assume you weren't sent here to do your employer's bidding but came on your own volition to wish me luck on my interview. Will you be watching me tonight, or has that function been assigned to someone else?"

"I volunteered to watch it. I've always been a huge fan of Mr. Jackson's. You know, we black folks need to support each other." Reynolds thought it now safe to smile, and did so graciously.

Matheson also smiled. Reynolds believed it to be genuine. The two men had tested each other, and neither was the worse for wear. Reynolds got up from his chair. "I better leave so you can prepare for tonight."

"I'm on at six and again at nine should you miss the initial airing or be inspired to watch it twice."

Reynolds started to leave when, to his surprise, Matheson offered his hand. Reynolds found himself taking it. The men stood eye to eye, hands clasped, and it seemed to Reynolds like another contest, perhaps to determine who'd be the first to blink or loosen his grip. They both ended the exchange at precisely the same moment, and Reynolds headed for the door, half expecting to hear a provocative comment about his wife.

"James?"

Here it comes, thought Reynolds. He turned, wanting to be ready with an appropriate comeback.

"Thanks for stopping by," the professor said.

Reynolds nodded, waiting for the second round to be fired.

"Oh, by the way," Matheson added, "do you think you'll be needing any tapes from the show?"

"For Cheryl?"

"Actually, I had in mind your colleagues at the office." Matheson sat on the top of his desk. "Although now that I think about it, I imagine they have ample equipment to record my activities."

Reynolds left with the distinct feeling that practicing law was far superior than teaching it, after all.

CHAPTER
10

THOMAS JACKSON ENJOYED his reputation as a respected black journalist and cable network anchorman known for straightforward interviewing. He seldom became flustered or angry—at least, not on the air. He got along fabulously with his coanchors and guests no matter how extreme their political views or how annoying their observations. He was, in other words, the ideal foil for Matheson. His understated manner played well with a television audience that needed to be appeased or reassured. In the unlikely event a guest threatened the comfort level of Jackson's viewers, he'd put them at ease by becoming shocked and outraged. His physical movements were stiff, arguably robotic, and therefore never dangerous. He had the requisite calm and soothing voice, and on those infrequent occasions when he showed emotion and laughed, he could be surprisingly charming.

Matheson spoke from a satellite news station in Jackson, an affiliate of CNN. For the past five minutes, he'd been fielding questions from Jackson, whose image filled a small studio monitor. He sat on a metal foldout chair whose legs were uneven. An intern had slid two matchbooks and a strip of cardboard underneath to prevent the chair from teetering whenever Matheson shifted his weight. Despite the lack of amenities, he felt relieved he wasn't in Atlanta being interviewed in person. He feared that if he'd been seated right next to the bland host, his own personality might have seemed overwhelming.

Matheson needed a balanced debate format, or at least the illusion of one. If the discussion came off too one-sided, he risked being characterized as a bully, an ungrateful "angry black man" taking advantage of an award-winning member of his own race. Up until this point in the program, he'd been careful not to score points at Jackson's expense. He would change tactics shortly.

"Professor Matheson, four men whose names and addresses you distributed were gruesomely murdered; two others are missing. Isn't it understandable that reasonable people might conclude you're directly responsible?" Jackson managed to ask the question without any fluctuation in his voice and, even more amusing to Matheson, without any facial expression.

"If reasonable people had fulfilled their duty decades ago, my course wouldn't need to be taught." The professor remained restrained and, notwithstanding the hot overhead lights, free of perspiration.

"No one would disagree with your right to teach such a course, but why insist on disseminating your list? Isn't that an invitation to commit acts of reprisal?" Jackson's eyebrow finally moved slightly.

"To teach about only those who were lynched places

black people in a perpetual state of victimization, where they're so demoralized they can't fight back, or worse, so frightened they won't fight back. Either way, they're permanently defeated. Education's about liberation, Mr. Jackson, not defeat." Matheson contained his passion safely beneath the surface, wanting his message to get through.

"As for your suggestion that my teaching methodology is in reality a subtle call to punish those who've committed the most heinous crimes against innocent men, women, and children, to that indictment I plead guilty." Jackson tried to interject a remark, but the professor continued. "The form of punishment I advocate isn't a private execution. It's a public ostracizing. I don't ask my students to take an eye for an eye—quite the contrary. I insist they stand eye to eye with the men who've brutalized their fathers and grandfathers, and denounce those crimes. I ask that they pronounce life sentences on these criminals to guarantee they'll never again commit violent acts against blacks without anticipating a moral, ethical, and political retribution."

Matheson looked straight into the camera. "There's a price to be paid for violating the laws of man as well as the laws of God. Since we're a country that honors both, I feel fortunate to have students who wish to conduct themselves as patriots and Christians."

Matheson delivered his message without coming across as a radical revolutionary or black-power fanatic. He portrayed himself as an attractive, articulate, and reasoned defender of the Constitution—or for that matter, the Old Testament. His persuasiveness even prompted a black cameraman to take his eye away from his equipment and exchange a nod of solidarity with a young Afro-American female assistant.

"Your father was a close friend and associate of Dr. King."

"I'm named in his honor," Matheson said proudly.

"Like Dr. King, your father's a passionate advocate of nonviolence."

Matheson knew where this was heading. "Since we're dealing with history, I might remind you and your viewers that the man we honor as the finest proponent of nonviolence was murdered preaching it. Had some of his admirers turned their cheeks less frequently and reached for their weapons more often, Dr. King might be alive today."

This first sign of defiance from Matheson unnerved Jackson. "Professor Matheson, you see nothing wrong in what you're doing?"

"I ought to be applauded." Amazingly, Matheson sounded humble.

Reynolds was watching the telecast at home. Turning up the volume, he admired an elaborate configuration of standing dominoes spread across his living room floor. They resembled an imposing army of black plastic figures defiled by white-dotted numerical representations.

"You seriously think you should be congratulated for your behavior?" For the first time in the interview, Jackson leaned forward.

"I certainly do," responded Matheson.

"By whom?" Jackson challenged. His stern demeanor was meant to signal—both to his viewers and the network's commercial sponsors—that if any applause was forthcoming, it would come without his participation or endorsement.

"Be careful, Thomas," warned Reynolds as he placed one of the dominoes on the floor.

"By the same people who hailed legislation permitting communities to know the identity and whereabouts of child molesters," answered the professor. The camera moved in more closely on Matheson until he filled the entire screen. "Shouldn't black people have the same rights as children and their parents to know who their predators are and where they live and work?"

"I tried to warn you," mumbled Reynolds as the camera captured Jackson, listening to voices in his earpiece offering him conflicting suggestions.

"Those child molesters were convicted in a court of law," claimed Jackson.

Reynolds wondered if that was the best response Jackson's team could have generated for their outgunned moderator.

"Had justice prevailed, the murderers on my list would've been waiting in line to greet them."

Reynolds had a hunch that tomorrow this interview would be endlessly debated around water coolers all across the country. By the time the cups were refilled, a new media star would be born.

"So this is payback?" asked the puzzled host.

"No, Mr. Jackson, this is justice."

Jackson, in a rare miscue, lost track of the red light and stared blankly into the wrong camera. He quickly corrected his error and used the lull in action to readjust his glasses. "And will the person or persons murdering the alleged 'murderers' on your list be brought to justice?"

"Score one for Tommy." Reynolds tried to maintain his optimism, but his hopes were fading fast. He watched Matheson create a sense of drama. The professor leaned back, tilted his head, shifted his eyes, and lightly touched his lower lip, preparing to share a truth that would make his listeners follow him anywhere. He possessed a sense of timing any actor would envy.

"Mr. Jackson, in recent years this nation's been embroiled in a violent campaign designed to protect the freedom and safety of its citizens. It pursues international criminals as well as those who harbor them and does so without mercy. When this country was attacked on its own soil, no one suggested we should turn the other cheek. We didn't seek to understand our enemies in order to love and forgive them. We branded them evil cowards and then did everything in our power to destroy them. Is there any greater evil than bombing a church and killing innocent little girls engaged in prayer? Are there any more despicable and cowardly terrorists than those who conceal their faces beneath white hoods while they lynch black men and women?"

The professor put the fingers of both hands together in a flexible pyramid and continued. "I'm not certain what will happen to anyone who feels compelled to take matters in his own hands. We'll just have to place our faith in the existing legal system and let American justice be our conscience as well as our guide."

"Damn, he's good." Reynolds placed the final domino in its desired position.

"Dr. Matheson, you made reference to the attack on America. Some people have suggested your actions jeopardize the unsurpassed unity experienced by citizens of all races."

This news anchor obviously hadn't learned his lesson, thought Reynolds.

"Unsurpassed unity when combined with unexamined fear and hypocrisy is a formula for genuine disaster," Matheson pointed out. "I doubt this ad hoc solidarity would have existed had fanatical racists taken over those planes and traveled a few miles uptown to a Harlem neighborhood or black elementary school. If that alternative scenario had occurred, do you honestly believe billions of dollars would have been devoted to destroying racist organizations in this country, let alone chasing neo-Nazis in Germany or skinheads in Great Britain and France?" Matheson waited for an answer Reynolds knew would never come.

"Professor Matheson, I'm afraid we're out of time. Thank you for joining us tonight." Jackson put down his pen and shuffled some three-by-five cards.

"It was my pleasure, Thomas; thanks so much for inviting me." Matheson could afford to be gracious.

The professor had let the cat out of the bag and thrown it in the face of millions of viewers. If the first casualty of war is truth, then what is the cost of a crusade against terror? Reynolds wondered. Perhaps it's the knowledge that in order to eradicate evil we must begin to emulate the evildoer. And if you label your enemy "evil" long enough, you justify even the most immoral act as noble. Wasn't Matheson living proof of that?

He retrieved his remote control and turned off the television. Just as the set went black, the unit slipped out of his hand and struck the domino that moments earlier had completed his architectural achievement. He watched helplessly as the piece set off a chain reaction. One domino knocked over the next, mimicking a thousand Radio City Rockettes collapsing in perfect symmetry.

CHAPTER
11

Appearing from behind a red satin curtain at the university's performing arts center, Matheson bowed to thunderous applause. He crossed the stage proscenium and stood behind the podium. Acknowledging the enthusiastic reception, he raised his hands several times to quiet the crowd, but they remained on their feet, cheering wildly.

Brandon and Regina, in the front row, saluted him in triumph. He looked into the sea of proud faces and noticed a figure standing at the back of the theater, a safe distance from the main activities. After a few moments, the man took a seat in the very last row. Matheson recognized Reynolds and gave him a slight welcoming gesture. Reynolds clapped three times slowly, then stopped to tip an imaginary hat in the professor's honor.

Matheson hushed the crowd and motioned for them to be seated. He adjusted the microphone attached to the podium. "I'm speechless, which is a day too late for Thomas Jackson."

The students laughed and applauded again.

"I take it from your generous reception a growing number of you subscribe to cable and are satisfied with your service?"

Regina climbed to the stage and proceeded to the wing. She pushed a button, and the curtain slid open. She flipped a switch, and dozens of spotlights illuminated a series of movie posters featuring several generations of Hollywood's leading men, from John Wayne, Gary Cooper, and Humphrey Bogart to Harrison Ford, Arnold Schwarzenegger, and Sylvester Stallone.

Reynolds studied the high ceilings, admiring the delicately etched designs on the carved wooden moldings. He counted the small private opera boxes sprinkled along the second and third levels. The upper balconies protruded a few feet from the walls. He wondered how many plays, poetry readings, and concerts had been performed in this magnificent venue; he predicted that the drama about to unfold would surpass them all.

Matheson picked up a long, narrow stick and held it in his left hand, then spread his arms as wide as they would reach. With his face lifted toward the rafters and bathed in a warm blue-and-gold–filtered glow, he performed his best rendition of Moses: "Behold the faces of the great American hero; bow down before them at the altar of eternal servitude or face the unrelenting wrath of Western European history." Matheson dropped the stick along with his impersonation.

"For those who think the stress of last evening's telecast may have driven me over the edge, let me assure you there's a purpose to my madness."

There always is, Reynolds thought.

"History devoid of analysis and truth ceases to be

history and instead becomes propaganda and myth, both of which are drugs far more powerful and dangerous than any narcotic or hallucinogen." Matheson walked in between the posters, at times disappearing behind each one. It created the effect of an invisible voice speaking on behalf of the exhibited images.

"The actors represented on this stage have gender and race in common. They personify the classic heroic figure that will seduce you with false images of beauty and morality and tempt you to replace the protective cloak of your heritage and history with a coat not of your making. They'll rob you of your desire to dream and, if you're not careful, capture your very soul."

Watching Matheson from afar, admiring his eloquence, Reynolds felt a nervousness nagging at him. He wondered to what end this teacher would use his extraordinary gifts.

"American cinema, literature, media, history—all have endorsed a code of conduct, a definition of right and wrong, that is embodied in the people we call heroes. And playing those heroes are the white male actors whose images you see before you. They let nothing prevent them from achieving victory, acquiring honor, defending their family, their country, their God. And they do so by any means necessary."

Matheson scanned the rows of faces in front of him, then shifted his attention to Reynolds for a moment.

"Our heroes—black heroes—aren't accorded the same respect, because they're not allowed the same means to achieve it. White heroes take up arms to battle their enemy while our heroes are expected to turn the other cheek and pray for divine intervention. There are a great many things you can do while on your knees, some of them pleasurable. But, my friends, gaining freedom and fighting for liberty are not high on the list."

Against his better judgment, Reynolds laughed with the students.

Matheson removed his jacket and hung it on the side of the podium. He walked to the edge of the stage and sat down. His legs hung over a shallow orchestra pit that had been converted by his wizardry into a heavenly cloud. "It's time we put our faces up there alongside those white faces that for so long have represented courage in the service of virtue. If our town is being terrorized, then it's imperative we dispatch our black Gary Cooper before the train arrives and the moral clock strikes not high noon but rather darkest midnight."

Reynolds searched the faces of Matheson's adoring students. He had no doubt they'd sacrifice their lives for this man. He worried they might also kill for him.

"Sojourner Truth called attention to the dilemma of race in relation to the obstacles confronting her more advanced white sisters, by uttering her now famous question. She wasn't speaking for herself, but for all black women when she asked, 'Ain't I a woman, too?' Well, with all praise to Sojourner, I humbly ask on behalf of our ancestors who were courageous enough to sometimes act cowardly so that we the descendants of their suffering would never have to: America, after all this time, ain't I a hero, too?"

The students leaped to their feet in sustained applause. Matheson also got to his feet and stood motionless, his slight fatigue dissipating as the clapping continued. He nodded an appreciative thank-you, then glanced to the very back row. The seat he focused on was empty. Reynolds was nowhere to be found.

Reynolds didn't know if he should wait any longer or return home. He was unsure why he'd decided to stand outside the auditorium in the first place. Maybe he owed Matheson the courtesy of a good-bye. He took a seat at the bottom of the steps leading to the arts center and enjoyed the sights and sounds of the campus at night. Students were leaving the building from several exits. He wondered if he'd selected the right one. He'd chosen the biggest, grandest portal opening into a lobby as big as a ballroom. Yes, Matheson would choose this path lined with rose petals tossed by young worshipers who would sing his praises as they followed him all the way to his horse-drawn golden chariot.

"You didn't stay to the end of the lecture," Matheson called out heartily.

Reynolds stood and was surprised to see the professor departing alone. The prosecutor smiled. "I'm not big on hero worship."

"Giving or receiving?" Matheson stepped down the stairs.

"You're enjoying all this, aren't you?"

"Immensely." The professor paused for a second. "May I buy you a cappuccino? There's a small café just off the campus that's open late."

The two men took a shortcut through the faculty lounge to a staff parking lot and eventually to the rear entrance of the coffee shop. They were served quickly at the professor's own private table. The waitress brought coffee, two slices of pie, and a freshly baked croissant, which emitted the aroma of cinnamon.

They exhausted a few minutes in small talk before Reynolds asked, "What makes someone like you?"

"The same thing that makes someone like you. Nature . . . nurture. Who's to say one's more important than the other?"

"My office was notified you've received death threats."

Matheson stirred his coffee. "It's a violent world."

"You're not worried?"

"My father taught me that death isn't to be feared."

"What else did he teach you?"

"That life is really frightening—although I'm sure he never intended to teach me that. It's a natural by-product of Christian training. Something to do with loving thine enemy while despising yourself." Matheson took a bite of his croissant.

"You don't strike me as a man who despises himself."

"Nor have I ever loved my enemy or blessed those who cursed me. Of all my accomplishments, I'm most proud of that."

A black woman in her fifties approached their table. She dismissed Reynolds with a perfunctory nod, then turned an admiring look at Matheson. "Excuse me, are you the professor who was on television last night?"

"I'm afraid I am."

"I just wanted to tell you how proud it made me feel to see a courageous black man finally stand up for his people. I intend to say a prayer and ask the Lord to keep givin' you whatever strength you'll need to go on teachin' those students the truth."

"That's very kind of you." Matheson seemed genuinely touched.

She smiled, then asked, "Could I impose and ask for your autograph?"

"I'd be both honored and delighted to give you one."

She found a piece of notepaper inside her purse and handed it to him. Reynolds turned away. Matheson removed from his jacket a Mont Blanc fountain pen with a gold inscription down its side, designed especially for him.

"Whom should I make it out to?"

"Calpurnia."

"Like Caesar's wife?" the professor asked with interest.

"I don't know anything about that, but it was a name good enough for my mother, her mother, and the mother before that."

Matheson laughed. "Thanks for reminding me that our contributions predate the Roman Empire."

"Predate everything else if you believe those old bones they dug up in Africa," she said.

Reynolds watched Matheson write his greeting. He'd mastered the art of reading upside down through years of stealing clues from opposing counsel while at the judge's bench, although deciphering Matheson's message from any angle required no deceptive skill. The man's penmanship was eminently legible—one could say, impeccable. *God,* Reynolds thought, *is there anything this man can't do well?*

Matheson wrote, *Dear Calpurnia, the real power of magic rests not in what we make disappear, but in what we discover. May your magic never fail you. Always, Martin Matheson.*

He gave the woman her paper, which she handled as

carefully as the holy scrolls. Thanking him profusely, she left with a glow on her face.

Reynolds looked at Matheson, who acted as if nothing unusual had happened. The professor took a sip of coffee and noticed Reynolds wasn't eating. He pointed to the food.

"You should try the pecan pie; it's to die for."

CHAPTER

12

REYNOLDS GRIMACED WITH determination and made a frantic dash across the hot clay court. With a desperate heave of his out-of-control body he viciously swung his tennis racket, barely missing the ball. He fell to the ground and slid headfirst, mashing his face into the newly installed white mesh net.

"Game . . . Set . . . Match." On the opposite side of the net Miller raised his racket victoriously toward the sun.

Reynolds rose to one knee and searched his body for any damage.

"A tennis court is different than a court of law," Miller proclaimed.

"Okay, I'll take the bait," Reynolds said, rising to his feet. "How is it different?"

Miller smiled. "The rich and powerful don't always win."

Reynolds stared back at his opponent. "That's it? That's your pearl of wisdom?"

Miller shrugged modestly. "It's also a place where *love* means nothing—seems a rather hopeless sentiment." With an unsportsmanlike chuckle he added, "As in *six-love,* the score of our final set!"

Waving off a troublesome gnat, Reynolds began walking away from Miller, who followed alongside. "Oh," Reynolds said, turning to his friend, "Cheryl's invited you to dinner."

"Why?" Miller asked suspiciously.

"Something about wanting our children to be exposed to different cultures, and you're about as different as they come."

"I'll assume that's a compliment," Miller replied, "but that doesn't ease my fears."

They started toward the back of the court to retrieve their leather bags and check their pagers.

"Is she trying to fix me up again?" Miller asked.

Reynolds laid it on thick. "I can absolutely assure you my wife has no ulterior motive whatsoever. She wants merely to provide you with a pleasurable dining experience in the company of friends."

"Whenever a lawyer speaks in long sentences without so much as a comma separating his thoughts, it's a clear indication he's got either a weak case or a powerful lie."

Reynolds waved good-bye and quickly made it off the court and into the parking lot.

Miller leaned against the fence to ponder his fate alone.

Miller removed his jacket and leaned close to Reynolds. "It wasn't Cheryl. It was you. That's low even for a prosecutor."

Reynolds took the jacket and hung it inside the hall closet.

"Soup's on," Cheryl announced. She stood next to Lauren Sinclair, who looked radiant and uncomfortable. Cheryl ushered all of them to their seats at the dining room table. She placed Miller next to Angela and directly opposite Sinclair, who sat next to Christopher. Reynolds took his customary position at the head while Cheryl sat at the other end. "Well, don't we make quite the family," she said.

"Cheryl," Miller said, "if you knew my real family, you'd know how happy I'd be to join yours."

Cheryl lifted a glass of water and held it toward him in a toast. He nodded gratefully, then turned his attention toward Reynolds. "So what's the latest on our esteemed Professor Matheson? I see that the powers that be have failed to silence him."

"Todd," Cheryl intervened, "I'd rather not talk about that in front of the children, if you don't mind."

Miller gave an apologetic nod.

"He's awesome," chimed an enthusiastic Christopher. "I hope he's still teaching when I go to college!"

Cheryl made brief eye contact with Reynolds, who turned toward his son with raised eyebrows. "How much do you know about the professor's class?" he asked.

"He's got a list of bad people and God's punishing them," answered Christopher.

"God doesn't punish people that way," Cheryl responded.

Angela dived in. "He sends them to hell, bucket-breath."

"Does not," replied Christopher.

"Does," answered Angela.

"Does not!"

"Does!"

"That's enough," refereed Cheryl. "You know so much about God, young man, you can say grace."

Christopher stared at his sister and mouthed the words *does not*. He bowed his head in prayer. "Dear Lord, thank you for the food we're about to eat and knowing which people to punish and which ones to leave alone." He gave another warning stare at Angela, who turned up her nose, asserting her superiority and defiance. The gathering mumbled, "Amen," and Cheryl passed around platters of food.

"James tells me you taught him a lot about the law," Sinclair said to Miller.

Miller nodded. "He would've made a great defense attorney except for one fatal flaw: He had an uncompromising desire to punish people."

"My dad's beaten Mr. Miller twelve court cases in a row," Christopher proclaimed.

"Let's not rub it in," Reynolds interjected. "And it was thirteen," he said with great enjoyment.

"Eleven. I plea-bargained two." Miller placed a spoonful of whipped butter on his corn muffin. "So, Lauren, how many innocent people have you successfully persecuted? I meant, prosecuted."

Cheryl placed a bowl of steaming potatoes under his chin, forcing Miller to inhale the aroma. "Mashed—just the way I prefer all my food," he said sincerely.

She dumped three large servings onto his plate. He quietly signaled "enough" and smiled his appreciation.

Angela passed a bowl of vegetables to her father without taking any for herself.

"Did you forget to put some of this on your own plate?" he asked.

"I thought since we had guests I should give up my portion," Angela responded sincerely.

"How thoughtful," Miller said. He took the bowl from Reynolds and studied it. "And I bet you really love spinach as much as I do." He passed the bowl to Sinclair without taking any.

Angela was reaching for the gravy when Reynolds grabbed her hand. He looked at it carefully, then glanced toward his wife. "Why are her fingernails blue?" He wouldn't let go of her wrist.

"To match her toenails," Cheryl answered.

Angela and her mother both rolled their eyes and uttered the same word, "Duh!"

Releasing Angela's hand, Reynolds lifted the tablecloth and peered underneath the table to check his daughter's feet. He dropped the cloth back into place. "Her toenails *are* blue." He searched the faces gathered around the table. "Why are my daughter's toenails painted blue?"

"To match her fingernails," Christopher explained.

Miller and Sinclair rolled their eyes and spoke in unison, "Duh!"

Reynolds shifted his attention to Miller, but his son interrupted. "Dad," Christopher asked, "can I get my ear pierced?"

"Not on purpose," responded Reynolds.

"Dad!" protested Christopher. "I'm serious."

"You want serious?" asked his father. "Here's serious. Absolutely not."

"Not both of them! Only one," explained his son.

"Not one. Not two. Not ever." Reynolds reached for some chicken, selecting a breast and a drumstick.

"But I wanna wear an earring!" Christopher pleaded.

"Wear clip-ons," Reynolds countered calmly, and then suddenly froze. "Forget what I just said about the clip-ons.

No earrings of any kind anyplace on your body, do you understand?"

"Oh, man!" Christopher's shoulders hunched upward, then settled back into place.

"Mr. Miller has pierced ears," Angela observed.

Reynolds took a biscuit and buttered it. "Mr. Miller also has a long ponytail, but I don't hear either one of you asking for one of those."

Miller reached for his braid of hair and placed it forward over his shoulder, patting it defensively.

"I think you have lovely hair, Todd." Cheryl touched Miller on the hand. "It gives you a mark of distinction."

"Then can I grow my hair like that, Mommy?" Christopher offered in compromise.

"Not in this or any other lifetime," his mother said unequivocally, then smiled politely at Miller.

Christopher reached behind his head and tried to manipulate his very short hair into some form of ponytail.

The rest of the meal went along smoothly, which meant that the diners barely avoided confrontations involving politics, religion, and most especially the criminal justice system. Sinclair tried to be civil. Miller tested, taunted, and complained. Reynolds, while showing his friend due respect, at the same time tried to tell Miller how much he'd changed.

"I remember when no one in my office wanted to go up against you," Reynolds said with a mix of nostalgia and regret.

"That's when I had righteousness on my side." Miller looked at Sinclair. "I wanted to save the world. Well, maybe not the world—the South. That's no small accomplishment." He put two spoonfuls of sugar in his cup, stirred the coffee, and sighed. "Life was so much more gratifying when my clients were victims instead of victimizers."

Sinclair touched a cloth napkin to her lips and commented to Cheryl, "Well, I can't tell you when I've had such a pleasant time."

"I hope you have greater credibility with a jury," Miller said, mildly amused.

"I was being courteous." Sinclair put down the napkin near the side of her plate. "But if I have to answer under threat of contempt of court, I got tired of your self-serving, melodramatic whining about an hour ago. If you didn't feel so sorry for yourself, maybe your clients might have a better chance." She turned toward Cheryl and smiled graciously. "It was a lovely dinner; thanks so much for inviting me."

"If I knew you were going to be insulting," Miller said seductively, "I might have warmed up to you a lot earlier."

"Good night, Todd," Cheryl stated with finality.

"Am I leaving?" he asked.

She nodded yes.

"Oh, well," he said, then mockingly imitated Sinclair. "It was a *lovely* dinner; thanks so much for inviting me." He looked at Sinclair and gave her a killer smile.

Reynolds retrieved Miller's jacket and helped him with it. Miller gave Cheryl a good-bye hug, kissed Angela on the forehead, and squeezed Christopher's cheeks. "Don't give up on that earring." He took Christopher to the side. "If you need a good lawyer to sue your father, I'm your man." He took Sinclair's hand. "And that's ditto to you." He kissed the back of her hand and gave a gentleman's bow, which allowed Cheryl to pinch his behind.

He looked at Reynolds. "I think your wife has a thing for me," he said lasciviously.

"We all do," replied Reynolds. "It's called a headache." He opened the front door. "I'll push your car," Reynolds whispered loud enough for everyone to hear him. "No need for you to suffer any further embarrassment."

"Thank you," Miller said sarcastically. "Particularly for the discreet manner in which you handled my humiliating circumstance." The two of them walked outside. "While we're on the subject of humiliation," Miller continued, "why don't you arrange one of our little Sunday night card games."

"I can do that. Let's shoot for next week. I'll check everyone's schedule."

Miller reached his car and pried open the door. "I sort of miss that baby doctor blowin' cigar smoke around the table just before he cheats." He wedged himself into the driver's seat and started pumping the accelerator.

"You need to get a life," Reynolds suggested.

"I've already had one; trust me, life's greatly overrated."

"Lauren was right: Wallowing in self-pity gets old real fast." Reynolds placed the weight of his body against the driver's door to help Miller close it.

Miller rolled down his window until it stuck. "She never said, 'wallowing in self-pity.' Her exact words were 'self-serving, melodramatic whining.'" He turned the ignition, and the car sputtered. "If you're gonna agree with her, have the decency to quote her accurately." Miller playfully nudged Reynolds. "Did you see that certain sparkle in her eyes when I walked by her? I think she wants me. . . . She's probably gonna follow me home."

"If she does, call the police."

"I don't trust the police. They're in bed with the DA's

office." The car backfired, then started. "Speaking of bed, if she asks for my number, give it to her."

"The woman holds you in contempt."

"Being held is not a problem." Miller poked his face out the window. "It's the letting go that hurts." Miller drove off, with the damaged-muffler sound increasing appreciably as the car gained speed.

Reynolds headed toward his house as Sinclair left it. They walked to her car.

"Your friend's obnoxious in a charming sort of way." She unlocked her car door.

"He used to give the most powerful and eloquent closing arguments I'd ever heard," he said sadly.

"What happened?"

"Same thing that happens to all of us: It became a job, not a calling."

"You care for him a lot."

"He's an honest defense lawyer. When was the last time you heard those words strung together in the same sentence? Plus he believes the sixties really happened. You gotta love a guy with that kind of sense of humor." He kissed her on the cheek. "Drive careful."

"Thanks for dinner," she said.

He watched her drive until the car disappeared around the corner. He remained outside for a moment and thought about Miller. He shook his head and smiled, then walked toward the front door, quietly singing, "Ain't gonna let nobody turn me 'round, turn me 'round, turn me 'round. Ain't gonna let nobody . . ."

CHAPTER
13

AFTER RACHEL RECEIVED the phone call, she applied some light makeup to her cheeks—nothing too fancy or obvious—then worked on her eyelashes. God had blessed her with naturally long ones that seemed to invite the wrong type of strangers to gaze into her soul. Or so they tried. Occasionally she attracted the right men, who'd stay longer than the next application of mascara. She had a good life, better than her mother's, better than she sometimes thought she deserved. But still there remained a second pillow, seldom used. She kept it by her side and waited for a good reason to fluff it. Perhaps tonight, she hoped.

A loud sports car pulled into the driveway and sputtered. She smiled and brushed back her hair. She opened the door and went outside, making herself comfortable and attractive on the front porch.

"Hi," Miller said. "I hope I didn't call you too late."

"There's too late and there's not at all." They both smiled the same sad expression. "Have a seat, Todd."

"You're not too cold?" he asked.

"Would you rather be inside?" she responded with an accusing tease.

Miller sat next to her on the swinging settee. "No, no, this will be fine for now." He leaned back and looked at her. "Just didn't want you to catch something. There's a chill in the air."

She wet her index finger and stuck it high above her head. "There's a lot in the air this evening. All of it ain't cold."

Miller twiddled his fingers, and the swing swayed back and forth.

"What's wrong, Todd?"

"Wrong?" He looked at her, puzzled. "Nothing's wrong. I was just thinking about you and thought, since I was driving out this way, I'd give you a call to see . . ."

"If I was lonely, too?"

He stopped swaying.

"Doesn't matter why you called," she continued. "I'm glad you did."

He smiled gratefully and started swaying again. This time she helped.

"You're dressed pretty spiffy. You have one of your late-night client meetings?"

"Dinner with friends, nothing special. Talked law most of the night. Or to be more specific, *justice*."

"You can't stop being an attorney even on a Saturday night."

"It's in my blood, three generations."

"You ever think what you might be if you hadn't become a lawyer?"

"Probably a blues singer."

She laughed and leaned closer to him. They both

stopped swaying. She shivered and lightly rubbed her arms. "Guess you were right about that chill," she said playfully.

"You think we should go inside now?" he asked cautiously.

She stood and took his hand. "Think we probably should've gone in when you first suggested it."

They entered the house, and she double-locked the front door. After they'd made love, she studied with amusement the pillow wedged between the headboard and his face, and released a sigh.

"What's the matter?" he asked.

"Nothing," she said with a smile. "I'm just relieved that pillow got used. I was getting sick and tired of seein' it puffed up so full and proper like a proud little man with a stuck-out, hairless chest."

He put his arm around her and drew her closer to him. She placed her head on his heart, and he held her.

"How come you never had any children?" she asked.

"I never wanted to be evaluated that honestly." He stroked her hair.

She kissed him on the cheek, then more softly on the lips.

"What'd you do that for?" he asked.

"I heard good lawyers avoid asking questions they don't know the answers to." She ran her hand down his leg. "You're a good lawyer, aren't you, Todd?" She grabbed his pillow and propped it under his head.

"Is it time for the defense to rest?"

"Not yet," she answered seductively, then moved her body on top of his. Her eyelashes fluttered twice. "Not yet."

CHAPTER
14

DELBERT FINNEY STARED at the tape recorder on the detective's desk. "You gonna turn that on?" he asked.

"Not right now," answered the detective, who was reviewing his notes. He circled two sections and asked, "How often did you say you visited Professor Matheson's home?"

"Just that once."

"Sounded like you really enjoyed yourself."

Delbert's smile lit up the small room usually reserved for interviewing criminal suspects. "Most beautiful place I'd ever seen. We watched movies on a giant screen built right into the wall and ate take-out chicken and popcorn. Nobody important ever paid that much attention to me or cared what I wanted in life."

"Did you tell the professor what you wanted, Delbert?"

The slender young man nodded his head. "Told him I wanted to be happy. Popular." He looked at his feet. "Not such a country hick. I wanted to be someone Sereta would like." He looked at the detective. "She's a freshman like me."

The detective wrote her name on his pad.

"Most of all I wanted to accomplish something to make my parents proud, pay them back for all the sacrifices they made."

The detective wrote down the information and circled it. "While you were there, did anything unusual happen?"

"The whole thing was special for me. When I left, he gave me a book of short stories by Langston Hughes and a volume of poetry by Paul Laurence Dunbar. I read 'em soon as I got back to the dorm. They were about people I knew, people like me. I never thought poetry could describe common folk and still be about love." He scratched the back of his shoulder. "I read some of it to Sereta," he said shyly. "We're dating now."

"Seems like you owe the professor a great deal."

"I was miserable at that school when I first got there. It was so big. I threw up every night. I was the youngest of eleven, the only one to go to college, and I missed my family. Yeah. I owe Dr. Matheson everything."

"Would you kill for him?" The detective studied Delbert. "You know any other students who might do the same?"

Delbert stared at the detective for an uneasy moment. "Can't read other people's minds or hearts, but as far as me, I'd do whatever the professor asked me to do."

The detective turned on the tape recorder. "You mind repeating that? After you finish, you'll be free to go."

"It's good to be free," Delbert said proudly. "Didn't always feel that way. That was something else Dr.

Matheson gave me. So go ahead and turn on your machine. Record that, too."

Delbert completed the interview. As he was leaving, he saw Brandon, who offered to give him a ride back to the campus after his turn with the detective. Delbert accepted the offer and wished Brandon luck. While he waited in the hallway, he exchanged greetings with other classmates and told them what questions to expect from the detective and how to answer.

In the City of Brotherly Love, where the Liberty Bell is cracked but not broken, an eighteen-year-old black man with a history of mental illness had died at the hands of two white policemen. The off-duty officers shot him thirteen times. The coroner's report suggested that one of the officers had fired his weapon as the man fell helplessly to the ground.

This news story might have gone unnoticed by District Attorney Vanzant and his counterparts across the nation had it not been for several disturbing developments that made the incident unlike any previous police shootings of unarmed black men. First, the community didn't erupt in violence. Second, protestors compiled a document referred to as "the list," modeled after Matheson's course. Local activists reviewed records of police shootings that had resulted in black fatalities going back a period of five years. The names and addresses of the white officers involved in those killings were published in newsletters and distributed throughout the city. Their photos and "unpunished crimes" were printed on wanted posters plastered on street signs and displayed in storefront windows. Minority officers were excluded from the list, which intensified hostility among white police, who refused to patrol certain communities at night and sought reassignments away from their black partners.

"Listen to this," Vanzant muttered as he quickly read an article faxed to him from one of his associates. "The head of the Fraternal Order of African-American Police held a news conference condemning the shooting and insisted reforms were long overdue, saying, 'I appreciate the frustrations experienced by people of color, and I believe many of these problems could be alleviated, if not altogether eliminated, by hiring and promoting more black officers.'"

Vanzant crumpled the article and surveyed his staff. "That grandstandin' son of a bitch ought to be fired. He's a damn disgrace to the uniform. Tryin' to make political hay out of a situation this volatile." He shook his fist. "You know they got people followin' the cops on that list wherever they go, even harassin' their wives and children?" He folded his arms behind his head and expanded his chest. "We gotta get out in front of this. Nip it in the bud before Matheson has fan clubs poppin' up all over the country."

Reynolds watched Winslow remove slices of cucumber from a Tupperware container.

Sinclair reviewed her paperwork. "We've got a few local congressmen drafting legislation to prohibit these types of efforts if they jeopardize law enforcement or create a danger to public safety."

Vanzant shoved a wad of tobacco into his mouth. "Fat chance of that seein' the light of day," he uttered with disgust. "Our friends at the ACLU have probably already filed a lawsuit to block it. Oughta put their useless names on a list and see how they like it." Vanzant rose from his chair and slowly moved to a narrow window, where he stood staring outside, hands on hips. "I wanna know the minute this happens anywhere else. I don't care what the issue is—if anybody starts to copycat Matheson, I want to be notified immediately."

Reynolds knew enough about Vanzant's style and body language to recognize that the meeting had ended and that his boss wasn't likely to turn away from the window until everyone left. Sinclair was the first to go, followed quickly by Winslow. Reynolds remained a moment, pondering these developments. Once again Macbeth's witches had risen from the earth, except this time they spoke with southern accents. If their sensibilities weren't exactly an-eye-for-an-eye Old Testament, at the very least they reflected a Wild West frontier form of law and order, where a black code of honor replaced the blue code of silence.

The struggle for civil rights had migrated north. It remained to be seen how long it would continue before troops were called out to permanently quell the disturbance. Reynolds exited the office, and Vanzant returned to his desk.

CHAPTER
15

EARVIN COOPER DIDN'T need the services of any cop, particularly a black one—not for advice and certainly not for protection.

"If you see or hear anything suspicious, you give us a call," the black officer said. He'd tried to be helpful and courteous, but he'd been greeted more warmly in the past by rabid pit bulls.

"Don't need you or anybody else to fight my battle," Cooper grunted before taking a step away from his front door. "You got any advice, save it for the lost soul fool enough to trespass on my property." Cooper slammed the screen door and marched toward his garage. He stopped at the officer's voice.

"Mr. Cooper?" the policeman said.

Cooper turned, his hands on his hips, defiant. He stood five feet five on a good day. In high school he'd played middle linebacker with a ferocity that had crushed opponents. He continued to see much of the world as a football field, where yielding an inch could mean the difference between victory and defeat.

"You didn't seem surprised to be on the list." The officer approached Cooper but remained at arm's length. "What'd you do to get on it?"

Cooper analyzed the black man who wore a uniform of authority. He made no effort to conceal his contempt as he cleared his throat and spit on the lawn. "You don't really want to know the answer to that, now, do ya?" He wiped his mouth with the back of his hand and stared at the officer.

The policeman nodded slightly. "Take care of yourself, Mr. Cooper." The officer proceeded to his patrol car and made a point of backing into a small flowerbed before he spun out of the driveway.

Cooper entered his garage and headed to the back wall, where he unlocked a metal cabinet. He removed a box the size of a small coffin and pried open the lid. He inspected his collection of guns and rifles, then removed several containers of ammunition and was beginning to organize his arsenal when his wife entered.

"Earvin, what that policeman want?" Ruth Cooper glanced at the weapons spread out on the cement floor and raised an eyebrow in quiet surrender. She knew enough not to ask about his guns. They'd made a pact many years ago: He wouldn't keep them in the house, and she wouldn't interfere with his visitation rights.

"There's a burglar in the neighborhood—just wanted to warn everybody." He didn't look at her while he loaded the first gun.

"A burglar?" she asked in disbelief. "Ain't nobody got nothin' to steal 'round here. That why you foolin' with this nonsense again? I don't want none of these in my home."

"It's my home, too, Ruth, and I ain't foolin' with nothin'. Just go back inside; make sure the doors and windows are locked."

"It's gonna be hot tonight," she protested. "I ain't gonna be able to sleep with the windows closed."

"Put on the damn fan."

"Makes too much noise."

"So does your mouth, but you don't seem to mind that." He stopped fidgeting with his guns and aimed his uneasiness at her. "You got a choice: Stay awake 'cause it's too hot or stay awake 'cause it's too noisy. Now, what's it gonna be?"

She made a sucking sound to indicate her disapproval. He grunted once, then arched his shoulders. After forty years of marriage they'd mastered the art of finding practical shortcuts to annoy each other while avoiding confrontations that might jeopardize their happy union.

Ruth took the potentially negative situation and turned it into a positive with the same skill she used to discover innovative recipes for leftovers. "Well, if I'm not gonna sleep tonight," she said with uncommon emphasis on her southern diction, "might as well soak extra long in that lavender water you like so much."

Cooper turned and faced her with renewed interest.

"Wouldn't hurt if you took some extra time tonight and made yourself smell 'specially good, too," she said flirtatiously.

He watched her leave the garage with her dress demonstrating a bit more sway than customary. He loaded a second gun and grinned widely.

CHAPTER
16

MILLER FINISHED HIS third bottle of beer and opened a fourth. Reynolds added a splash of cranberry to a glass of orange juice and sipped it while he studied the faces of his opponents.

"He's exactly the last thing we need stirring up trouble and acting like one of those drug-dealin' gangbangers going around frightening decent, hardworking people," declared an agitated Thornton Starr, the host of this evening's poker game.

"Be careful, Doc, you're talking about Todd's clients," cautioned Winston McKay, a real estate broker who had made his fortune buying below-market homes from whites fleeing integration, then selling them to his fellow blacks at exorbitant profits.

"No decent black attorney would represent them," explained Thornton. He puffed on his Cuban cigar blowing smoke at Miller.

"That's 'cause you've got all the black lawyers in

town handling your malpractice suits," Miller struck back. He put two cards facedown on the table and dealt himself two more.

"Only malpractice claim ever brought against me was from a crack baby's mama, and that got thrown out of court. I only deliver 'em; I can't stop junkies from poisoning their children while they're still in the womb," Thornton said with a deliberate drawl that helped accentuate his disgust.

"I say Matheson ought to be congratulated for what he's doing," suggested Winston. "This country always wants to sweep the dirt under the carpet. It's about time someone had the guts to look under the rug and prove the house is still dirty."

"I suppose you're one of those fools who believe in reparations for slavery," scolded Thornton.

"Government finds money for every other group. It's not like we haven't earned it." Winston drank the remainder of his cognac.

"That's the problem with black folks," said Thornton. "Always looking to dredge up our suffering as if anybody gave a fuck. Spend all their time begging for reparations when they ought to be finding a way to get a pay raise at work. I'll take one card," he said as an aside. "And you can forget about our so-called leaders trying to solve any real problems. Show me a civil rights leader earning less than six figures annually and I'll show you a piss-poor businessman. If you can't get rich pimping the poor, you better trade your M.B.A. for a divinity degree." He relit his cigar. "Hell, even an atheist can make a fortune if he pastors a church."

"I'd forgotten how cynical this group was," observed Miller.

"Not to mention racist," added Reynolds.

"I'm not racist," Thornton said defensively. "I just don't like people who act like niggers—don't care what color they are or how many degrees they've obtained."

"Maybe Matheson put the wrong people on his list," advised Miller. "Might've been better off going after the enemy within."

"I'll take two," announced Winston.

Miller dealt him the cards, then drank the rest of his beer.

"Better get ready to see his own damn name at the top of somebody's agenda. Must think he's teaching at one of those Ivy League schools in New England, where they like their faculty radical and their coeds naked and multi-cultural. He's lucky these redneck crackers haven't lynched his black ass. No offense, Todd," apologized Thornton, who puffed twice on his cigar.

"None taken," assured Miller. "Some of my closest relatives are redneck crackers and have never given it a second thought."

"They're not the only ones don't use their minds," continued Thornton. "Black folk run around like a bunch of headless chickens."

"Maybe that's because our leaders have been assassi-nated," proposed Winston.

"Or bought off," submitted Reynolds.

"And what happens when one of our leaders gets mur-dered? Instead of doing something constructive, every year we take off the whole month of February and listen to his relatives talk about him." Thornton put out his cigar. "When the Kennedys get assassinated, you see their children runnin' around giving don't-ask-what-your-country-can-do-for-you speeches? Hell, no. They act like they got some sense and move on with their lives.

"Now, you tell me, just 'cause a man's a plumber, does that mean when he dies I'm supposed to ask his son to finish fixing my pipes? If your daddy's a martyr, that doesn't give you the right to open up a franchise in his name and start charging fees for yourself. Lord, there's something terribly wrong with the way we market martyrdom and wallow publicly in our collective pain and struggle." He moved some chips to the side. "I'll buy Coretta a damn red dress myself if she'd promise to smile more often and get out on the dance floor." Thornton lit a new cigar.

"I think I've had too much to drink," commented Miller. "Thornton's starting to make sense; I know that can't be right."

"None of you want to admit it, especially Todd over there," pointed Thornton, "but the trouble facing my people is mostly self-induced and group-inflicted."

"What's this '*my* people' stuff?" Miller asked as he dealt Reynolds three cards. "You've married more white women than I've dated."

"And I've divorced every one of 'em," clarified Thornton. "I may stray, but I always come back home." He studied his cards and held them close to his chest.

"Now, that's the Thornton I know," said a relieved Reynolds. "Doesn't make a lick of sense and is incredibly proud of it."

"Go ahead and joke," pouted Thornton.

Reynolds looked around the table at the others. "Am I joking?" he asked with great sincerity.

Thornton tossed five blue chips and three red ones into

the pot. "Y'all can match that or do the smart thing and fold while you still got chump change in your wallets."

"I think you're bluffing again." Reynolds confidently threw his chips into the center of the table. "I'll see that and raise you." He picked up several green chips and individually dropped them. "One, two, three, four, and five big green ones!"

"I'm out," said Miller, who tossed his cards onto the table. "I've learned the hard way a prosecutor doesn't take a risk unless he's got a winning hand."

Winston placed his cards down. "Too rich for my blood."

Thornton studied Reynolds, then looked at Miller. "Something tells me you two been working together all night, and I'm about to put an end to your unholy alliance." He reached across the table and retrieved some additional poker chips from a wooden case. "I'm gonna see those five green and raise you ten more." He puffed away until his face disappeared behind a cloud of smoke.

Reynolds was tempted to pursue the matter, but after rechecking his cards he surrendered. "If you need the money that much, go ahead and take it."

"Don't ever try to fool a pediatrician, especially one who's been in practice for thirty years." Thornton placed both hands around the pile of chips and pulled it toward himself with a grin partially blocked by the cigar that dangled from his mouth, dropping ashes onto the table. "Been readin' faces since they first peeked out the uterus, and seen every expression known to man."

Miller scratched the bottom of his foot. As usual, all the guests were forced to remove their shoes before entering the doctor's home, in a fruitless effort to keep the cream-colored Berber carpets clean. "I think I'm allergic to your rug."

"Don't worry, it's not an allergy," assured Thornton. "One of the dogs has fleas."

"You let dogs roam around the house with fleas, but your friends have to take off their shoes?" asked Winston.

"I *know* where my dogs have been," answered Thornton. "You gentlemen want to get in another hand before the pizzas arrive? Winston will lend you some money."

"Can't afford the interest he'd charge," said Reynolds.

"You can take out a second mortgage—use it for collateral," offered an accommodating Winston.

"Don't take this personal, Winston," advised Reynolds, "but I don't trust you."

The men laughed. Thornton filled Winston's glass with more brandy. He handed a cold bottle of beer to Miller. Reynolds passed on a refill of juice. "Seriously, James," said Thornton, "this problem with Matheson must be making your life miserable."

"Why's that?" Reynolds asked uneasily.

"'Cause he's making it difficult for every successful black man, and that has to be doubly true for someone in law enforcement, especially at a time when everyone's loyalties are questioned. Hell, I still get asked what I think about Islamic fundamentalists. I'm a damn Baptist; what these crackers think I think?" He looked at Miller and raised his glass in an apologetic toast. "Sorry, Todd."

Miller raised his bottle. "If you only knew what these *crackers* thought about me." He swallowed some beer.

"All I'm sayin' is, we finally found someone to take our place on the bottom of the heap, and along comes this fool professor and focuses the attention right back on us."

Thornton took a quick puff. "Now I've got to pledge allegiance three times a day in public."

"Everybody knows you're a patriot. You still got your flag on your Rolls, don't you, Doc?" Winston asked good-naturedly.

"Sure do," answered Thornton. "And I'll let you in on a little secret: I got me a Confederate one in the glove compartment, just in case of emergency. My motto is, be prepared and stay flexible."

"I think you've twisted flexibility just about as far as it'll go," remarked Reynolds. "Which may be our only hope."

"You know what your problem is, James?" asked Thornton. "You're a black man with integrity, and that's a mighty lonely place to be." He looked at the men around the table with a twinkle in his eyes. "Or so I've been told." Everyone except Reynolds laughed.

"Now, as far as this mess with Matheson," continued Thornton, "it's one thing we got to live down these ignorant punks weaned on criminal activity, but you can't get no more educated than a Ph.D. He's our best and brightest. If he goes wrong, what does that say about the rest of us to white folks who are just waiting to say, 'I told you so'?"

Reynolds looked at Miller. "Todd, when a white person screws up, do you feel personally embarrassed or responsible?"

"Yes," confessed Miller.

"I forgot who I was asking," corrected Reynolds. "You're Caucasian twice removed."

"Don't forget," Winston joined in, "Matheson's father is a pastor."

"That's exactly my point," Thornton shot back. "If

he's a bad seed, then none of us are ever gonna be trusted. He's setting the race back another hundred years."

"Yeah," said Winston, "but remember when you were young and went looking for a hot tenderoni? What was every full-blooded man's dream?"

The men looked at each other. Miller guessed, "That you'd have enough gas money to drive around and search?"

"That you'd find a preacher's daughter!" Winston proclaimed excitedly. "You knew she'd be so repressed all you had to do was touch her button and bam! You wouldn't be able to walk straight for a whole week."

"Why are we listening to your boyhood fantasies?" asked Reynolds.

"Wait a second," interjected Thornton. "Winston's onto something. Same principle applies to a preacher's son, except a man reacts differently to being repressed."

"Yeah," agreed Reynolds. "He studies hard and goes to medical school."

"You don't want to listen, suit yourself," Thornton said, annoyed. "But you won't convince me you're not paying a heavy price for that man's actions. Before this is over, there's gonna be a lot of nervous and angry people in this city, and that's a combination killed more black folks than King Cotton."

"Thornton," Miller interrupted, "can I ask you a personal question?"

"Be my guest, and don't forget that's who you are."

"Are you a Republican?"

Thornton put his hands on his hips and lectured Miller. "I'm for anyone who lowers capital gains and eliminates the estate tax." He looked around and included the other two men. "I don't need no black fist in the air or no poor hands in my pockets; just let me keep and invest my money, and we don't ever have to discuss civil rights again."

The doorbell chimed.

"Saved by the bell," Miller said thankfully.

"Dinner is served," announced Thornton, much to the relief of Reynolds, who'd come close to losing his appetite.

The rest of the evening the men avoided political and religious discussions, although Thornton did his best to interject the matter of race with every new slice of pizza. At midnight they'd had enough and thanked their host for an enlightening evening. They located their respective shoes and exited through the rear door so as not to scuff the imported marble in the foyer.

Reynolds drove while Miller sat silently in the passenger seat. Miller's sports car remained in his mechanic's shop over the weekend to get an "oil change and massage."

"You've been noticeably quiet; that's not like you."

"My friend," Miller said in a depressed voice, "I haven't been like me in quite some time." He paused and looked inquisitively at Reynolds. "Did what I just said make sense?"

"For someone who's had a six-pack of German beer and half a bottle of domestic wine, I think you're perfectly coherent."

Miller rolled down his side window and inhaled a breath of fresh air. "You ever ask yourself if it's worth it?"

Reynolds stared straight ahead. "Every day."

"And is the answer ever yes?" Miller wondered.

"To tell you the truth, it's a rhetorical question. That

means it's not supposed to be answered," responded Reynolds.

"My father told me never to trust a black man who began any sentence with 'To tell you the truth.'"

"Why did he include only blacks?"

"My daddy's a bigot."

Reynolds slowed down to turn a sharp curve. "My father told me never to believe any white man who began any sentence."

"Began any sentence with what?" asked Miller.

"That's it. Any sentence, if started by a white man, was enough for my father to dismiss as an outright lie."

"How come he included only white men?"

"He was wise," answered Reynolds. "And, he hadn't met Dr. Thornton Starr or his moneymaking real estate sidekick."

Miller laughed. Reynolds stopped the car at a red light. He rolled down his window. A car pulled alongside. The stereo from the vehicle blared full blast, playing a rap song with the word "nigger" interspersed frequently with the phrase "black bitch motherfucker." Reynolds and Miller turned toward the source of the noise and discovered a blonde, blue-eyed girl in her teens, joyously moving her head back and forth to the rhythm.

The white girl noticed Reynolds and smiled politely. He nodded hello. She blew a small pink balloon of bubble gum, then gathered it in and resumed chewing. The light turned green, and she drove through the intersection.

Reynolds's foot remained on the brake. He looked at Miller. "We have met the enemy," he said diplomatically.

"And it be us," agreed Miller. "Where's Marvin Gaye when he's needed most?"

"His father killed him," answered Reynolds.

"That's what fathers do best to their sons, although it's usually over an extended period of time." He looked at Reynolds with an irrepressible grin. *"Make me wanna holler, throw up both my hands."*

Reynolds floored the accelerator and burned rubber. He dropped off Miller before taking the long way home. He always needed additional time alone after playing cards with "Baby Doc." Tonight he'd need more than usual. Civil rights discussions often required an extra twenty minutes to wind down.

Thornton belonged to every black bourgeoisie organization in the city. When he criticized them, he did so with a great deal of authority and a significant amount of expertise. The good doctor's firsthand experience shaped his jaded views regarding the state of black affairs. He understood better than most that Gucci shoes were not exactly meant for marching, which explained in part why today's community leaders flew first class and slept in five-star hotels. That reality, along with his views concerning the marketing of martyrdom, resonated with Reynolds in a way that left him increasingly depressed and pessimistic about the likelihood of African-American progress.

A year before, at the insistence of his wife, he'd taken the entire family on a tour of civil rights museums. She felt the history lesson would give their children a sense of the struggle. He argued that the concept of a continuing "struggle" represented little more than a euphemism used frequently to explain failure.

He resisted the trip but eventually relented, to his utter chagrin. The first two stops were Montgomery followed by Birmingham, cities responsible for more than their fair share of human misery, therefore requiring extra large facilities to adequately warehouse it. That suffering formed the basis for the exhibits now permanently enshrined in sanitized buildings that charged admission for the privilege to relive the torment. Reynolds noticed that the first site happened to be in close proximity to a zoo on one side and a newly constructed public aquarium on the other, which gave the term *theme park* a whole new meaning.

During their visit several street vendors were arrested for selling souvenirs without official permission from the protectors of copyright infringement laws. Evidently, the words spoken by slain black leaders couldn't be listened to without payment of royalties to family survivors. Reynolds considered this a bit odd since most assassinated black men had died fighting for the rights of the oppressed. They had intended their beneficiaries to be the family of man, not their own personal estates. Reynolds managed to buy a Dr. King coffee mug, a tape of his famous speeches, and a Malcolm X T-shirt at discount before the unlicensed entrepreneurs were hauled away by the franchise guardians. The institutionalization of human suffering had indeed become big business.

His home state had given birth to the blues, and while it might be heresy to think this way, Reynolds believed the singer of the blues always felt better than the people forced to listen. The songs of despondency were synonymous with his people's history, interchangeable and indistinguishable from one another. And as he'd learned from his father's life experience, once you dwell on the struggle, you invariably and inevitably drown in it.

In Reynolds's estimation, the crisis in black leadership could be traced to various grave sites, many without the benefit of headstone or manicured plot. Death left an unexpected legacy, a warning heeded by those who dared to wear the mantle of the fallen hero. The price paid for worshiping at the shrine of dead martyrs included the inescapable knowledge that when you lead, you die. No matter how that message might be packaged, whether in a holiday parade or a funeral procession, that self-defeating conclusion remained essentially the same.

That lesson had influenced today's newly installed leaders, who, whether self-appointed or democratically anointed, stood a greater chance of being killed by a television crew's camera than by an assassin's bullet—and, in truth, a few had almost trampled each other to death in the race to be the first to the microphone. They feared a fall of their stock portfolio more than any downward movement of a sheriff's nightstick. And while they denounced poverty with an elegance matched only by their custom-tailored designer wardrobes, their lavish incomes were derived from, and contingent upon, the very system that maintained it.

Oh, what a tangled web is weaved, reflected Reynolds, when service to the poor conceals a lucrative scam and faith-based devotion masks a clever tax shelter. No wonder Matheson became so popular so quickly. When the moral compass hasn't worked in a while, movement in any direction tends to be viewed as a hopeful sign. And when you've been lost so long, you'll follow any path that leads you out of despair to the promised land and a victory over your enemy, even if that foe is undefined and unavailable.

In the absence of any truth, a lie will serve as an acceptable, even desirable substitute. If that lie's told often enough, it becomes the standard by which you measure your history, your value, your life. Matheson offered an alternative to both the blues singer and the song: Swing instead of sing, and then make someone else pay the piper. Reynolds feared that in short order this would become a tune to which many would tap their feet and dance to their hearts' content.

Reynolds arrived home and pulled into his driveway. He walked across the lawn and, when he reached his front entrance, remembered something Thornton had said. A vision came to him of Dr. King's widow in a red party dress, moving to the beat of a carefree drummer. Wouldn't that be a sight to behold? he thought. It might soothe the spirit and even be enough to ignite a fire, spark a new movement no longer dependent upon bowed heads, closed eyes, and broken hearts.

He didn't know precisely what role Matheson would play in closing the door to perpetual mourning and opening another door to something potentially more destructive. But, as the saying goes, "You've got to dance with the person who brought you." Matheson's might be the first song or possibly the last, but Reynolds hoped everyone would leave the prom better off for hearing it.

CHAPTER
17

MATHESON CANCELED HIS appointments today because he wanted to be alone. His increasing celebrity had begun to interfere with his teaching duties. He needed some quiet time to grade papers and complete a new course syllabus for next term. He'd told his secretary to turn off the lights in the outer offices; then he sent her home early. He skipped lunch and worked at his desk until late afternoon. He was thinking about taking a break when an attractive young woman entered. He'd seen her before at several campus functions and guessed she might be a sophomore.

"Can I help you?" he asked.

"My grandfather's on your list." She walked to the chair in front of his desk and sat down. "I'd like you to take him off."

Matheson studied her. She sat perfectly erect and brushed the blond hair away from her face. Her hand trembled slightly. He noticed a minor flinch of her left shoulder, which signaled tension, and when her eyes avoided his gaze, he sensed more than nervousness.

"You are . . . ?" he inquired politely.

"Melissa Grayson," she answered forcefully. "My grandfather's Chester Grayson."

"Did he send you?"

"He has no idea I've come."

Matheson looked at her for a moment. She was telling the truth or had learned to lie very well. Given her bloodlines, he wasn't prepared to give her the benefit of the doubt. He slid open his desk drawer and searched through a file. He removed a folder and placed it on top of his desk, then nudged it slowly toward her.

"Do you want to read about your grandfather, or do you already know about his sordid past?"

"He's helped raise me all my life. I don't need to read about him to know the kind of man he is."

"Who he is, isn't terribly important. What he was and, more to the point, what he did, *is*." He opened the folder. "Family's important to you?" he asked kindly.

"Yes."

"It was important to them, too." He placed several black-and-white photos along the front of the desk and positioned them so they'd face her. He touched the first picture. "The man your grandfather murdered had three sons. The oldest was seven. His wife was pregnant with his daughter, the one he'd never see, or hold, or bounce on his knee."

Melissa looked away, then stared at the floor.

"Did your grandfather ever bounce you on his knee? I'm sure he must have. And, I'm equally sure you giggled and he laughed and probably someone snapped a photo."

He pushed a second picture near her. She didn't look

at it. "Perhaps it was like that one. Children laughing. Happy. Not a care in the world. Rushing to greet their father, who has his arms filled with presents and love and hugs and a promise of a future he couldn't deliver."

She looked at the photo, then at him. "My grandfather's a good man, Professor. He's one of the most decent and gentle men I've ever known."

"He castrated a black man, then threw his testicles into a fire." This time Matheson looked away. "That man was studying to become a doctor, someone who'd take a vow to heal the sick. A policeman killed his oldest son, the one with the brightest smile in that picture, after a botched robbery attempt. His middle son became a heroin addict and overdosed before his fifteenth birthday. The state institutionalized his youngest son. They diagnosed him as crazy because he stood on a bridge one night screaming about how much he hated white people."

Matheson looked at her without any anger. When he finally spoke, he conveyed only sadness. "And the daughter who'd never been held by her father? She sought comfort in the arms of any man who'd hold her, whether they paid her or not." He leaned toward her. "Your grandfather didn't kill just one man. He destroyed an entire family." The sadness disappeared, replaced by defiance. "I don't give a damn how much he's changed. I'm not taking him off the list."

After a moment of silence during which Melissa dug her nails into her thigh, she took the file and began to go through it. Matheson searched her face for some type of expression. She gave no clue to her feelings. He wondered if she was actually reviewing the folder or just wanted to avoid his eyes.

"Do you conduct similar research on all the victims?"

The question surprised him. He waited for her to look at him, but she kept herself occupied by shuffling the documents.

"Yes."

"You've spoken to their families?"

"Whenever I could."

She placed the file back onto his desk. She looked at him and spoke calmly. "Do they have as much hate in their hearts as you?"

Her eyes held no indictment, making Matheson's response more difficult. "You think this is about hate?"

Her eyes changed suddenly. They became bright and intense, a jeweled, dark blue fire that consumed the room. "Who the hell made you God?"

"If I *had* been God, you'd never have known your grandfather."

At the casualness of his reply, she slumped back into her chair as if struck hard in the stomach. She waited for a moment, rose quietly, and headed for the door.

"Miss Grayson, I'll take him off the list."

She stopped to look at him. He stood behind his desk.

"All he has to do is admit publicly what he did fifty years ago. He doesn't have to say he's sorry. He doesn't have to apologize. There's no one left in the family to pay restitution to. He just has to admit he murdered a man. And he doesn't even have to say why."

He walked slowly toward her. He opened the door and waited for her to accept the offer or leave. She didn't move.

"I'll do you one better, Melissa. He doesn't have to announce it publicly. He just has to admit it . . . to you."

Her eyes closed briefly. She opened them and spoke softly. "Whatever my grandfather did when he was young, I know he's paid for it every day. I only hope, Professor, that you'll suffer as much for your sins."

He remained motionless for several moments after she left. When he finally moved, he became aware for the first time of her perfume. The fragrance reminded him of the bath bubbles his mother used to pour into the water; as a child he refused to wash unless the cherry-vanilla bubbles overflowed the top of the tub. He hadn't thought about that for many years. His mother had left him before he turned eight. From that point on, he took showers.

He returned to his desk and picked up the folder. It felt heavy. He removed a photo of Grayson and stared at his face. Melissa had her grandfather's eyes and mouth. He wondered what else she'd inherited. He closed the folder without replacing the photo, which he slowly tore in two.

CHAPTER
18

EARVIN COOPER RACED out of his home brandishing an ax handle. "Get the hell away from here!" he shouted at the two young black men on his front lawn.

Delbert held the base of a signpost as Brandon finished hammering it into the ground. Delbert headed quickly away but stopped when he noticed Brandon hadn't followed.

Cooper stood face to face with the powerfully built black who was calmly holding a hammer. "Take that thing out my lawn," Cooper said without looking at the sign.

"Take it out yourself," Brandon responded. "If you don't know what to do with it, maybe you can burn it. You're pretty good with fire, aren't you, Mr. Cooper?"

Cooper gripped the ax handle and raised it a few inches. Brandon waited patiently and tapped the hammer against his side twice.

Delbert joined Brandon. "We better go," he said.

"Better listen to your friend and get your black asses off my property," Cooper warned. "Or you can come back later and I'll have more than this stick in my hand."

"Maybe I'll just do that," answered Brandon. "You be sure to be here and welcome me yourself."

"I'll be here, boy. You can count on it."

Brandon and Delbert proceeded to the car parked across the street. Cooper followed a safe distance behind and scribbled the license plate number on his hand. Brandon sped off, his tires kicking up dirt and gravel.

After the car disappeared, Cooper returned to the sign-post and read: *A MURDERER LIVES HERE BUT NOT FOR LONG.* He stared at the sign, then placed both fists around the ax handle and began hacking the sign into pieces.

CHAPTER

19

THE LITTLE BOY outran the sounds of terror that drowned out the steady pounding in his small chest. But he couldn't outrace his fear or the bloody fingers reaching for him. He closed his eyes and tasted the salt from his tears and prayed his suffering would be short. He couldn't tell if his legs were still moving. The punishing earth beneath his feet had long ago numbed his lower body. He felt slender fingers on his shoulders. With one last effort at courage he opened his eyes and unsuccessfully attempted to scream. He turned and frantically pounded the black man's chest. The boy heard dozens of rapidly approaching footsteps finally coming to his rescue. He saw the blazing cross and felt a sense of relief followed by exhilaration. He relaxed his fists and stared at his hands, which were now stained with blood.

Reynolds awoke to find Matheson patiently standing over him.

"I hope I didn't startle you." Matheson stepped to the side and let the sun blind Reynolds. "Your wife told me I could find you here."

Reynolds slipped out of the hammock that hung comfortably between two large trees in his backyard. "Don't tell her I wasn't raking leaves." He did a stretching exercise to loosen up the tightness in his shoulders.

"Your secret's good with me," Matheson said, then stepped back into the sunlight. "You looked distressed. I imagine prosecutors often have problems sleeping well."

"We sleep just fine, especially when we put away the bad guys. Must've been something I ate. Chili peppers usually make me toss and turn." Reynolds smiled politely. "So, why are you visiting me on such a lovely Saturday afternoon?"

"I was hoping you might join me for a casual ride around town. Give us a chance to chat, get to know each other."

Reynolds cocked an eyebrow and tried to read Matheson's face. He considered the invitation, then shrugged. "Sure, let's go for it."

The two men drove for twenty minutes. Luckily, Matheson owned a terrific sound system along with musical selections that made conversation unnecessary. Reynolds was equally impressed with the car, an immaculate classic Mercedes convertible two-seater.

"You must spend a small fortune keeping this car in mint condition. What is it, a sixty-seven?"

"Sixty-eight. Actually, I have a new one, but I like to take this out on weekends."

"Didn't know being a professor was that lucrative."

"I supplement my salary with books and lectures. But

the real reason I drive expensive cars is, I enjoy pissing off my colleagues." Matheson turned off the radio. "It's amazing the difficulty some folks have accepting a black man's success."

"Who would've thought?" Reynolds said.

"Thought what?"

"That you'd enjoy pissing people off."

Matheson laughed and inserted a new CD.

Reynolds smiled and leaned back, gently touching the headrest. "Where are we going?"

"To the hood, James. To the hood." Matheson pressed down on the accelerator, and the car's speed increased quickly, forcing Reynolds to sit more rigidly against the red-leather bucket seat.

They drove through West Jackson, Reynolds quietly viewing the barricaded stores and abandoned buildings along Lynch and Maple and Sunset Avenue. They arrived at a street called Hope, but there was little of it for the men who stood at the corner, waiting for darkness to arrive. Reynolds knew these folks intimately. He prosecuted them every day. They were the human signposts whose messages were long ago read and deemed unimportant. Day or night, they waited in front of boarded-up businesses that had deserted them along with any dreams they might have had for a future.

The only playground in the neighborhood had been designated too dangerous for children and was confiscated by young men with neither fear nor anything else of value to lose. During the day they sprinted back and forth on an asphalt court shooting jump shots; at night they shot dope or each other. Freedom didn't exist here. Even the nets that hung from the basketball hoops were made of steel chains that clanged instead of swished whenever a ball fell through their rusted links.

Reynolds and Matheson exited the Mercedes and stood next to each other. A young black girl, no older than eight, walked toward the opposite corner. Matheson watched her as he spoke to Reynolds. "You see that girl across the street?"

"Yeah."

The girl greeted two older boys, who followed her into an abandoned building.

"You might as well arrest her now," Matheson said softly.

"She guilty of a crime?"

"She's beautiful. That can be the ultimate crime on these streets. Or an invitation to commit one."

"If anybody's inviting a crime, it's not that little girl. It's you," Reynolds responded with a degree of anger that surprised him.

Matheson remained calm. "One rich, used-up ex-athlete with a penchant for white powder and whiter women gets acquitted, and the whole country loses its collective mind and vows to reform the legal system while making his life miserable. You have any idea what a two-hundred-year system of jury nullification has done to this community?"

"I know about poverty, Martin. About hopelessness and fear and the crimes that stem from them." Reynolds waited in vain for Matheson to look at him. "If you brought me here to show me that, then you're wasting your time. I sure as hell don't need a lecture from you about being black or poor."

"I didn't bring you here for a lecture, James. I brought you here to see what we've created. Broken buildings, broken lives, broken promises. One envelope with a trace of a biological or chemical weapon can send an entire country into hysteria, but we flood this place with drugs and guns and terror and nobody gives a damn!"

"Killing a bunch of old white men is gonna change that?"

"Somebody's got to make the people who live here believe their lives are important, that you can't destroy them without paying a price. Sandburg once said, 'Slums always seek their revenge.'" Matheson looked across the street. "Sometimes they need to be pointed in the right direction."

The young girl exited the building carrying a small plastic bag in her hand. She hustled down the street and met an older woman who took the bag from her. They dashed across a vacant lot and moved behind a large trash bin. A few moments later a car pulled out, driven by a black man. The woman had joined two men in the rear seat. The girl sat in the passenger seat, her face pressed against the glass, looking at Reynolds as the car sped past.

Matheson walked behind Reynolds and onto the basketball court. The men stopped playing and approached with wide grins. Reynolds watched them exchange a variety of soul handshakes and slaps and fist-knockings with the professor. One of the men tossed the ball to Matheson, who quickly hit a fadeaway jump shot from just inside the three-point line.

"Doctor Knowledge, you ready to shoot some hoops for real?" the man asked. "I can get you some sneaks, and if you wanna play for money, I can even make sure they fit."

"Jerome, you know I don't want to take advantage of your youth and inexperience," Matheson joked.

"If you beat me, I'll sign up for some of those courses at the college just like you want."

"Education is not for the vanquished, Jerome. Enlightenment is neither a by-product nor a reward for losing."

"Tell the truth!" someone shouted.

"Truth is like history. It's defined by the people who win." Matheson took a step toward Jerome. "When you're ready to experience that type of victory, I'll enroll you myself."

One of the younger men retrieved the ball and tossed it to Jerome. He dribbled it twice, then wrapped both arms around the ball, holding it firmly to his chest. "If we lived on the bottom of the ocean"—Jerome looked at Matheson with admiration—"none of us would be as deep as you, my brother." He gripped the ball with one hand and with the other saluted the professor.

"I'm coming back tomorrow," Matheson warned. "Be sure to practice that pitiful thing you call a hook shot."

"You just pump up those Air Nikes you got. Last time you jumped I almost saw the ground." Jerome laughed, then looked over at Reynolds. "He a friend of yours, Doctor?"

"In time, Jerome." Matheson gave a reassuring nod to Reynolds. "In time."

Matheson walked away from the men, who immediately returned to their game. Jerome received a hard body check under the basket and threw an elbow that connected on someone's chin.

Reynolds watched for a moment, then addressed

Matheson. "Somehow I thought you were preparing to challenge me one-on-one."

"I'm sure that would make some people happy. But I'd rather have you on the same team, James." Matheson looked at Reynolds and spoke seriously. "I mean that."

"I hope that's possible, Martin. I really do."

"You don't sound terribly optimistic," Matheson replied.

"I learned a long time ago never to predict a jury verdict. I've been surprised by the outcome too many times."

"And disappointed?" Matheson asked.

"On occasion, even heartbroken."

"That could be a good sign. It means you have a heart. Although it does depend somewhat on the reason for your grief." Matheson turned his body to the side and leaned closer to Reynolds. "Just exactly who do you cry for, James?"

"I cry for the victim, Martin."

"Then we have more in common than I'd hoped." Matheson gave Reynolds a reassuring pat on the shoulder and walked to the street corner. Reynolds looked back at the basketball scrimmage, which had turned even more intense. For a moment he thought being a part of that game might be preferable to joining the professor on some unknown journey. He hesitated, then followed Matheson down Hope.

"Are we going someplace in particular?" Reynolds asked.

"We *are* someplace, James." Matheson stopped. "It's called the future. Unless we change it." He resumed walking.

"You gonna leave your car there?" Reynolds asked as they were about to turn the corner.

"If you're not safe among your people, you're not safe anywhere."

"I take it that means you're covered by theft insurance," said Reynolds.

"With no deductible," confided Matheson, flashing a generous smile. "Come on, I'll treat you to lunch."

Reynolds shrugged. *I've come this far; might as well go the whole nine yards.*

The two men ate at a local soul food luncheonette. The woman who ran the place with her two sons knew Matheson and served him extra-large portions. The aroma of barbecued chicken and hickory-smoked ribs permeated the tiny establishment, which had a small eat-in counter and three lopsided wooden tables with bench chairs. Most of the people who entered came for takeout and didn't have to suffer the lack of air-conditioning.

Reynolds sat in a cramped space near a portable fan blowing warm air from a side window. Matheson kept his back to the door, making it easier for patrons to give him an affectionate pat on the shoulder or offer a congratulatory "Go get 'em, Doc" or "We're with you all the way."

"How's your brisket?" Matheson asked.

"Delicious," Reynolds replied between bites. "I haven't tasted greens and corn bread this good since . . . Well, now that I think of it, I don't remember if I've ever tasted them this good."

"There's a lot of love in this place, James. And every bit of it goes into what Eunice Williams calls down-home cookin'."

"You've known her a long time?"

"Her mother operated a diner sixty years ago and passed on the family recipes to Eunice, who's been teaching her sons, who will teach their daughters, and so the tradition lives on." Matheson drank some ice-cold lemonade. "My father used to come here when he was young. This whole area consisted of shops, restaurants, and theaters—all owned and operated at one time by black folks. Now this is the only shop that remains. Everybody else went the way of the dinosaurs, except it wasn't fire and floods that did them in but the ravages of a poorly conceived integration strategy."

"I doubt your father would consider himself a contributor to their extinction."

"I'm certain he wouldn't. But that doesn't change the reality of what we gave up to get to where we now are."

"You seem to be doing just fine," Reynolds countered. He ate some greens and savored the taste while waiting for the fencing match to continue. For some reason, it stopped.

"James, I really didn't want this afternoon to deteriorate into our rather counterproductive tit-for-tats. I'm more guilty of instigating those arguments than you are, and I apologize."

Reynolds felt uncomfortable. He could handle an arrogant Matheson, but the humble version made him nervous.

"More than anything else," continued the professor, "I'd like you to understand what I'm doing."

Reynolds set his knife and fork on the table and searched for an appropriate response. "Martin, what troubles me most is your indifference to ruining the lives of the very students you claim to care so much about. One or more of them is probably committing these murders, and you—"

"I know my students aren't responsible for any of

those deaths, James. And I'll take that knowledge to my grave."

"How can you be so sure?"

"Because I know," the professor answered.

Reynolds studied Matheson but could find nothing in his expression to indicate why he felt so certain. "For the moment, let's accept you're right. They had nothing to do with the murders. Still, they're celebrating every death. You've got them caring more about revenge than they—"

"They care about *justice*, James. They aren't celebrating revenge any more than the families of victims of violent crimes celebrate the death penalty. When those family members attend state-sponsored executions, they don't go there looking for blood. They're searching for closure. And when that switch is pulled or that needle injected, do they finally experience a sense of relief?" Matheson leaned back and released a sigh. "Yes. I imagine they do. It may not bring their loved ones back, but in some small measure it protects the ones still alive and the ones yet unborn. If you can't understand me, James, then you can't understand the system you represent or the job you do or the citizenship you hold. Don't blame me for being an American—blame America." Matheson smiled sadly, then leaned closer toward Reynolds. "Do you know what they call a person who bombs a terrorist?" he asked.

Eunice brought more corn bread to the table. "How's your meal, Professor? Hope your friend's enjoyin' his food as much as I enjoyed makin' it for him."

Reynolds smiled politely. "I've enjoyed it more than I can say, thank you very much. I'll be sure to come back."

"And bring plenty of company," Eunice said, pointing

behind her. "I got extra chairs out back." She placed her hand on Reynolds's shoulder. "Hope you saved some room for sweet potato pie or peach cobbler."

"One slice of each, please," said Matheson. "We'll share." He nodded at Reynolds.

"Comin' right up fresh from the oven," said Eunice, heading back to the kitchen.

Matheson smiled and looked at Reynolds. "It's not as American as apple pie, but it's all right to deviate occasionally from some traditions." Matheson held up his glass of lemonade and toasted Reynolds, who returned the favor.

CHAPTER
20

SHIFTING HIS WEIGHT to accommodate a sack of newspapers slung over his left shoulder, Robert Johnson cradled his favorite fishing rod, which was protected by a long black leather case he'd received last week for his thirteenth birthday. He'd be fishing now if his younger brother hadn't come down with a stomach virus. He could have ignored Joseph's plea to take over his paper route, but their mother had taught them that obligations needed to be fulfilled and brothers were supposed to help each other no matter what.

He tossed a newspaper on a front porch and never broke stride. He probably wasn't going to catch any fish this late, but he loved being near the water and intended to make up for lost time even if that meant he wouldn't be home before nightfall. His mother worked on Saturdays, and his brother would cover for him if she got back earlier than expected.

The two brothers were extremely close, and though

Joseph was only nine, Robert considered him his best friend. They'd do anything for each other, including but not limited to deceiving their mother for a noble cause such as fishing, football, or sneaking into the movies without paying.

Robert tossed another paper, toward a house surrounded by a bright white fence. It banged against the front door and ricocheted behind a medium-sized hedge. He glanced at his wristwatch and sighed. He hoped it hadn't landed in a wet area. Sprinklers were watering both sides of the walkway, and he didn't have any extra papers to spare. He promised Joey he'd deliver them all so his brother would stand a good chance of being newspaper boy of the month. It meant a whole week's bonus and bragging rights likely to increase tips for the rest of the year.

He left the sack of papers on the sidewalk to ensure they'd remain dry. Unwilling to abandon his fishing rod, he carefully extended the case and maneuvered it efficiently in front of him, avoiding the spray from an overactive sprocket wheel attached to a long green hose. He made it through safely and tucked the end of the case between his arm and ribcage, simulating his preferred method for snagging trout. The front door sprang open and startled him. He never heard the explosion but saw a bright red-yellow flash just before he was thrown in the opposite direction of the fishing pole.

The case floated high and lingered over his fallen body, eventually landing a few feet away. The water from the gyrating sprinkler sprayed him and threatened the leather case. He instinctively reached to protect it when he noticed the water around him turn red. He felt a hole in his chest and raised his head to see an old man at the front door, holding a shotgun.

Robert's head sank back to the wet earth. His body started convulsing in competition with the out-of-control sprinkler head. Chester Grayson slowly approached the teen and knelt beside him in stunned disbelief. He tossed the shotgun to the side and cradled the boy in his arms. Robert shook for several moments until his body became perfectly still. Grayson looked up toward the heavens and screamed as his granddaughter, Melissa, rushed from the house to offer assistance.

"The man acted in self-defense," argued Vanzant.

"That's for a jury to decide," responded Reynolds.

"You really expect this office to issue an indictment against a seventy-two-year-old man who was frightened out of his wits?" Vanzant said with more energy.

Lauren Sinclair moved toward the window of Vanzant's office. "Melvin, if we don't do something, it'll seem like he got away with murder a second time and nobody cared." She looked at Reynolds for support, but he wanted out on this one. "At least bring it before a grand jury," she continued. "If they decide there's enough for us to go forward, a trial will get out all the facts."

"We already know all the facts," answered Vanzant. "We got us a bunch of terrified old men sleepin' with loaded shotguns who'll blow away any stranger who sets foot on their property!"

"Any black stranger," corrected Reynolds.

"By all accounts the guy's been a model citizen. He's given his time and money to all kinds of charitable organizations, black and white." Vanzant walked toward Reynolds, who was seated in the far corner of the room.

"James, you look me straight in the eyes and tell me you think any jury is gonna convict that man."

"Wasn't that the criterion used fifty years ago?"

"Goddamn it!" shouted Vanzant. "This is the twenty-fuckin'-first century!" He'd resorted to swearing, once again hoping it would mask his fear.

Reynolds stood face to face with his boss. "Even in the twenty-first century, you shouldn't be able to kill a black teenager for carrying a fishing pole."

Vanzant didn't budge. "Maybe you need to go back to law school. Brush up on the sections dealing with state of mind and criminal intent."

"By any chance, is that near the sections on reasonable force and involuntary manslaughter?"

"Gentlemen, we're not going to resolve this by giving each other law exams," Sinclair intervened.

Vanzant approached her. "From Chester Grayson's point of view, did he or did he not have reason to fear for his life?" He turned around and pointed his finger at Reynolds. "Why don't you ask that question of your professor friend?"

"He's not my friend," replied Reynolds.

"Then what the hell were you two doin' drivin' all over the city?" Vanzant asked.

"How'd you know that?"

"We got a court order to follow his ass!"

Reynolds looked accusingly at Sinclair. She turned away. He waited for a moment before addressing Vanzant. "Was I the only one in the office who didn't know?"

Vanzant didn't feel the need to respond, so Reynolds headed for the door. "Where are you goin'?" Vanzant asked.

"To a funeral." Reynolds opened the door and faced Vanzant. "Wouldn't it be easier if you ordered surveillance on my ass, too?" He left, slamming the door behind him.

Vanzant proceeded to his desk and opened a small pouch. "Let Grayson have the weekend," he said resignedly. "We'll issue a warrant for his arrest on Monday." He sat down and inserted a wad of tobacco inside his cheek.

Sinclair took a seat near the window and removed her eyeglasses. "How long are we going to keep Professor Matheson under surveillance?" she asked.

Vanzant rested both feet on the corner of his desk. "We could only get authorization for seventy-two hours. Right now he's free as a bird without a worry in the world." He balled up a piece of paper and tossed it at the wastebasket. It hit the rim and bounced out.

The thudding sounds became more intense and far more desperate. Matheson struck the large leather punching bag that hung from a metal-reinforced stand. He wore only gray sweatpants, sneakers, and small red boxing gloves. The perspiration glistened off his back and chest under the hot lights of the university's gymnasium. The rubber soles of his shoes squeaked against the blue mats covering the hardwood floors. His body moved quickly from side to side as he leveraged his full weight behind each fierce and unforgiving punch.

He grunted every time he struck the bag, this followed by a deep, mournful release of air and pain. His fists rhythmically pounded the oversized bag, low then high, low then high. Suddenly, he stopped and stared at the listless bag that swung slowly back into place. He looked ready to fall to his knees, exhausted, nearly defeated, but he forced his body to continue. He took a step back, then, with new energy summoned from some hidden reservoir, leaped into the air and rapidly spun his right leg into the unsuspecting bag. The bag lifted off the secured hinge and crashed to the floor.

Nine-year-old Joseph Johnson collapsed into his mother's arms at the sight of his beloved brother resting peacefully inside a walnut-colored casket. He screamed and wept as Mrs. Johnson led him to a seat in the front pew. Reynolds sat near the rear of the church and heard the boy, in between his despairing sobs, plead for someone to "kill that white man!" who took away his only brother and best friend. Some members in the congregation nodded their heads, either in mourning or agreement. Turning, Reynolds spotted Matheson a few pews over, seated alone with his head bowed.

The minister spoke, but Reynolds heard nothing other than the weeping of the young boy. After a while he blocked out the sounds and saw only the visible signs of grief: people dressed in black, a woman's tear-stained face covered partially by a veil, a child's clenched fist.

The innocent had once again suffered, he thought. They always did. Matheson's great crusade would be bloodier than imagined and claim more victims than those listed on a single sheet of paper. Reynolds was now sure of that. He closed his eyes and wondered how he could bring an end to all this. When he opened them, he noticed that Matheson was no longer in his seat.

He looked around and found the professor holding the grief-stricken Joseph. The boy's body no longer shook.

His weeping had stopped. Even his calls to punish the man who killed his brother had ceased.

Matheson placed his arm around the boy's shoulders, and Joseph sat taller, more erect. He leaned the side of his face against the professor's chest. The boy's parents gratefully moved aside to give Matheson additional room to comfort the child.

Reynolds wanted to pray but couldn't. As an alternative, he bowed his head and kept it that way for the rest of the service.

CHAPTER
21

CHESTER GRAYSON STUDIED his naked body in the mirror of his locked bathroom. Intensely vain as a young man, he could no longer deny what time had done to a once firm physique. Old age is a cruel master, he'd discovered. He turned off the water that filled three-quarters of his newly tiled tub, then tested it with his right hand—his left had flared up with arthritis and remained unreliable. The steam from the basin together with the fog on the mirrors usually served as better barometers than his weather-beaten skin.

He placed his right foot into the hot water and forced himself to tolerate the pain. He placed his other foot into the tub and sat down as quickly as his tired body allowed. He leaned back, letting the water engulf his skin, which immediately turned bright pink under the extreme temperature. He'd already poured several capfuls of his wife's moisturizing lotion into the water. Under normal circumstances he'd rather stay filthy than subject his body to such feminine devices, but he assumed the softener would prevent staining. Bad enough if his wife should find him there, it would be particularly unkind if she had to scrub whatever residue he left behind.

He picked up the pearl-handled straight razor that had belonged to his grandfather and admired the detail, the craftsmanship. People used to care about their work back then. They knew they were creating a legacy and wanted to feel proud about it.

He slashed his left wrist, then submerged the gnarled hand beneath the oiled surface. His eyes darted toward the ceiling, disinclined for the moment to see the water changing color. The sight of blood had often sickened him. It reminded him of the day he'd become a savage, egged on by a crowd and intoxicated by too much to drink and his own overwhelming fear. Someone had placed a knife in his left hand and dared him to "stab the nigger." He'd meant to slice the black man across the leg, thereby proving his manhood and loyalty to friends he would never speak to again. When he raised the weapon over his head, the man had looked at him and pleaded, "Tell my children I love them. Tell them I—" Grayson had let the knife fall before the man could finish his request. Then he became a madman, cutting, slashing, and screaming in an effort to drown out the man's cries.

He stared at the bathwater and thought about how long it had taken him to wash off the man's blood. There were times when he still saw traces of it hidden within the wrinkled birth lines of both his palms. He later learned the man had studied to become a doctor. Imagine that, he thought, smiling.

Grayson intended to leave behind a note to his wife, to his two sons, and especially to his granddaughter,

Melissa. He wanted to say he loved them, but he couldn't write the words. After all, he'd never delivered the message to the man's children as requested, and payback seemed only appropriate. He owed the man at least that much.

He lifted his left hand from the bloody tub and placed it onto his chest. He'd suspected that God had rendered the hand useless as punishment, a constant reminder of his terrible deed. Blood pumped from his wrist in rhythmic squirts, graphically painting the surrounding porcelain canvas. The color faded from his face and lips. He wondered if the man's widow found the money he'd stuffed inside her mailbox the Sunday after her husband's funeral.

The room darkened. The ceiling swirled, then opened. The sky beckoned, but he knew the heavens wouldn't welcome him. He'd devoted much of his life to seeking repentance, only to fail when tested. His cowardice had caused another tragic death and claimed the life of a newspaper boy. He dared not ask for forgiveness again. He slowly sank deeper into the water and heard a voice from the past or perhaps the future: *"Tell my children I love them. Tell them I—"*

The doorknob jiggled. His wife wanted to know if he needed anything. His eyes remained open as red liquid slowly buried his face and seeped into his ears and mouth.

News of the suicide spread rapidly throughout the DA's office, and when it reached Vanzant he released a sigh of relief. The death freed him of the obligation to conduct a controversial trial. News organizations around the country had deluged his office with requests for interviews. He'd even received phone calls from the international press. The possibility of putting Grayson on trial had caused his migraines to return. If ever anyone had been caught between the proverbial rock and a hard place only to receive a last-minute reprieve, it was District Attorney Melvin Vanzant. He could now reassume his daily duties without the added pressure of having to seek a murder indictment against a frightened old man.

Vanzant left his office early and treated his wife to an unexpected lunch at her favorite restaurant. He ordered the finest bottle of imported wine on the menu and drank it slowly. He didn't know how long his luck would continue—probably not very long at all. But for the moment he'd enjoy his good fortune even if it happened to coincide with a tragic death. You took your victories where you found them.

By contrast, Reynolds brooded over Grayson's death the entire day. He postponed a lunch appointment and two staff meetings in favor of sitting alone at his desk. He pressed his fingertips together and rested them on his lips as he contemplated the sheer magnitude of events. Everywhere he went, people discussed the professor's course, the revenge murders, the justice system, the American way, and now, of course, the man who took his own life. "Too late," some argued. "Too sad," countered others.

Reynolds flipped through his Rolodex and located a number. He picked up the phone and dialed. Surely, he thought, after all this suffering, even the professor would listen to reason now.

Matheson ignored the ringing phone and sat quietly in his den organizing his work. He listened to a woman's professionally dispassionate voice on the radio: *"In another bizarre twist to an already tragic tale, Chester Grayson committed suicide at his home yesterday evening, shortly after the funeral services of Robert Johnson, the thirteen-year-old he was accused of shooting to death."*

Matheson moved aside a plate of food that had gone untouched and studied several photographs of black children on stretchers being removed from the basement of a burned-out church.

"Johnson reportedly was delivering the morning newspaper as a favor to his younger brother," the impersonal voice continued. Matheson read news clippings of the church firebombing.

"No motive for the killing has been officially established. . . ."

The phone stopped ringing.

"Neighbors interviewed immediately after the boy's death suggested Grayson had grown increasingly troubled after his name was linked to an unsolved civil rights murder that occurred nearly five decades ago, when the reformed Klan member was in his early twenties."

Matheson searched through a file folder.

"According to family members, Grayson denounced his former racist behavior and had led an exemplary life since the mid-sixties. Ironically, he'd been unaware that his name had been deleted from Professor Martin Matheson's newly distributed list of suspected murderers less than twenty-four hours before the shooting of the young newsboy."

Matheson turned off the radio and removed an eight-by-ten photo from a manila envelope. He wheeled around his leather chair and faced a large bulletin board attached to the wall just behind him. The board was covered with photos. On one side hung pictures of black victims—lynched, burned, mutilated. Directly next to them rested a poster filled with photos of white men.

Matheson retrieved a silver thumbtack and, in a recently vacated space under a neatly hand-printed banner that read, *UNPUNISHED MURDERERS*, attached a photo of Earvin Cooper.

CHAPTER

22

RUTH PLACED SEVERAL heaping spoonfuls of steaming hot vegetables with melted cheese on her husband's plate. Earvin Cooper didn't have much of an appetite. He'd been unable to eat much ever since that black policeman visited him with the news that he'd been placed on some crazy professor's list.

"You want butter for your vegetables?" Ruth asked.

He slid the plate away and muttered, "They're too soggy."

Ruth rolled her eyes and released one of her customary "What am I going to do with this man?" sighs. "They're exactly the way I've made 'em for the last forty years, which is exactly the way you've always liked them," she snapped.

He didn't respond.

"Earvin, is everything all right?" she asked. "You been actin' strange for almost—"

He threw his napkin onto the meat platter in disgust

and rose abruptly, knocking over his glass of milk and spilling the contents across the dining room table. "What's the damn world come to? A man can't even get his food made the way he wants!" He stormed into the kitchen and headed for the back door.

"Earvin, where you goin'?" Ruth's voice betrayed fear.

"Check on the animals!" he snapped.

"You ain't never checked on the animals this late." She tried to reach him, but he'd already made it outside into the warm night air.

Cooper entered the darkened barn after making a brief stop inside his garage. He held a flashlight in one hand and a gun in the other. He slowly searched each separate area, starting with the stables. His two horses ignored him and used the time to nibble at some grain in their feed troughs. A cow looked at him with its large brown eyes and casually swished its tail, turning away from the bright yellowish beam.

The hens didn't appreciate the interruption and fluttered aimlessly in small circles. Cooper shined his light at the vacated nests and discovered several eggs. He tucked the gun into his waistband and proudly stuck out his chest. "'Bout time you started earnin' your keep," he uttered with a grin.

A noise distracted him. He grabbed the handle of his gun, prepared to remove it quickly if need be. He traced the left corner of the barn with the light, then moved it to the opposite corner. He noticed one of the bales of hay had fallen from its stack. He pointed the light higher and found a newly made, elaborate web constructed inside all four corners of a window frame. A large black spider worked its way toward a captured moth until the light temporarily froze it. Its body pulsated for a moment and waited for Cooper's next move. He removed a gold Zippo lighter from his trousers and flicked it twice.

"Can't have a picnic without barbecue," he remarked, then extended the flame toward the center of the web. Just before his hand reached the intended target, Cooper noticed a shifting image in the glass, followed by a shadow that concealed half the silver web. His fingers tightened around the flashlight's thick cylinder just as the lighter was viciously knocked from his hand. He swung the flashlight but missed the assailant, who punched him in the face.

Cooper removed his gun, but it was kicked out of his hand with lightning speed. It landed on a vacated nest and crushed several eggs. Cooper threw the flashlight at the stranger, then rushed him with the football skill he'd acquired decades earlier. They tumbled over several bales of hay. Cooper lashed out in a desperate frenzy and struck the intruder on the head and chest.

The lighter had ignited a small fire near the stables, which spread quickly, fueled by dry straw and brittle wood. Cooper landed hard on his back but immediately recovered and locked his arms around the stranger's waist in a tight bear hug. Their two silhouettes wrestled near the flames as horses kicked furiously and hens scampered hysterically.

Punches were thrown in the darkness, striking flesh and bone. The two figures crashed against the side of the barn. Cooper drove his knee into the assailant's stomach and pounded his fists into the back of the stranger's head.

Cooper took a bruising elbow to his face, followed by a brutal punch to his kidney that forced him to stagger backward. The assailant moved quickly to the side and disappeared. Cooper hustled to the door and opened it, allowing the moonlight to break through. Grabbing a pitchfork off the sidewall, he turned around rapidly, primed to strike.

A Molotov cocktail was hurled across the barn and struck Cooper full force against his massive chest. He flung the pitchfork, which barely missed the stranger and embedded itself in the burning wood. The pitchfork continued to vibrate as Cooper's body erupted into flames. He made one last futile attempt to reach the moving shadow. Overcome by fire, he scrambled to the floor, rolling and writhing in agony.

The assailant jumped through the flames and unlocked the stalls. The horses stampeded over the smaller animals. Other livestock frantically escaped through the smoke-filled opening. Flames fully engulfed the barn, which crackled and popped like a pile of logs in a giant fireplace.

Ruth ran toward the inferno, screaming her husband's name. Cooper crawled outside, body ablaze and hideously contorted. A few feet from his wife's outstretched arms he collapsed onto the smoldering and scorched earth. Ruth watched helplessly as blue and red flames shot toward the sky and dark smoke blocked out the fading moon. She fell to her knees, totally unaware of car tires screeching away from the place she once loved to call home.

CHAPTER
23

PRESSURE TO STOP Matheson from teaching his course intensified after Grayson's suicide. Every politician in the state, with the exception of a few black ones, had been inundated with phone calls, E-mails, and letters demanding he be fired from the university. Cooper's death caused editorial writers from around the state to insist "all law enforcement place their territorial interests aside and work together diligently to capture those responsible for these horrific murders and put an end to our long dark nightmare." As the subject of national newscasts, the murders even forced the president to answer questions raised by the White House press corps.

The state's attorney general coordinated efforts with the FBI and local law enforcement. Since the majority of the murders had taken place in Jackson County and its surrounding area, Vanzant assumed a major role in heading up the primary task force. Forensic specialists had begun gathering information, and Dr. Charles Hunter, a nationally renowned criminal profiler, had compiled and analyzed data on Matheson's students, close colleagues, and the professor himself. He'd prepared a preliminary summary of his findings, which Vanzant asked him to share with the staff.

"Right now," reported Hunter, "our strongest theory is that the killer is one or more students either enamored of or devoted to Matheson. Given the strength required to overpower the victims, the murders were likely committed by a male, but we haven't ruled out female participation in the crimes. Whoever it is wants to curry favor with his or her hero or cult leader. He or she is probably from a broken home without a strong male presence, an underachiever in both academics and sports, has few friends, especially from the opposite sex, and is inclined to be adamant, possibly fanatical, about politics or religion." Hunter took a sip of coffee.

"I've also offered a scenario you might find intriguing. It's possible that a highly educated white male, late twenties or early thirties, imitating the infamous John Brown, committed these crimes to correct perceived injustice and alleviate self-guilt. Since whites are far more likely to commit serial murders than blacks, and in this case could move easily in and out of white communities unnoticed and unsuspected, I recommend local police investigate Caucasian civil rights advocates or former members of racist organizations who'd actively disavowed their affiliations."

"That would be an extremely short list," joked Reynolds.

"Don't take this the wrong way," Vanzant said, "but I think that theory's unadulterated bullshit. I'll put my money on that football star who abandoned dreams of glory to study under Matheson. I saw that kid play his freshman year. Phenomenal. Absolutely phenomenal," he continued. "He would've been the first pick in the draft no matter what year he decided to declare. Now, you tell me, a young guy gives up millions of dollars to play a sport he trained for his entire life, walks away from fame, fortune, and fuckin', for what—to study with his mentor? Is that the action of a normal person or someone under the spell of his guru? Ain't that the definition of a fanatic, or zealot, or groupie, or . . . ?"

"Murderer?" Hunter asked.

"He's big, he's quick, he's strong, and he's devoted to pleasing his personal messiah." Vanzant waited for someone to agree with him.

"He also was at the scene when Rankin's car exploded, and Cooper's wife said her husband wrote down his license plate a few days before the fire," added Woody Winslow. Uncharacteristically, he was munching on something unhealthy—a powdered-sugar jelly doughnut.

"Gentlemen," Vanzant announced solemnly, "I believe we've narrowed our list of suspects."

Brandon and Delbert walked across the student parking lot. "Wanna come over to my parents' for Thanksgiving?" Brandon asked.

"I promised my mom I'd go home for the holidays."

"I guess I'll have to find someone else to eat my vegetables," Brandon teased. He gave Delbert a playful shove. "You sure you're not sneaking off with Sereta to get married?"

"I wouldn't be keepin' it no secret. I'd be screamin' her name from the tallest building in Jackson."

"You got yourself a good lady, Delbert."

"Got me a pretty good best friend, too. Don't know

why you'd hang around with someone like me, but I ain't complainin'."

Brandon was about to respond but noticed two patrol cars slowly circling a section of the lot. He moved cautiously, trying not to bring attention to himself.

"You mind if I don't give you a ride back to the dorm?" he asked Delbert.

"What's the matter?"

Brandon focused on the two cars that had stopped next to each other. One of the policemen spotted Brandon and pointed in his direction. The driver of the other car turned and stared at him as well. They steered their cars around an entry gate and traveled the wrong way, in the middle of opposing traffic, toward the two students.

"Get out of here, now!" Brandon shouted at Delbert, then jumped over a hedge and dashed toward his car. Before he unlocked the door, he heard the first police siren, followed a split second later by another. He hurriedly entered the car and jammed his key into the ignition. He started the engine and quickly shifted into reverse. His foot slammed against the accelerator. The car raced backward, striking a parked vehicle. It spun forward, scraping the front end of a van, then sideswiped an SUV pulling out of its space.

The two patrol cars maneuvered through the crowded lot and converged on Brandon's sedan. Delbert tried to block one of the officers' vehicles with his body but at the last moment dove out of the way and landed hard on the pavement. His books skidded underneath a large trailer.

Students rushed from the area and barely missed being struck by Brandon's automobile as he zigzagged in between rows of parked cars, driving toward a narrow access road.

One patrol car blasted through a construction barricade and speeded across a patch of gravel before climbing an elevated mound of dirt and sliding into a pile of cement bags. The fine, light gray dust burst into a thick cloud, spraying granulated particles high into the air. The police vehicle emerged from the haze of flying debris with windshield wipers struggling mightily.

Trying to catch his friend, Delbert sprinted across the lot but had no chance. He watched Brandon drive out of the university lot onto a public road less than a hundred feet in front of the rapidly approaching patrol car.

Brandon ignored a flashing red signal at an intersection, causing oncoming traffic to slam on brakes and screech to a crashing halt. Front and rear bumpers ferociously banged against each other. A hood flew open and sailed over two unscathed vehicles, landing full force on a new pickup truck.

Both police cars were now actively engaged in the chase, driving onto the corner sidewalk to avoid the surrounding accidents. Brandon saw their red lights swirling as the two patrol vehicles edged along either side of his sedan in an effort to cut him off. Brandon sped up, then pushed his brake to the floor. The two cars passed, providing an opportunity for him to head in the opposite direction.

Brandon backed up and made a tight turn, but the car stalled. He'd restarted the engine when the first patrol car barreled into the rear of his sedan and crushed his vehicle against a street lamp. Brandon's head whipped forward and struck the windshield. The air bag exploded as the second police car wedged itself against the car's side, effectively cutting off any escape.

The radiator erupted, releasing streams of scalding

water and hot steam. Four police officers emerged from their vehicles and surrounded Brandon's car with weapons drawn. "Put your hands up over your head and keep them there!" screamed the officer closest to the driver's window. Brandon complied with the demand and lifted his hands over his bloodied face.

He groggily sensed the front door being ripped open and hands tearing at his body while he sat in the front seat, incapable of offering resistance. Two policemen removed him from the car and threw him to the ground, facedown. Someone drove a knee into the small of his back and twisted his arms behind him. He heard a clicking sound, then felt handcuffs lock around his wrists. The glimmering green liquid from his ruptured cooling system burned his skin. He raised his face off the ground to speak and saw a baton move quickly toward his head, followed by a sharp pain, then darkness.

CHAPTER
24

REYNOLDS HAD FILLED one legal pad with notes and begun a second when his phone buzzed twice. Annoyed, he picked up the receiver. "I asked you not to—" He listened intently. "Send him in." He cradled the receiver for a moment, then hung up the phone. Quickly straightening his desk, he proceeded to involve himself with various stacks of papers.

He heard his office door open and close. "Be with you in a moment," he said without looking up from his work. He finished scribbling information on the side of a court transcript, then, placing his ballpoint pen inside his jacket pocket, started to rise. When he saw Matheson's injured face, he sank back to his seat.

"What happened to you?" Reynolds asked in amazement.

Matheson walked slowly toward Reynolds and took a seat on the opposite side of the desk. He lightly touched his face, which was marred by a series of deep bruises and minor abrasions. "I seemed to have upset some of our more temperamental citizens."

"You file a report?"

"I did indeed. The police were mildly amused and totally uninterested. As you can imagine, I'm not very popular with law enforcement."

"By the looks of your face, you're not popular with all sorts of people." Reynolds studied Matheson. "You go to the hospital?"

"No bones were broken, and I wouldn't give my enemies the satisfaction of seeking medical attention." Matheson touched a swollen area underneath his left eye. "I consider these marks badges of honor. I intend to display them with pride."

"You're gonna show them for a while regardless of your intent. You don't have much choice in the matter."

"There's always a choice, James. You simply need the courage to make it."

Reynolds wasn't in the mood for another lecture. "So what brings you here? My secretary said it was urgent."

"One of my students has been arrested. I was hoping you might look into it . . . see that he's treated fairly."

"Brandon Hamilton?"

"Yes. He's not who you're looking for. He's not a murderer."

"He acted like a person with a great deal to hide. He also caused quite a bit of damage in the process of leading the police on a very dangerous pursuit."

"Brandon paid a visit to Earvin Cooper's home two days ago and left behind a protest sign. I'm sure you know about that."

"I have the report," replied Reynolds.

"Then you're probably aware Cooper confronted him

and wrote down his license plate number." Matheson extended his left leg gingerly and winced slightly in pain. "After he learned of Cooper's murder and saw the police looking for him, he panicked."

Reynolds observed Matheson's discomfort and wondered how seriously the professor had been injured. "He placed a sign on Cooper's property suggesting he wasn't going to live long. That's a pretty serious threat that managed to come true. You give your students psychic powers as well as an understanding of history?"

"If you teach history properly, you can predict it with great accuracy." Matheson folded his arms across his chest. "And in the spirit of getting one's facts correct, the sign read, 'A murderer lives here, but not for long.' It referred to his address, not his life. The goal was to drive Cooper from the community."

"Burying him would certainly accomplish that."

"Brandon's guilty of trespass. That's all."

"At the moment he's guilty of resisting arrest, numerous driving infractions, and leaving the scene of several accidents."

"He exercised poor judgment. Given the circumstances that's completely understandable."

"A jury might have to decide that. For his sake as well as yours, I hope they agree with you."

"So you're not charging him with Cooper's murder?"

"That hasn't been determined," said Reynolds. "But witnesses also placed him at the scene of the car-bombing that killed Arnold Rankin. Several people there described him as smiling while the elderly victim burned to death."

"Justice brings a sense of satisfaction even when it's significantly delayed," said Matheson. "After murderers are punished I sometimes smile, too. Does that make *me* a murderer?"

"It makes you a lot of things, none of which are desirable."

"Whatever you may think of me, I know the capabilities of my students. Brandon's a good kid. I'd be grateful for any help you can offer—assuming you can do that and keep your job."

"I appreciate your concern over my livelihood."

Matheson noticed the awards and citations arranged on the wall behind Reynolds's desk. "Very impressive." He walked toward the wall to inspect each plaque. "Most of these are from white organizations. You must have a terribly effective cracker sling."

"Cracker sling?" Reynolds asked. He was both annoyed and curious.

Matheson turned toward him. "A very good friend of mine worked at a prestigious law firm. He, of course, was the only black but continued to express his determination to be promoted to full partner. I asked him how he intended to accomplish that. He confided he'd contrived a rather useful invention which he characterized as a 'cracker sling.'"

"Like the one David used to slay Goliath?" asked Reynolds.

"An arm sling," clarified Matheson. "He'd wear it at every important staff meeting. Claimed he needed it for a recurring injury, tennis elbow or something else equally believable." He approached Reynolds. "Whenever one of his colleagues said something particularly irritating or downright infuriating, the sling restricted his natural impulse to inflict bodily injury."

"Did it help him make partner?"

"No," said Matheson, smiling. "But it kept his ass out of jail."

Reynolds laughed but not as genuinely as Matheson. "He ever use the sling to prevent him from hitting a black person?"

Matheson stared at the window. "We've never had to restrain ourselves from attacking each other." He returned his focus to Reynolds. "But then, you know that better than most. Your job might not exist if it were otherwise."

"I'm afraid my profession would thrive regardless of who struck the first blow," Reynolds said quietly. "As far as Brandon Hamilton, he's in enough trouble whether or not any additional charges are filed against him." He stood behind his desk and faced Matheson. "I'll give you a call when I learn anything."

"I'd appreciate that, very much." Matheson extended his hand. Reynolds reached for it, and the two men shook firmly while maintaining solid eye contact.

"I hope I didn't say anything that caused you distress or brought discomfort," said Matheson. "I wouldn't want you to continue to have the wrong impression about me."

"I'm sure you've left me with the impression you'd like me to have."

"That's comforting to know."

"Better get those cuts attended to," remarked Reynolds. "You wouldn't want any permanent scars from your misfortune."

Matheson gave a quick nod then proceeded to the door.

"Oh," called out Reynolds. "Wouldn't be a bad idea if you had that leg checked as well. Couldn't help but notice you favor one side when you walk." He smiled warmly.

Matheson nodded again, this time more warily, and left the office. Over the next hour Reynolds unsuccessfully attempted to complete his remaining work. After starting one task only to abandon it for another, he decided to forsake the effort and begin anew in the morning.

Throughout his drive home, he thought about the "cracker sling." There must have been a time when he needed one, maybe two. How had he finally managed to control his emotion? He did know that white folks often mistook passion for anger. And in the early days he had struggled mightily to keep his passion in check. He leaned forward less often and spoke more softly, always making serious points while smiling. He tried not to look too tall and extended his hands palms up, never curling his fingers, because the temptation would be too great to proceed further and form a fist. Once a fist is formed, whether or not it's thrown is immaterial. Those clenched fingers would be enough to taint his career, his relationships, and his future. Like a criminal record, they'd follow him from one job to the next, provoking whispers: He's "capable of violence." His "temper is volatile." He "almost struck a man," "a white man," "his boss."

No. He didn't need a "cracker sling," not anymore.

Matheson's unsettling suspicions about him and a great many other black men were essentially correct. Their success depended in large part on their ability to restrain themselves. Not with a sling or a harness or a straitjacket but with a barely held silence or a dishonest nod of approval or a bitter-tasting smile that would choke a more honorable person. To Matheson, these upwardly mobile professionals had sacrificed their passion in order to make people who despised them comfortable.

Reynolds knew that Matheson was right on at least one other subject: Black folks never needed a sling to prevent them from striking out and destroying each other. But there were infinite ways to self-destruct. He couldn't help but wonder how many good and decent people would be harmed as a result of one professor's twisted effort to make history accessible to the masses.

Reynolds pulled into his driveway and turned off the car engine but left the battery engaged. He sat motionless, listening to the music playing on his radio. He recognized the melody as a Miles Davis tune and remembered an interview the legend had given several years before his death. A reporter asked how Davis would spend his time if he had only one hour to live. Miles answered, "I'd choke a white man to death, slowly."

Reynolds laughed when he first heard the story, as had, no doubt, many other black men who'd heard the tale. He still recalled Cheryl's response when he relayed the comment to her. "My God, how tragic." She shook her head in disbelief and repeated, "How incredibly tragic." He knew then and there why he loved her so much, and he feared what he might become without her and their children in his life.

He noticed Cheryl standing under the light at the front entrance to their home. She smiled and waved. Witnessing those two actions, he knew he'd be able to set aside the burdens of the moment. He knew, too, that he'd make love to his wife tonight. What he didn't know was that the lovemaking would be especially passionate and would last much longer than usual.

CHAPTER
25

T HE FOOTHILLS OF the Appalachian Mountains, located in the northeastern corner of the state, offered budding geologists unlimited research opportunities. Students took advantage of the varied terrain, studying the massive boulders and spying on unsuspecting college girls who sometimes swam nude in the bubbling streams and clear lakes just beneath the rocky outcroppings. This area was far removed from the harsh realities of urban life. In the distance the legendary Delta blues seemed to start from a steep bluff and drop off sharply in a deep, mournful wail. Heavyhearted lyrics conjured images of flat and fertile land where a more optimistic future might be found.

In between the towering pines and rugged hardwoods that laced either side of the riverbank, a father paddled a canoe while telling favorite stories to his seven-year-old son. Yoknapatawpha County may have existed in the imagination of William Faulkner, he said, but every

proud and loyal Mississippian had a piece of that ficti-
tious land in his heart. He spoke of the king of rock 'n'
roll with a special reverence. Elvis had grown up in a
humble two-room home not far away in Tupelo, but he'd
proved the American dream possible. The boy knew this
already and really wanted to hear about the Indians
who'd once inhabited the region. "Did they really take
your scalp and eat the hearts of their victims?"

His father laughed. He assured his son it was all true
but told him not to worry. "The savages were defeated
long ago, and the ones who managed to survive have
been civilized."

The young boy asked what "civilized" meant.

"Tame, no longer a threat or danger," his father
replied.

He thought about his dad's answer, then asked if he
could help paddle. His father smiled proudly and handed
him the oars. "Steady strokes," he ordered. "Just keep
moving them together."

The boy tried valiantly, but one oar always made it
back before the other, forcing the canoe to move in ever
widening circles. Frustrated, he yanked the resistant oar
with both hands and brought to the surface a bloated and
decayed human torso.

Several hours later, federal agents and local police
were sprinkled throughout Natchez Trace National
Parkway, searching for evidence in marshy habitats that
offered a haven to waterfowl and other seemingly protected species.

"The body discovered this morning in a lake just outside Oxford has been identified as Theo Crockett, who's
been missing since early September," Vanzant read from

a prepared statement into a collection of microphones. The DA's press facilities didn't have sufficient space to accommodate the large group of reporters, forcing many to view the proceedings on a monitor in an adjoining meeting room.

"This brings the total number of homicides associated with the so-called unsolved civil rights murders to six. A seventh potential victim, Travis Mitchell of Polarville, remains missing." He looked into a crowd ready to pounce at the first opportunity. "I'll be happy to answer a few questions."

"Mr. Vanzant!" a woman shouted. "Have murder charges been brought against Brandon Hamilton for the death of Earvin Cooper, and is he also a suspect in any other of these killings?"

"At this time I'm not at liberty to discuss any charges that have been or may be filed against Mr. Hamilton or anyone else."

"Can you tell us the status of police investigations into the murders?" asked a reporter from the state's largest daily.

"The police have worked tirelessly on this case from the very beginning. They're coordinating forensic efforts with state and federal law enforcement with the full cooperation of our office." Vanzant looked into the news cameras with the assurance of an old pro. "Evidence is being collected and analyzed that will greatly assist us in apprehending, prosecuting, and convicting the person or persons involved in these cowardly acts of violence."

"Does your office plan any action against Professor Matheson?" shouted a voice from the back of the room.

"As of this moment, Professor Matheson hasn't violated any law. However, I don't think I'm alone in feeling that he bears moral responsibility for these senseless killings as well as the pain and suffering inflicted upon all decent, law-abiding citizens throughout this state. I'll take one more question."

"Is it true your office pressured the university to stop Dr. Matheson from continuing to teach his courses?" asked a black reporter who'd pushed his way to the front.

"My office isn't in the business of pressuring the university or any other institution. But the mere fact that public funds are used to pay the professor's salary, which enables him to continue preaching hate and possibly advocating or inciting violence, is both a travesty and a tragedy. I'm hopeful trustees of the university will work with our legislators to correct that as quickly as possible."

In a sudden burst of flashbulbs, Vanzant concluded the session and headed quickly to the exit.

A group of white protestors carried signs outside the university's humanities building that read, STOP PREACHING HATE, NO MORE VIOLENCE, TIME TO FORGIVE, and MATHESON'S THE REAL RACIST. A growing number of black students angrily encircled the group. Posters were forcefully ripped away, and several physical confrontations ensued. Campus security requested assistance from local authorities, who had started to arrive in patrol cars and police vans just as the violence broke out. They rushed to the scene with batons raised, but the black students immediately pulled back when Matheson appeared at the doorway's entrance and ordered them to stop. He walked down the steps and approached the police.

"Hey, Professor!" someone called out. Matheson saw a white man in his early thirties appear from the middle of the crowd. He moved closer and spit in the professor's face.

Matheson quickly grabbed the man by the throat and spun him around. He slapped the man hard across his cheek and pinned him against a tree. "This isn't the Civil Rights era!" he said a few inches from the terrified man's face. "And I'm not my father!" Matheson pressed the man against the tree. "You understand?" The man nodded, and the professor slowly let go.

The white demonstrators stood in stunned disbelief. The black students proudly exchanged smiles. Matheson removed a handkerchief from his back pocket and wiped off the spit. Two policemen walked steadily toward him.

"Professor Matheson," called out the larger one.

"Yes?"

"You're under arrest."

Matheson tossed the handkerchief in a trash receptacle. "The man spat on me. If you want to arrest someone, I suggest—"

"I'm afraid that's not the reason you're being taken into custody, Professor." The second policeman, a young black officer, spoke softly and respectfully.

Some black students slowly began to surround the police while others moved to protect Matheson. The professor calmly raised his hand and signaled for them to relax. "These men are only doing their duty. It can be a burdensome task, but if my father were here I'm certain he'd remind us, 'This, too, shall pass.'"

Regina and Delbert moved closer to their professor's side. Matheson looked at the students. He glanced at the humanities building and quickly scanned the adjacent area. He turned to the police. "Officers, I'm ready if you are."

The police led him away as most of the students stood silently and watched. Delbert moved from Regina and struck the demonstrator who had spit on the professor. Campus security converged on the two men and separated them before any more punches were thrown.

Cheryl sat motionless on the edge of the couch, eyes intently watching the black female reporter who appeared on her television screen. *"In a stunning development, Professor Martin Matheson, son of prominent minister and civil rights leader the Reverend Samuel Matheson, was today arrested and charged with the murder of Earvin Cooper.*

"Unnamed sources close to the investigation have confirmed that personal property belonging to Professor Matheson was found at Cooper's murder scene. Also discovered was blood evidence linking Matheson to the crime."

The front door opened, and Reynolds walked in, carrying his briefcase and looking morose.

The reporter continued, *"District Attorney Melvin Vanzant refused to rule out filing additional murder indictments. And when asked about—"* Reynolds turned off the television.

"My God, James, this is impossible. There's no way I'm ever going to believe Martin's capable of murdering a bunch of old men. They're harassing him over teaching those courses, and it's unfair. Isn't there anything you—"

"Cheryl, we need to talk." Reynolds placed his briefcase on the coffee table and sat on the couch next to his wife.

"This doesn't make any sense. Why, after all this time, would he kill any of those people?"

"I'll have to answer that to the satisfaction of a jury of his peers."

"What are you talking about?"

"I've been assigned the case."

CHAPTER
26

MILLER WALKED DOWN the prison hallway flanked by two white guards. They'd been polite in the past, even jovial, but not tonight. Miller lightly touched his handkerchief to his forehead, wiping off some perspiration. His stomach churned, and the muscles in his back tightened. It had been a long time since his body reacted this anxiously to meeting anyone, particularly a client.

They reached a narrow room with a large, thick glass partition reinforced by steel mesh. An armed guard remained stationed inside a security area. When he saw Miller, he electronically buzzed the gated door. One of the police officers held it open until Miller entered. The door shut, and he discovered Matheson, seated patiently at a table that was bolted securely to the floor. Miller placed his briefcase on the metal bench and sat opposite Matheson.

"Why'd you ask for me?"

"You had the most colorful ad in the yellow pages."

"I don't advertise."

"You're still the most colorful. I think it only appropriate that a white lawyer defend me."

"In the event you're convicted, you'll have an entire system to blame," theorized Miller.

"That'll give you additional incentive to win. You get to free me and absolve the system at the same time. Who knows? You may even find salvation for yourself." Matheson studied Miller for a moment. "I researched your background; you have an interesting family history."

"I don't think I like you very much." Miller waited for a response.

Matheson shrugged. "Could give you greater credibility with the jury. They'd see you disagreed with my methods but believed in my innocence."

Miller unlocked and flipped opened his briefcase. "While you were conducting your research on me, did you happen to notice I marched with your father several times?"

"You must've gotten terribly tired," said Matheson, smiling. "So, tell me, after you became a missionary were your feelings hurt by the natives when they rejected your teachings?"

Miller bit down slightly on his lip. "If this is your way of ingratiating yourself, it's actually working." He removed a pencil and yellow pad from his case. "You want to talk about your trial now, or should we continue walking down memory lane?"

Matheson relaxed against his chair. "After I plead not guilty at the arraignment, I want to waive the preliminary."

"I advise against that," warned Miller. "Any lawyer

would." He wrote a note on his paper. "You can learn a great deal about the prosecution's strategy."

"Their strategy is to convict me. Mine is to get out of here. We go straight to trial," Matheson stated emphatically.

"I took the liberty of checking with the DA's office before coming here. They're running tests on the dynamite caps found in your garage. If they match with Rankin's car bombing . . ."

"I bought them at a construction supplier. They're not difficult to purchase."

"Two dozen special agents are investigating every move you've made in the last six months. They found gasoline receipts that place you in Greenville the day Taylor and Hopkins were lynched."

"I was in Dallas the day Kennedy got assassinated. They gonna blame me for that, too?"

"How old were you?"

"Five. I was a deadly shot with a water pistol." Matheson looked at the window and saw both officers peering through the glass. He gave a friendly wave. The two men turned their backs on him. "So far, you've given me more incentive to act expeditiously. The longer I'm confined, the greater the likelihood I'll be charged with additional murders. Let's get this one settled as quickly as possible."

"If you're found not guilty, they can turn around and indict you on the others. Even if you manage to win this case, there's no guarantee you'll be released for long."

"If they choose to pursue me after my acquittal, then their real motivations will be clear to everyone. When that happens, they won't find any person foolish enough to do their dirty work, not even *our* mutual friend Mr. Reynolds."

"You *really* did do your homework on me. I'm impressed."

"I'm in the profession of dispensing assignments; I ought to be able to do my own when the occasion demands." He handed Miller a sheet of paper. "That's a list of some students who can assist you. Typing, research, whatever you need. I've already asked one of them to put together a photographic display."

"Of what?"

"The pictures I distribute to my class. If the prosecution's going to show graphic photos of the murder victim, I want to even the score for the jury."

Miller briefly studied the information. "Looks like you've been planning your defense for quite a while."

"It pays to anticipate your adversary's next move."

"What gives me the feeling you've anticipated the next three or four?" Miller asked.

"Because you're the lawyer I knew you'd be," responded Matheson. "Insightful and committed to fighting injustice wherever you find it."

"Did you want to write my opening statement?"

"No, but I'd like to review it. Feel free to drop it off any night—I'm up late."

Miller smiled to himself and shook his head in disbelief. "What made you so sure I'd take your case?"

"Cases like these are as rare as, oh, shall we say, white southern-born liberals." Matheson closed Miller's briefcase and leaned it against the table leg. "I knew you'd take it, because you've been waiting for it all your life."

Maybe it was the smugness of the observation or the accuracy of his insight or a combination of both, but

Miller now knew he didn't like Matheson one single bit. But it didn't matter. He'd represent him. He'd cut off his left arm for the chance.

"In addition to your services on my behalf, I'd also like you to represent a student of mine. He was arrested for Cooper's murder, and since they've now accused me, I see no reason why they need to detain him any further." He handed Miller a sealed envelope. "All the information's in there. I'll be happy to secure his bail—put up my home as collateral if necessary."

"You may need that for your own bond," suggested Miller.

Matheson laughed.

"Did I say something funny?"

"Not even the most devout liberal can be that naive."

"Try me."

Matheson reached out and touched Miller's arm. "They've no intention of releasing me. They wanted to find a way to lock me up and they've accomplished that. There's no chance I'll leave this place unless a jury orders it. It's your job to get the jury to do what the state finds far too dangerous." Matheson stood and signaled that the meeting was over. "Convince them to give me my freedom, Mr. Miller."

Miller rose from his seat and collected his things. "Out of curiosity," he asked, "are you guilty?"

"A man who'd commit such monstrous crimes certainly would be capable of lying about having committed them." Matheson stared straight into Miller's eyes. "So, why bother asking?"

Miller forced himself not to blink first. "Just wanted to know what kind of man I was dealing with."

Matheson moved closer and stood directly in front of

Miller. "I'll be happy to tell you." He paused for a moment and took delight in making Miller wait. "I'm not a liar."

Miller took the materials Matheson had given him and grabbed his briefcase. He faced the professor. "Then you'll be the most unusual client I've had in the last twenty years." He signaled the guard, who buzzed the door open. He walked to it and turned to Matheson. "Well, Professor, it looks like you've got yourself a lawyer."

"I'm sure you won't let me down."

"I'll do my best," replied Miller. "I'd hate to think of the consequences if I should fail. You might even be tempted to put me on some list."

Matheson smiled. "As I said, I already conducted a thorough search into your background. You'd be the one and only person in your family on the patriarchal side who'd have nothing to fear."

The two men looked at each other for a moment.

"At least, not from me," added Matheson.

"You ready to leave?" an officer asked.

Miller glanced one more time at Matheson, then closed the door and left.

CHAPTER
27

REYNOLDS SAT AT his kitchen table and poured Miller a glass of orange juice.

"Don't you have any beer?" Miller asked.

"It's seven-thirty in the morning."

Miller looked at his watch. "Then I'll have the hard stuff."

"You need to stay sober."

"No one should be that needy." Miller drank the juice.

"I'm going out to inspect your client's home this afternoon. Wanna meet me there?"

Miller glanced around the room. "Where's the wooden horse?"

"No tricks. No deceptions. Just extending you a courtesy."

Miller poured himself more juice. "I have to get a court order to be anywhere near one of your evidence-collecting trips. Now I get a personal invitation. Why the change of heart?"

"Let's just think of it as a goodwill gesture."

"Or a public relations ploy. Are you trying to use me, James?" Miller sipped his juice. "I was planning on being there with binoculars and a film crew, but if you need me to validate the fairness and integrity of your office, I'll play along."

Reynolds smiled. "Tell the truth, Todd. You've waited a long time for a case like this."

"In my wildest imagination, I never thought there'd be a case like this. But yeah, I'd wait for it. Forever."

"If we handle this wrong, we could tear the community apart, maybe the whole country. You know that, don't you?"

"The country's been torn apart for years and it doesn't even realize it."

"You think we can help mend it?" asked Reynolds.

"No, but I've been wrong before." Miller finished his juice. "My grandfather would turn over in his grave if he'd any idea what I'm about to do to the family name."

"I thought you told me he was a respected judge."

"And a lifelong member of the Klan. My dad followed in his footsteps serving as legal counsel to the White Citizens Council."

"You must've had one hell of a family reunion."

"I was definitely the outsider as a child. Had one close friend, a skinny black kid named Sanford who smiled constantly and walked as if his shoes were too small— because they were."

"Did Daddy Miller approve?"

"I made the mistake of inviting him into my bedroom one afternoon. We played blissfully until Dad arrived and caught us laughing and hugging each other. Sanford gave me a friendly kiss on the cheek that sent my father into a rage. I imagine he felt that black boy had violated his home and soiled my purity or, at the tender age of seven, my manhood."

"What happened?"

"He kept screaming at me. Demanded I beat him. I started swinging wildly, trying to block out my father's voice and Sanford's cries. I don't know where I hit him or how many times. I didn't even notice his blood on the carpet. If it hadn't been for my mother's intervention and Sanford's whimpering pleas, I don't think I would've stopped." Miller looked away for a moment and tried to regain control of his emotions. "I'll never forget Sanford's eyes. There was such sadness in a place where there should've been unrelenting hate."

Reynolds hesitated. "Was he all right?"

"Just a bloody nose and a few scratches. But I never saw him again. My father ripped up the stained carpet and burned it in the backyard so there'd be no trace of the incident or sign of a friendship destroyed by one tiny childhood embrace." Miller paused, then cleared his throat. "You know that quote about men living lives of quiet desperation?"

Reynolds nodded.

"It's not true. The desperation's very loud."

"Hi, Mr. Miller." Christopher stood at the doorway.

Miller studied the young boy and smiled; then his eyes filled with tears. "Hello, Christopher," was all he could say. He left without looking at Reynolds.

Police vans lined the street outside Matheson's home. Yellow tape cordoned off an area that had quickly become a magnet for curiosity seekers armed with handheld video cameras. The growing crowd of onlookers was ordered to stay fifty yards away from the residence while detectives and lab technicians conducted an investigation of the premises.

Detective Lanny Shaw, a twenty-year veteran, greeted Reynolds at the front steps and advised him of the progress of the search. Miller arrived seconds later, but two officers quickly stopped him.

"He's authorized to enter," Reynolds informed the group. "But if he tampers with any evidence, shoot him."

Miller approached Reynolds. "You go in yet?"

"I wanted to share this Kodak moment with you. Have you met Detective Shaw?"

"I've had the pleasure of discrediting his testimony on many occasions. It's nice to see you again, Detective."

"Always a pleasure, Counselor."

"Well, let's take a look at what we've got." Reynolds motioned for Miller and Shaw to follow. They entered Matheson's brightly lit home through a large circular foyer, which contained a colorful variety of well-maintained plants. A spiral staircase provided access to the second floor. They proceeded down a walkway and glanced at the original paintings displayed on the richly paneled walls. The fine-art gallery led to a sunken living room. They stepped down two marble steps and were surrounded by cases filled with books and wood and bronze sculptures. They observed a wide-screen television built into the back wall, which featured an elaborate audio and video editing system. The men admired the features.

"Looks like a murderer's room to me," quipped Miller. "Definitely a killer CD player, wouldn't you say, Detective?"

"I'd kill for it," answered Shaw.

A rookie policeman approached. "Mr. Reynolds? I think you need to take a look at the den."

"Detective," Reynolds said, "why don't you maintain control of this area. I'd like a photographer sent to the den as quickly as possible."

"We've already got two there, sir," said the policeman.

"Then I'll try not to make any more obvious suggestions and let you continue to do your jobs," apologized Reynolds. "Officer, lead the way."

Reynolds and Miller followed the cop down a long hallway and into the den. The area stood in stark contrast to the elegance and comfort of the living room. Cold, dark, and undecorated, this place felt confined and depressed, with no furnishings other than a desk, chair, and two file cabinets all crammed together into the farthest corner of the room. Due to lack of fresh air, the place had the odor of a closet filled with old sweaters and worn shoes.

Police photographers were taking pictures of the area near the desk but stepped aside to allow Reynolds and Miller access. They studied two large displays containing photographs of blacks murdered during the Civil Rights Movement on one side and the alleged murderers on the other. The display of murderers was further subdivided into those "executed" and those "still alive." The photos of the blacks were particularly gruesome, especially when compared to the smiling faces of the white men who'd allegedly murdered them. Both Reynolds and Miller stared intently at the exhibit, unable to look away or at each other.

Banners attached to the bottom of both displays contained quotations by Thomas Jefferson. Underneath the display of tortured and mutilated black victims were the words *I tremble for my country when I reflect God is just.* Beneath the photos of smiling white men hung the inscription *The tree of liberty should be refreshed with the blood of tyrants.*

Reynolds found a gold replica of the scales of justice between the two displays. It held a heavy weight on one side, which caused the scales to tilt in favor of the whites. He placed a weight on the opposite side, and the scales were now balanced.

"If justice were only that simple," remarked Miller.

"We make it more difficult than it has to be," Reynolds responded.

"You ain't seen nothin' yet." Miller placed another weight on the opposite side, and the scales tipped in the other direction, leaning toward the black victims.

The men remained in the den for another ten minutes. On his way out, Reynolds asked the police photographer to send copies of his work to the DA's office as soon as possible. He also asked Detective Shaw to furnish him with duplicates of the display-mounted research materials, including exact reprints of each photo.

Reynolds and Miller spent the next hour touring the rest of Matheson's residence and agreed to meet later that afternoon at Earvin Cooper's home.

When they arrived at the Cooper home, most of the area had been cleared, but there remained a small portion sealed off as part of the crime scene. Members of the Criminal Investigation Department were present along with forensic scientists from the special unit of the FBI. Reynolds spoke with some of the staff, then walked with Miller alongside the burned-out rubble.

"You think this nightmare's ever gonna end?" asked Miller.

"I'm not exactly an expert on solving nightmares," answered an equally reserved Reynolds. "Ever since I was a kid, I've had this dream of a black man chasing me."

"You're *supposed* to have that dream. It's the bogeyman, and he's always black."

"I wake up before he can hurt me."

"That's supposed to happen, too," Miller said. "That way you can look for him during the day. If you don't find him, any black man will do."

Reynolds stopped walking and looked inquisitively at Miller. "You sure you don't have a little Afro-American blood in you?"

"It's the South," said Miller, shrugging. "All things are relative, especially your kin."

Ruth Cooper anxiously approached the two men. She pointed her finger at Reynolds. "You the one gonna prosecute that professor?"

"Yes."

"He took away the only man I ever loved."

"You must be Mrs. Cooper," Reynolds said sympathetically. "I'm very sorry for your loss."

She assessed the damage to the property and gazed at the barn in ruins. "I hope his nigger soul burns in hell." She walked away from the two men.

Reynolds watched her proceed toward her home and enter it, slamming the door behind her.

Miller tugged on the sleeve of Reynolds's jacket. "Thanks for not introducing me," he said.

CHAPTER
28

VANZANT GATHERED HIS senior staff in a small auditorium located in the building's basement. Reynolds and Sinclair sat together in the front row and listened to their boss as he held a hand microphone and roamed the stage. "Christmas vacations are canceled. New Year celebrations are put on hold. At my request, the attorney general has provided staff to assist our efforts to find evidence that implicates Matheson in the other murders. We've got a dozen federal agents investigating more than three hundred leads phoned in to a special hot line established by the governor."

Vanzant stopped pacing. "The State of Mississippi versus Martin S. Matheson is our number one priority, and a finding of guilty is the only acceptable outcome. He didn't just kill an individual. He's defied the forces of government by substituting his judgment for our entire judicial system. Justice itself is on trial, and I promise you, it's gonna prevail."

Reynolds didn't expect to get much sleep in the next few months. He'd have to forsake precious time with his family, so he wasn't in the mood for any more of Vanzant's political blustering. But he endured it for another twenty minutes—along with Sinclair, who'd been assigned to assist him. After Vanzant concluded his "pep talk," the two spent the afternoon reviewing materials and developing a tentative schedule to interview prospective witnesses. They hoped to establish more than a circumstantial case against Matheson to increase the likelihood of gaining a conviction. For the moment, that was all they had.

Under normal conditions they might have waited longer before bringing a murder indictment against the professor, but that luxury didn't exist. The public wanted to put a halt to Matheson's courses, and they clamored for someone to be arrested. When the opportunity presented itself to accomplish both, Vanzant seized on it. It was now left to them to prove beyond a reasonable doubt that the son of a prominent minister and advocate of nonviolence had committed murder. In a little over three months, they'd have their chance before a jury of Matheson's peers.

That hardly provided sufficient time to prepare for most misdemeanor assignments, let alone adjudicate an emotionally charged murder case. But the defendant had exercised his right to a speedy trial, and it was so ordered without any further delay from the prosecution. A great deal of work needed to be accomplished in a limited amount of time, and Reynolds couldn't afford to waste any of it.

"Here's Matheson's résumé." He handed the paperwork to Sinclair. "We need to get copies of his books, articles, speeches—anything that gives us a fix on his beliefs or personality."

"I don't get it." Sinclair shook her head in amazement. "Why would a guy like Matheson butcher a bunch of old men?"

"Why did Hannibal Lecter eat people?"

She raised her eyebrow in wonderment. "He was crazy?" she answered tentatively.

"Matheson has a genius IQ combined with a hero complex. That could result in some nasty repercussions." Reynolds picked up a cardboard box and placed it on a large work desk.

"Nasty enough to make him a murderer?" Sinclair asked.

"Let me put it this way"—he removed forensic reports from the box and organized the files around the conference table—"if he invites you to dinner and serves fava beans just before uncorking a fine Chianti, excuse yourself from the table and get the hell out of Dodge."

"I'm glad to see you haven't lost your sense of humor." She helped him with the documents. "You're going to need it."

"Along with a new pair of glasses." Reynolds retrieved several books from a package and started reading the first one.

Sinclair glanced at the paperback. "Why are you researching James Baldwin? I thought he believed in non-violence."

"He also believed most black people hated white people."

"Baldwin said that?" Sinclair exclaimed.

Reynolds put the book to his side and touched her

shoulder consolingly. "He meant it in a kind and affectionate way."

Sinclair sat at the end of the table. "I've heard of tough love, but that strikes me as a bit extreme."

Reynolds edged closer to her and opened to a page in the paperback where he'd previously placed a bookmark. "Matheson quotes Baldwin as saying any black man who saw the world through the eyes of John Wayne wouldn't be a hero but a raving maniac."

"What does that give us?" she asked.

"Motive."

She took the book from Reynolds and started reading.

CHAPTER
29

PROMISING TO MAKE the trial even more colorful was the assignment of Judge Tanner to the case. To no one's surprise, he refused to allow cameras in his courtroom, preferring instead to protect the State of Mississippi's illustrious heritage. A reopening of old wounds would serve no useful purpose other than to give the northern liberal press a series of free shots at a chapter of southern justice better left closed.

Reynolds welcomed Tanner's intervention for reasons more to do with the future than the past. No matter the outcome of the case, the fragile nature of black-white relationships would be forever changed in this community. Better to contain the damage locally than let it spread nationwide.

Reynolds and Miller appeared before Tanner in his chambers. The judge allowed only one representative from the prosecutors' team—a ruling that Reynolds believed reflected no particular evenhandedness on

Tanner's part. If anything, it reaffirmed the judge's uneasiness around attorneys who were of the "softer and gentler persuasion," Tanner's term for female counsel. Southern chivalry still existed, and it required women to be grateful as well as compliant toward its most ardent advocates.

"Gentlemen, I want this meeting to remain off the record, so I've dismissed the court reporter for the remainder of the day."

Miller and Reynolds exchanged an uncomfortable look.

Tanner spoke informally. "I'd like to avoid problems, particularly embarrassing ambushes from either side. So I suggest in the spirit of cooperation we conduct a dry run without the pressure of public exposure. That'll give me an opportunity to rule on several motions and get a sense of how vigorously I'll be challenged." He smiled graciously. "It'll also allow you to appreciate how strongly I feel about certain politically delicate issues. Let's just say, if you know where the judicial minefields are located, you'll stay out of those areas altogether. Seem fair enough?"

Both lawyers nodded reluctantly. Reynolds understood that the judge would rather bully the attorneys inside his chambers than come across as obstinate before the jury.

"Splendid," said the judge, who leaned back into his chair. "Now's as good a time as any to test the waters. Mr. Reynolds, you first."

"I ask the court to deny bail for the defendant and to have him remain in custody throughout the duration of the trial."

"Mr. Miller, let's hear your argument."

"Your Honor, since the professor doesn't have significant financial resources and would pose no risk of flight, I request bail be waived entirely or set at a moderately low figure."

"Mr. Miller," Tanner said in a voice that foreshadowed a lecture, "sometimes there's a risk of flight, and on occasion there's a greater risk a defendant will hang 'round and make everybody's life miserable. I believe, given the circumstances of this crime, the community will be better served by keeping Professor Matheson confined. I'd like to make it easier to guarantee everyone's safety, including your client's."

"Are you really concerned about my client's health, or is this just an effort to prevent Professor Matheson from exercising his First Amendment rights?" challenged Miller.

"He can speak all he wants," Tanner offered. "But, he'll be talkin' to three tiny walls and a row of iron bars in his cell. His days of inspiring students will have to be put on hold for a while, Mr. Miller."

"Your Honor, if my client were white, I doubt very much he'd even be arrested with the relatively minor circumstantial evidence the state's presented thus far."

"Counselor, if your client were white, he wouldn't have had black students takin' his course, and we wouldn't be here today." Tanner's voice became less strident. "Now, I admit, the state's got a difficult case, but it's not due to the absence of evidence. You and I both know there are plenty of folks dressed in those lovely orange jumpsuits servin' time based on a fiber from a throw rug or a mere strand of hair that appeared to be a possible match." Tanner rubbed against the bottom of his chair.

"Yes, Your Honor, we can agree on that," Miller said,

"but we can also agree those defendants were poor and uneducated."

"Prison ain't made 'em no richer, so I hope for their sake they picked up some books while they've been incarcerated and gotten smarter." Tanner mumbled something and rocked forward. "Now, as far as this case, I'm expecting a rather speedy trial. Mr. Reynolds, I hope you don't intend to draw this out."

"No, Your Honor," agreed Reynolds. "We don't anticipate calling any more than six to eight witnesses."

"Fine and dandy." Tanner jotted a note. "I don't want any comparisons to that case in California whose name I dare not mention. Suffice it to say, you can't put jurors through a case that lasts as long as the Nuremberg trials and expect one or more won't find a doubt and call it reasonable." The judge sharpened a pencil. "And don't allow your cocounsel to change her hairdo or wardrobe more often than you change your theory of the case." Tanner tried the new point on his legal pad. It broke off when he used it, and he grudgingly put it aside for a pen.

"Judge Tanner," Miller interjected, "I object to you providing advice and encouragement to the state designed to help achieve a guilty verdict against my client. I find that highly inappropriate and potentially prejudicial against the defense."

"No need to get all riled up or try to establish a misleading record as a basis for your possible appeal." Tanner rubbed the bridge of his nose. "Now, Todd, don't you go on and get your feelings hurt; I'm about to give you some helpful advice, too. You're as free as Mr. Reynolds to cherish it and draw it to your bosom or reject it and risk havin' it come back to seek revenge on another part of your body."

"Your Honor, I'll be grateful for any insights you have to offer that will ensure my client receives a fair trial."

"Wonderful," punctuated Tanner. "My recommendation is that you don't piss me off in front of the jury."

"That's it?" asked a frustrated Miller.

"I can expand it to include my private chambers."

"That won't be necessary, Your Honor," Miller capitulated. "I appreciate your first offer and will consider it seriously."

"It's advice you can take to the bank. And if you don't follow it, that's precisely where I'll send you to pay any fines I impose for contempt of court." The judge turned around his yellow legal notepad and displayed it on the outer lip of his desk so that both Miller and Reynolds could see it. He pointed to the left margin. "Now that I've given you both the benefit of my substantial wisdom, I call counsel's attention to the two letters runnin' down the side of my paper right next to your motions. You with me?"

"Yes, Your Honor," both attorneys answered.

"*R.R.*—got several of them already." Tanner's fat little fingers played the accordion alongside the paper's edge. "You see all these?" He pointed out the initials. "That's my abbreviation for *Reserved Ruling.*" He put the notepad down. "As long as y'all don't give me too many convoluted citations to look up, or ask for too many complex decisions before we even start the damn trial, I promise to rule on your requests in a timely fashion." He cleared his throat. "Follow me thus far?"

The two lawyers looked at each other a bit confusedly.

Tanner took a drink of ice water and ran the liquid over his teeth before swallowing. "However, if I start havin' to write a lot of these twin *R*s, that's when life gets unduly complicated." He leaned back in his chair and flapped his arms, freeing space for his black robe to spread its wings and fly. "I discovered a long time ago, the best solution for a complicated problem is to apply a simple remedy. So once I fill up a whole legal page with my *Reserved Ruling* initials, this is what I'm gonna do." He took a red marker and started circling the initials. When he finished an entire page, he once again showed the pad to both attorneys.

"I've just changed my exceedingly patient and cooperative twins into a series of dangerous railroad warnings." He fanned himself with the pad. "I'm not responsible for what happens to anyone who wants to risk crossin' the tracks or challengin' the train to a race. However, that's a contest you can't win." He rested the pad against his stomach and folded his arms around it in a loving embrace.

"So, gentlemen, don't complicate this case any more than necessary. If you do, I guarantee you won't see what hit you—but rest assured, the damage inflicted will be quite severe." He tossed the pad in front of him and leaned forward. "The wheels of justice may grind slowly, but trust me, they do grind." He smiled warmly. "Do either of you have any further motions you'd like me to consider at this time?"

The two lawyers didn't respond.

"I thought not. May God bless you and keep you from harm." Tanner tucked his yellow legal pad under his right arm. He carried it in the manner of a football headed for a trophy case and walked to a cabinet. He slid open a door, lowered a drop shelf, and removed a bottle of brandy and three glasses.

"I don't do this often," the judge announced, "but it

might be a good idea if we share a toast, since I have a queasy feelin' this case might test our skills and collective patience beyond all reasonable limits." He filled the glasses halfway.

"Judge Tanner," said Reynolds, "I'm afraid I don't drink."

"That's as good a reason to have fear as any I've heard." Tanner pulled out a can of Coke.

"I'll drink his, Your Honor," volunteered Miller.

"Spoken like a true defense lawyer. But I don't want you leavin' here and causin' any accidents." He handed Miller his drink. "'Specially in that car you drive." The judge gave Reynolds his soda. They stood in a three-spoked circle as Tanner raised his drink. "To the pursuit of justice."

They clinked together their two glasses and a can and declared in unison, "To justice."

CHAPTER
30

DURING HIS FIRST three weeks of confinement, Matheson remained in solitary, totally isolated from the general inmate population. Several white prison gangs had threatened his life. Blacks, who greatly outnumbered all other ethnic groups combined, issued a retaliatory warning that if the professor was harmed in any way, the lives of all whites, including correctional officers and staff, would be endangered.

Matheson insisted he be allowed to participate in public activities and eventually signed a waiver agreeing not to hold the state liable for any injury sustained while outside protective custody. During meals in the cafeteria, black prisoners offered the professor their desserts or extra portions of meat. They'd gather around his table and ask questions about his college course and the nature of the crimes committed by the men on the list. Instead of answering, Matheson discussed matters of greater concern.

He started with the institution of slavery. If it existed today, he hypothesized, blacks would be quartered in housing much like these prisons; the latest and most advanced technological equipment would be utilized to monitor their movements and quell any potential uprisings. He speculated how drugs would be used to control the most defiant among them. The irony wasn't lost on these inmates, most of whom had lost their freedom due to the use or sale of narcotics.

He asked how many of them had children and how often their sons and daughters had seen them before they'd been incarcerated. He wanted to know if they supported them, financially or emotionally. Many of the men stared at the floor they were forced to disinfect twice each day. "Imagine a time when children were ripped away from their parents," he told them, "and sold to anyone who had money in their pockets or hatred in their hearts." He wanted them to envision their daughters being brutalized in the middle of the night and contemplate "how their voices sounded when they screamed for help." Then he posed the question: "Were those screams any different than the ones you elicited from your black victims?"

He talked about the Diaspora and the journey across a mysterious ocean during which their ancestors were chained together, huddled in darkness within the bowels of a ship. He described the slaves "lying among the dead and the dying, sleeping in their own defecation and sharing a nightmare tame in comparison to the reality that awaited." He suggested they look around the room at each other and consider the environment they'd created for those who shared their name and, in all probability, their fate.

"The worst type of slaves," he claimed, "were the ones

who not only volunteered for the job but also enlisted the people who trusted and loved them."

Did they know that less than two centuries ago masters inserted iron devices inside the mouths of field hands so they wouldn't be able to communicate with one another while working? And were they aware that the "sun heated the metal so intensely it tore away dry skin from blistered tongues each time it was removed"? He inquired if anyone wished to hazard a guess as to how those slaves might feel if they knew their burned-out throats were sacrificed so that their offspring might have the freedom, if not the luxury, to call their brothers "niggers" and their sisters "bitches and whores." How many of these inmates, he wondered aloud, had knife or gun wounds inflicted by the descendants of slaves? "Would those scars have hurt any more had they been caused by the lash of a bullwhip or the burning metal of an owner's branding iron?"

Then he stopped talking and requested the men share their stories. He listened carefully and without judgment to several multigenerational tales of families who'd been in and out of prisons their entire adult lives. Sometimes father and son, or brother and brother, or uncle and nephew would be serving time together, separated by the distance between similar county, state, or federal facilities but united by equally harsh sentencing for identical crimes. A grandfather spoke of waiting for a grandson to join him in prison. He recounted the day the boy lost his name to an assigned number, the last three digits of which he'd frequently played and twice won in the poor man's illegal lottery.

Mothers and wives and sisters and daughters increasingly acquired their own unique numerical "ID bracelets,"

thereby repeating the multigenerational prison ritual.
Only this time it wasn't the men but the women recycled
rather than rehabilitated.

Those who escaped the harshness of imprisonment
suffered the indignities of visiting their loved ones in a
cold, guarded room, forced to endure the mechanical rape
of handheld metal detectors moving relentlessly across
their bodies and between their legs. They took off
sweaters and discarded belts. They removed jewelry from
their wrists and around their necks and stored it in lock-
ers to be supervised by guards who deemed prisoners of
no value. Before receiving authorization to enter the visitation area, old women pulled out their bobby pins and
hoped they still looked presentable. Young girls left behind plastic barrettes or colorful hair ribbons and exchanged them for embarrassment and tears, which their
mothers quickly ordered them to conceal.

Before too long these visitors, who'd grown accustomed to their dignity being stripped away, asked to meet
Professor Matheson. They'd read so much about him
from letters sent home, as well as from newspaper accounts of his impending trial, they now thought of him as
family. On regular visits they brought him books and
extra magazines. They asked for permission to write to
him and ended each letter with the assurance he'd always
be in their prayers. On special visits they baked him co-
conut cake, his favorite, and a variety of pies and cookies
he shared with everyone, even the guards. He'd been invited to become their children's godfather. They hugged
him when they arrived and wept for him when they left.

One Saturday evening after visitations had ended, a
Muslim inmate approached and offered to convert
Matheson to Islam. He replied that they should all set

aside their gods and discover if love was possible without the existence of a deity. "God's been used so often to tolerate evil," he said, "to accept it as a plan conceived by a divine force, designed to test the depths of one's faith." For a moment he wanted them to conceive of a world without God's will—a time when they had to assume responsibility for acting without a grand design or an all-powerful being recording their actions for the specific purpose of rewarding or punishing them in an afterlife. What would happen if this life was all they had? If their immortality existed only in the hearts and minds of those whom they'd touched with honor and respect?

"Would you love differently?" he asked each man. "Would your good deeds be less worthy or important? And if you lived without a belief in God yet acted the way a God would demand, wouldn't you reap and possibly deserve even a greater reward?"

The Muslim thanked Matheson for posing questions that caused him to rethink and renew his faith, then asked if he could leave a copy of the Koran for the professor to read at his convenience. Matheson indicated he'd already read it several times but would accept the book as a gift that reflected the good wishes of a friend. That night Matheson opened the holy book and found a newspaper clipping of a burned-out house. The brick structure remained intact with two sets of windowless frames supported by steel bars. The front entrance also had been consumed by fire except for an iron gate inserted within the doorway.

At breakfast the next morning, Matheson asked the man why he'd kept the article. He answered that as a teenager he'd robbed the home several times. There wasn't much worth stealing, he said sadly, "a radio, an old television, some CDs." A woman lived there as a single parent raising three young daughters including an infant. She had evidently spent two weeks' salary to purchase and install the steel bars inside her windows and front door in order to protect her belongings.

Less than two days after the installation, an electrical wire overheated and caused a fire to spread quickly throughout the small home. The mother grabbed her three children and attempted to exit the burning house but remained trapped by the very system designed to protect them. Neighbors tried frantically to remove the screaming children, to no avail. By the time firefighters entered the home, the entire family had perished in the blazing inferno.

He'd had nothing to do with setting the fire and therefore technically hadn't killed them. Yet, he knew if it weren't for his continued thefts, she wouldn't have needed the security gates that turned her home into a prison and her prison into a death trap. To a truthful heart, that made him as responsible for taking their lives as if he had started the fire himself and barricaded all the exits to their salvation.

He'd placed the article inside the Koran in the hope that Allah would grant him forgiveness. When the professor first asked the men to imagine the screams of their children being brutalized in the middle of the night, the inmate had thought of that mother and her three little girls. He heard their screams and felt the fire that consumed their lives erasing an entire family from the face of this earth.

He looked at Matheson with tears in his eyes and asked the professor if he'd felt responsible for the murders of those white men on his list. Without any hesitation Matheson answered yes, and further replied that he'd never ask his God for forgiveness, only understanding and, perhaps, mercy. He returned the Koran to the young Muslim brother but asked to keep the newspaper article.

"I'd be grateful to you, Professor, for relieving me of my grief," said the prisoner.

Matheson posted the article on the cell wall over his bed, where it would remain until he learned his fate.

At the end of the professor's first six weeks virtually every black inmate had attended at least one of his regularly scheduled sessions. They sat in foldout chairs or on long metal benches or on the floor. When a particularly large crowd assembled, they stood quietly along the walls, with the tallest inmates in the back. They abstained from smoking in the meeting room and agreed not to retaliate against any warring factions for the duration of the talks plus one hour. They found the additional grace period unnecessary since there were no reports of violence among blacks on the days that Matheson spoke.

They listened attentively to the professor and often took extensive notes that they later studied and often committed to memory. Each subsequent question-and-answer period lasted increasingly longer. Matheson encouraged the men to seek answers within the group and to take comfort in the knowledge they weren't alone in their problems or in the common struggle to find meaningful solutions.

The guards allowed the meetings to go beyond designated time curfews since to do otherwise risked negative reactions from those present. Black guards volunteered for extra duty on nights the professor conducted his business. On more than one occasion, what Matheson said to the men or what they said to him moved a few officers to tears.

As the trial date approached, the prisoners became increasingly anxious regarding Matheson's future. While they wished him freedom, they also thought about their own lives and the possibility of enduring prison without him. He'd promised not to forget them, but they'd heard that before, from spouses and mothers and brothers and children who'd suddenly stopped visiting or writing or accepting collect phone calls. They were related by blood and yet had been abandoned, betrayed. They'd no such claim on the professor, so "why should he be any different?" they asked.

"Because he is," the Muslim told his fellow inmates. "Because he is."

They nodded in agreement and shared a prayer.

CHAPTER
31

REYNOLDS LOST TRACK of the time he'd been in his den reviewing the photos taken from Matheson's home. It had been dark outside when he started, but now the sunlight forced him to close the drapes.

When he'd first sat down, he removed everything from his desktop except for a lamp. He opened several photo albums and stacked them on top of each other. He selected pictures from the largest one and spread them out in front of him so he could take notes. He didn't write a single word for a long while. He didn't do much of anything except stare at the gallery that lay before him.

He didn't want to stare at the photos, but the harder he tried to look away, the longer the horror held him, drawing him closer to a place he feared he'd never leave. The images had a hypnotic quality. If he didn't know better, he'd swear he saw the victims' eyes move to avoid his, as though they were ashamed of their bodies now contorted by an unprovoked collision with hate. Their deaths were grotesque, yet in their anguish he found a stunning silence that converted rage into an illusion of peace.

It was odd—remarkable, even—that once emotions moved beyond terror and sadness, something indescribably beautiful entered. Perhaps it was faith, or maybe a profound connection with the oneness, the sacredness, of life. Whatever it might be, this much was certain: It raced to fill the void that, if allowed to exist a moment too long, would be occupied forever by madness. He understood that no one with an ounce of passion could study these photos without being consumed by them. And once they absorbed your spirit, it would be difficult if not impossible ever again to distinguish between vengeance and honor.

Reynolds touched the first picture and paused briefly over each body. He went on to the next, then the next, continuing until he felt them die again. He caressed each frozen image: someone's child, somebody's father, a wedding ring on a charred finger, a face without eyes, an infant savagely separated from its mother's protective womb with one merciless swing of an ax, destroying any chance that it might survive long enough to learn why it was despised with such viciousness.

He turned the pages of one album to reveal additional atrocities so great they numbed his senses. That very numbing provided him the necessary power and courage to proceed. He saw a woman and her son hanging perfectly still from the same bridge that once connected and often welcomed strangers to a safe harbor and the community they'd desired to call home. Their necks were bent and broken. The sides of their faces touched their shoulders, seeking support or comfort but finding only despair.

He saw what was left of a man roasted alive. His blood had been boiled so hot by the burning embers of hatred that it exploded and splattered a crowd still busy distributing severed fingers and other prized body parts as souvenirs.

He stared at a bent serrated knife usually reserved for splitting and gutting hogs. It protruded from a young girl's abdomen. An oversized corkscrew of twisted steel had punctured her thighs numerous times and ripped away her flesh and muscles by repeatedly pulling out large chunks of her body. Her insides were randomly flung across the earth like red-stained ripened crops to be harvested by the devil himself.

He traced the scars on the back of a young boy whipped to death then mutilated beyond recognition except for the remains of his skull. It had been fractured with such force that one eye dangled outside its socket while the other lay buried beneath a blood-soaked eyelid swollen shut by the brutality of what it had seen.

He'd become a vulture cautiously circling to inspect the dead and dying before acquiring the nerve to move more closely and feast off their remains. Was he violating them, or paying tribute? He turned his attention away from the victims and studied the crowds, whose only apparent anxiety came from the fear they wouldn't be included in any subsequent photos taken near their slaughtered prey. Their frenzied white faces blended into one lurid and psychotic smile, which transformed a scene of debauchery into a tragic rendering that made forgiveness impossible and the future unworthy of hope.

What would possess a group of people, even one that had become a vile mob, to descend into such a deep depravity that they'd invite their own children to attend and actively participate in the butchering of a human life, then proudly pose so that the evil act might be recorded forever, if not in the annals of history, then at least in their cherished family albums?

Reynolds waited for an answer but knew none would be forthcoming no matter how many pictures he studied or how long he stayed in this photographic mausoleum of the violated and defiled. He wanted to cry somehow, but couldn't. He wanted to kill someone, but that would make him just like the smiling white men he now despised. He thought of his precious children and wondered what he'd have done had their faces been among the victims in these photographs. He had no doubt he was capable of killing anyone who harmed his family; the only question was how long he'd make them suffer.

So, if he'd do that for *his* children, why wouldn't he do it for the children in these pictures, or for the fathers and mothers who would never hold them again? Weren't their lives important, too, their suffering worthy of redress? And if he failed to protect them, wouldn't all children, including his own, be less safe? What if Matheson had in fact freed him from the obligation of ever having to answer those questions for himself? Did that make the professor a criminal, or did it turn Reynolds and countless others like him, who substituted outrage for action, into cowards?

He delicately arranged the photos in three equally spaced rows that formed one large, shattered portrait of pain. This time the eyes of the dead refused to turn away, forcing him now to feel ashamed. The image slowly blurred as the newly created mosaic of murdered men, women, and children began to be filtered through the tears of a prosecutor whose duty required him to punish them again. Except now, he'd rob them of their right to feel vindicated by denouncing, then penalizing the only person in this world who'd convinced them their lives mattered and their deaths merited avenging.

He would represent the people of the state of Mississippi and seek justice against Matheson in a court of law, but who would speak for the people in these photos to defend and uphold a theory of justice that never encompassed them? Who would explain why their murderers were being accorded greater protections in death than these victims ever had in life? The first teardrop fell, followed by the second, then the third, and Reynolds pushed away the photos to protect them from further distress.

He turned off the small table lamp, leaned back into his chair, and thought of a sociology exam he took in college. He was asked the definition of a societal problem. He answered, "Something bad that happens to white people." Once again, society would vent its outrage at the murder of whites while ignoring the history that got them killed. This time he wouldn't let that happen. Somehow, he'd find a way to give these black people a voice, to see to it that someone wept for them, too.

He would call them as prime witnesses, resurrected examples of what can happen to a justice system when it devalues certain lives and, in the process, creates a monster that owes its allegiance to no one, not even to the thing that created it. Reynolds would slay that monster once and for all. It was the only way he knew how to honor them, by honoring the sanctity of life. Matheson had violated that sanctity, and in so doing had betrayed the very people he purported to avenge. And for that, Reynolds would make him pay.

He closed his eyes and invited the testimony of those who'd waited so long to have someone call their name with the respect they deserved. Reynolds couldn't leave quite yet. He needed a little more time alone with them in the darkness, where he might better experience their torment in an effort to bring closure to his own.

Cheryl found her husband sitting on the porch. She'd fallen asleep waiting for him to finish his work. When she awoke and saw that his pillow had never been used, she knew exactly where to find him.

"Want some company?"

He never looked at her but nodded yes.

She sat next to him and took his hand. "You don't need to be the one doing this, you know."

"I don't want a white person bringing him to justice."

"Why not?" she asked, surprised. "You think the community won't accept a guilty verdict if it comes as a result of a white prosecutor?"

"The community's not likely to accept the verdict no matter who's assigned the case. I just don't want the lead prosecutor to be white. Something about that would seem unfair."

"Unfair?" She let go of his hand and gave him some space.

"Maybe *ironic* is a better word. White prosecutors never really went after the murderers of those black folk. If they go after him with all their energy and the full force of the law, it would be like the victims were being lynched all over again."

"And if you do it, won't it be the same, maybe even worse?"

He still hadn't looked at her. "If I do it, I do it for them.

In a strange way, I feel like I'm representing them, too."
He gave a tired smile and finally turned to face her.

"What are you thinking?" she asked.

"About my dad. He used to say you have to be twice
as good as the white man to be treated the same. Even
then, they'd go to their grave before acknowledging you
might be equal to them, let alone better."

"I hate to be the one to break this to you, James," she
said, touching his arm. "But all black parents tell their
children that. Sometimes they don't mention color—by
the time you've reached five or six, they assume you can
figure out some essential things on your own." She
nudged him playfully, but he stared at the floor.

"You believe that stuff about the oppressed always
being better off than their oppressors?" he asked.

"In this world or the next?" she asked half teasingly.

"This one," he said, remaining serious.

She thought about it for a moment. "I guess I do.
Spiritually—maybe in other ways, too." She studied
him. "Is that why it has to be you? You want to prove
we're better?"

"I wanna prove there's nothing wrong with justice—
the problem exists with some of the people who've ad-
ministered it. And those black people who suffered, they
have to know they died for a reason. To make it right." He
looked at her again. "To make the system work, for
everybody."

"James . . ." She hesitated for a moment. "How can
you be so sure he did it?"

"Because I would have, too." He moved closer to her.
"If I'd been him and spent all that time studying the anguish and the pain and the brutality and not had anyone
to pull me back from the abyss of raw hatred . . ." He

rubbed his face with his hands. "I hope to God I never get that close to the edge."

"I don't think you could ever change into someone I couldn't love," Cheryl said very quietly.

"You couldn't love me if I turned into a murderer."

"If you turned into that, you'd no longer be the person I married." She removed a piece of lint from his shirt. "You'd be a stranger to me, our children, most of all to yourself."

"I've tried over thirty murder cases in the last ten years. You know how many were death penalty?"

"Seven," she quickly answered.

He smiled. Of course she knew, he thought to himself. He'd been a nightmare to live with during each one. "No matter how vicious the crime or repulsive the act, I always understood how someone could be that sick, could murder another human being. That demon exists in all of us if pushed far enough." He leaned back against the wooden post. "I've seen it in the faces of some of the most contemptible men ever convicted. But here's the really scary part: I've also seen it when I've looked at the relatives of the victims. All that rage needing to be released."

"Why are you putting yourself through this?"

"Because I'm afraid what Matheson did really is the norm. He tapped into some insanity that makes it all right to hate the hater and feel vindicated." He took a deep breath and looked beyond the boundaries of his backyard. "The line between justice and revenge disappeared a long time ago, Cheryl. If we fail to reestablish it now, I don't know if we'll ever be able to." He walked over to the other side of the porch. "I've got to show the jury that line while we're still capable of seeing it."

"Don't put that burden on yourself, James. You're one man prosecuting a single case. If you think you can change the world with this verdict, you've lost before you begin. Whatever happens with Matheson, you can get over it and go on with your life. But if you think you're fighting some righteous cause with the world hanging in the balance"—she crossed to his side and held him—"honey, that's not anything you'll ever recover from. And we still got a whole lotta livin' to do and two beautiful children to raise."

"And have we taught them to be twice as good just to be treated the same?"

"Three or four times, and even then it might not be enough to outdo their parents."

He gave a hint of a smile.

"Well," she continued, "I can't speak for their daddy, but I know if they want to surpass my achievements, they—"

He put his hand over her mouth and brought her close to him. He removed his hand slowly, and when her mouth became fully exposed, he kissed her gently, then more passionately.

"Mommy?"

They stopped suddenly and turned to discover Christopher. He looked annoyed.

"Angela won't let me watch my videos on the TV in the living room."

"Go watch them in your room," his mother said, still flustered from the interruption.

"I don't wanna. My TV's too small."

"Go watch in the den," she suggested.

"I don't like to be in there by myself."

"Go watch in Angela's room," his father recommended

as Cheryl gave her husband an incredulous look and raised her head while closing her eyes.

Christopher grinned mischievously and ran back into the house. Cheryl opened her eyes and stared at her husband.

"Did I mess up?" he asked.

"Big-time," she responded.

"Oh, well," he sighed, then grabbed her. "Where were we?"

She pulled back. "You were about to save the world, and I suggest you practice with your daughter, who—"

"Christopher!" they heard a blood-curdling scream.

"Who probably isn't going to handle your compromise too well," Cheryl finished.

They heard Christopher scream, "Daddy said I could!" Followed by Angela yelling, "Daddy's not that stupid!"

CHAPTER
32

FOR THE PAST three months Miller had prepared for the trial almost nonstop. He reviewed all the state's evidence and hired forensic specialists to evaluate findings and conduct independent testing on the results. He read materials Matheson collected for his class, and studied copies of the photos discovered at the professor's home. Students volunteered to gather research and assemble visual displays he anticipated utilizing in his opening. Posters and photographic exhibits now cluttered his entire home. He'd never had this much help before in trying any case.

Miller removed an unopened milk carton from his refrigerator and checked the expiration date: thirty days ago. He shook the carton and felt a thick, lumpy slush. It annoyed him that things spoiled before they were opened. He believed expirations should apply *after* unsealing a perishable item. He started to separate the top of the carton, to pour the contents down the disposal, but thought better of it. He placed the container on the kitchen counter and looked at his cat, who gave him one of her all-knowing stares that combined pity with a sense of superiority.

He admired dogs, which was why he'd never owned one. He knew they had a tendency to love their masters no matter how poorly they were treated, so he wisely decided not to test the limits of their loyalty. He couldn't stand cats, but they did have the singularly positive attribute of not making him feel guilty when he treated them like dogs.

This member of the lion family had arrived at his doorstep on his birthday more than six years ago and wouldn't leave until fed. He soon learned, to his utter dismay, that once a cat shares dinner on your porch, you might as well place its name on the lease. They were also independent creatures, which contributed to Miller's disdain. It made him feel inadequate that a cat could take better care of itself than he could.

On the first night she moved into his home, he named her Miranda, then read the cat her rights. They included, among other things, the mutual obligation to respect each other's private space, private thoughts, and private needs. Miller maintained his part of the bargain, but Miranda intruded whenever her clairvoyant mind deemed it necessary. He had no difficulty understanding why certain cultures worshiped cats while others despised them, although these opposite emotions were caused by the same basic principle: Cats were either possessed by demons or capable of recognizing them in others. Either way, they were dangerous and needed to be idolized for life or destroyed at the earliest risk-free opportunity. But since there's never a truly risk-free period in anyone's cow-

ardly life, you learned to live with your fears while si-
multaneously paying tribute to them. In that regard, having cats was a lot like having family.

Having concluded that even Miranda deserved more
than rotten milk, Miller picked up the carton and
dropped it into the plastic wastebasket. If good milk
could go bad without ever being opened, what chance
did kids have who were exposed to all types of contam-
inations? As he pondered the question, he cleaned
Miranda's litter box for the first time in a long while,
then fed her some tuna. He put two ice cubes into an
extra-large bowl, filled it with water, then searched for
his car keys. He wondered what had become of his childhood friend Sanford, and continued to think about him
until he reached his destination.

The trip took slightly more than two hours, the last
thirty minutes of which were spent on poorly paved
roads. The Gulf Coast embraced the contradictions of divergent histories. The past could be reflected in the rusty
shrimp boats that dotted the riverbank, barely able to provide sustenance to a family of four, let alone adequately
feed an entire marketplace whose appetite for the old
ways of doing things had drastically changed. The future
in all its splendid glory consisted of floating dreams better known as riverboat casinos. Gambling had invaded
Mississippi with a vengeance and harvested the poor
more efficiently than Whitney's invention had stripped
cottonseed from the state's other prized crop.

Miller planned to phone before he left home, but why
give the devil advance warning, especially when it controlled visitation rights? He thought it best to surprise the
man, catch him off guard. It wouldn't necessarily level

the playing field, but it might allow him to be competitive, stay in the game longer than he'd managed to do on other visits. Like most sons, Miller had tried valiantly to please his father, but never could. So at some point in his life he had simply decided to do the next best thing and disappoint him at every turn. The disappointment evolved quickly to infuriation and gradually to indifference, eventually culminating in disinheritance.

Miller had followed the footsteps but decidedly not the path taken by his patriarchs. He became a lawyer or, if he believed his father, a disgrace to his profession. He fought for civil rights with the same intensity he'd lashed out at Sanford, and for the same reason. His father remained the driving motivation behind all of Miller's important adult actions. If he couldn't please him, then he'd fail him unconditionally. And he'd keep failing until he finally learned the source of his father's bigotry—and the target, if any, of his love.

He drove through the narrow entrance leading to the complex where his father resided. It had been called an elderly nursing home five years ago, then a retirement community two years later, and now simply a senior lifestyle residential retreat. He'd visited many prisons that were far more honest about who lived behind the guarded gates and why. The facility employed a cordial staff. White folks handled the money while blacks carried the bedpans. It used to bring him abundant satisfaction to know his father depended on black people to assist him in performing the most basic of bodily functions. Now it brought only great sadness and deep regret.

Miller avoided the valet and parked the car himself. He wanted to delay this for as long as possible, and the journey through the maze of gardens and walkways gave him time to reconsider the visit. He could always get back into his car and return home. There'd be no harm done. He would have wasted a few hours, but he'd already spent much of his life avoiding the man who'd disowned him by calling him everything but a child of God or his son. No. The man hadn't called him his son since the day Miller obtained a law degree and notified his parents what he intended to do with it.

The knot in his stomach tightened. Several residents were seated in lawn chairs near a pink marbled water fountain. They resembled small porcelain statues wrapped in plaid flannel robes. He wondered if his father might be outside, sweet-talking a younger woman or telling tales of his youthful exploits. If he knew his father, his listeners would be enthralled, charmed by the man who generated genuine adoration from mere strangers and unadulterated fear from his own family.

Miller proceeded to the main building, where he registered as a family visitor. A friendly student nurse issued him a gold pass on a cloth necklace and told him to wear it around his neck at all times while traveling anywhere on the property. He assumed the trainee feared someone on the grounds might mistake him for a resident and force-feed him Valium before giving him a haircut and a bath. He stroked the back of his ponytail and placed it over his right shoulder. He wanted to make sure it would be the first and last thing his father noticed. *That should drive the old man crazy.*

He'd been told to meet with one of the administrators, since the doctor wasn't available on Saturdays. There he would receive an update regarding the senior Miller's "situation," along with other helpful information on how to interact with him. He decided to skip that enjoyable task, feeling that no one could give him a better briefing on the condition of his father than his father himself. In any event, he already knew the best way to communicate with the man who had brought him into this world only to almost drive him out of it: from a distance or not at all.

He maneuvered his way through an obstacle course consisting of walkers, wheelchairs, and motorized strollers until he found a safe hallway with minimal mechanical traffic. He hated these places. They reminded him of hospitals, except the patients in this warehouse weren't being cured, since no cure existed for their particular ailment. This halfway point between a holding area and a resting place had a certain antiseptic quality made less stringent by a smattering of potpourri and a whiff of aerosol spray. Miller guessed the scent might be either French vanilla or wild country blossom, since both fragrances worked equally well to temporarily mask the aroma of an unclean house.

He didn't know what to expect when he entered room 53 for the first time in five years and discovered his father seated with his back to the door, staring out the window.

"Dad?" Miller waited for an explosion. When that didn't happen, he assumed his father would simply ignore him, act as if he didn't exist. He wouldn't allow his father that luxury. "Dad, it's me, Todd."

"Toddpole?" his father asked in a gentle voice.

Miller smiled, in part from nervousness but mostly from genuine surprise. "Toddpole?" Miller said the word with an amused nostalgia as he moved closer to this figure who still hadn't demonstrated enough decency to turn and face his son.

"You haven't called me that since I was a little—" He froze when his father wheeled around to greet him. There was a glimmer of recognition and a glimpse of a smile weakened by time and a lack of practice. This couldn't be Richard Stanton Miller. Not this withered little man with the translucent skin that revealed pale purple-green veins struggling desperately to complete their mission.

Miller's father had been a tower of strength, defiant in every way imaginable. When he spoke to a jury, they had no choice but to believe him. Tall and eloquent, confident and knowledgeable, passionate and unforgiving, he couldn't be beaten by any adversary save one. After eighty-five years his father had met his match. He'd lost the most important battle of his life to the universal equalizer, time. And that defeat made him gaunt, hollow-eyed, and something not even his avowed racism had ever completely accomplished: pathetic.

"You clean up your room?" the soft voice asked.

Miller tried to respond but couldn't speak without releasing a lifetime of tears.

"You know how your mama fusses whenever you don't clean up like you're supposed to."

Miller turned away. His shoulders slumped a little more with each word he spoke. "It's clean, Dad."

"Including your toys? You sure you put them all away?" His father grabbed the sides of the chair to lift himself but stopped and settled back into his spot. "If you break them I'm not buying you any more." His father turned and once again faced the window.

Miller quietly moved to a chair next to his father's bed and sat down. He looked at the small night table that had three framed photos: a wedding picture of his father and mother, his grandfather posed outside a courthouse, wearing his judge's robe, and a picture of Miller as a child standing next to his proud, smiling father, who had his hand on his son's shoulder. Miller felt the first tear moisten his cheek. He placed his fingers on his quivering lips and wept quietly.

He didn't remember falling asleep but had the distinct impression of a parched mouth kissing him gently on his forehead, followed by the careful placement of a blanket around his upper body. He kept his eyes closed until his father's shuffling ceased. Miller rose from the chair and thought about leaving without disturbing the figure who'd returned to the window. He concluded he wasn't that much of a coward.

He tried to engage his father in a conversation that entailed more than the distant past, but after a few promising attempts Richard Miller disappeared to a space reserved for memory and dreams. Whether the place was real or imagined, Miller hoped his father would find peace there and, perhaps, another chance.

The car ride back home seemed filled with shadows. Clouds lingered overhead, threatening to release a sudden storm that hadn't been forecast. Miller had on occasion read news accounts detailing the lives of the most rabid racists from the early stages of the Civil Rights Movement, the ones who bombed churches and crippled or murdered children and blinded babies. Many of them had avoided prison only to enter, at an early age, advanced stages of dementia. He wasn't sure whether that represented a punishment or a blessing. Now he'd witnessed his own father ravaged by Alzheimer's, and realized that the suffering had been left to the son.

He'd wanted his dad to curse him or strike him or be the terror he'd grown up despising. It would give him energy for the battle that lay ahead. But when he found him shrunken in a wheelchair, with a mind disconnected from today, he realized he'd been living a lie. He'd never stopped loving or needing his father's approval. Despite his best efforts, he'd never hated him. This discovery made him feel ashamed, terribly lonely, and perhaps more than anything else, betrayed. How long had he lived this pretense of self-righteousness and moral outrage?

He shouldn't have visited this place, but in reality he'd never had a choice. Matheson had flung the past in everyone's face, and perhaps it was only right that his defense counsel take the first blow. He hadn't realized how often he'd need to turn the other cheek, and certainly had had no idea how much it would hurt. His father had no memory of the things that tormented him most, and Miller dared not remember the times that he himself cherished.

True enough, they were brief, those glorious exchanges between a loving father and an adoring and obedient son. But they were there. How ironic that they'd returned to a mind no longer capable of distinguishing reality from madness—or perhaps no such distinction ever existed. Hadn't the world of his father been both real and insane? How else to explain a gifted and highly educated man harboring such sickness?

Miller wondered if his father or grandfather had ever done anything that might have put them on Matheson's list. If they had, their actions would forever remain an unsolved mystery. If they hadn't, they certainly knew friends who belonged there. That fact alone enabled the commission of evil acts and may have even endorsed or encouraged them. When a governor stands at the entrance of a schoolhouse and proclaims, "Segregation today, segregation tomorrow, segregation forever," he's officially sanctioned the lynch mob whether he intended to do so or not. When respected community leaders remain silent in the face of atrocity, they've become the mob in spirit, if not in deed, and have no need to touch the rope.

It was a strange legacy shared by the descendants of the South, all of whom were one or two degrees of separation from being a child of a victim or a father of a perpetrator, or both. Miller reflected that for his entire professional life, he'd been cursed to represent defendants who looked guilty whether they were or not. Poor, black, and uneducated, their stories stood little chance when weighed against the testimony of reliable eyewitnesses and the judgment of dedicated jurors who feared the same dark skin.

Now, at long last, he'd been gifted with the ideal client: influential, intelligent, handsome, and articulate. Matheson didn't fit the profile of a criminal except for skin color, and this one time Miller could make that liability disappear, or at least cloak it within the framework of reasonable doubt. Would an acquittal of Miller's prized defendant achieve some semblance of payback for all those innocent men convicted? More to the point, would it be the final act of defiance by a son toward his father—a man currently hiding in the secret recesses of his own diseased mind? Miller didn't know the answers to those questions, but he'd soon discover them.

For better or worse, he accepted that his life would never be the same. He'd been a southern oddity. Now he would be a celebrity. Back when they'd been on speaking terms, his father had advised him that a traitor shouldn't publicize his home address. Well, his list of enemies would likely increase, and they'd have no trouble finding him. What they would find still needed to be determined. He prayed it would be a man he'd be proud to know, one who would have the integrity, if not the innocence, of a child his father had once lovingly called "Toddpole."

CHAPTER
33

T HE NORTHERN MEDIA descended on the area, exhibiting behavior that would have given locusts a good name by comparison. They devoured everything in sight, from hotel rooms to restaurant seats to the best downtown parking spaces. And they managed to do it with an arrogance and rudeness that surpassed even the lowest expectations of the local population.

One high-level reporter from a major New York paper entered a coffee shop near the courthouse and asked the owner where he might find some tofu. Aubrey Munson, the bell-shaped proprietor, gave him directions. "Go to the red-light district. You'll find that and a whole lot more." The reporter left the shop in an indignant huff, and the regulars laughed for five minutes.

Aubrey knew enough about tofu to know it would never see the inside of his mouth, let alone his stomach. He had feigned ignorance because the snooty journalist addressed him like a retarded child. In fact, the reporter had treated everyone in the store with contempt from the moment he'd walked in wearing his square-toed, hand-sewn leather Italian shoes with the extra-thick heels to make him look taller.

Aubrey had received a jury summons, as had most of his neighbors. They'd all thought long and hard about using those official notifications to start a barn fire but decided civic duty outweighed resentment toward the process. He actually hoped he'd get picked. He told the lunch crowd about his last jury experience. "Involved incest," he solemnly informed them. "I lost ten pounds. Stomach muscles knotted up every time I looked at that pitiful excuse for a father. If it'd been left to me, I would've saved the taxpayers a lot of time and heartache and put a bullet through that pervert's brain—maybe an extra one for good measure. Even let that scumbag's daughter, a pretty little thing, watch if she wanted. Hell, now that I think about it, I woulda' helped her squeeze the trigger if it brought back some of her childhood."

Aubrey saw himself as a reliable business owner, a decent Christian, and a man of action. If asked to serve in the Matheson case, "I'd do it in a heartbeat. Wouldn't be intimidated by the press, the lawyers, or—like I told my wife—those student agitators who are tryin' to turn that nigger into a hero."

Yes. It'd be a privilege to join eleven other honorable citizens to ensure that justice triumphed. Given his previous experience, there'd be no reason why "I wouldn't be selected to chair the group." As the man in charge, no matter what the final outcome, he'd be the first one interviewed. Might even get invited to fly to California and meet Hollywood stars who'd want to play him on the big screen. "*Jury Foreman:* The real-life story of Aubrey

Munson." Now, wouldn't that be a hoot? As he began to consider these larger issues, he discreetly asked some of his more trusted customers if he'd "been too harsh on that fella from New York."

Every single patron reassured him the odd man with the strange appetite "got precisely what he deserved." Still, politics being what they were, Aubrey wondered if he'd made a mistake offending a potentially powerful ally. It never paid to mistreat a person who had unlimited access to a printing press. Aubrey shrugged, as if to say, "It's too late now."

He'd read that the lawyers for both sides agreed to use a juror questionnaire developed by some high-priced consultant. There were questions on it like "What are your feelings about interracial dating?" and "How do you celebrate Dr. King's holiday?"

"What in tarnation does that have to do with a murder case?" he asked the reporter who'd called him at home to conduct a local survey—an opinion poll of sorts. She didn't know, either. Thought it reflected attitudes of either racial tolerance or prejudice.

"First of all," Aubrey had replied, "interracial dating is a no-no that comes directly from the Bible. So, that answers that. Second," he went on, "the man has a holiday; people take off work, and I ain't never met nobody bigoted against vacation." He waited for her to respond. She didn't. "Where's the damn problem?" he pushed. She thanked him very much for his time and told him the interview had ended. He wanted to know when it would be published so he could get a copy. She wasn't certain, but she'd be sure to send him one. That promise had been made three weeks ago, and he still hadn't seen any of his quotes—so much for trusting the media.

He made a fresh batch of coffee and collected all the unused sugar pouches from the counter and returned them to their jelly jars. He checked to see which straws hadn't been removed from their paper wrappings and shoved them into the silver holder. He changed his blue apron and put on a freshly starched white one just in case any of those photographers wanted to take pictures of his place later today. He glanced in the mirror behind the cash register and pushed his hair back. Probably need to get it cut soon, he thought, then counted the money in the register to see how much business had improved since all this mess started.

CHAPTER
34

REYNOLDS AND HIS family attended early morning service at the Reverend Matheson's church. The choir sang "Search Me, Lord." The unusually brisk air felt warm in comparison to the arctic chill that greeted them once inside. *"Go ahead and search me, Lord. . . ."* The congregation remained cordial to the children and courteous but distant toward Cheryl. *"Shine the light from heaven on my soul. . . ."* Reynolds, on the other hand, saw nothing but scorn followed by backs that turned on him quickly and often. *"If You find anything that shouldn't be . . ."* The Reynolds family sat in their normal seats in pew eleven, but there were several vacancies on either side, and spaces in front and behind that created a circular divide. *"Take it out and strengthen me. . . ."* The Reynolds clan had become an island unto itself, surrounded by hostile waters and shunned by once friendly neighbors. *"I wanna be right. I wanna be saved. And I wanna be whole."*

The Reverend Matheson gave a subdued sermon, which fit the occasion. It had something to do with the struggle between Cain and Abel, good and evil, trust and betrayal. Several times Reynolds thought he should stand or raise his hand and be identified in the unlikely event that anyone in the place hadn't gotten the clear parallels. When the service ended, Reynolds tried to make a quick exit, but one of the deacons cornered him at the rear of the church. He relayed a message that the pastor had requested him to wait.

Reynolds asked Cheryl to take the children to the car and wait for him. He stood alone in one corner of the vestibule until the Reverend Matheson arrived.

"I appreciate your seeing me, James."

"This isn't going to take long, is it, Reverend? My family's waiting, and I need to—"

"I'll make it brief," the Reverend Matheson cut him off. "It would be better for all concerned if you stayed away from the church for a while. I've made arrangements with Pastor Hayward in Madison. He'll be happy to handle your spiritual needs."

"Any reason in particular I'm no longer wanted as a member of your congregation?"

"I believe you know the answer to that, James. If not, I suggest you pray for guidance."

"I'm just doing my job, Reverend."

"I wonder how many crimes against humanity were justified with that phrase." He inched closer toward Reynolds. "How does it feel to be a Judas?"

Reynolds didn't flinch. "I could never be Judas, Reverend. That would make your son Jesus. And you know how ridiculous that sounds."

Several members of the choir walked past and

acknowledged the pastor, who blessed them as they left. He returned to Reynolds, who'd been kept on hold, and addressed him in a sad, resigned voice. "Might be a good idea if you and your family found another place to worship on a permanent basis. I don't believe I can offer what you need." He turned and left.

Reynolds stared down the long center aisle of the church and noticed a large statue of Jesus on the cross. *Search me, Lord. Go ahead and search me, Lord.*

Several customers walked out of Rachel's café, after Miller entered. It had been a long time since he'd caused that reaction. He proceeded to the lunch counter with a jovial smile and a light bounce in his step. He'd learned during the good old days of tossed bottles and loud jeers to act as if you were on your way to a picnic rather than a civil rights demonstration. It wasn't that much of a stretch, since most protests could have easily ended up with him as the main course—someone's idea of a fashionable cookout.

Miller sat patiently at the counter, attempting to attract Rachel's attention. The café had thinned out considerably since his arrival, and Rachel had started cleaning all the vacated tables covered with plates containing half-eaten meals. Miller hummed a pleasant tune, but she ignored him. He tapped the edge of the counter, a rolling drumbeat of steadily moving fingers. It elicited no response.

"I can wait for it to get less busy if you'd like," he finally said.

"It would be better for both of us if you got your coffee somewhere else." Her voice was harsh. She never looked at him.

Miller knew Rachel well enough to know this hurt her

more than it hurt him, and it hurt him more than he'd ever imagined.

"I'm a lawyer. I'm supposed to help people," he stated with an implicit plea for understanding.

"I'm a waitress." She pointed to a sign above the cash register. "I reserve the right to refuse service." She still hadn't looked at him, but her voice cracked and her face became flushed.

"You exercising that right?" he asked, then moved three seats to the right and sat in front of her. She tried to move, but he grabbed her hand. "I asked you a question," he said resolutely. "Do you intend to exercise that right?"

She pulled her hand away from his. They'd finally made eye contact. He thought he saw tears in her eyes, or maybe they were in his.

"I already have," she answered, then walked away.

He remained at the counter for a few moments, his legs weak and his feet unable to move. The café blurred a bit, and he refocused his eyes on her silhouette behind the kitchen curtain. She was bent over slightly, her hands pressed to her face and her body shaking.

His vision blurred again. His legs steadied enough for him to stand, and he headed for the door.

CHAPTER
35

REYNOLDS AND MILLER spent the greater part of a week reviewing responses from prospective jurors to a twelve-page questionnaire. Miller didn't believe in the process. In fact, he thought it a colossal waste of time. People lied easily when they completed forms. As with any other test, they answered based on what would get them a passing grade and not on what they believed. He preferred to analyze a person's body language, not his penmanship.

Reynolds found them useful as an initial weeding-out tool. You could quickly dismiss the group too stupid to lie, and have additional time to probe the veracity of those who gave clever answers they couldn't recall. The art of selecting a jury had been greatly overrated. In most trials, if you had the evidence, you obtained a conviction; if you didn't, the defendant went home free. But in certain special cases—the ones where law sometimes gave way to raw emotion—the jury composition made all the difference in the world.

"An agent offered me a book deal," Miller told Reynolds as they waited inside the courtroom for the next panel of potential jurors.

"A lawyer with an agent," mused Reynolds. "That's like a devil with a publicist."

"Joke if you want to," Miller cautioned, "but after this is over, you and I are going to be famous."

"One for winning and one for losing," agreed Reynolds.

"I know how I want to be introduced." Miller leaned closer to Reynolds. "How much money you think it'll cost to buy off the jury?" he whispered.

Before Reynolds could respond, Tanner entered the courtroom and took his place behind the bench. The media and interested spectators once again jammed into their seats. If the court became this crowded for jury selection, Reynolds shuddered to think what chaos awaited once the trial commenced in earnest. Several guards were stationed throughout the courtroom, and special metal detectors had been installed at each entrance. The stairwells were monitored, and only one of three elevators provided access to the area. At the urging of federal officials, the judge authorized undercover security to mingle inside and outside the courtroom. There'd been a steady increase in the number of death threats aimed at Matheson. To further complicate matters, the new weapon of choice, the Internet, carried rumors of invading armies of supporters and opponents plotting to storm the building, either to free the professor or kill him.

Tanner called the proceedings to order, and a group of men and women wearing plastic badges were escorted to the jury box. Reynolds and Miller took turns interviewing panelists under the watchful eye of Matheson, who sat at the defendant's table dressed in a dark blue suit, crisp white shirt, and red power tie.

They'd gone through another two dozen without any agreement and spent the last ten minutes grilling Hardy Wilkins, a white carpenter with an easygoing personality and pleasant style. Miller asked a series of questions having to do with notions of fairness and objectivity and finally concluded on the theme of retribution. Wilkins considered the issue for a moment, removed his glasses, and cleaned the lenses. "I don't believe in revenge," he said, then returned his glasses to the bridge of his nose. "A guy pokes out your eye. Then you poke out his eye. 'Fore you know it, got a bunch of damn blind people lookin' for someone to hit." Some of the spectators chuckled, which made Hardy self-conscious. "Well, not exactly lookin', but you catch my drift."

"This juror's acceptable to the defense, Your Honor," Miller informed the court, and noticed Hardy's grateful smile.

"And to the people," agreed Reynolds.

"Well," uttered a relieved Tanner, "we're finally making progress. Let's bring in juror number forty-six while we've got us some momentum buildin'."

The lawyers went through a third and a fourth batch of jurors before calling Carter Bullins, a potbellied plant manager who supervised the slaughter of chickens. When the questioning began, his pale white skin suddenly glistened. Reynolds sensed that the man enjoyed his opportunity to enlighten the court on how the real world functioned without legal protocol or fancy, convoluted concepts.

"If those men did the crimes, the lynchings, then they got what was comin'." Bullins placed his hand under his chin and picked at an open sore. "If you ask me, don't think it was the professor."

"How did you arrive at that conclusion?" asked Reynolds.

Bullins flexed his shoulders and looked at Matheson. "Never met a man with that much education worth a damn when it came time to doin' an honest day's work."

Matheson smiled. News reporters, obviously pleased to have something worthy to quote, wrote in their notebooks.

"Thank you very much for your insightful comments," Judge Tanner said. "You're excused."

"Defense was leaning in favor of selection," Miller asserted with a huge grin.

"I'm sure you were," sighed Tanner. "Mr. Bullins, you may go back to the poultry factory. I'm sure the chickens miss you very much."

Bullins swung open the gate to the jury panel and left the courtroom with a swagger.

"Speaking of food," remarked the judge, "I think this might be as good a time as any to take a lunch break. Bailiff, please inform the next two panels they should return to the court no later than one-fifteen. We'll reconvene at that time."

Miller conferred with Matheson for a few moments before the guards escorted the professor to a holding cell. Reynolds and Sinclair reviewed their jury list and circled several names, all of whom they intended to challenge when the process resumed.

Miller strolled over to the prosecutor's table and tried to sneak a peek at the paperwork. Sinclair quickly placed the information inside a folder and rested it against her chest.

"Miss Sinclair, it's so nice to see you again," said Miller, smiling warmly.

"The feeling's mutual, Mr. Miller," answered Sinclair.

"Is that where you keep all your secrets?" he asked. "Pressed tightly against your . . . heart?"

"I find it a very useful location to hide evidence. It's the last place defense counsel would search." She smiled.

"Is that because we don't believe prosecutors have hearts?" Miller replied, then winked at an amused Reynolds.

"Not at all," she answered. "It has more to do with your profession's not wishing to travel in unfamiliar territory."

"I just came over to say hello and to tell you something of great importance," Miller said gallantly.

"I'm all yours," responded Sinclair.

"You read my mind," replied Miller. "The bad news is, we won't be able to date until my client's acquitted." He leaned forward and spoke quietly. "The good news is, it won't take long." He took a gentlemanly bow and returned to his table.

Sinclair faced Reynolds. "I really want us to win this case." She looked at Miller, who had taken his briefcase and turned to wave at her. "In the absolute worst way," she said to Reynolds with renewed commitment.

The selection process resumed shortly after two o'clock. Several more panelists were interviewed and dismissed. Around three-thirty, Mrs. Florence Blanche Whitney, a widow of "thirty-three years this winter," began answering questions posed by Miller initially, then by Reynolds. Whitney, a black woman in her late sixties, presented an interesting choice to both sides. She didn't have much formal education but had a wisdom born of experience "tryin' to raise seven sons, four daughters, and twenty-six grandchildren so they'd be a pleasure for decent, God-fearin' folks to know."

Reynolds liked her and thought that with the size of her family, she'd certainly have the stamina to argue her views with eleven other jurors. Still, he couldn't be sure what those beliefs might be, and he wanted to be delicate in the way he explored them. Whether she was to be selected or not, other panelists were listening to his questioning. He knew the importance of not offending any prospective juror or that person's colleagues, especially when the person in question represented the grandmother you'd pick to grace the cover of a greeting card.

"Mrs. Whitney," Reynolds said respectfully, "you've lived in this state all your life?"

"Never had the money or enough suitcases to leave."

"You've seen a lot of things change, I imagine."

"Some for the good, some not," she said, massaging her fingers.

"Have you ever had any particular difficulty with white people?"

Mrs. Whitney looked at Reynolds curiously, then to the judge with some confusion.

"Mrs. Whitney, do you understand the question?" asked Tanner.

"I believe so," she answered. "He wants to know if I've ever had difficulty with—" She stifled a laugh and tried not to smile.

Tanner tried to help. "Just try to answer the question to the best of your abil—"

She lost it and laughed hysterically, which caused the spectators in the courtroom to laugh. She tried to stop, but with each effort she laughed even more. The bailiff chuckled. Tanner hid his smile behind the sleeve of his black robe. Reynolds stood perfectly still in the center of the room with his hands to his sides and his neck immobilized. He wanted to find a graceful way out of this, so he embarked on the easiest path.

"This juror's acceptable to the people, Your Honor."

"Mr. Miller?" asked the judge, who discreetly wiped away a tear of laughter.

Miller stood and announced, "We welcome her with open arms."

"I thought you would," commented the judge. "All right, Mrs. Whitney, you can step down and make yourself comfortable." He wrote her name on his tally sheet. "Counsel, let's proceed."

In eight hours the attorneys interviewed just under a hundred panelists and agreed on only two. Matheson had been present throughout the whole day but stayed surprisingly low-key, offering comments to his counsel on only a handful of the members of the jury pool. Reynolds didn't believe that pattern would continue much longer.

At the session's conclusion Tanner registered his annoyance at the lack of progress. "Gentlemen," he warned, "if you don't start selectin' jurors at a quicker pace, I'll assume the questioning and make the appointments myself. I want everyone to be in court at eight o'clock in the morning, and you can expect to work through the evening if necessary."

He reviewed his notes. "In an effort to meet media demand, I've agreed to provide a live audio feed of the proceedings. Under no circumstances will I allow video to be transmitted on closed-circuit monitors and risk the signal being intercepted and broadcast to the public. I don't want that to happen and will severely sanction anyone who violates any of my directives."

He dismissed the participants at five-thirty and accepted an invitation by the media to have his picture taken, though he refused interviews. He also allowed his assistant to distribute his résumé along with a synopsis of his significant rulings. To be even more helpful, he attached some of his notable quotes and gave the press permission to use them freely with the proviso that adequate attribution be given at all times.

At eight o'clock that night, Robyn Rochon arrived wearing a teal knit dress that clung to her cinnamon skin. Reynolds offered her something to drink, and she requested a bottle of water at room temperature. As he searched his office, he tried to remember the last time he'd seen her face on the cover of a fashion magazine. He found an unopened carton of bottled water and removed one bottle. She graciously thanked him and sat in the chair near his desk. He took his seat and noticed she was carefully observing his office. "Is something the matter?" he asked.

"I was just looking for the hidden cameras or recorders," she answered politely, then took a sip of water, which made her perfectly shaped lips glisten slightly.

"Ms. Rochon, I can assure you I wouldn't tape you without your knowledge or permission."

She smiled and gazed around the room a second time. Reynolds studied her for a moment and thought she and Matheson must have made an extraordinary pair. "I appreciate your agreeing to see me," he said.

"I didn't think I had a choice. I assumed if I refused

you'd find a way to legally force me to appear. So I thought it best to come and dissuade you from doing that."

"Have you visited the professor?" Reynolds asked.

"He wouldn't place me on the visitors' list. I sent him a note of support, but I'm sure you were able to read that before he did." If she felt any resentment, it remained attractively packaged.

"As far as I could gather, you were the last woman involved with Dr. Matheson."

"Thank you," she responded with a glimmer of a smile. "That's nice to know."

"How long were you two in a relationship?"

"I should probably ask you. Just how much of my life have you investigated?"

Reynolds concealed both a smile and his admiration. "My records indicate two and a half years, that seem right?"

"Two years, eight months," she corrected him.

"And it ended over a year ago?"

"Thirteen months, two weeks, four days, give or take."

"You always have such a good memory?"

"For things that are important and events that hurt like hell." She took another sip of water, then placed the bottle on the desk.

"I take it you loved him?"

"I disagree with your use of the past tense, but outside of that we have no argument." She shifted her body in discomfort or impatience. "Mr. Reynolds, since you're delving into intimate matters, do you mind if I ask you a personal question?"

"Seems only fair."

"Did you volunteer for this case, or were you assigned?"

He braced himself for the "Uncle Tom" accusation. "Would my answer make a difference on how you viewed me?"

"I view you as the enemy. Your answer would only reveal how dangerous you are." She stared through him with almond-shaped eyes, and he finally saw the belligerence.

He leaned back in his chair and realized he'd never call her as a witness unless he had absolutely no choice. "Have you ever lost a friend or relative to violence, Ms. Rochon?"

She glanced away for a second. "I had a younger brother who was robbed and murdered."

"I'm sorry to hear that," he said sympathetically. "I hope he had as effective an enemy as me working on his behalf."

She placed her hands together, and her expression softened. "What do you want from me, Mr. Reynolds?"

"Why did the two of you break up?"

She gently touched her mouth. "You ever hear Dr. Matheson give a lecture to his students or speak to the community?"

Reynolds nodded yes.

"He resented black leaders who'd offer their help only if they got paid. He said they'd arrive late like royal peacocks, claiming their commitment to the struggle, then leave early in chauffeured limousines. Martin never accepted a dime from any community organization. He donated his money and time to anyone who needed advice or support or just someone who genuinely cared and wasn't afraid to demonstrate it."

"That doesn't sound like a person you'd leave," remarked Reynolds.

"I didn't," she confessed. "He left me. It wasn't that we ever formally ended the relationship. It's just after a while loving the people reduces your capacity to love the person."

"I find it hard to believe a man wouldn't make the time to be with you no matter how many people needed him." The words escaped before he could rearrange them more professionally.

"I'm afraid I was the one who wouldn't spend the time. After he started researching and preparing his course, I refused to enter his den. There were so many horrible pictures. I'd get sick every time he found a new batch. Eventually, I couldn't even visit his home or watch him as he worked, or . . ." She diverted her eyes. "Or stand to hear him cry." Her voice trembled. "I wish I'd been stronger." She looked at Reynolds. "I wish that with all my heart." Her face saddened, but it remained flawless. "He was the most passionate man I'd ever loved, and yet the most gentle. And those damn pictures took away his ability to touch or be touched."

Reynolds didn't know what to say. Thankfully, she broke the silence.

"If you're planning on calling me as a witness, I'll never say anything to hurt him, even if it means I have to lie."

"To protect him?" Reynolds asked.

"To save him," she answered.

Reynolds nodded his head in understanding. "Will you be coming to any of the trial?"

"I don't think I could bear that. But I'll tell you something"—she gathered her purse and rose to her feet—"if he's not acquitted, I'll be the first one leading the candlelight vigil until he's released."

Reynolds stood and extended his hand. "It was very nice meeting you, Ms. Rochon."

She shook his hand and left.

Reynolds sat in his chair, leaned back, and placed his feet on the corner of the desk. He stared across the room for a long time, then studied files of information he'd collected on possible witnesses. Matheson's commitment to the community and devotion to his students were true. Reynolds had received more than enough testimonies on his behalf to be certain of that. He identified with the professor's disdain for those "leadership conferences" or "state-of-black-America think tanks," which usually were held in plush resorts. Up until five years ago, he himself had annually attended the best two or three.

The keynote speakers and panelists were often recycled versions of one another, activists and intellectuals touring as part of the caviar circuit. And when they spoke, they more often than not resembled incoherent performance art—the declamatory equivalent of the NBA Slam Dunk Contest, where style rules over substance, and an inordinate amount of energy is expended for two insignificant points. The irony, of course, was that the ensuing celebration left them poorly equipped to defend against their opponents who scored efficiently and often.

Reynolds faulted these inspirational/motivational presenters for seldom producing written remarks, which only partially contributed to their frequent lack of logic as well as subject-verb agreement. For all the fancy chicken dinners served and the time spent in heated and emotional debates, Reynolds inevitably left these sessions assured of three things: There was no new information exchanged, no plan offered, and no reason for white folks to worry.

So after sufficient heartburn and heartache, he stopped attending formal gatherings designed to enrich the defenders of the poor. Actually, Reynolds openly shared these sentiments in his last keynote address at a forum on black issues. He received exuberant applause and no more invitations to participate in future sessions—indisputable proof that whistle-blowers remained the most admired and unemployable people on the planet. Or as the saying goes, truth crushed to earth shall rise as an unrecognizable vapor.

He looked at his watch and knew Angela and Christopher were once again asleep without his giving them a good-night kiss. By the time he got home, his wife probably wouldn't want one. He thought about Matheson losing the ability to touch, and realized there were countless ways to achieve that frightening condition. Reynolds desperately wanted to avoid them all.

CHAPTER
36

THE NEXT MORNING'S headlines described the first day of jury selection. The story shared the front page with the other important news of the day. The body of Travis Mitchell was found, badly decomposed, in a marsh ten miles west from his home in Polarville. His limbs had been hacked off and placed inside a plastic garbage bag discovered near the rest of his remains. Upon being notified of the grisly finding, Mitchell's wife had fainted, and remained under a doctor's care.

Mitchell had been accused forty years ago of murdering and mutilating a fifteen-year-old black boy for allegedly whistling at his wife. An all-white jury acquitted the former deputy sheriff of the charges stemming from the incident, although its foreman was quoted as saying, "He probably did it; under the circumstances, what kind of man would he be if he didn't defend his wife's honor?" The article went on to report that Mitchell had two sons and a grandson who currently worked in law enforcement.

Miller requested an urgent meeting with the judge in chambers. "Your Honor, I personally observed prospective jurors reading the paper while they waited in the assembly room."

"Mr. Miller, your client might be well served by people who don't read, but that standard doesn't apply to the court." Tanner took a sip of tomato juice. "After jury selection, I'll instruct them not to read or listen to news accounts, but I'm rejecting any recommendation to sequester the group during the trial. I'll revisit the idea once we reach the deliberation stage." He looked at Reynolds, who'd been sitting quietly. "Any objection?"

"Not at this time, Your Honor," Reynolds answered.

"I suggest we carry on with our respective duties." Tanner finished his juice, then motioned the lawyers toward the door.

The morning session proceeded efficiently. Reynolds and Miller accepted two additional jurors, both black: August Cobb, a retired insurance salesman; and Vernetta Williams, a nurse and mother of three. Reynolds stayed clear of young black men but, for the moment, did keep Blaze Hansberry, a twenty-four-year-old African-American woman, on the list. She professed to be born again; that this should be necessary at such a tender age left the prosecution team with a few reservations. Reynolds agreed with Sinclair that even dyed-in-the-wool sinners didn't contemplate absolution and a rebirth until they reached middle age.

After the second morning break, Aubrey Munson took his turn with the lawyers. Munson had gotten this far because he lied extensively on the questionnaire. He indicated he had no difficulty with interracial dating and felt the world was a better place because of diversity. He also enjoyed paying tribute to Dr. King and considered it his favorite holiday next to "Christmas, Easter, and, of course, the Fourth of July."

"Do you believe you could set aside any preconceived notions about this case and render a fair and impartial decision based solely on the evidence presented?" asked a skeptical Miller.

"Not only do I believe it," responded Munson, "I'd swear to that fact before God Almighty just as I did when I last had the privilege of performin' my civic duty." He reminded Miller he'd been a juror in a prior difficult trial and had managed to maintain his objectivity "till the last dog died."

Miller consulted with Matheson and red-circled Munson's name. "I'm gonna use a peremptory challenge. This guy is lying through his teeth."

"I want you to select him," declared Matheson.

"Martin, trust me on this. There's no way that—"

"I want him on the jury. Period." Matheson sat back in his chair and put Munson's name on his notepad under the Yes column.

Miller turned to face the judge. "This juror's acceptable to the defense," he announced weakly.

"Mr. Reynolds, do we have a second from you?" asked Tanner, who had already begun to write Munson's name in the category marked *Satisfactory*.

"The state has no objection to this juror," Reynolds informed the judge after briefly checking with Sinclair.

Munson's slight smile disappeared quickly after glancing at Matheson, who had turned to wave at Regina and Delbert, seated in the row behind him.

Tanner decided to work through lunch, giving the lawyers added incentive to find at least three more jurors before their afternoon break. They found two: Faraday Patterson, a black factory worker in his mid-fifties, divorced with no children; and Cindy Lou Herrington, their first white female, a homemaker and seamstress, mother of two "grown and, praise God, livin'-on-their-own daughters."

Before the dinner hour they'd managed to select two more women: Octavia Richmond Bailey, a black librarian, forty-eight, never married; and Harriet Keela Dove, an administrative assistant, white, thirty-nine, married three times.

Tanner checked with the bailiff regarding the jury panel's availability and made some notes on his chart. "Gentlemen," he said to the attorneys, then noticed Sinclair, "and gentle-lady, I've been advised we're running low on the number of citizens remaining on our panel. We'll have to supplement the pool with new recruits in the morning." The judge tried to locate one of his notes. "Mr. Reynolds, have you decided on that juror you asked the court to set aside? I can't recall her name."

"Blaze Hansberry, Your Honor," Reynolds answered. "We'll make a decision on her no later than midday tomorrow."

"Fine. That concludes our proceedings for today," Tanner announced. "We'll meet tomorrow to complete jury selection. To be on the safe side, I suggest we include four alternates."

"The state agrees with that number," advised Sinclair.

"I wasn't seeking agreement, Ms. Sinclair, but the court will take notice of your unsolicited endorsement." Tanner rubbed his neck with the tips of his fingers. "I'd like to begin opening statements no later than Thursday of next week. That means exhibits need to be reviewed by both sides Tuesday morning. Any disagreements will be resolved by me with my usual judicial flair." Tanner stood behind the bench. "We've accomplished a great deal today, counsel. Let's hope the trial goes as smoothly. Mr. Miller, I presume by now you've reviewed the state's witness list."

"I have, Your Honor." Miller rose from his seat and addressed the judge. "A finer group of men and women couldn't be found if I subpoenaed them myself. And I would've if the prosecution hadn't beaten me to the punch."

Tanner looked at Reynolds and Sinclair. "Defense counsel is pleased with your witnesses; that should give you pause." The judge proceeded from the bench. "I wish you a pleasant evening, and may your night-light never dim beyond its natural limitations." By the time he entered his chambers, he'd completely taken off his robe.

Sinclair sat back in her chair, stretched out her legs, and released a sigh of relief. Reynolds looked at the rear of the courtroom and saw Brandon Hamilton proceed directly toward Matheson, who appeared genuinely delighted to see his young student. The professor gave Brandon a fatherly hug, and the two men smiled broadly. They exchanged as much information as possible before being interrupted by two deputies.

Regina carried a stack of files and gave them to Miller but couldn't reach Matheson before the guards led him away. She sat down, dejected, and then noticed Reynolds staring at her. The two made sustained eye contact before Miller and Brandon sat next to her. Miller placed an outline of activities on the table, and both students reviewed and discussed their respective assignments.

Sinclair tapped Reynolds on the arm and nodded in the

defense table's direction. "Shouldn't one of them be at school and the other in jail?" she asked with little energy.

"The Lord moves in mysterious ways." He noticed the Reverend Matheson, still in his seat with his head bowed in prayer.

"Can we go home now?" Sinclair pleaded.

"I've already ordered Chinese takeout."

"We had Chinese last night," she reminded him.

"Yeah, but it was cold by the time we ate it."

"What makes you think it'll be any different tonight?"

"Because I told them to deliver it at midnight."

"Oh, then we can save any leftovers for breakfast."

"There you go!" Reynolds reached for Sinclair's hand and helped her from the chair. They walked out of the court, both ignoring Miller's pleasant wave.

Matheson put together his own defense strategy, including how he wanted Miller to handle the opening. Miller complained about both the plan and the forced selection of Munson on the jury. The two men met in the lawyer's room reserved at the jail. They were allowed limited time, and Miller didn't want to misuse it with arguments he couldn't win, so he changed the subject.

"I've gotten calls from every high-profile black attorney in the country. They've offered their services free of charge."

"They can't stand the fact I've got a white defense counsel handling the most publicized civil rights case since the murder of Emmett Till. What about black organizations? I assume they've remained safely noncommittal."

"No one's formalized a position one way or the other on your guilt. But they've given news conferences condemning historical injustice that—and I'm quoting now—'has given rise to a climate of mistrust, despair, and outrage.'"

Matheson smiled. "Their speeches are meant to inflate their own importance and increase their dwindling memberships. They're probably praying for my conviction. I'd be much more useful to them as a captive martyr."

"Why do you say that?"

"If I were free, they'd have to choose between alienating their community base or compromising substantial donations from their white benefactors. They've spent decades perfecting the fine art of criticizing institutions while soliciting money from them. So far, they've been able to tiptoe around charges of blackmail and extortion by claiming it's a reasonable business expense to eliminate past vestiges of racial discrimination. Aligning themselves with someone like me pushes the envelope a bit further than civil rights etiquette allows."

"I take it you enjoy their dilemma?"

Matheson provided a hint of a smile. "Maybe, a wee bit."

Miller started feeling a kinship with this man. How could he not be drawn to someone who enjoyed disrupting both the people and the palace guard?

"You've gone through your own trials and tribulations with black organizations, or am I unearthing unpleasant territory?"

"We've had an interesting dance," admitted Miller.

"Needed one moment, abandoned the next?"

"Something like that."

"Did they resent you, or did you resent them?"

"Never had time to give it much thought. I do recall a young black nationalist telling me there wasn't room for Caucasians in his version of the Movement. Accused me

of being like a promiscuous white girl wanting to sleep
with all the black studs to embarrass her family."

"I take it a lot of black men should be incredibly grateful you weren't a woman."

Miller laughed at both the honesty of the observation
and the audacity it took to make it.

"We all have our frailties, Mr. Miller. Take your comfort where you find it," Matheson said graciously.

"Blessed are the weak, for they shall inherit the earth."

"I'm not a biblical scholar but I believe the correct
word is *meek,* not *weak,*" corrected the professor.

"I'm not a linguistic expert," confessed Miller, "but
that's a distinction without a difference."

Now it was Matheson's turn to laugh, and he did so
with a grudging admiration. "We're getting along surprisingly well, aren't we?"

Miller agreed and left with the professor's plan outlin-
ing, in specific detail, how he wanted his defense to be
presented.

CHAPTER
37

THEY ARRIVED BY the carload. Those who didn't have their own transportation rented vans, sharing the expense with fellow passengers. Some hitchhiked from as far away as Chicago. Rival gang members drove in the same vehicles, listening to music created by their favorite hip-hop artists in tribute to Matheson. Reminiscent of the early-sixties invasion of the Freedom Riders, many traveled on buses with placards that read STOP A LEGAL LYNCHING, and EDUCATION'S NOT A CRIME. Instead of singing songs of protest, they rapped words of defiance. At one point the evening before, an entire caravan of college students from Birmingham and Montgomery had lit up Interstate 59 before proceeding to Highway 20 and the state with which they shared both a common border and a history of racial violence.

While most were under the age of twenty-five, a sizable contingent of veterans from previous civil wars had also made the pilgrimage. They brought sleeping bags, tents, and a variety of camping equipment that police feared contained much more than cooking utensils and pocketknives. Many in the local black community offered to provide housing for those unable to find adequate shelter. This most unlikely of family reunions had caused nearly as much excitement as the impending trial and undoubtedly contributed to the unavailability of weapons and ammunition at virtually all surrounding sporting goods stores. White townsfolk had quickly purchased everything in stock and placed additional orders on-line or through direct catalog sales.

Mississippians had experienced a great deal in their storied existence, but nothing had prepared them for this onslaught. Radio talk shows expanded their regularly scheduled coverage to handle the significant increase in phone calls from outraged citizens. "Instead of complainin' about the past, why don't these blacks go into their own communities and stop the killin' and drug-dealin' there?" offered one irate woman. A man who claimed to be "pure, unspoiled, untainted white" called to say the professor was living proof that no matter how much you educated them, "a nigga will revert to bein' a nigga each and every time." Despite the constant interruptions of the radio host, a supporter of Matheson shared his views: "I don't care what you or these other racist crackers say, that professor will go down in history as one of the greatest men who ever lived. For the first time in my life, I'm proud to be black!" The next caller, wanting to be referred to as "a patriotic American," offered his dissenting opinion. "As far as I'm concerned, the only good thing about having another black on the planet besides myself is that I'll always know where to look for my worst enemy. The professor's a disgrace, and anyone

who supports him ought to be tossed out the country."
Subsequent callers debated whether that message came
from an "ignorant white person trying to sound black" or
a "self-hating black wanting to be white."

In that highly charged atmosphere, Reynolds and
Miller selected their final three jurors, all of whom happened to be African-American: Jefferson Lynch, a fifty-
year-old landscaper and handyman; Faison Sheppard,
forty-four, a high school basketball coach; and, after a
great deal of soul-searching and second-guessing, the
prosecution decided to roll the dice and pick the young
born-again dental hygienist, Blaze Hansberry. The alternates would be chosen with far less scrutiny after lunch.
As it now stood, the racial composition of the jury consisted of four whites and eight blacks, equally divided by
gender.

Reynolds made the mistake of stopping by his office
before returning to the courtroom for the afternoon session. Vanzant intercepted him in the corridor. "How the
hell did you allow eight blacks to get on the jury?"

Several staff members walked past the two men,
avoiding eye contact or the need to offer greetings.

"I selected the best jurors available, the ones I believe
will listen to all the evidence and render a fair decision."

"Fair?" Vanzant scratched the back of his head and did
a half turn. "They're probably members of his fan club!
Did you bother to ask if any of them had relatives taking
his class or if they belonged to his father's church?"

"*I* belonged to his father's church; that didn't stop you
from selecting me."

"And you're beginning to make me regret that decision." Vanzant spun back around to face Reynolds. "You

wanna tell me what possessed you to choose a jury like that?"

Reynolds put some distance between himself and his boss. "Blacks are far more likely to convict Matheson than whites."

"You base that on what?" Vanzant placed his hands on his hips, exposing a stomach that hung freely over his belt.

"Whites don't want to believe someone like Matheson could commit those crimes. It would make them too nervous." Reynolds reversed his strategy and took a step closer to Vanzant. "Blacks know it's possible. That's why we pray so often."

"Maybe you're just tryin' to stay popular with your people."

Now the two men were only inches apart. "You don't like the way I'm handling this case, take me off it!"

"You'd like that, wouldn't you?" Vanzant pointed his finger at Reynolds and came dangerously close to touching his chest. "Your ass is on the line, and that's precisely where I intend to keep it!"

Reynolds massaged his temples, then looked at Vanzant. "You ever hear of a cracker sling?"

"No, should I have?"

"Yes. Many times." Reynolds walked away and headed for the men's room.

Woody Winslow approached his visibly miffed boss. "You all right?" he asked tentatively.

Vanzant rubbed the bottom of his chin. "You know what a cracker sling is?"

"No idea," Winslow responded. "Is it some type of racial epitaph?" He chewed a handful of granola.

"The word's *epithet,* and it better not be," warned

Vanzant. "'Cause I got some slurs of my own I've been savin' for the right occasion." He looked down the same hall Reynolds had used to make his getaway. "I want you to attend every minute of that trial and report back to me at the end of each day. You understand?"

"You want me to be part of the team?"

"If I wanted you to be part of the team, I would've said that," Vanzant snapped. "Just sit in the back of the courtroom and take good notes and stop makin' all that damn noise when you eat!" Vanzant walked away as Winslow took his last crunch.

Reynolds returned to the courtroom, and the rest of the afternoon went smoothly. Four alternates were chosen, and the jury panel received their instructions from the judge. Opening arguments would begin Thursday afternoon or perhaps Friday morning, depending on the number of motions *in limine* remaining to be resolved. Tanner gave the jurors a long lecture instructing them not to discuss the case with anyone. They were to advise him immediately of any violations of his orders. He told them to be particularly cautious of the press and warned he'd dismiss anyone seen talking to a member of the media, regardless of the subject matter. He told a few jokes and praised the attorneys on both sides, then sent everybody home with a quote about the importance of jury service. It kept democracy safe and "made this country what it is today."

Matheson coughed lightly at the judge's last comment, and Miller quickly gave him a glass of water to prevent Tanner from issuing any negative remarks. Blaze Hansberry glanced at the defendant and offered a brief but friendly smile, causing Reynolds to feel a sharp pain in his side. He wasn't sure if the discomfort came from within or as a result of Sinclair's poking him with the end of her pencil. He avoided looking at her "I-told-you-so" expression.

That evening Reynolds had dinner with his family for the first time in several weeks, although he hardly touched anything on his plate and his attention drifted frequently. Angela looked at him, then at her mother, who signaled that this wasn't the time to ask for anything.

Christopher, however, ignored the warning (assuming he'd noticed it at all). "Dad, what's *authentic* mean?" he asked.

"You know how to use a dictionary, don't you?" intervened his mother.

"*Genuine,* or *real,*" answered an uninterested Reynolds.

"That's good, isn't it?" Christopher asked despite a raised eyebrow from his mother.

"Ordinarily," his father said while pushing his food from one side of the plate to the other. "It depends on how it's used."

"I heard Mr. Taylor tell another teacher at school that Professor Matheson was an authentic hero."

Reynolds placed his fork down and stared at his son. "What else did you hear him say?"

Cheryl shifted uneasily in her chair.

Christopher chewed his fried chicken. "Something about him being like Noah's ark." He washed it down with fruit punch.

"Why would he say that?" asked a mystified Reynolds.

"Oh," Christopher exclaimed as his face brightened,

"now I remember, not Noah's ark. He said Joan of Arc. This lady who got persecuted for her beliefs."

Cheryl released a long sigh.

Reynolds glanced away, disgusted, then looked at his son. "By any chance, did he teach you how to diagram a sentence, or improve your understanding of fractions, or how to correct a dangling participle?" His voice conveyed increased agitation. "Or anything else he's supposed to be doing with the damn tuition money I give him, which is enough to feed an African village for a year?!"

"Honey, calm down," Cheryl said.

"I am calm!" shouted her husband. He took a deep breath and spoke more softly. "I'm just wonderin' what else this guy is teaching impressionable kids."

"What's 'impressionable'?" asked Christopher.

"You get one new word a day," warned Cheryl. "Okay?"

"Pass the Matheson," Reynolds said.

Cheryl looked at her husband strangely. Angela raised her eyebrows in disbelief. Christopher put his hand over his mouth and stifled a giggle.

"What?" Reynolds asked. "Why's everybody looking at me? I just asked for some macaroni; is that a crime?"

"You haven't eaten the Matheson you've got, Dad," joked Angela, which made her brother laugh.

Looking at him with concern, Cheryl handed Reynolds a bowl of macaroni before he could respond. "James, I think it might be a good idea if you got some rest tonight."

"Yeah, Dad," agreed Angela. "You look tired."

"I don't need any rest, and I feel perfectly fine," he replied stubbornly. "I just came home to have dinner with my family, and I have to hear about some fourth-grade teacher's idea of heroes and martyrs and God knows what else he's filling our son's head with."

"My head's not filled with anything, Dad," Christopher said reassuringly.

"You got that right," agreed his sister, who then took an extra serving of stuffing.

"Children," interjected Cheryl, "hurry up and finish your meals. I want to talk with your father."

"If you want to talk with me, you can do it in front of them." Reynolds pushed his chair away from the table. "It's obvious everybody else with an uninformed opinion speaks freely around our kids, so why should you be any different?"

"Because 'everybody' is not their mother nor are they married to you, and I don't appreciate your suggesting my opinions are uninformed," Cheryl said sharply.

Angela and Christopher exchanged apprehensive looks.

Cheryl gave both of them a warning stare. "You may leave the table now."

They started to rise from their seats but froze on their father's order. "I told you to stay!" They sat down and waited for their mother's countermand.

She didn't look at her children but neatly folded her napkin, leaned back into the chair, and relaxed her body. She stared at her husband and spoke calmly. "You want to tell us what this is all about?"

His chin nearly touched his chest, and he pouted for a moment. "Not really," he said to the floor.

Cheryl turned her head halfway and signaled to her children to leave. They both hesitated for a moment, then left quickly. She waited for Reynolds to look at her, but his eyes remained diverted in every direction but his wife's.

"You acted this way the first time you ever tried a case," she said quietly. "I remember thinking, if you were going to be that difficult to live with, our marriage wouldn't last past your third trial."

He gradually shifted his eyes and looked at her. "You weren't exactly Miss Congeniality during the first pregnancy. To top it off, you were overdue and I had to live with your malformed body and maladjusted personality an extra two weeks."

She sat ramrod straight. "You said you *loved* the way I looked."

"I would've told you the truth, but I was afraid you'd sit on me."

She folded her arms across her chest. "So now that we're sharing secrets, you want to let me in on what's troubling you tonight?"

He rubbed his face with both hands and took a deep breath. "I had an argument with Vanzant about the number of blacks on the jury. I don't think we've got the evidence to convict. I may have made a mistake selecting a young black woman to be on the panel. Judge Tanner thinks it would be a good idea for the lawyers to wear flak jackets on the way to court. And the governor's thinking about calling in the National Guard to handle any disturbances during the trial or after the verdict's announced."

Exhibiting absolutely no emotion, she looked at him. "Yeah, but what's troubling you?"

He smiled and touched her hand. "Were you really thinking about divorcing me during my first trial?"

"No. I was thinking of killing you." She paused for a

moment. "I guess this isn't a good time to bring that up. The issue of killing, I mean."

He shook his head and tried to release a quiet laugh, but he felt too weak and depressed. "Maybe I'll call you as a witness. Use you as an example of good people who do bad things."

"Did you really not like my body when I was pregnant?"

"You looked like a Russian submarine, except you made more noise. A lot more."

She rose from her seat. "Go ahead and subpoena me. It won't be too difficult to convince the women on the jury that we're all capable of murder if the right buttons are pushed."

He watched his wife walk away and thought about her advice.

CHAPTER
38

THERE WOULDN'T HAVE been greater security if the president of the United States had visited town accompanied by a delegation of Israeli and Palestinian leaders. Every highway and alternate route leading into the city had remained gridlocked since six o'clock this morning. Police and news helicopters hovered above the courthouse and its surrounding area in a constant parade of aerial surveillance. Vendors set up souvenir booths along the main walkways. Demonstrators for and against Matheson screamed obscenities at one another. A few celebrities from entertainment and sports arrived in stretch limousines. One lead singer from a popular rap group nearly initiated a riot as fans converged on his entourage seeking autographs and a chance to touch him.

A daily lottery system determined who would be admitted to the trial. After the press, family, and special guests received their allotments, hundreds of people lined up for the chance to be awarded one of twenty-six available slots. A few of the lucky winners were offered thousands of dollars in exchange for their all-day pass. The price of admission was expected to increase dramatically for the reading of the actual verdict. And in the event Matheson took the stand in his own defense, the bidding would start at an estimated $25,000.

As Reynolds made his way through this madhouse of dueling news crews fighting for interviews and ticket brokers looking for the best deals, he couldn't help but think of the money that could be generated if this circus had been part of a pay-per-view extravaganza. It would probably go a long way to eliminating hunger in the poorest communities in the state. Or perhaps it might be used for something even more valuable: finding a medical cure for the condition that motivated these people to be here. He didn't know if the audience had come to cheer for the Christians or the lions, or, for that matter, whether they'd be able to tell the difference. He only knew this wasn't the way to arrive at an impartial verdict. He doubted that a jury could function uninfluenced by the threatening storm. The system hadn't been all that reliable when the jurors were cloaked in anonymity. Given the starlike status attached to the major participants, how in the world could justice occur?

The trial started promptly at ten o'clock on an overcast Friday morning. "Good morning," Tanner greeted the court, then instructed the jury, "The prosecution will now have the first opportunity to lay out their theory of the case and summarize the evidence they intend to present. After they conclude, the defense will be provided equal time to address you. Please keep in mind that while these opening statements are important, nothing said by either side constitutes evidence. That'll be provided through witness testimony, which you and you alone will evaluate at the proper time." He looked at Reynolds. "The state may proceed."

Sinclair handled the opening. She spoke for slightly over two hours, using a variety of exhibits. The prosecution had failed to arrange a tour of Matheson's residence. Reynolds wanted the jury to observe the professor's "work room," up close and personal, to gain an appreciation for the brooding environment in which past atrocities had been recorded and future murders predicted or planned. He thought it would be helpful to provide a different impression of the handsome and charismatic defendant—an intimate insight into what he did at night.

Early in his career Reynolds had prosecuted a brutal rape case involving an adolescent girl who had accused a wealthy businessman of the assault. The defendant happened to be married to a beautiful debutante. He also had two adorable children, an impeccable reputation in his community, and a secret room in his basement filled with pornographic videotapes of young children being molested. Once the jury saw that evidence, they were ready to believe the worst. Reynolds hoped Matheson's room would have the same impact, but the judge disallowed the request. Tanner didn't want to provide the media any more opportunities to sensationalize the case. In addition, he sought to protect the jurors from being photographed by the tabloids. He couldn't guarantee their privacy after the trial ended, but he'd do what he could to safeguard it until then, even though his gut told him half were already practicing posing in the limelight.

So, instead of a tour, Sinclair had put together a display of Matheson's study, positioning the exhibit so that the jurors would see it throughout her presentation. She distributed photos of Earvin Cooper's burned corpse and foreshadowed the testimony of a forensic pathologist whom the state would call as their witness. She expected him to describe for the jury "how Mr. Cooper struggled valiantly against the defendant and was able to inflict a great deal of punishment likely to cause noticeable injuries on his assailant." Sinclair then unveiled several enlargements of photos taken at the police station the night Matheson reported his attack. "Which, coincidentally," she informed the jury while standing between photos of Cooper's burned corpse and Matheson's swollen bruises, "occurred the very evening Earvin Cooper engaged in a desperate and sustained battle for his life."

Reynolds studied the twelve members of the jury during important sections of Sinclair's presentation. They were attentive, and most took copious notes. A few sneaked looks at Matheson, and two or three of the black members of the panel occasionally glanced at Reynolds. He assumed they were waiting for him to do or say something, and he wanted them to keep that thought. He'd once participated in a high school play where the director told him the key to a successful performance rests on the actor onstage who hasn't yet spoken. "That actor," announced the instructor, "controls the audience."

Over time, he'd learned that the same principle applied in a courtroom. It helped to have jurors wonder about him and anticipate his next move. Hopefully, when he finally broke his silence, the real drama would unfold, leading to a satisfying resolution in the third and final act.

After Sinclair completed her presentation, Tanner provided an early lunch break. He didn't want Miller to be interrupted with a long delay in the middle of his opening argument. For security reasons, the jury ate in a private dining hall, with food catered by court personnel. A clumsy attempt to truly integrate the jury around one long table failed when the jurors rearranged their reserved seating assignments. The four whites clustered together while the blacks moved freely among themselves, depending upon the specific topic of discussion or expressed interest. Alternates secluded themselves in a distant corner of the room.

Mrs. Whitney, the oldest jury member, took Blaze Hansberry under her wing. "You remind me of one of my granddaughters," she said affectionately. "She put those braids in her hair, too. Ain't they difficult to wash?" she asked.

Blaze laughed and assured Mrs. Whitney, "My hair's clean and my soul's cleansed."

Mrs. Whitney didn't doubt the power of the Lord but hinted, "A hot-comb wouldn't hurt none."

When the jury returned, the exhibits were gone but nothing else in the courtroom had changed, including the presence of an overflow crowd. The bailiff called the court to order, and Judge Tanner notified the jury they'd now hear from the defense. He took a sip of water. "Mr. Miller, are you ready to present your opening on behalf of your client?"

"I am. Thank you, Your Honor." Miller rose from his chair and stepped in front of the defense table. Reynolds expected him to stay relatively close to his client so the jury wouldn't have difficulty observing them both. If you have the biggest cannon you don't need to shoot it. You simply showcase it prominently.

"Let me first begin by thanking each member of the jury for your willingness to represent the people of this state and ensure justice is done." He touched the back of his ponytail. Reynolds assumed one of two things: Either Miller needed magic more quickly than usual, or he was playing to the sketch artist seated behind him in the front row.

"Have you ever given a young child a puzzle?" The jurors searched their memories. Reynolds saw a few of them nod affirmatively. "Nothing too complicated. Colors are bright. Pieces are large. Each one fits inside the contours of a thick board, and when it's put together it looks just like the picture on the box. Remember watching the child try to figure out what to do with all the pieces once they'd been dumped on the floor?" Miller paused for a moment and searched the twelve faces that remained glued to his.

"The first response is one of excitement and wonderment as the child's little fingers pick up a section and try to push it and squeeze it and smash it till it connects with some other section. In a matter of moments what started out as sheer ecstasy turns quickly to frustration and anger and tears. But after sucking fingers and tugging on ears to find equilibrium, the child turns right back around and tries again." He extended his hands and smiled. "Of course, he or she might have to spend a minute or two finding those pieces that have been thrown against the wall."

Mrs. Whitney laughed quietly and nudged Blaze, who smiled.

"But with your help the child manages to locate everything," Miller continued. "The little one struggles a bit more, comes close to giving up again, and just when you think it was a big mistake to choose that gift"—he clapped his hands together—"miracle of miracles, two pieces fit together, then three, then four, and before you know it, the child's staring at the most beautiful picture of a green-and-purple dinosaur ever assembled."

He stretched out his arms wide and held his head high. "The child shouts, 'Mama' (or 'Daddy,' or 'Grandpa'), 'come see what I made!'" He wiggled his index finger accusingly at them. "And you rush over, all proud, and tell your puzzle builder what a great job he or she did, and before you can find your Instamatic to record the greatest achievement of their lives, what does your gifted progeny do?" Miller looked at the jurors and arched his eyebrows, waiting for the answer. "That's right. The precious child yells, 'I wanna do it again,' and proceeds to rip the puzzle totally apart to start the entire process all over."

The jurors laughed. Miller put his arms across his chest and rocked back on his feet twice before coming to a relaxed stance. "Well, the law's a little like that. We try to turn justice into a simple puzzle that can be completed without too much heartache." He took his first step toward the jury. "The state will present you with their pieces in the form of evidence they contend results in a picture of guilt." He placed his palms together and unevenly interlocked his fingers. "I'll try to explain to you why the pieces don't fit."

He moved two steps closer to Reynolds and Sinclair. "Sometimes the prosecution's evidence isn't quite as strong as they initially assumed. They'll be tempted to change some of the pieces." He looked directly at the prosecutors, then faced the jury. "But you won't let that happen, because, unlike a child, you're not allowed to bend and twist the truth so it'll become your version of the facts." His voice rose with indignation.

"This isn't a simple game anymore; a man's life is at stake; a man's freedom's in jeopardy. And who, precisely, is this man?" He crossed to the defense table and stood behind Matheson. "The state will have you believe he's a murderer," he spoke softly, "a man who advocated violent revenge and in the end decided to take justice into his own hands." His voice became slightly louder. "But, ladies and gentlemen of the jury, no matter how hard you try and force those pieces together, they'll never fit the true picture of Professor Martin Matheson." Miller pointed at Reynolds. "He may be a puzzle to the prosecution, but he's no mystery to the community."

Reynolds watched Octavia Bailey and Vernetta Williams move their heads side to side the way a congregation acknowledges a profound truth revealed by the pastor. It's a rare moment when shaking your head no really means an unequivocal yes.

"He's a dedicated scholar with a passion for education and a fierce determination not to allow history to be distorted or forgotten." Miller became more emphatic and deliberate in his delivery. "He's a black man unapologetic for his intellect and unwilling to remain silent about what he knows, no matter how uncomfortable it makes us— and make no mistake: We've been made to feel terribly uncomfortable."

Miller approached the jury and put his hands on the railing. "In the prosecution's opening, they showed you photographs of the professor's work area at home. They made you look at the horrific burnt corpse of Earvin Cooper, the tragic victim of a senseless homicide. And then, ladies and gentlemen, very cleverly they displayed the photo of my client, who himself was the victim of a violent and cowardly assault." He took his hands off the railing and slowly paced in front of the jury box, looking at each member as he spoke. "You want to know why they did that?" He waited for a moment. "Because they want to take distinct pieces from three different and unrelated puzzles and have you believe that it creates an image of a criminal."

Miller walked to a slide projector. "Well, let me show you Professor Matheson's only crime." He flipped on a switch. A brutal image of a naked black man in flames flickered onto a large white screen and caused a number of jurors as well as others in the courtroom to gasp.

Reynolds jumped to his feet to offer an objection, but Tanner moved on his own. "Mr. Miller," the judge said with authority, "turn that off and approach the bench with opposing counsel."

Miller turned off the projector and joined Tanner at the bench. Reynolds and Sinclair also arrived and engaged in an animated discussion. Matheson studied the jury. All except Aubrey Munson were straining their necks to get a good look at the activity occurring among the lawyers and Tanner. Munson watched the professor. The two men made eye contact for several moments before Munson retrieved his pad and wrote a brief note.

Reynolds tried to maintain his calm, but his emotions were greatly tested. "There's no reason to show photos of lynchings over thirty years old!" he told the judge. "Our jury includes eight blacks. How do you expect them to feel when they're forced to see those?"

Miller seized the moment. "If Mr. Reynolds is suggesting African-Americans won't be able to discern the truth after reviewing all relevant evidence, he should've stated that for the record in the opening argument."

"Your Honor," said a frustrated Sinclair, "how can you—"

"Thank you, Attorney Sinclair. As always, I appreciate

your wise counsel, but I'm going to call a brief recess so we can continue this in chambers."

The attorneys returned to their places. Tanner informed the jury there were some procedural matters to resolve and promised to reconvene as quickly as possible. The judge met with Reynolds and Matheson in his chambers and requested that the court reporter take minutes. Tanner didn't conceal his dismay as he asked, "Mr. Miller, do you have a legal basis for admitting these photos?"

"I've prepared a brief for your review that cites case law." Miller handed the judge a thick file. "The defense maintains that Professor Matheson is being victimized because of his unpopular beliefs and teaching methods. We have a right to pursue that theory and to demonstrate to the jury exactly what brought him to the attention of local authorities."

"What brought him to the attention of local authorities was his blood at the crime scene," insisted Reynolds.

"I look forward to your presentation on DNA testing," challenged Miller.

"As will I," snorted Tanner. "You'll have my ruling within the hour. I'll give the jurors most of the afternoon to digest their food while I do the same to your briefings." Tanner leaned his body forward and pointed at Miller. "If I decide in your favor, I expect any presentation will be handled in the most respectful and least inflammatory way possible."

"I fully appreciate that concern, Your Honor. And I will certainly comply with the spirit of your request," Miller said diplomatically.

"I can tell you that under normal circumstances I'd grant your motion 'bout as quick as I'd allow a blind man

with arthritis to give me a shave and haircut." Tanner un-
wrapped some chocolate candy and popped a piece into
his mouth. "But given the unprecedented attention paid to
this case, I don't want anyone thinking Professor
Matheson didn't get the benefit of the doubt."

"Your Honor, if I can—"

"You already did, Mr. Reynolds, through your cocounsel's presentation. If anyone opened the door to the
professor's course and to his use of the photos, it was the
state. Now you're gonna have to live with it." He looked
at Miller. "Within reason. Is that understood?"

"Absolutely, Your Honor," promised Miller.

"We're going to have a shortened work schedule next
week. Because of scheduling conflicts as well as some logistical problems, we've got half sessions on Thursday
and Friday." Tanner opened his center drawer and removed a calendar. "Mr. Reynolds, you should look at
your witness list, and if you wish to revise it in accor-
dance with our time constraints, I'll allow that, assuming
there's no objection from defense."

"They can come early, late, or not at all," postured
Miller. "In the words of Joe Louis, 'they can run but they
can't hide.'"

"I believe Mr. Louis had difficulty being understood in
his later years," commented Tanner. "Try not to follow in
his footsteps." Tanner ate another piece of candy. "Mr.
Reynolds, what's your poison? You wanna stay as
planned or make changes?"

"I'd like to discuss it with Ms. Sinclair at the break, Your
Honor, but I don't anticipate making any adjustments."

"Mr. Miller, if I allow you to continue with your slide
show, how long do you intend to shock our sensibilities?"

"Judge, as you well know, some sensibilities are more

easily shocked than others." Miller looked at Reynolds. "I'll do my best to disturb everyone's within an hour."

"An hour?" objected Reynolds. "That's outrageous! There's no justification to put this jury through a barrage of—"

"Try forty-five minutes, Counselor," Tanner offered the compromise. "Or I'll invoke Article Four, Federal Rules of Evidence, Section Four-oh-three, and deny your request on the grounds the evidence is prejudicial, confusing, and an undue waste of court time. Do I need to provide you with any additional citations?"

"No, Your Honor, that's quite sufficient," agreed Miller.

"And I'm tellin' you now," warned Tanner, "if you start playin' the violin or any other background music while you show those photos, I'm pullin' the plug. Catch my drift?"

"Does pulling heartstrings count as music?" Miller asked.

"Mr. Miller, I'm tempted to tell you what to pull, but I'll wait for a more appropriate time. I suggest you both leave me to my chores so we can salvage the afternoon." Tanner started reading Miller's brief. The judge waited until both lawyers were gone, then returned the pages to the file. He placed his feet on the corner of his desk, leaned back, and closed his eyes.

CHAPTER
39

As REYNOLDS EXPECTED, the ruling went against the state, and Miller took full advantage of it. For the past sixty-five minutes the slide projector had displayed one horrific image after the other. Miller described each picture, his voice crackling occasionally with emotion. At times, he'd show the photo without speaking, particularly when the brutality of the crime was directed against women or children. The sound of the projector, combined with the beam of light, cast an eerie presence throughout the courtroom.

"This man was taken from a local jail with the assistance of a deputy sheriff. A mob mutilated his body."

Reynolds studied the jury, grateful he'd have a full weekend before he needed to face them. On the other hand, he worried these images might stay in their thoughts for the next three days. If so, the case was doomed before it began.

"They poured gasoline over his remains," Miller said

in a tone of quiet reverence, "and burned him at the stake." He let the jury study the slide until a few turned away. "As was the case in so many of these crimes, no charges were ever brought against the perpetrators."

"Mr. Miller," Tanner interrupted, "are you almost finished?"

"Just one more slide, Your Honor." Miller nodded to Regina, who provided technical assistance and operated the projector. She pressed the Advance button, and a new slide appeared on the oversized screen. A group of whites surrounded the lynched body of a black man who hung from a tree, one hand severed, neck broken, a knife plunged into his heart. In the background a few yards away glowed a large burning cross.

Miller pointed to the projected image. "I call your attention to the broken and tortured body of a truck driver, a family man. He committed no crime other than being black. And for that violation, he suffered this unspeakable atrocity." He walked to the opposite side of the screen. "Notice the people who stand around his bleeding corpse. Smiling, carefree, posing proudly for a picture with the man they've just sacrificed in tribute to their ideology of bigotry and hate."

Reynolds had kept his head lowered throughout the last section of Miller's presentation, looking up only to concentrate on the impact it had on the jurors.

"This is part of our shameful history," Miller said with his back to the screen, his long shadow cast in the direction of the jury. "A history Professor Matheson felt compelled to share with his students so that it might never be repeated."

Reynolds stood. "Your Honor, this jury has been subjected to more than enough of these brutal and sickening displays of the past." He approached the screen and stared at the photo. "I ask you to put an end to this gruesome and tragic—" He suddenly stopped. His knees buckled, his body bent slightly, and he brought his hands to his chest. His eyes remained fixated on this flickering photographic depiction that in one form or another had haunted his dreams throughout most of his life. The fiery cross seemed to dangle from the night sky just as it had in his frightened imagination. He studied the man's beaten face. Where had he seen it before? He focused on the mutilated hand. Did it somehow contain the secret to the mystery of the bloody fingers that had constantly pursued him? "Your Honor, can we have a brief recess?" He bowed his head. "I feel . . . ill."

"Mr. Miller, you may turn off the projector," instructed Tanner. "Bailiff, can we have the lights, please?"

The lights were turned on, which caused the jurors to readjust to the brightness. Rather than look at the screen, they focused on Reynolds, who, up until this intervention on their behalf, hadn't spoken a word since the trial began. No one paid greater attention to Reynolds than Matheson, who studied him with keen interest.

"Mr. Reynolds, are you gonna be all right?" asked Tanner.

"I apologize, Your Honor," he answered weakly. "I just need a few moments."

Sinclair went to his aid and gave him a glass of water. He took a sip and glanced at the jury. Vernetta Williams, the nurse within the group, appeared ready to scale the jury box and come to his rescue.

"Perhaps this is an appropriate time to adjourn." Tanner shifted through some paperwork. "The jury is admonished not to read news articles, watch television

accounts of the trial, or discuss this case among yourselves or others. Have a restful weekend. I'll see you
Monday, nine o'clock sharp." He rose from his seat and
grabbed a thick folder. "I'd like to see counsel in chambers. I'm confident you haven't forgotten how to get
there since your last visit of . . ." He looked at his watch.
". . . two hours and forty-seven minutes ago."

Tanner left the bench and headed quickly to his chambers while the bailiff escorted the jury out of the courtroom. Munson walked with Hardy Wilkins, the only
other white man on the panel, and gave him a friendly pat
on the back.

Matheson motioned for Regina and, when she arrived,
took her aside. "Find out as much as you can about that
photo," he whispered. She nodded. He glared at Reynolds, who'd recovered by now and made his way toward
the judge's chambers.

Miller and Reynolds once again took their seats in
front of Tanner, who sat behind his desk.

"Gentlemen," said the judge disdainfully, "as Ricky
advised Lucy, you got some 'splainin' to do." He gripped
the edge of his desk and stared at Miller. "Counsel, I
thought we agreed to handle your *forty-five-minute* presentation with dignity and decorum and not attempt to in-
flame the jury."

"I tried to do that, Your Honor. Mr. Reynolds obviously pulled some theatrical stunt to try and—"

"Outdo your theatrical stunt," stated Tanner. "He was
quite effective. I think he bonded with the jury. And, if he
tries it again, he just might have to post bond."

"I'm sorry, Your Honor. I think it was probably something I ate." Reynolds avoided eye contact with both
Tanner and Miller.

"You'll be eatin' crow in front of the jury if you push me too far. I don't know what the two of you are doin' out there, but if you want to be dramatic in my courtroom, you gotta wear one of these here robes. Otherwise, you'll both be dressed in jail fatigues. Understood?"

"Yes, Your Honor," responded the attorneys.

"Now, gentlemen, we all know there's an elephant in that courtroom, and he keeps invitin' his six bigger brothers. They may all be victims of homicide, but they're very much alive in the minds of this jury." Tanner unbuttoned the top of his robe and ran his palms along both sides of his head, pressing his hair back as far as it would go. "Mr. Reynolds, unless I missed somethin' very important, I counted only one murder charge against the defendant."

"That hasn't changed, Your Honor," answered Reynolds.

"You're both treading dangerously close to a mistrial before either one of you calls your first witness. All this talk about other victims ain't gonna help the jury focus on Earvin Cooper or his murderer."

"Judge," replied Miller, "I'm obligated to provide the most vigorous defense of my client that I can possibly present. The state raised the issue of motive and has attempted to taint Dr. Matheson with the murder of every person on his list."

"Just the ones who wound up dead," corrected Reynolds. "In case you haven't noticed, there haven't been any more murders since your client's arrest."

"That underscores my point," argued Miller. "Professor Matheson is being linked to multiple homicides through innuendo and wild speculation. The fact there haven't been additional murders suggests nothing more than a possible relationship between the course being taught and some psychopath inspired by it." Miller appealed to Tanner. "Judge, as you so aptly recognized in granting me permission to continue my presentation, Mr. Reynolds opened the door to this subject, and I fully intend to demonstrate the lack of—"

"I expect this to be a murder trial, not a history lesson," Tanner said angrily. "Either one of you play the race card, the only place you'll be practicing law in the South is south California. Now, get the hell outta here 'fore I make you go fishin' with me in the mornin'." Tanner removed his robe and rubbed his neck.

"My grandson don't like puttin' worms on the hook. And if you ain't learned by now, I don't take kindly to bein' baited." Tanner watched both men head for the door. "Oh, by the way," he added as an afterthought, "the bailiff slipped me a message after we reconvened." He unfolded a small note and glanced at it casually. "You both received death threats."

Miller and Reynolds stood perfectly still.

Tanner walked to his liquor cabinet. "Some black folks want Mr. Reynolds dead, and a few white folks would like to return the favor by killing you, Mr. Miller." He poured himself a glass of brandy. "We also got us some fair-minded people just want to blow up everybody." He took a sip and looked at the two lawyers. "Have a pleasant weekend."

He turned his back on the lawyers, who remained at the doorway for a moment and then left.

CHAPTER

40

REYNOLDS SAT IN his darkened den, listening to Billie Holiday singing "Strange Fruit." The music flowed quietly from a small cassette player. *"Southern trees bear a strange fruit . . ."* He held a copy of the photo last exhibited by Miller in court and lightly moved his finger along its edge. *". . . blood on the leaves and blood at the root."* Enough moonlight filtered through the window to allow him to stare at the image of the black man hanging lifelessly from a tree. Perhaps it was a poplar tree similar to the one mentioned in the song's haunting lyrics.

"Why are you sitting in the dark?" Cheryl asked, interrupting his concentration.

"It wasn't dark when I first sat down," he answered.

She switched on the overhead light and entered the room. "What are you listening to that for?"

"It's what Matheson listened to when he worked at home."

"That might drive anybody to kill." She walked toward him, unaware of what he held.

"So you're finally coming around to accept he did it?"

"I didn't say that. I said . . . My God!" She saw the photo and studied it in horrified revulsion. "What kind of animal would do that to a human being?"

Her husband placed the photo down on his desk. "What kind of human being is produced when people are treated like animals?"

Cheryl turned away. Reynolds noticed her discomfort and knew it had to do with more than the photo. "You still don't think I should be prosecuting him, do you?"

She hesitated. "You're being used. You know that?"

He didn't respond.

"If you win, you're going to be despised by black folks."

He looked at the floor, but she gently lifted his chin and made direct eye contact. "If you lose, whites are gonna doubt your ability and question your loyalty. Either way, everything you've worked to achieve will be destroyed." She softened. "You really want to risk all that for somebody else's political agenda?"

"He's guilty," he said firmly.

"How can you be so sure?"

"We've already been over this, Cheryl," he snapped. "I've been with him!" he said with a degree of anger that surprised him. He softened his tone. "Been in his home. I've seen the photos plastered on the wall like some sick monument. You look at them too long, it's like drinking poison."

"Drink it slowly enough, you build a tolerance," she said.

"But you destroy the soul," he responded softly.

She picked up the photo and brought it closer to him. "How long have you been looking at this?"

"I'm not sure, maybe all my life."

She put the photo facedown on the desk. "You and Martin have more in common than you want to admit. Just make sure you're prosecuting him and not yourself." She kissed him and left.

He closed his eyes to fully appreciate the song's sorrowful concluding lyrics. He envisioned birds scavenging for the sacred fruit, or watching it rot beneath the burning sun, only to be washed away by the cool night rain. He opened his eyes and studied the photo, wondering just how bitter this strange crop had become with time.

He ejected the cassette cartridge from the player and put it carefully into its case. He placed the photo in a gray manila envelope, retrieved his keys from his jacket, and left the room, carrying the photo with him.

CHAPTER
41

REYNOLDS DROVE HIS car slowly through a winding residential neighborhood in Natchez. He looked at the digital clock in his instrument panel and hoped his mother wouldn't be too tired to answer his questions. It had been a while since his last visit, well over a year—actually, now that he thought about it, closer to two. Cheryl enjoyed bringing the children to his mother's home. Christopher always liked going into the room where his father had grown up. He found it hard to imagine his dad as a child confined to a room without a television or computer or PlayStation. There *had* been a record player, though!

Reynolds smiled as he remembered his mother taking it out of his old closet and showing it to a stunned Christopher, then around five. She'd given him three chances to guess what it was. After his third choice—a rotisserie for pancakes—she placed a funny-looking vinyl disk that looked like a flattened black CD on the thing called a turntable. Christopher's eyes gleamed with amazement when he heard scratchy music blare from two cloth-covered box speakers that hung on side hinges, connected by long, thin, entangled plastic-coated wires. He asked his grandmother to play the song twelve straight times. After the fifth repeat, he started anticipating where the needle would skip or ride a bump. "Cool!" he said, with each accurate prediction.

Reynolds pulled into the driveway and turned off the car engine. He left on his headlights and observed his parents' home in the darkness. It had seemed much larger to him in his youth. He once thought he could run in his backyard for days before reaching the end. Now he realized there wasn't enough room to throw a football very far. He noticed his mother standing at the doorway. He turned off the lights, then exited his car, carrying a night bag and a large gray envelope.

His mother appeared younger than her sixty-five years. Even in the darkness he admired her clear skin that neither needed nor often used artificial ingredients to make her look lovely. Her silver hair glowed majestically in the moonlight and curved around her head in short, tight curls.

"James, I've been so worried ever since I got off the phone with you."

"Why?" He kissed her on the cheek, and they both entered the house.

"You sounded so strange. I was afraid something happened to Cheryl or the children," she explained.

"You mean you weren't worried about me," he teased, then dropped his bag onto the floor. He held the envelope to his side.

"I know there's nothin' ever gonna hurt you." She

grabbed his shoulders and turned him completely around. "Let me get a good look at you." She studied him carefully. "Have you lost weight? I made extra chicken and baked macaroni for you to take back to my grandchildren, but I think you could use some tonight. I'll heat up some greens, too."

He smiled sadly.

"James," his mother said seriously, "is something wrong between you and—"

He extended the envelope to her. "I think you know about that," he spoke softly.

She looked at the envelope with concern, then took it from him. Reynolds walked away from his mother and gave her some privacy. When he turned to look at her, he discovered her holding the photo to her breast, startled. She placed her left hand to her mouth.

"My God, who'd do such a thing?"

"I thought *you* might be able to answer that," he said.

"I've never seen this before in my life." She held the photo out to him. She wanted him to take it back.

He approached her, but his hands remained at his sides. "Not the photo, Mama." He stood close to her. "The incident . . . the man, hanging from that tree."

She didn't want to look at the photo again, but she did. She moved to an end table and retrieved her eyeglasses. She put them on and studied the picture carefully.

"I used to wake up seeing his face," Reynolds spoke as his mother's eyes stayed fixed on the photo in her increasingly unsteady hands. "He was always chasing me. No matter how fast I ran, he'd be right behind, his fingers reaching for me, tearing at my clothes."

Reynolds touched the side of a chair his father would have loved—wide and soft with high, cushy arms. He sat on the ottoman. "I fooled myself into believing he existed only in my nightmares," he said, lightly rubbing his unshaved face. "You'd come into my room and tell me he—"

"Wasn't real," she said, completing his sentence for him. She held the photo carefully and walked to her son. "I said that he was only in your—"

"Imagination." This time he finished her statement.

She sat next to him and held the photo on her lap. She looked at it occasionally in between her short, deliberate breaths. "I even started to believe it." She shook her head, ashamed. "Especially when you'd go weeks at a time without waking up frightened. There were nights when you slept so peacefully, followed by mornings when you woke up screaming you'd never sleep in your room again." Her eyes filled with tears. He touched her hand. She put her fingers around his.

"What happened to me?" he asked, barely above a whisper.

"You wandered away from your school group, got lost." She held his hand more tightly. "They'd organized a field trip at the county preserve. We searched all night for you. Your father and me were so afraid we'd never see you alive again. All we could do was pray and leave it in God's hands to bring you home safe." She let go of his hand and walked to the mantel, which contained childhood pictures of Reynolds, including one of him seated on his father's lap. He joined her and studied a framed picture of himself as an adult playing happily with his children.

"Your father and some other men found you unconscious the next morning and rushed you to the hospital. I was there at your bedside when you woke up screamin',

'No! No! Please stop! Please!'" She bowed her head and wept uncontrollably. Reynolds held his mother and comforted her.

"It's all right, Mama. Everything's all right. You don't have to talk about this anymore." He lifted her into his arms and placed her gently on the couch. He found a quilt and covered her, remaining by her side until she fell asleep.

Reynolds entered his old room, which had been converted to an extra guest bedroom for the grandchildren. Despite his mother's best intentions, he'd never allowed Christopher or Angela to sleep there. He said he didn't want to share his special secrets with them just yet. They'd have to wait until they got older. Then, and only then, would they be worthy of discovering the magic of his childhood.

His wife knew there was more to his edict than he'd ever admit—much more. She tried to get him to reveal his real reasons for denying their children—and, for that matter, herself—access to his past. She'd never been successful and long ago had decided not to force him to unlock whatever mysteries he'd worked so hard to keep hidden. For that, he'd remained grateful.

He pulled back the curtain and opened the window that had once promised him a quick escape from any unwelcome visitations disrupting his sleep. On more than one occasion, he also used it to avoid a well-deserved whipping. In the end, his father or mother would find him outside, peeking from behind the large oak tree, and they'd make him endure twice the ordinary punishment for the additional trouble he caused. He'd learned to dread "seek and destroy missions" long before he ever fully appreciated "search and rescue." When he turned away from the window, he discovered his mother standing at the doorway, holding the photo.

"What did you want to know?" she said bravely.

He sat on the edge of the twin bed and bowed his head. "Who was the man they hung?" he said quietly.

"I don't know," she answered firmly.

He looked at her and knew that while capable of evasion, she'd never directly lie to him, not even over this.

"I never wanted to know," she continued with absolute conviction.

"Was I found near him?"

She nodded. "They said he did things." She swallowed hard. "Terrible things to young children. We didn't believe them. They just needed an excuse to kill that man. So they created a horrible lie."

Reynolds's eyes searched for the window, but he knew he'd traveled too long and too far to escape now. "You recognize any of the men in the photo, the ones standing around his corpse?"

She walked toward him and pulled out a desk chair. She sat down and pressed her back against the rigid set of wooden bars. "I've been lookin' at it for a while." She pointed to a white man who wore a long, light coat and a ten-gallon hat. He stood at the base of the lynched man, almost touching his bare foot.

"This one never was no good," she said with a level of animosity that lingered in the air. "We all knew enough to stay away from him. Far as I know, he hasn't changed."

"He's still alive?" he asked, interested.

"Let it go, James," she warned. "The only thing that comes from reopening old wounds is an infection ten times worse than the original." She rose from her seat and headed to the door. "I'll make us something to eat."

"What's his name, Mama?"

She diverted her eyes to the floor. "Eat some food and rest for a while. If you still want to know in the morning, I'll tell you then." He nodded his head in agreement. She left the room.

CHAPTER
42

*T*HE BOY RAN *faster than he'd ever thought possible, and yet the bloody fingers never tired. No matter what he did and despite his best efforts, the fingers followed his every move. The night sounds were almost deafening, but the boy could still hear his heart pounding and feel the warm breath on his back. "Help me!" He heard the words, desperate and afraid. He felt a hand tug at his chest. He saw blood and the rapid movement of a sharp blade illuminated by a cross. He felt something or someone strike him against the side of his face. His body kept falling and falling; then he heard laughter, followed moments later by a scream and something shining in the dark.*

Reynolds awoke on the bed in the room of his childhood. His perspiration had soaked through the pillow and stained the blanket underneath his body.

He sat up and looked around his old bedroom and decided the nightmare had plagued him long enough; the time had come to turn the tables and chase the ghost. He took a shower, had breakfast with his mother, and then left to acquire the information he'd traveled all this way to obtain.

The Greek Revival mansion overlooked the Mississippi River. It sat on a scenic bluff that must have made it a spectacular plantation in its day. Gothic white pillars lined the front entrance. Elderly black men in spotless uniforms worked next to tall concrete and marble columns. Reynolds half expected to see a marching band in red jackets playing "Dixie" while the servants danced and shuffled for the amusement of their master. Sarah, an older woman, introduced herself to him in the courtyard, wearing a maid's outfit with a white apron that caused Reynolds to think of *Gone With the Wind*.

"Follow me, sir," she said, curtsying slightly. She walked pigeon-toed down a pathway that led through a garden of yellow and peach-colored roses. So this is the New South, he thought, as he walked on loose multicolored gravel sprinkled in between large round stepping-stones. They passed a guest house with several recessed porches. He wanted to hate this place but found the architecture remarkable. He wondered how many black hands had toiled to make the fine millwork and how many backs were broken to lay the bricks that surrounded the structure.

He followed Sarah to a large, ornate gazebo adjacent to a sparkling pool. A white man sat comfortably under a blue-striped canopy. He wore a tan linen jacket and straw hat and drank iced tea with the flair of an aristocrat. Reynolds would bet his life the man had a neatly pressed Confederate uniform hanging in his closet alongside a custom-tailored robe fashioned from the finest white silk sheets.

"Are you Gates Beauford?" Reynolds asked while standing under direct sunlight.

"If I'm not, my mama's gonna be one shocked lady." Beauford looked at Sarah, who smiled on cue.

"I'm James Reynolds."

"Yeeeesss." Beauford prolonged the word and gave it many meanings, none of which Reynolds liked. "I've been watchin' you on TV. Impressive, very impressive. Sarah, you know we got us a celebrity? Why, that's the lawyer who's gonna put away that black professor for killing all those innocent elderly gentlemen."

She looked at Reynolds, trying unsuccessfully to hide her disdain. Beauford noticed her demeanor and spoke sternly. "Sarah, bring our special guest some lemonade. . . . Make sure it's from a fresh batch."

Sarah rolled her eyes and proceeded to the main house.

"She's a little slow but been with the family a long time. Would be cruel to let her go now. I doubt she'd even know how to take care of herself." Beauford squeezed a wedge of lemon into his tea until all the juice was gone.

"She manages to take care of you. Wouldn't be that big a leap to take care of her own needs." Reynolds spoke politely.

Beauford studied him for a moment, then stirred the ice cubes in his glass. "Oh, my, where are my manners? You must be melting in that hot sun. Do find yourself a cozy spot beneath the shade and rest a spell."

Reynolds took a seat opposite Beauford, separated by a round outdoor table with a frosted Plexiglas top and porcelain lamp in the middle.

"So, what brings you all the way out here from the big city? It must be something important for a man of your stature to visit my humble home."

Reynolds opened the envelope and removed the photo. He slid it across the table and positioned it in front of Beauford, who showed no reaction other than to scratch the back of his head just beneath his hat.

"Nice photo, don't you think?" Beauford asked. "I mean, given the conditions—night, dark forest, old cameras—I'd say it came out as good as could be expected."

"That's you in the front, isn't it? Standing next to the man you lynched." Reynolds stared into Beauford's eyes and found no discomfort and no remorse.

"I believe so. But let me check just to be certain." Beauford lifted the photo, held it in the sunlight at arm's length, squinted. "Yeah, that's me." He put the photo on the table and looked at Reynolds. "I was young, more outgoin' then. I value my privacy now. A great deal." He stirred his drink, then handed the photo to Reynolds. "I suggest you destroy that for your own good. Wouldn't want anything unfortunate to happen to you."

"This isn't the past, Mr. Beauford. I can take care of myself." Reynolds leaned forward. "You, on the other hand, might want to get yourself a good attorney."

Beauford cocked his head to the side to examine Reynolds, then smiled dangerously. "The world's goin' to hell in a handbasket. That's what happens when people don't know their place." He closed his eyes briefly and spoke nostalgically. "Wasn't all that long ago we had a

Sovereignty Commission, funded by the legislature to take care of potential trouble before it got outta hand. Governor and lieutenant governor were members; worked closely with the sheriff and other decent folk. That's when government was part of the solution instead of the problem." Beauford used a white cloth napkin to dab the perspiration on his upper lip. "Don't tell me about the past, boy. Contrary to what you might believe, we ain't left it."

Sarah arrived with a cold pitcher of lemonade and two frosted glasses, but Beauford raised his hand for her to stop. She saw the photo and looked at Reynolds, then at her employer.

"You can take that back, Sarah. There's been a change in plans. Mr. Reynolds will be leaving, immediately." Beauford remained focused on Reynolds. Sarah glanced again at the photo, then left quickly.

"I want to know what happened," Reynolds stated firmly.

Beauford pressed his index finger against his nostril and moved it in small circles. "A man needed to die. He got some help. A lot of it." Beauford sat back, more relaxed. "The world went on," he spoke casually. "Might even have been a better place. What's that sayin' about youth bein' impetuous?" He shrugged his shoulders. "We were impulsive. Afraid before we had to be." He partially covered a yawn. "Hell, if we'd just waited, been a little more patient, you all would've killed each other." He removed his hat and brushed back his blond and gray hair. "Just like vicious dogs trained to protect where they piss." He picked up a paperback book that rested on a nearby lounge chair. "You said your name was Jimmy?"

Beauford flipped through the pages until he found his bookmark, a thin red ribbon.

"James," corrected Reynolds.

Beauford nodded that he recalled. "James," he said invitingly, "get the fuck off my property." He returned to reading his book.

CHAPTER
43

CALLED AS THE state's first witness, Federal Agent Marsh testified for nearly three hours in a professional if not rehearsed manner. He covered his area of expertise and explained forensic science in lay terms. He proudly discussed the role of the FBI and detailed how the Bureau's laboratories were the best in the world. He used a pointer to highlight a series of crime scene photos of Cooper's barn, attached to a large poster display. He placed a red circle around a magnified picture of a Mont Blanc fountain pen wedged between two rocks at the burned-out site. There were identifying numbers recorded on each photo.

"You were able to conduct fingerprint analysis on the pen?" Reynolds asked as he stood at a podium and faced the witness.

"Yes. We managed to take several complete impressions."

"And were you able to match those fingerprints taken

from the fountain pen found at Earvin Cooper's murder scene?"

"Yes. The prints perfectly matched those of the defendant, Dr. Matheson," said Marsh, looking directly at the jury.

"Was there any reason to believe the pen may have belonged to the defendant?"

"It's a very expensive pen that evidently had been specially designed and ordered as a gift to the professor from some of his students. It had his initials inscribed in gold on the cover, and a personal message engraved on the side."

"Do you recall the message?"

" 'Without justice there is no honor.' "

"Thank you, Agent Marsh. I have no further questions at this time." Reynolds resumed his seat.

Tanner turned toward the defense table. "Mr. Miller?"

"Agent Marsh, you have no idea whatsoever how the fountain pen got in Mr. Cooper's barn, do you?" Miller started quickly, asking the question while in the middle of rising.

"It could have fallen from the defendant's pocket during a struggle," Marsh answered.

Miller proceeded to the podium but stood in front of it. "It could've been dropped by the horse who was lending it to the cow who wanted to write a message to one or more of the hens, but my question suggested you have no real knowledge or facts as to how the pen was left there, isn't that true?"

"I offered you one plausible scenario; I'm certain there are many others."

"We can definitely agree with that." Miller headed toward the display. "Permission to approach the witness, Your Honor."

"Granted," said Tanner.

"Agent Marsh, could you study photo number twelve of the state's exhibit, please?"

"Would you like me to step down?"

"If that would make it easier for you."

Marsh left the witness stand and moved to the side of photo 12. He studied it without blocking the jury's view.

"Would you explain to the jury why the earth underneath where the pen was discovered is completely scorched and yet the pen itself is in good enough condition to lift fingerprints?"

Reynolds immediately looked at the jury. The four black men in the group showed reactions ranging from Faraday Patterson's smirk to Faison Sheppard's noticeable scowl.

"It may have been protected as a result of it being wedged between the two rocks. Or it's possible the pen wasn't in that position or location when the ground was ablaze," speculated Marsh. "It could've been forced there by the explosion or water pressure from fire hoses or any number of other explanations."

"Including being planted—excuse me, dropped—long after the fire was extinguished?"

"That's highly unlikely."

"Can the witness resume his seat, Counselor?" asked Tanner.

"Of course," replied Miller. "Particularly if he's able to maintain the chair in as good condition as this fountain pen."

"Mr. Miller," warned the judge, "keep your personal

observations to yourself. You'll have a chance at the end of the trial to make all the commentary you wish."

"Thank you, Your Honor." Miller walked toward the jury. "Agent Marsh, are you aware of whether or not anyone from your office took foot impressions at the scene of the crime?"

"My office assisted local detectives as well as forensic scientists from the state's crime lab. I believe we took a number of those impressions."

"Isn't it true that the only set of foot impressions you were unable to account for belonged to a person with a size-thirteen shoe?"

"That's correct."

"Mr. Cooper wore a size nine, so it's safe to assume you ruled him out."

"The foot impression did not belong to Mr. Cooper or any known persons who had authorized access to the barn or its surrounding area," answered the agent.

"Those footprints didn't belong to Mr. Cooper, yes or no."

"No." Marsh shifted uncomfortably in his seat.

"Thank you." Miller approached Matheson and stood beside him. "Do you happen to know Professor Matheson's foot size?"

"It was measured as a nine and a half or ten."

Miller puckered his lips and raised his eyes toward the ceiling in thought as he carefully made his way back to the jury box. "So, let's see, using the terminology that you agents are so fond of, a nine and a half or ten, when carefully compared to a thirteen, is not a scientific match." He turned to face Marsh. "Is that a fair characterization of the evidence?"

"I believe the sizes speak for themselves."

"So if the shoe doesn't fit, you must acqu—"

Reynolds jumped up to object. "Your Honor!"

"I didn't say it; I didn't say it." Miller placed his hands up in surrender, then placed them on the jury railing. "But I will state in my own words that if the shoe's the wrong size, then you must surmise a murderer's still on the rise." He looked at Reynolds. "Much to the state's surprise."

Sinclair attempted to stand, but Reynolds put his hand on her shoulder. He'd already decided that any objections should be saved for matters more important than Miller's antics, which he hoped might backfire.

"Mr. Miller, I've cautioned you about your running commentary. If I neglected to mention that also includes a prohibition against bad poetry, let me do so now for the record." Tanner looked at his watch and wrote a note on his ledger. "Proceed with your cross-examination."

"I have no further questions of this witness." Miller crossed to his table and smiled at Reynolds as he took his seat.

"Mr. Reynolds?"

"Nothing further, Your Honor."

"The witness is excused. Agent Marsh, you may step down," instructed the judge. "We'll take our lunch break. The jury's to follow the court's admonition regarding discussing this case. I'll see you back here at one-thirty. Perhaps by that time Mr. Miller will have devised a more suitable way to entertain us."

Tanner struck the gavel and left the bench.

CHAPTER
44

T HE AFTERNOON SESSION started on time. The state
called Officer Hezekiah Macon as its second witness,
to provide chain-of-custody testimony and to identify
one key piece of evidence discovered at Cooper's murder scene. On his way to the stand he made brief eye
contact with the professor, whose class he'd once rudely
interrupted on police business. Matheson waited until
the officer finished taking the oath before giving him a
friendly nod.

Macon spent the first twenty minutes discussing his
training, experience, and years on the force. Reynolds
asked him to list the number of awards and commenda-
tions he'd received, which caused him to speak proudly
and at great length of his background and service. After
the customary introduction designed to create a sense of
ease between witness and jury, Reynolds proceeded with
the substance of the case.

"Your Honor, permission to approach the witness."

Tanner nodded approval. "Proceed."

Reynolds carried a small transparent bag that contained a narrow black object. "I submit into evidence state exhibit eleven-A."

"So identified," uttered the judge.

Reynolds gave the bag to the witness. "Officer Macon, do you recognize the object inside that plastic bag?"

"It's the fountain pen found at the site of the murder."

"Had you ever seen this pen prior to it being discovered at Earvin Cooper's property?"

"Yes. I saw it in the possession of the defendant."

"What makes you so certain of that?"

"I attended an interview Professor Matheson had at police headquarters in late September. He used the pen to sign some paperwork. One of the detectives commented on how attractive and unique it was and asked if it was very expensive."

"How did he respond, if at all?"

"He said it was custom-made and, to his knowledge, one of a kind, but its real value was based on it bein' a gift from the first class of students he ever taught."

Reynolds glanced over Matheson's shoulder at a row filled with students. Next to them sat the Reverend Matheson.

Macon continued. "He went on to say something about it being priceless as a result of that."

"Officer Macon, as you sit here today, are you absolutely certain the pen discovered at the scene of Earvin Cooper's murder is the same one-of-a-kind custom-made pen that belonged to the defendant, Martin Matheson?"

"I am, sir."

"No further questions, Your Honor."

"Mr. Miller, your witness," declared the judge.

Miller rapidly pursued his first question. "Officer Macon, do you know Sergeant Jill Fischer?"

"She's our desk sergeant."

"Your Honor, I'd like to introduce into evidence defense exhibit seven-B, and I ask permission to approach the witness."

"The exhibit is so marked, and you may approach." Tanner took a breath and watched Miller hand Macon a sheet of paper.

"Officer, please take a moment and review that."

Macon skimmed the paper.

Reynolds sneaked a peek at Matheson and noticed a slight smile.

"Could you tell the jury the nature and content of that paperwork?" Miller asked, as if the answer bore great significance.

"It's a lost-property form filled out by Professor Matheson and signed by Sergeant Fischer."

"What did Professor Matheson report as lost, and when and where did he lose it?"

"He indicated he left his fountain pen at our office durin' his interview."

"The same fountain pen we've been discussing in court?"

"It would seem so," the officer admitted.

"The one found in Mr. Cooper's barn the night of his murder?"

Macon hesitated, then replied, "Yes."

"And please remind the jury the date the interview occurred with the professor."

"I believe it was on or around September twenty-eighth."

"A full eight weeks before the murder of Earvin Cooper."

"That sounds correct."

"According to that form, was the pen ever found and returned to Dr. Matheson?"

Macon scanned the paperwork. "Evidently not."

"You interview a great many suspects as part of your official duties, isn't that true?"

"Yes."

"A significant number have extensive criminal records?"

"Unfortunately."

"Ranging from petty theft to murder, I'd imagine?"

"The range of crimes is pretty diverse. Just like the people who commit 'em."

"If one of those criminals was interrogated in the police station the same day you interviewed Dr. Matheson, and stumbled upon an expensive pen, what's the likelihood that person would've returned it to the lost-and-found?"

Macon crossed his arms. "I've no way of estimatin' that."

"How long have you been in law enforcement?"

"Fifteen years."

"Has it been your experience that when thieves, rapists, and murderers happen upon an expensive item, they immediately bring it to the attention of police, then volunteer to fill out a report?"

"It's possible." Macon uncrossed his arms and leaned back.

"Many things are possible, Officer, including arresting a respected and distinguished professor and accusing him of the most heinous crimes based upon little more than the discovery of a lost or stolen pen!"

Reynolds rose to his feet. "Your Honor, the state objects."

"As well it should," Miller agreed.

"Mr. Miller, save the philosophical stuff for your closing argument," Tanner said, barely controlling his anger. "Objection sustained. Ask your next question, Counselor."

"During your fifteen years as a seasoned and experienced police officer, how many times has a criminal approached you to return an expensive item?"

"I don't believe that's ever happened," Macon answered.

Miller walked in front of the jury box. "So it's possible, perhaps even likely, somebody with a criminal record who'd been detained at your station found the pen and either kept it for himself or gave it to someone who visited him while in custody."

Macon looked at the jury. "That's highly unlikely."

"Officer Macon, you're not suggesting someone who worked at the station found the pen and later placed it at Mr. Cooper's barn to implicate the professor, are you?"

"If someone in law enforcement found the pen, it would've been returned to its proper owner."

"Officer Macon, is there any particular reason you didn't inform this jury you were one of a handful of officers who arrived at Mr. Cooper's home shortly after his murder?"

"I was never asked."

"There's no need to become modest. You spent the first half of your testimony telling the jury of your many achievements. You're a highly decorated officer, isn't that true?"

"I've had my fair share of honors."

"And you played a major role in sealing off the crime scene area, didn't you?"

"Along with several investigators."

"How important is it to maintain what is often referred to as the 'integrity of the crime scene' as quickly as possible following the commission of a crime?"

"Very," answered an increasingly annoyed Macon.

"Please tell the jury why that's the case."

"To make sure evidence isn't compromised or lost."

"You don't mean 'lost' in the same way that Professor Matheson lost his pen at your station, do you?"

"I'm not convinced the professor ever lost it," Macon replied harshly. "Seems odd he'd be that careless with something he'd just finished tellin' everybody meant so much to him."

"So are you telling the jury it's your theory Professor Matheson filled out a lost-property report because he had nothing better to do with his time?"

"Maybe your client, the defendant, lied about losin' it. Or he could've owned another one just like it that he dropped at the murder scene."

Miller looked at the jury for a moment, then shook his head sadly. "Professor Matheson is an extremely bright and organized educator. He'd have needed to be fairly absentminded and clumsy for your theory to be true."

"Brilliant people do stupid things after they've murdered someone."

"Couldn't be too stupid." Miller moved closer to Macon. "He secretly ordered a pen identical to the one he had, because using his clairvoyant powers, he knew he'd lose it at your police station and would need an extra one to leave behind at the scene of a crime." He turned his back on Macon and addressed the jury. "And, oh, by the way, for good measure he placed it inside a burning building just in the right location where it could be found in pristine condition with his initials engraved on the top and his fingerprints imprinted all over the bottom." He looked at the witness. "Is that really what you want this jury to believe?"

"I'm speculatin' just like you are, Counselor."

"But you're a police officer under oath, and as such you're attempting to testify to the facts as you know them, not as they might be conveniently distorted to prove the state's theory."

A frustrated Reynolds once again rose to his feet. "Your Honor, I have to object to Mr. Miller's continued badgering of the witness."

"Was I badgering Officer Macon?" Miller asked innocently. "If I was doing that, I certainly apologize. After all, this is only a murder trial where Professor Matheson risks losing his freedom and possibly his life, and I wouldn't want to be rude in challenging the evidence."

"Would counsel be so kind as to approach the bench, please?" ordered Tanner.

Miller faced the jury and shrugged his shoulders helplessly, then joined Reynolds and met the judge at the bench. Tanner leaned over so far, his nose almost touched Miller's forehead. "You're skating on thin water, mister."

"Your Honor probably meant to say 'ice,'" corrected Miller.

"I'll say 'contempt of court' if you interrupt me again

or start makin' speeches when you're supposed to be askin' questions. Now, if you got some evidence the real murderer just so happened to be visitin' the police station the day your client lost his pen"—Tanner turned his back to the jury—"or if you're gonna imply a police officer planted incriminating evidence against Professor Matheson, you better offer a whole lot more than theatrical implications and inferences—or I'm about to rule all of your questions out of order."

"Your Honor, with all due respect—"

Tanner cut him off. "Whenever somebody starts off a statement '*With all due respect*,' I got a pretty good feelin' I ain't gonna be shown any. Matter of fact, I'm likely to get downright insulted. And, Mr. Miller, it does not pay to insult a judge while he's wearing a robe in his own courtroom. Now, you finish up with this witness or you move your line of questions in a different direction." Tanner sat back in his chair.

By the time Miller turned to face the jury, he displayed a smile that indicated great satisfaction and pleasure with whatever discussions he'd completed with the judge. Reynolds, in contrast, looked as if he'd been the one chastised.

"Officer Macon, I just have a few more questions on another matter. What was it, precisely, that brought Professor Matheson to your police station on September twenty-eighth?"

"My partner and I were asked to visit the defendant while he was teachin' one of his classes. We asked him to come with us to discuss what was happenin' as a result of his list."

"You asked him to come with you?"

"Yes."

"And you handcuffed him in front of his students so he might feel welcomed and comfortable as he made the journey from his classroom to the backseat of your patrol car?"

"My goal was to prevent students from gettin' involved in police business. I wanted to avoid a confrontation that might get additional people in trouble."

"And you accomplished that through intimidation and humiliation?" Miller asked innocently.

"I thought if we demonstrated we were there on a serious matter, it would eliminate any potential conflict."

Miller shook his head in agreement and offered a helpful suggestion. "Wouldn't it have been easier to pistol-whip him?"

Reynolds rose. Miller waved him off. "I'll withdraw that comment. Thank you, Officer Macon, for your enlightening views; I'm certain the jury found them helpful."

"And, Mr. Miller," added Judge Tanner, "I'm certain our state coffers will appreciate being made richer by two hundred and fifty dollars, which is the sanction I hereby impose on you for being in contempt of court."

Reynolds observed the jury. As if he didn't have enough problems with heroes, now the judge had turned Matheson's attorney into a martyr as well.

"In that case, Your Honor, I'll avoid having my wallet assaulted any further. I have no more questions of this witness." Miller strolled to his seat with the noticeably increased admiration of several black jurors. Aubrey Munson, as usual, looked greatly annoyed.

Tanner poured a glass of water and downed two aspirins. "Mr. Reynolds, do you have any redirect?"

"Yes, Your Honor, thank you." Reynolds walked toward the witness. "Officer Macon, you don't like the defendant, do you?"

"I have no reason to either like or dis—"

"Officer, this isn't the time to be courteous!" snapped Reynolds. "You don't like the man, do you?"

Reynolds's outburst caused the jurors to sit up straight and pay renewed attention.

Macon looked down at the floor. "No, sir, I don't."

"You believe he murdered Earvin Cooper."

Miller rose quickly. "What this witness believes is immaterial to—"

"Counsel for the defense was very much interested in what Officer Macon believed on a variety of subjects," Reynolds said firmly. "I think it's only fair for the state to pursue the same line of questioning."

"The objection is overruled," Tanner said with some satisfaction. "Officer Macon, you may answer."

"Yes. I believe the defendant murdered Mr. Cooper."

"Did you come to that conclusion because you don't approve of the course Professor Matheson teaches?"

"No."

"Do you think he's a murderer because you don't like him?"

"No, sir."

"Have you rendered an opinion as to who murdered Earvin Cooper based on the evidence discovered at the crime scene?"

"Yes, sir, I have."

"And you state under oath that you believe the man who took the life of Earvin Cooper is Martin Matheson, the defendant?"

"I do."

"Did you plant evidence at the scene of the crime?"

"I did not."

"To your knowledge, did anyone else involved with this investigation attempt to falsely implicate the defendant in the crime of which he now stands accused?"

"No."

"You realize if you planted evidence, you'd be guilty of committing a felony that would cost you your career, your livelihood, and your freedom."

"I know that," answered Macon with conviction.

"And you're telling this jury you wouldn't be willing to go to prison to frame an innocent man, even if you didn't like him?"

"I would not."

"Even if you despised or hated him?"

"Even then." Macon looked squarely at the jury. "I wouldn't jeopardize everything I've been sworn to uphold. I wouldn't do that to my profession, to my family, or to myself, no matter how I felt about the professor."

Reynolds waited for a moment and discreetly surveyed the jurors in the back row. They believed the officer, he thought, but would it matter? "I appreciate your honesty, and I'm hopeful the jury does as well. I have no further questions of this witness." Reynolds walked past the defense table, ignoring both Matheson and Miller, and took his seat next to Sinclair. He didn't want to display too much righteous indignation—just enough to elicit empathy from the jury.

Tanner looked at Miller with an expression that suggested the answer to his upcoming question had better be no. "Mr. Miller, do you wish to recross?"

"That won't be necessary, Your Honor."

"Officer Macon, you're excused," said Tanner.

Macon left the witness stand and exited the courtroom.

Tanner turned to the jury. "I'm going to let you go a little early today. I'd rather do that than keep you late or dismiss you in the middle of someone's testimony. As you know, we'll conduct half-day sessions tomorrow and again on Thursday. Hopefully, we'll be able to complete at least one or two witnesses both sessions." He took a large swallow of water. "As you've just experienced, on occasion in the heat of battle, tempers flare and lawyers in the pursuit of their advocacy may force a judge to comment negatively or, as was the case with Mr. Miller, impose a fine or sanction."

He leaned closer toward the jury and spoke with a father's firmness. "You should not, under any circumstances, construe that action by me as demonstrating a preference for one lawyer over the other. Nor does it imply I have a view regarding the credibility of a particular witness, or, for that matter, a position on the innocence or guilt of the defendant."

Reynolds carefully studied the reactions of the jury and wondered if the judge would have been better off avoiding this subject altogether.

Tanner looked at the attorneys and smiled. "As both the prosecution and defense will agree, I've had to take a lot of lawyers to the woodshed during my time as a judge, but it doesn't mean I don't like or admire them. They've got their job to do; I've got mine." He turned to the jury. "And, ladies and gentlemen, you certainly have yours. You are instructed to do that job on the basis of the evidence submitted to you. Any exchanges between myself and another participant in this room shall have no bearing whatsoever on your deliberations or the outcome of this case."

He panned the jury. "Having looked into each of your

faces, I'm assured we understand and accept our distinct roles. Am I correct in that belief?"

The jurors nodded yes or answered in the affirmative.

"Then we can all rest peacefully in the knowledge we'll be here tomorrow to see who gets fined next."

CHAPTER 45

CHERYL HAD BEEN reading a magazine when she heard a car pull into the driveway. She straightened the pillows on the couch, quickly fixed her hair in the mirror, and hurried to the front door.

Reynolds walked in slowly and barely kissed his wife on the cheek. He proceeded into the living room and collapsed on the sofa. Cheryl took a seat next to him.

"Did it go as poorly as reported on the news?"

Reynolds let out an exasperated gasp. "A big-foot police officer stole Matheson's pen then planted it at the barn. We do blood evidence tomorrow." He shook his head in defeat. "Miller will claim contamination, police incompetence, corruption, and then dismiss the reliability of DNA testing."

"Martin must feel relieved," she said.

"I'd like to permanently relieve *Martin* of that pretentious smirk on his face."

"You have another face to worry about."

"Whose?"

"Young boy, nine years old, named Christopher." She looked at him. "Sound familiar?"

"It rings a bell." Reynolds rose from his seat. "Is it bad?" he asked, concerned.

"It's a man thing," she replied. "I'll let you be the judge."

"Please don't use that word or any other that might remind me of where I've been today," he pleaded. He headed down the hallway and knocked on his son's bedroom door. He entered and discovered Christopher standing next to the window, looking out. When the boy turned around, Reynolds noticed a swollen eye and a bruise on his forehead. He approached his son and took a seat on the edge of the bed.

"You wanna talk?" Reynolds asked gently.

"I threw the first punch," Christopher replied with little comfort.

"You're supposed to throw the last."

"It *was* my last."

"How many guys?"

"Four. They all thought Matheson was a hero and they said you were a Tom."

"That's when you threw the punch?"

"No. They said you were an asshole. Cared more about winning than finding the truth."

"You hit 'em then?"

"No. They called me a punk. That's when I hit 'em."

"Oh . . . Well, as long as you're defending our family's honor . . . Can you eat?"

"What did Mom make?"

"Tuna casserole."

"No."

Reynolds stood next to his son, and they both looked out the window. He placed his arm around Christopher's shoulders. "Wanna sneak out for a pizza?"

"Won't Mom get upset?"

"What's she gonna do about it, beat you?"

"Hey, Dad"—Christopher frowned—"could you quit with the cute stuff?"

"Sorry," said Reynolds. "Just wanted to look at the bright side."

"That's easy for you to say, you still got two good eyes."

They walked to the door, and Reynolds opened it, then placed his hand on his son's shoulder. "So, you wanna tell me again about that punch you threw?"

"It was a beauty, Dad, except I didn't follow it up with anything."

Reynolds nodded understandingly. "I know the feelin'." They both left the room.

CHAPTER
46

TUESDAY MORNING DR. Nelson Stokes explained the intricacies of DNA. He told the jury that every individual has his own unique genetic makeup, which distinguishes him from anyone else who's ever lived, is currently alive, or will be born anytime in the future. "Think of it as God's special nicknames for all His children," he said, to the appreciation of Blaze Hansberry. Reynolds thought the rest of the jury found him condescending.

Stokes described the various tests performed, then showed examples of enlarged laboratory plastic strips, which offered a comparison of Dr. Matheson's DNA with the blood evidence discovered underneath Earvin Cooper's fingernails. He identified the pattern of thin lines that formed "a scientific match with the defendant, providing conclusive proof that Dr. Matheson and the victim were engaged in a bloody confrontation."

Miller offered numerous objections, most of which were overruled. But his constant interruptions had the desired effect of making the doctor's tedious presentation even more unbearable.

Tanner gave the jury an extra ten minutes for their morning break and an extra half hour for lunch. When they returned for the afternoon session, it took Reynolds less than thirty seconds to mercifully conclude his questioning.

"Dr. Stokes, you conducted DNA tests on blood found underneath Mr. Cooper's fingernails, is that correct?"

"Yes."

"What are the odds the DNA you analyzed belongs to anyone other than the defendant?"

"Seven and a half billion to one."

"Thank you, Doctor."

Tanner appeared as relieved as the jury that Reynolds had completed his portion of the examination. He turned to Miller. "Counselor, you may begin your cross of the witness."

Miller stood and gave a comforting nod to the jurors and walked toward the witness. "Dr. Stokes, you'll have to forgive me if I ask some rather naive questions, I'm just an old country lawyer. I don't know much about DNA except for what I learned by watchin' case after case of high-profile defense teams pretty much destroyin' the reliability of all that testin' you do."

Reynolds knew once Miller started dropping his "g's" he was setting up the witness for the kill.

"Now, from the little I know about this evolvin' science, I'm somewhat concerned, and maybe you can alleviate my fears. Isn't it true that the people responsible for handlin' genetic material need constant trainin'?"

"That's true for all occupations involving technology, and yes, it's particularly the case with this form of science."

"I happen to have a list of county and state employees who initially collected then conducted the preliminary analysis on the DNA evidence you spent all morning long describing. I took the liberty of reviewing their training and the type of equipment they used." He moved to the defense table and retrieved several computer printouts. "Your Honor, permission to approach."

"Granted."

"Defense would like to introduce exhibit seventeen-A into evidence."

"Court reporter will so mark and record," instructed Tanner.

"Dr. Stokes, might you take a moment and evaluate that information, and if you can, would you kindly explain to the jury whether or not in your expert opinion the laboratory technicians on that list have maintained the proper ongoing professional training required to fulfill their duties?"

Stokes read the material. He frowned noticeably, and his eyebrows arched several times during his review.

"Dr. Stokes, I take it by your facial expressions you have some concerns you might like to share with the rest of us."

The witness became stoic. "The training hasn't kept pace with the technology in all instances, but I'm certain these people are qualified to perform the jobs they were hired to do."

"Oh, I wouldn't belittle our hardworking and dedicated state employees who do the best they can with poor training, limited resources, financial cutbacks, and outdated equipment." Miller folded his arms across his chest. "That equipment I just mentioned *is* outdated, wouldn't you agree, Doctor?"

Stokes shifted uncomfortably in his seat. "There's better and more advanced equipment in the scientific marketplace, but what they use is perfectly adequate."

"Somehow the phrase 'perfectly adequate' doesn't exactly generate an abundance of confidence. If you were having a heart transplant, would you feel comfortable having the surgeons use 'perfectly adequate' equipment?"

Reynolds stood. "Objection, Your Honor. We're not discussing heart transplants."

"I agree with counsel," said Miller. "We're dealing with a man's life and freedom, but I'll withdraw the question."

Reynolds sat down and decided he wouldn't object again unless absolutely necessary.

"If I could"—Stokes tentatively raised his hand— "might I address your concerns regarding the equipment?"

Miller smiled politely. "Please try."

"Thank you. Regardless of any perceived problems either in personnel, training, or equipment, I want to remind the jury that I personally conducted these tests, which formed the basis for my opinions. I can assure the court that my laboratory utilizes the most advanced and precise technology available."

"Thanks for reminding us of those facts," said Miller, looking none too thankful. "Perhaps you can help resolve another concern. I was taught in basic introduction to science, 'Garbage in, garbage out.' Does that principle still apply?"

"It does," answered Stokes reluctantly, "but—"

"That's what I thought," said Miller, cutting him off. "Now, I reviewed the report you furnished the court. And frankly, I may have misunderstood some of the information."

"That's quite understandable," offered an annoyed Stokes.

Miller ignored the remark. "One of the samples you use to determine statistical probability is based on African-American males."

"Correct."

"So, when the report indicates a sample base of five, does that represent millions?"

"No. Five is the accurate number."

"Five people?!" Miller expressed incredulously.

"That may sound insufficient, but—"

"It does indeed. Tell the jury the backgrounds of those in the sample."

"The backgrounds?"

"It states in your report they were African-Americans. Can you tell us if they were born in this country? Were they the products of interracial marriages? Any health problems that might affect the tests?"

"They live in Detroit."

"So they were foreigners?" Miller's question caused an immediate outburst of laughter.

"Mr. Miller, could you save the humor for another time and place?" warned Tanner.

"I'm sorry, Your Honor. I hadn't realized how funny this was until Dr. Stokes answered my questions. I'm through with this witness."

Tanner gave Miller a stern stare that lasted several

moments after he took his seat. "Any redirect, Mr. Reynolds?"

"Yes, Your Honor, just a few questions." Reynolds had already decided he'd need to call two or three additional scientists to compensate for Stokes's unimpressive testimony, but he wanted to make a reasonable effort to rehabilitate this witness.

Stokes reviewed the nature of statistical sampling and discussed the number of tests conducted on thousands of human subjects around the world. He described the sophistication and reliability of the tests and the type of DNA data pool the worldwide scientific community could draw upon in rendering their conclusions. Reynolds asked how many times in his experience mistakes in handling DNA, or outdated equipment, had resulted in the misidentification of a defendant on trial. "Zero times," answered Stokes. "It might exculpate a guilty person, but it would never cause an innocent one to go to prison. Mistakes in the laboratory don't create someone else's DNA."

Reynolds thought he'd done as much as he could to restore credibility to his witness, and finished his redirect.

"Mr. Miller, any recross?" asked the judge.

Miller rose from his seat. "I'll be brief, Your Honor."

Tanner looked at his watch. "I'm sure the jury will appreciate that."

"Dr. Stokes, you indicated that mistakes in analysis could never misidentify a subject and therefore contribute to an innocent defendant's being wrongly imprisoned."

"That's correct," responded Stokes. "As I said, the lab

can't create DNA. It can only analyze what already exists."

"But mislabeling occurs all the time, doesn't it? Hospitals operate on the wrong person, remove or replace a healthy organ, or send a baby home with someone else's parents."

Stokes shook his head and waved his index finger. "That's a completely different subject, and you know that, Counselor."

"I realize you're a renowned specialist in your field, Doctor, but I didn't know you could also read my mind." Miller addressed the jury. "*I* can't even do that with precision, and trust me—I've tried."

Reynolds watched August Cobb and Faraday Patterson nudge each other and smile.

"Do you happen to know how Dr. Matheson's blood was made available so that you and others could conduct DNA tests?"

"I'm not sure I understand your question," responded Stokes.

Miller retrieved two sheets of paper. "Defense introduces exhibits thirty-four-A and -B."

"So marked," ruled Tanner.

"Your Honor, may I approach the witness?"

The judge nodded. Reynolds looked at Sinclair, concerned.

"Dr. Stokes, please take a moment and review that paperwork."

Stokes skimmed the two sheets and looked up at Miller.

"Isn't it true that Dr. Matheson voluntarily provided two blood samples while he was being treated for injuries sustained in an attack?"

Stokes looked at the information again. "It would appear so."

"And where was he when those samples were taken?"

"Based on the information contained in this report, apparently the blood was taken at a police station."

"And you have no way of knowing what happened to that blood after it was in the custody of the police, do you, Doctor?"

"I would have no reason to know, sir."

"You're telling this jury that although you personally analyzed DNA evidence, you don't care what happened to it or how it was handled before it got to you; is that your testimony?"

Reynolds rose angrily. "Objection!"

"That is not my testimony! I said . . ." Stokes exhibited his first real sign of anger and confusion.

"There's an objection, Dr. Stokes," Tanner interrupted.

"I apologize, Your Honor," replied the flustered witness.

Tanner looked at Reynolds. "Your basis."

"Intentionally misstates Dr. Stokes's testimony, and further, Your Honor, I believe Mr. Miller is raising another totally unfounded inference regarding police conduct in this case."

"I'm sure Mr. Miller isn't going to travel down that road, unless he can provide more than mere speculation to this court. Am I reassured of that fact, Counselor?" Tanner stared at Miller.

"Wouldn't think of doing otherwise, Your Honor."

"As far as your initial objection, Mr. Reynolds, the court sustains it," ruled Tanner. "Mr. Miller, you may proceed with this witness."

"I have no further questions."

"Mr. Reynolds?"

"I have none, Your Honor."

"Very well," remarked Tanner. "The witness is excused."

Stokes left the court in a huff.

"This concludes the session for today. We'll meet tomorrow and attempt to complete as much testimony as we can before we go into our half-day schedules for the remainder of the week." Tanner turned his attention to the jury. "You're reminded of the court's previous admonishment regarding discussing any facet of this case. Have a good evening and try to get yourselves some well-deserved rest."

Miller joked with some of the spectators behind him while Reynolds and Sinclair remained seated at their table in defeat.

Reynolds was preparing to leave when he noticed Regina holding up a large tan envelope and smiling at Matheson, who nodded in appreciation.

It had taken her longer than expected, but she'd finally located the information. Though it had required her to travel to the main library in Natchez, the trip resulted in not one but two articles of interest. The first described the grisly lynching of Thaddeus Edwards, a thirty-six-year-old truck driver and father of six daughters and one son. The victim had been mutilated and stabbed through the heart. His body was discovered still hanging from a tree in the state park just off the main trail leading to the picnic area.

While copying the article, Regina had noticed a small column at the bottom of the page, with a heading that caught her interest: FIVE-YEAR-OLD NEGRO BOY FOUND

ALIVE. She skimmed this second story and stopped at the name James Reynolds. She learned that the boy, known at school as "Jimmie," was the only child of Lydell and Sonya Reynolds. She readjusted the microfiche machine, pressed the Print button, and made a copy.

CHAPTER
47

WEDNESDAY'S SESSION STARTED with a bang or, more accurately, the threat of one. All occupants left the courthouse in an orderly fashion as members of the bomb squad searched every inch of the facilities, starting on the fifth floor and working their way down to the basement. Miller approached Reynolds and Sinclair, who stood outside near the parking lot at a reasonably safe distance from the main activity.

"Burning down the building won't save you," quipped Miller.

"It's not a fire drill," Sinclair informed him. "We've got a bomb threat."

Miller leaned close to Sinclair and lightly sniffed. "Maybe someone didn't like your perfume."

She gave him a hostile look.

"Although I am rather fond of the bittersweet scent losing prosecutors exude."

She stared at Reynolds. "James, I know he's your

friend, but I'm gonna hurt him. I'm really gonna hurt him."

After the court proceedings were canceled for the day, Reynolds and Sinclair returned to their office to regroup. Miller lingered behind and strolled through the festive crowd. With his hectic schedule he hadn't previously noticed the outdoor community that had emerged since the beginning of the trial.

Territories were allotted for various factions and political causes. The media reserved the best locations, setting aside space for catering and celebrity trailers. Food vendors and artists fought daily for the remaining spots, while entertainers and troubadours roamed freely, accepting donations for each performance, trick, or face-painting.

Miller stopped at a booth and perused so-called Third World propaganda in the form of leaflets, newsletters, and books. He read about the government's "AIDS conspiracy" and their "secret plans at genocide aimed at people of color." He shook his head at the notion that his government could successfully plan *anything,* let alone manage to keep it secret for longer than seventy-two hours.

He walked to another area and browsed a series of charcoal sketches, original posters, and oil paintings. Some of the exhibiting artists were quite talented, while others simply stamped slogans on canvas or cheap T-shirts and sold their products to the highest bidder, providing discounts for volume purchases.

He headed toward his car after discovering two posters displayed on easels next to each other. Both posters revealed the same basic drawing of a lynching. The first showed a man's black silhouette hanging from a tree; the body cast a long white shadow. The second reversed the images; the hung victim was depicted as a white silhouette that cast an equally long black shadow, perhaps slightly longer.

Miller expressed interest in both until informed by the artist that he'd sold out of the white version but would have more in stock before the trial ended. Miller promised the man he'd come back later, then proceeded to his vehicle without making any more stops.

Sinclair and Reynolds attended a strategy session with Vanzant. They'd listed the names of all their witnesses and discussed the possibility of adding others.

"What about that guy Matheson threatened at the university just before he got arrested?" Vanzant asked. "He's available to testify, and it would show the professor's violent nature."

"What's he gonna say?" responded Reynolds. " 'I spat in the professor's face and he should've handled it more serenely'?"

"James is right," agreed Sinclair. "After they learned what he did to Matheson, they'd threaten him, too."

"Maybe we were wrong not to charge him with Arnold Rankin's bombing death," said Vanzant.

"A gas receipt and a year-old purchase of dynamite aren't sufficient to indict him," countered Reynolds.

"Yeah, but cumulative evidence might be enough to sway some of the jurors." Vanzant reached for his pouch of tobacco and discovered it was empty. "When it rains, it pours," he said despondently.

"Had we indicted Matheson on any of the other murders with the evidence we've got, we would've lost all credibility with the jury," argued Sinclair. "We haven't got that much as it is."

Vanzant pulled out a folder and handed it to Reynolds. "Maybe this will help."

Reynolds and Sinclair both studied the contents.

"Let's get him on the stand pronto," ordered Vanzant.

"We'll have to bump the pathologist's report," said Sinclair.

"From what I've been told about this jury," remarked Vanzant, "they've had their fill of scientists and doctors. Let's give 'em a taste of common folk."

Reynolds sat back. "I got a bad feeling about this."

Vanzant looked at the two attorneys. "I've already scheduled him. He'll be your next witness." He walked toward his desk and flicked on his fan.

Reynolds took it as a sign to leave. He picked up his materials and left with Sinclair. Once they reached the safety of the hallway, he pulled her aside.

"We're not gonna have time to meet with this guy or prepare him for testimony or even determine if we should put him on."

"I know." Sinclair nodded sympathetically. "But it looks pretty straightforward. Anyway, our not having had time to interview him means we aren't obligated to give Miller any more information than we've got in that file." She walked with Reynolds down to her office. "If we knew for certain Matheson would take the stand, we'd use it as impeachment and not share it with Miller at all. But we can't afford to take that risk."

"I know Todd too well," Reynolds warned. "When he's prepared, he's dangerous. When he's not, he's a barracuda."

"That explains it," said Sinclair.

"Explains what?"

"Ever since I met him at your home, I've been trying to figure out where I first saw him. It was swimming with the other sharks."

CHAPTER
48

BOBBY GELON SAT in the witness chair and answered all of the questions posed by Reynolds. Gelon, at five-four in shoes, peeked over the dark wood railing at the jury and spoke in short, gruff sound bites. He rocked back and forth occasionally, which caused his bald pink head to disappear then reappear between responses. He told the jury he was forty-two, but Reynolds knew they didn't believe that, either.

"It's your testimony the defendant purchased a pair of size-thirteen work shoes from you?" asked Reynolds.

"Five months ago, sure did."

"How can you be certain that person was Dr. Matheson?"

"Never forget him," Gelon said indignantly. "Seemed like the man went out his way to be rude and obnoxious. Had a real chip on his shoulder. Thought for sure he wanted to pick a fight."

"No further questions." Reynolds sat with an uneasy feeling.

"Mr. Miller, your witness."

Miller started to rise, but Matheson pulled him down. "Ask him about his employment practices," he whispered, "whether he's had any discrimination lawsuits." He pushed a file toward Miller, who opened it and quickly scanned the pages. He looked up from the file and gave the professor a curious look.

Miller rose and approached the podium, carrying the file. "Mr. Gelon, how long have you owned your shoe store?"

"Been in the family fifty years. My granddaddy trained my papa. He trained me. I'm trainin' my two boys."

"You employ non–family members?"

"Got twelve. Half of 'em part-time."

"How many are black?"

"Your Honor, Mr. Gelon's hiring practices are of no concern to this court," argued Reynolds.

"The jury has a right to determine if his motives go beyond civic duty," rebutted Miller.

"The witness may answer," ruled Tanner.

"I ain't got no blacks workin' for me. Never have." Gelon's rapid-fire response caused several jurors to smile in amusement, while it had the opposite effect on others.

Miller paused and scratched behind his right ear. "You seem pretty proud of that. Did your father ever hire any blacks?"

"Your Honor, Mr. Gelon's father didn't sell shoes to the defendant," objected Reynolds.

"The defense would like to introduce several lawsuits filed by African-American consumers and applicants for employment that clearly demonstrate a pattern of discrimination in the business practices of Mr. Gelon, his papa, his granddaddy, and in all likelihood in the future, his two boys."

"Mr. Miller, you will show proper respect in my courtroom. Understood?" Tanner didn't flinch.

"I'm sorry, Your Honor. I'll share these documents with the state. Perhaps we can stipulate their admission this afternoon."

"That'll be fine," agreed the judge.

"Mr. Gelon, were there any other employees or customers in your store when you say Professor Matheson purchased the boots?"

"Nope," replied Gelon nonchalantly. "Just before closin' and I was by myself."

"How convenient," Miller replied. "Could you tell this jury why you waited so long before calling the district attorney's office?"

"Didn't know my information was valuable."

"By 'valuable' do you mean you wanted to see how much it was worth to a tabloid newspaper or a television station?"

"Objection," argued Reynolds.

"Sustained," ruled Tanner.

"You think coming forward in such a high-profile case might be good for your business?" asked Miller.

Gelon rocked out of sight, then reappeared. "Hadn't given it much thought till you asked the question just now."

"Well, since you're thinkin' 'bout it," Miller said sarcastically, "would you hazard a guess if your appearance will be good for your store, bring in new customers?"

"Don't rightly know, but I'll be happy to leave my business cards at the door," answered a grinning Gelon.

"And let me expedite that for you as rapidly as possible," Miller said with disgust. "I have no further questions of this witness. Mr. Gelon can get back to his family business." Miller took his seat but avoided looking at Matheson.

Reynolds declined the opportunity to redirect. Tanner excused the witness. The rest of the afternoon the jury heard from the state's pathologist, who described the injuries sustained by Cooper and the cause of death. He speculated on the duration and effectiveness of the victim's struggle and the type of injuries he may have inflicted on his assailant. He explained his autopsy reports and utilized three large easels to display anatomy charts. The doctor was proud that his work had been the subject of a documentary broadcast on a premium cable network. He described various methods a pathologist could use to reconstruct a body and informed the jury that a careful autopsy not only revealed answers to how a person was murdered but also offered important clues to who may have committed the homicide.

After Reynolds finished direct, Miller asked the doctor why the Association of Crime Scene Reconstruction had expelled him eight years ago for unethical behavior, and "was that also the reason why the Southwestern Association of Forensic Scientists censured you the following year?"

Miller notified the judge he had no more questions.

Friday afternoon consisted of more of the same. Two DNA experts testified for the state and explained the basis of their scientific judgment that the blood found on the victim's body matched the defendant.

Tanner dismissed the jury a half hour early and advised them to have an enjoyable weekend. He kept the lawyers for an additional hour and forty-five minutes to review motions and make rulings from the bench.

The session ended at 6:15, and the prosecution team headed back to the DA's office, where Reynolds sat dejected in their conference room.

"You want a cup of coffee?" Sinclair offered.

"No, thanks. Given my luck, caffeine will make me drowsy."

She filled a large ceramic mug for herself. "Wouldn't be a bad idea to get some rest."

"After this is over, all I'm gonna do is stay in bed. I might not sleep, but at least I'll be balled up in a fetal position."

"You think Matheson might've owned two pens exactly alike? We could check the most exclusive writing and stationery stores."

"You really want to know what I think?" He stood up and walked to a duplicate poster display of the Cooper crime scene. "I think Matheson created an elaborate trap and we fell right into it. He never lost that pen. He knew all along there'd come a time when he'd need to use it."

"Whoa, slow down, Mr. Prosecutor." She put an extra sugar in her coffee. "That's a bit too far-fetched even for the most avid conspiracy theorist."

He approached her and pleaded his case. "He made sure Officer Macon was the one who originally noticed the pen; then he filed a lost-and-found report without ever checking with him."

"So?"

He sat down next to her. "He volunteered to have the

police take a sample of his blood under the pretense it might help them capture his assailants."

"Why would he give the police incriminating evidence and put himself in jeopardy?"

"Not himself. Us. He counted on a jury having no faith in the justice system, and with good reason. This whole trial is taking place because the courts failed to punish the man Matheson's accused of murdering. That message isn't lost on those jurors."

"You think he planned the perfect crime that far in advance?"

"Not the perfect crime, the perfect cover. He wanted to be caught. He just didn't want to be convicted."

"No one's that diabolical, James."

"Look, I know you think it's far-fetched, but the man selected a small shoe store isolated in some remote town. He ordered the largest pair of boots available, paid cash, then argued with the only person in the store, who just happened to be a known racist with a public record of discrimination complaints." Reynolds studied Sinclair's face and could tell she was at least considering his theory. "You believe there's any way Matheson would patronize that shop unless he intended to set us all up?"

"The store owner has a motive to lie. Miller demonstrated that."

"You believe Gelon wasn't telling the truth?"

"The guy's a bigot. Maybe he wanted his ten minutes of fame and some free advertising," she said without conviction.

"That guy didn't drive all the way down here and make up some story about selling shoes to Matheson, and you know that."

"Maybe I do," admitted Sinclair. "But I'm not sitting

on the jury." She stepped away from Reynolds. "It just strikes me as too bizarre. I mean, why would Matheson volunteer the blood samples?"

"He assumed they'd find his blood at the murder scene."

"In a burned-out barn? My God, James, will you listen to yourself? I know you're frustrated—we all are. But you're imagining a sinister master plot behind everything that's happened. Murdering old men is bad enough, but not even the devil could be that cunning or evil."

"I'm telling you, Lauren, he's played us like a violin, and the concert isn't over yet. Matheson deliberately left behind enough evidence to get himself arrested, knowing full well he'd undermine its credibility. The man developed a scheme to destroy our case before we ever put it together."

"If half of what you're saying is true, then Melvin was right not to indict on any other counts of murder. If he gets off on this charge, we've got six more bites at the apple."

"If he's acquitted on this one, we'll never make another murder charge stick."

"Then he's won," Sinclair said in resignation.

"Not yet," advised Reynolds. "There are still some people whose testimony Matheson may not be able to tarnish."

"I thought we were through with our witness list."

"I'm working on a long shot."

She watched him walk to the end of the conference table, where he grabbed his coat and retrieved a small phone book.

CHAPTER
49

REYNOLDS DROVE THROUGH an impoverished area of Natchez, unable to pass the slow-moving garbage truck that left behind more trash than it removed. Though only a few miles from his mother's place, this neighborhood could have been dropped from another planet. Homes were little more than tar-paper shacks. Unsafe porches teetered on decayed wood. Torn and frayed welcome mats prepared visitors for greater disrepair once inside. Front and side yards were dumping grounds for broken-down cars, secondhand parts, makeshift furniture, and worthless appliances. Reynolds discovered an occasional garden or vegetable patch overshadowed by piles of discarded plastic junk and scrap metal.

The garbage truck made a tight turn and rolled over a child's bicycle. As it went around a narrow corner, it struck the edge of the curb and bounced hard, scattering additional litter across the road. Reynolds searched for street addresses, but many of the numbers were missing.

He relied on bent and dented mailboxes to help navigate him through unfamiliar terrain. His car slowed down and pulled in front of a large house. He couldn't tell whether the scaffolds surrounding the home represented renovation or decay. Either way, they seemed insufficient for the repair of a structure so damaged by time and neglect.

Reynolds exited his car and took along his briefcase. He observed two young black girls on the front lawn. The older one, around nine, jumped rope. The other, probably her younger sister by two years, mimicked her. When Reynolds approached, they stopped playing and stared at the well-dressed black man.

"Frank Edwards live here?" he asked.

They looked at each other and giggled. Reynolds heard the sound of wood being chopped. The older girl threw her rope to the ground and raced her sister to the rear of the house. Reynolds picked up the jump rope and followed them.

Frank Edwards handled his ax with efficiency. Chips of wood flew with every swing. His deceptively thin body masked a strength forged by hard work and a lifetime of fighting poverty and disappointment. He brought the ax blade down with extra force and cut a chunk of wood in two. He studied Reynolds for a moment, then swung the ax again, driving it into the top piece of a woodpile. He wiped the perspiration from his forehead with his shirtsleeve, and his eyelids closed halfway. "Let's go inside."

Reynolds gave the jump rope to the youngest girl, who used it to tease her sister.

The two men entered the kitchen through a side door. Several punctures and large rips had rendered the screen useless, inviting mosquitoes and other flying insects to enter and exit at will. The temperature felt ten degrees hotter than outside, and the kitchen smelled of ammonia and roach spray. Edwards took a glass from a rubber dish holder near the sink and turned on the faucet. He ran water over the outside of the glass, wiped it clean with a towel, and filled it with water.

"I been readin' 'bout the case." Edwards handed the glass to Reynolds. "Don't know how you could try and put that man away. You bein' black and all."

Reynolds drank the water and found it surprisingly cold and refreshing. "How much do you remember about your father?"

"I remember the hole he left. That professor, he filled some of it. Not all. Just a tiny piece."

Reynolds finished the drink and handed the glass to Edwards, who issued his statement without any anger. "I ain't gonna do nothin' to help you, if that's why you came by."

Reynolds placed his briefcase on the kitchen counter and opened it. He removed the photo of the lynching and handed it to Edwards, who held it at a distance, then slowly brought it closer to his body. He swallowed hard, and his eyes filled with tears.

"I thought you should have that," Reynolds said respectfully.

Edwards looked through the screen door and saw his two daughters fighting to use the jump rope. He gazed at the photo. "I used to go there," he said softly. "Stare at the place. The tree. Sometimes, I'd see him. Hangin'. Swayin'. Mouth open. Like he wanted to say somethin'." He peered at Reynolds. "I never thought he'd look this bad." He returned the photo to the briefcase and snapped it shut.

"I think I knew your father," Reynolds said. "When I was young, I remember seeing him."

Edwards took Reynolds's glass and moved to the sink. "They accused him of hurtin' children. Doin' sick things to little girls." He rinsed the glass and placed it upside down on a brown mat. He turned to face his visitor. "My daddy never did nothin' but make 'em laugh."

He stood by the door and watched his children take turns with the rope. "He'd always have 'em over the house. Tellin' 'em stories. Holdin' 'em on his knee. My mama told him not to touch the white ones, to just let 'em play by themselves. He'd get angry and say all God's children got a right to be hugged." Edwards approached Reynolds, and they stood face to face. "What you really come here for?"

After he heard the answer, Edwards loaded his daughters into his pickup truck, and Reynolds followed them for less than ten miles on Highway 61. They exited at Stanton and proceeded to Natchez State Park. The trip took about twenty minutes. Edwards passed the main entrance and drove the length of two and a half football fields before pulling into a small rest area. Reynolds parked his car alongside the truck and exited his vehicle first.

Edwards stepped out of the truck and pointed toward a clearing between some thick bushes. "There's a narrow trail that leads to a larger openin'. It's about a quarter mile past the first cabin you see, maybe a little more." He nervously rubbed the side of his face.

Reynolds had climbed out of the truck and stood in front of it. He didn't want to put the man through any more suffering. "I appreciate your help. I'm sure I can—"

"I'll walk with you partway," offered Edwards. "Show you how to get there. Won't go no further than that."

Reynolds nodded in gratitude.

Edwards told his girls to stay inside the truck until he returned. He headed toward the opening and pushed back some branches, then made his way to the path.

Reynolds moved to the truck's passenger side, reached inside his pocket, and removed some money. He handed it to the oldest daughter. "You wait till you get back home. Then give that to your daddy. Okay?"

The older girl thought about it while the younger negotiated a deal. "Can we tell him you said to buy us somethin' with it?" Her sister nodded to second the motion.

Reynolds noticed the younger girl was holding a white doll with bright blue plastic eyes and golden yellow hair. "Then you can get a brand-new doll to replace that one," he suggested.

The little child looked at her older sister, who shared her bewilderment, then focused her confusion on Reynolds. "Why would I do somethin' stupid like that?" she asked, exasperated.

Reynolds smiled sadly and signaled his agreement. He rushed to join Edwards as the girls did their best to divide the money.

CHAPTER
50

THE COURTROOM FILLED to capacity earlier than usual. Anticipating the inevitable, reporters had already written their stories about the state's resting its case. The buzz all morning dealt with whether Miller would bother to put on a defense, let alone call Matheson to testify in his own behalf.

The bailiff brought the room to order, and Tanner entered from his chambers. The judge instructed the jury to be seated, and noted for the record that all the participants were present. The jury appeared in a jovial mood. The men, as planned, wore blue shirts, and the women displayed something red. Mrs. Whitney wrapped a rose scarf around her shoulders. Vernetta chose to wear a red jacket. Blaze squeezed into a tight two-piece outfit that made her particularly popular with Faraday Patterson and Jefferson Lynch.

The judge paid the group a compliment and indicated they'd made good choices. He noted that one jury several months ago had decided to wear all black, which "scared the bejesus outta the poor defendant and didn't make me feel my usually bubbly self." After a minute or two of pleasant bantering, he got serious and invited Reynolds to continue with the state's case.

Reynolds walked slowly to the podium and faced the judge. "The state calls April Reeves," he announced in a clear voice, surprising many in the court who'd expected this phase of the trial to conclude.

Upon hearing the name, Matheson seemed to turn stone cold. The rear door opened, and a dignified black woman in her early sixties entered. She proceeded down the aisle of a hushed courtroom. All eyes remained focused on her as she approached the witness stand and raised her right hand.

"Do you swear to tell the truth, the whole truth, and nothing but the truth, so help you God?" asked the clerk of the court.

"I do," she replied confidently.

"State your full name for the record."

"April Patricia Reeves."

"You may be seated," Tanner said politely. "Counselor, please proceed with your witness."

"Thank you, Your Honor," Reynolds said, shuffling through some papers. After a few moments he closed his file and took several steps away from the podium and toward the witness stand. He positioned himself an equal distance from the jury and Mrs. Reeves in an effort to partially block Matheson's view.

"Mrs. Reeves, where do you currently reside?"

"Atlanta, Georgia. I've lived there for almost twenty years."

"Do you know the defendant?"

"I certainly do."

"And what's the nature of your relationship?"

"He's my son," she declared proudly.

Excited murmuring occurred throughout the courtroom. Tanner banged his gavel once and immediately restored order. "Unless you're giving testimony or serving as counsel in this trial," he chastised those seated in the chambers, "I strongly recommend everybody remain quiet." He made himself more comfortable. "Mr. Reynolds, please continue."

"Is there a reason why you have a different last name from your son's?"

"Martin's father and I were divorced more than thirty years ago. I remarried."

"Mrs. Reeves, could you tell us the reason your marriage ended?"

Miller rose and almost knocked over the pitcher of water on the defense table. "Your Honor, this isn't divorce court."

"Is that an objection to the question, Counselor?" Tanner asked.

"Yes, Your Honor, on the grounds of relevance."

Tanner released a frustrated sigh and directed his remarks to a patient Reynolds. "Where are you going with this?"

"Your Honor, it's important that the state be allowed to pursue this line of inquiry to establish a basis for Professor Matheson's racial animus." Reynolds spoke calmly and with a sense of assurance. He hoped his tone would conceal his true feelings of insecurity and dread.

Tanner thought about it for a moment and scribbled a note. "I'll allow it for now," he said reluctantly. "But I reserve the right to reverse myself. The witness may answer. The court reporter will read back the question."

The reporter reviewed her notes. " 'Mrs. Reeves, could you tell us the reason your marriage ended?' " She appeared as interested in hearing the answer as everyone else in the room.

Reeves moved slightly forward and addressed the jury. "I had and continue to have great respect and affection for my ex-husband. But he was consumed with his work." She glanced at the Reverend Matheson, who had his head bowed.

"As a civil rights activist?" Reynolds inquired.

"Yes. I wanted to be supportive, but he insisted on exposing Martin to violent demonstrations. It led to many conflicts between us."

"At what age was your son first exposed to these violent demonstrations?"

"He was a baby, no older than five. Samuel felt the Movement needed children."

"By Samuel, are you referring to your ex-husband, the Reverend Matheson?"

"Yes."

"You indicated the Reverend needed children for the Movement. What role were they to play?"

"Martin's father was certain that if the world saw the hate directed toward innocent children, including our son, that such violent encounters would change public opinion."

"You disagreed?"

"I was a mother, not a strategist."

Reynolds glanced at the jury and noticed Mrs. Whitney nodding in approval. "How did your son's participation in the Civil Rights Movement at such an early age affect him?"

Miller once again rose, except this time he held the pitcher of water. "Your Honor, I object. Mrs. Reeves is not an expert in psychology."

"You've obviously never been a mother," replied Tanner, which elicited some laughter from the jury and court observers. "Overruled. The witness may answer."

"At first our son was very proud and excited. He felt he was participating in a great cause. And he was." She succeeded in making eye contact with Matheson and smiled warmly. He gave her a reassuring nod.

"Did his feelings ever change?" Reynolds continued.

"It was after he'd been called . . ." She hesitated. "A racial slur," she said uncomfortably. "I believe it may have been the first time he ever heard that word. At least, directed at him with such force."

"How old was your son at the time?"

"Five or six. A truck driver had yelled at him. The man was quite huge, with massive arms and a powerful build. It was hard to imagine someone that size screaming at a child so young, and with such fury."

Reynolds moved closer to the jury and allowed Reeves to have an unobstructed view of Matheson. "What did your son do? How did he react?"

"He was too frightened to do anything. But late that night I heard him crying in his room." She suddenly became uneasy, her voice more emotional.

"Would you like to take a moment and drink some water, Mrs. Reeves?"

"Thank you." She poured a glass of water and took several sips, then removed a tissue from her purse.

"I just have a few more questions, Mrs. Reeves. And then I'll stop, okay?"

She nodded gratefully.

"You mentioned you heard your son crying in his room the night of the incident. What happened next?"

"I went to him. And held him. And tried to convince him everything would be all right."

"Was he convinced?"

She shook her head. "He made me promise I wouldn't tell his father that he'd cried." She again looked at her ex-husband, who still avoided her. "He didn't want to disappoint him."

Reynolds walked past Matheson and stared at him for a moment, but the defendant didn't return the look. "Did he say anything else?"

"He wanted to know what he'd done to cause grown men to hate him so much."

Reynolds studied the jury. Some of the women were wiping away tears. Men looked at the floor. He glanced at Matheson, who stared at his mother with a son's concern.

"Did your son ask you any more questions?"

She looked at the Reverend Matheson, who now stared at her with interest. She shifted her attention to Reynolds. "He wanted to know why his father hadn't come to his defense, to protect him from that kind of evil."

Reynolds spotted Miller listening intently. "How did you respond?"

"I tried to find a way to explain it to him, but before I could begin, he started crying again. His body shook with pain and humiliation. I just held him and tried to comfort him."

"Did you tell your husband?"

"I pleaded with him not to take Martin to any more demonstrations." She faced the jury. "Maybe I was wrong. Selfish. But I didn't want my son scarred by racial hatred. I didn't want him to be the target of that animosity, ever again."

"No further questions." Reynolds moved to the prosecutor's table and sat next to Sinclair, who'd used up her second tissue.

The courtroom remained silent until Tanner interrupted. "Mr. Miller?"

Miller stood and took a few careful steps toward Mrs. Reeves. He looked at her sympathetically. "Mrs. Reeves, you love your son, do you not?"

"Very much."

"Know him the way only a mother could?"

"I believe I do."

Miller vacillated for a moment, then asked his question. "Is your son capable of the kind of hate necessary to commit the crime of which he is accused?"

Reynolds stood. "Calls for speculation."

"I'll allow it," Tanner ruled. "Answer the question, Mrs. Reeves."

She looked at Matheson, then turned directly to the jury. "The son I held in my arms, the son who cried himself to sleep while I told him I loved him, that son, my son, is not capable of that hate." She turned back to Miller.

"Thank you, Mrs. Reeves." Miller joined Matheson and sat down. "I have no further questions."

Reynolds stood before Tanner could address him. "Your Honor, just a few additional questions."

"Proceed."

"Mrs. Reeves, you're here as a result of being served a subpoena, isn't that true?"

"That's correct."

"You don't want to say anything that is damaging to your son, is that safe to assume?"

"I'm here to tell the truth as I swore to do." She looked at Matheson for a moment, then addressed Reynolds. "I can't imagine the truth being harmful to my son."

"Mrs. Reeves, just moments ago you told this jury you were trying to protect your son from the harsh realities of racism and bigotry and violence."

"He was a child then."

"And yet the ugly truth hurt him and eventually also destroyed your marriage. So it seems the truth can be harmful to everyone, even two loving adults." He watched her bow her head and didn't want to push any further, but had to. "Wouldn't you agree?"

She raised her head and answered, "Regretfully, I would."

Reynolds sought the safety of the podium and stood behind it. "Mrs. Reeves, you testified you didn't want your son scarred by racial hatred. Do you believe your son—not the child but the man, the defendant in this courtroom today—do you believe he's been scarred by that hatred?"

She folded her hands together and sat erect. "Mr. Reynolds, I believe everyone has been scarred by that hatred. The ones who have been scarred the most may not even be aware of it." She looked at her ex-husband, who stared at his son.

"Thank you, Mrs. Reeves," Reynolds said sincerely. "I have no further questions, Your Honor."

"Mr. Miller?" inquired Tanner.

"I'll spare Mrs. Reeves any more testimony," answered Miller.

The judge dismissed the witness and called for a lunch recess. The jury lingered behind, leaving their box as slowly as possible. Reynolds knew they were waiting for the obvious reunion. He'd hoped this would happen outside their presence, but why should his luck change anytime soon?

Mrs. Reeves proceeded directly to the defense table and shook hands with Miller, then embraced her son for a long time. The two guards stood by respectfully and watched the emotional embrace. After a moment, the Reverend Matheson joined them. He hugged his ex-wife just as the last two jurors left the room. The Matheson family joined hands with Miller, bowed their heads, and prayed, led by the Reverend Matheson.

After the recess, the state rested its case, and Miller asked for an adjournment so that he might consult with his client and advise the court in the morning whether the defense would also rest. Tanner granted the request and dismissed the jury for the rest of the day.

Miller met with Matheson in the court's holding room. "I'm going to ask for a directed verdict," he informed the professor. "It's pretty standard fare, but I think we might have a chance, even with this judge."

"I don't want to take that risk," advised Matheson.

"What risk?"

"That he might rule favorably on your motion," answered Matheson.

"Excuse me," said Miller, looking bewildered, "but isn't that why we went to trial . . . to win?"

"I don't want a victory based on an edict from a judge who feels the state hasn't reached some imaginary threshold," responded Matheson. "I want you to put on a defense."

"We don't *need* a defense," Miller said. "The state hasn't proven anything. The longer the trial goes on, the more time they have to discover additional evidence or locate a new witness or . . ."

"They can't find what doesn't exist," Matheson said sharply. "We follow the plan. It's served us well thus far."

"Martin, you're making a mistake in prolonging this trial. Either the judge rules in our favor, or we rest and the jury hands you an acquittal. Either way, you walk out of here a free man."

"I'm disappointed in you, Mr. Miller. As a fighter for civil rights you surely must know that freedom is never given; it has to be taken. I intend to do that." Matheson stood and patted Miller on the shoulder. "We keep the trial going until I've told my side of this story."

"I'll put on our defense, but I don't want to hear anything about you taking the stand," warned Miller.

Matheson smiled. "We'll cross that bridge when we get to it," he said with a glimmer in his eyes. He waved the guards into the room and stood motionless as they secured chains around his hands and ankles.

Late that night, Reynolds stood in front of the kitchen cabinet and stared at the door he wanted to open. He turned away and rested against the refrigerator. Cheryl entered the room and watched him for a moment.

"Anything you need me to do?" she asked.

He studied her, then shifted his gaze to the floor. "Would you have allowed Angela or Christopher to demonstrate during the Civil Rights Movement?" He walked toward her. "I mean, if this were forty years ago, and they were needed for a protest to desegregate a school or a lunch counter or a bus"—he made eye contact with her—"and there'd be the possibility of violence, even death, would you have let them participate?"

She considered the question and shrugged her shoulders. "Actually, I had in mind making you some coffee or a sandwich. If I knew this was gonna be one of those children-in-the-lifeboat questions, I might not have volunteered." She smiled, but he didn't.

"I wouldn't have allowed it," he answered. "Not to face those angry crowds and the taunts and the threats. No way would I have exposed them to that hate."

"They wouldn't have had a choice," she replied. "Back then, kids were in the struggle whether they wanted to be or not. I don't think I could've denied them the right to confront cowardice with courage and hate with love." She leaned back and released a deep breath. "But I would've been on the rooftop with a rifle, just in case they needed their mommy."

He smiled weakly, then sighed. "I need their mommy now."

"Is that a protest or a demonstration?"

"Depends if I have to overcome or just come over," he answered teasingly.

She extended her index finger and beckoned him. He turned out the light and took her by the hand, and together they marched out of the room.

CHAPTER
51

SOMETIME AFTER SIX on the morning of April 4, the day that marked the assassination of his friend Dr. Martin Luther King Jr., the Reverend Matheson saw his church, which he'd built with his own hands, burn to the ground. Three hours later, he stood outside and stared at the structure ravaged by flames. The fire department had done all they could. A bomb had ripped off the church's rear doors, and fire spread quickly throughout the main chapel. A second bomb, planted near the side of the building, had created a gaping hole in the ceiling and exploded the stained-glass window containing the image of Jesus reaching toward the heavens.

Cars parked near the church were destroyed or severely damaged by the blast. The hood of one car folded in two. An avalanche of bricks and concrete flowed into walkways that once provided access to the children's Sunday school service. Water flooded the area and caused narrow streams to carry away tiny pieces of the church along with uprooted earth and ash.

Police were on the scene interviewing neighbors and searching for clues. Reynolds drove his car as close to the area as possible. He turned off the engine and exited his vehicle, then headed directly to his former pastor. The Reverend Matheson stared at the rubble of the home he'd spent a lifetime safeguarding for God. He stood on a street cracked and shattered by the force of the explosion.

"Whoever did this, I promise you we'll find them," Reynolds said with determination.

"Like this country's found all the others?" replied the Reverend Matheson softly. He placed his unsteady hand on Reynolds's arm. "I baptized your wife in this church . . ."

Reynolds provided support to keep the Reverend Matheson on his feet. "You can build it again. All of us will help."

". . . and both your children." The Reverend Matheson looked at Reynolds. "I've never done anything to hurt you. Why are you trying to destroy my son?"

"You may not believe he's a murderer, but in your heart you know he's responsible."

"The people responsible are the ones who committed those murders over thirty years ago. The ones who encouraged them or looked away—judges, juries, politicians, sheriffs, businessmen, housewives." He looked at his church in ruins. "The arsonists and bombers who hid in the shadows of indifference and cowardice." His eyes filled with tears. "The same ones who today are outraged and appalled never offered a single word of protest when it would have mattered. When it could've made a difference. Don't blame my son for a world he didn't create. He only called attention to it."

The Reverend Matheson's knees buckled. Reynolds held on to him and motioned for one of the officers to provide help. The proud preacher stepped back and refused assistance.

"I've stood on my own two feet and fought battles more difficult than this. If I have to lean on anything, it'll be my faith in God." He stood more erect and steady. "He's brought me this far, and no bomb or racist or false prosecution of my son will force me to turn away from what I believe to be right." He looked in the direction of the destruction. "Now, you go on and do what you have to do. This is still the Lord's house, and I want to pay tribute to Him."

Reynolds walked away but stopped when he heard his name called.

"James," the Reverend Matheson said firmly, "I will keep you and your family in my prayers."

Reynolds nodded his head in appreciation. "And you shall remain in mine," he said affectionately, then walked away without ever looking back at the fallen church or its weary pastor.

CHAPTER
52

VANZANT HELD THE photo of the lynching of Frank Edwards's father. "It was thirty-five years ago," he said, frustrated.

"It was murder," answered an unwavering Reynolds.

"You've already got a case; worry about that one." Vanzant tried to return the photo to Reynolds, who refused to take it.

"I want Beauford arrested," Reynolds said firmly.

"For getting his picture taken?" Vanzant argued. "For being there? There's no proof he was involved."

"Let a grand jury decide that. If he didn't do it, he knows who did," pushed Reynolds.

"And what if he claims he can't remember or says the persons responsible are dead? What do you want us to do then?" Vanzant paced in front of his desk. "For Christ's sake, James, the police have murders that happened this morning and they don't have enough resources to investigate those adequately. Now you want me to add this to their workload?" He held out the photo.

"Just look into it. That's all I'm asking," requested Reynolds.

The two men stared at each other for several moments, and Vanzant finally relented. He placed the photo on top of his In box. "I'll call the sheriff myself, but I'm not makin' any promises."

Reynolds let out a sigh of relief. "I appreciate it."

"I guess I owe you one after Gelon," admitted Vanzant.

Reynolds smiled. "If you ever want a good pair of boots, he gave me a discount card."

Vanzant laughed. It was the closest the two had been in quite some time. "Who's Miller gonna call as his first witness?"

"Trust me," said Reynolds, massaging his temple to release stress. "You really don't want to know."

Vanzant sank into his seat and stared at the photo of the lynching. "You said the guy with the big smile was named Beauford?"

Reynolds nodded in agreement. "Gates Beauford. I wrote his address on the back."

Vanzant turned over the photo and wrote down the information on a slip of paper. He picked up the phone and dialed a number.

As his first witness Miller called Dr. Charles Hunter. "Dr. Hunter, what is your current employment?" Miller asked.

"I work for the Federal Bureau of Investigation."

"In what capacity?"

"I'm a behavioral assessment specialist, or what might

be commonly referred to as a profiler. I collect information on a variety of serious crimes and, based on my personal and professional experience, establish a personality profile of the type of criminal involved."

"And you had special training to do this?"

"The Bureau has extensive training programs in all facets of crime investigation. As you know, we're considered the foremost agency in the world when it comes to crime fighting." Hunter came across as extremely confident, bordering on arrogant, with the smugness made famous by FBI agents.

"In addition to your agency training do you have any other experience or education that qualifies you to perform your work?"

"I have a Ph.D. in psychology with a specialization in personality disorders. I also have a master's degree in criminal justice."

"And where did you obtain your degrees?"

"Princeton University."

"Princeton?" Miller asked. "Isn't that in . . ." He paused with a pained expression and spoke without any accent. "New Jersey?"

"Yes," answered Hunter with a trace of resentment.

"Were you unable to gain admittance into one of our fine southern universities?" asked Miller.

Reynolds rose to his feet but didn't have to formally object.

"I'll withdraw that comment," volunteered Miller.

"Let's not make a habit of having to do that," Tanner said sternly.

Reynolds knew Miller was attempting to get under Hunter's skin and feared he might be succeeding.

"Dr. Hunter, isn't it true you were assigned to assist

the state's office of the attorney general in investigating a series of murders associated with Professor Matheson's list?"

"Yes."

"And did you and your colleagues develop any profiles regarding the person or persons most likely to commit these murders?"

Hunter reviewed the types of people profiled and the reasons they were considered. He described the rationale behind targeting Caucasian activists or radicals. He admitted under grueling examination that he himself had identified several of Matheson's students as likely suspects, including Brandon Hamilton and Delbert Finney, who just happened to be the next two witnesses on Miller's list. After Hunter finished going over all the categories listed as meeting the personality profiles of the murderer, the only person who seemed to be excluded was the professor.

"So let me see if I understand you correctly," summarized Miller. "The type of person likely to commit these heinous acts, including the murder of Earvin Cooper, would fall into the category of (a) a leader who saw himself as a person of action, like a football hero, or (b) a complete loner, isolated from his community and wanting desperately to do something to curry favor, like a shy, quiet kid from a rural section of the state, or (c) a white person."

"That's not what I said, sir," Hunter protested.

"I can have your testimony read back to you if you like. But let's spare the members of the jury the time. I'm sure they can request those portions of the court transcript if they feel a need. Now, let me ask you one or two more questions." Miller opened a folder at the podium and made some notes. "In your substantial experience in these types of matters, have you ever come across a serial killer who liked to wear boots three sizes too large for his feet, and if so, what kind of personality would that suggest?"

Several of the jurors smiled, while others snickered.

Hunter placed his hand under his chin and responded with obvious annoyance. "It would suggest the personality of someone who wanted to conceal his role in the crime."

"Well, Dr. Hunter," Miller postured, "you don't need to have a Ph.D. from Princeton to know that if your goal is to conceal something you'd be better off wearin' smaller shoes, not big ol' giant ones."

Miller continued toying with Hunter until he'd gotten his wish. The profiler lost control of his temper, whereupon Miller asked the judge for permission to treat him as a "hostile witness," which Tanner approved. The designation allowed Miller to lead Hunter even more than he'd already managed to do. By the time Hunter left the stand, Miller had used one of the investigation's chief advisers and experts to undermine the state's theory of the case. He'd now set the stage for the students to march into the courtroom and show the jury the true psychological profile of their professor and the effect he had in shaping their personalities.

Reynolds asked for an early lunch break in a weak effort to delay the inevitable.

CHAPTER
53

H E MADE AN impressive witness even before he spoke his first word. Clad in a dark blue suit that fit perfectly around his broad shoulders, he walked to the witness stand with a dancer's grace. When he raised his hand to take the oath, he struck a young soldier's pose.

"Could you please state your full name for the record?" asked the court clerk.

"Brandon Edward Hamilton."

"The witness may be seated," said Tanner. He nodded toward the defense table. "I believe the court's ready for your direct, Mr. Miller."

"Thank you, Judge Tanner." Miller moved to the podium. "Mr. Hamilton . . ." Miller hesitated and took a small step to the side. "Do you mind if I call you Brandon?"

"Not at all, sir."

"You're a graduate student at the university where Professor Matheson teaches, is that correct?"

"Yes. He's my dissertation chairman as well as my mentor."

"You have a good relationship with Dr. Matheson?"

"I'd do anything for him. He's been like a father." He looked at Matheson, and both men smiled. "Maybe it would be better if I said older brother."

Matheson laughed, as did most in the courtroom.

"Yes, I think that might be a more prudent choice of words," Miller said. "Particularly since he still chairs your doctoral committee." Miller displayed a warm, friendly smile to the jury, then focused on Brandon. "How and when did you first become a student at the university?"

"I started five years ago as an undergraduate on a full football scholarship."

"Were you offered any other scholarships at the college?"

"Yes. In baseball, basketball, and track."

"And what about other universities? Did you have an opportunity to go to school elsewhere?"

"I received scholarship offers from numerous universities around the country. I believe they totaled well over a hundred."

"And were they all for your athletic ability?"

"Yes."

"Had you ever been offered a scholarship because of your academics?"

Brandon smiled slightly. "Not until I started applying for graduate school."

"I noticed you smiled at my question, but we'll get to that in a moment. Could you tell the jury when you first met Professor Matheson?"

"I registered for one of his courses at the beginning of my sophomore year."

"What was your major at that time?"

"Playing sports, primarily." He looked at the jurors with some embarrassment. "Technically, I majored in sports psychology, but I'd be hard-pressed to tell you what that consisted of."

"And why did you enroll in one of Dr. Matheson's classes?"

"He had a great reputation on campus, and to be quite honest, I thought taking a black studies course wouldn't be that demanding."

"Were you wrong?"

"I'd never worked that hard in all my life." Brandon's eyes closed halfway as he shook his head at the recollection.

Matheson laughed, and a number of the jurors chuckled.

"It was also the most eye-opening experience I'd ever had." Brandon looked at each member of the jury individually. "Professor Matheson's the type of teacher you dream about having but usually never do. I was fortunate to meet him when I did." He glanced at Matheson. "I think I'd be a very different person if he hadn't played a role in my life—one I probably wouldn't have liked too much."

"How did Dr. Matheson influence you?"

"I'd been thinking about leaving campus and turning pro. I had a great freshman year and set several collegiate records in multiple sports. A number of football and basketball scouts wanted me to quit school and make myself eligible for the draft."

"Did Professor Matheson talk you out of leaving?"

"Even if I needed to be persuaded, that wasn't Dr. Matheson's style. He believed students should make their own choices, but only after considering all the options and consequences." He looked at the journalists clustered in the first few rows. "He's the only teacher who ever treated me as if I had something of value to offer besides scoring touchdowns or dunking basketballs." He smiled at Mrs. Whitney. "Once I began to take academics seriously, I discovered how much I didn't know."

"And you wanted to learn more?"

"I wanted to learn everything. I realized I'd allowed myself to be exploited at the expense of my education. So I resigned from sports, took out several student loans, and selected a real major. I asked Dr. Matheson to be my adviser."

Miller leaned against the lectern and generally treated Brandon much more casually than he'd treated any other witness. "Did he agree?"

"On one condition. He told me I needed to display as much dedication to developing my mind as I'd devoted to excelling in sports."

"Were you able to accomplish that?"

"With his help and faith in me, I went on to win two international academic fellowships. When I got notified of the first award, it was the proudest moment I'd ever experienced. It surpassed any feeling I'd accomplished in sports." He paused for a moment and tried to contain his emotions.

The members of the jury were touched by Brandon's testimony. Vernetta Williams dabbed at her eye with a tissue; Cindy Lou Herrington, Harriet Dove, and Mrs. Whitney provided motherly smiles and encouragement while several of the men smiled in admiration.

"Brandon, were you ever in trouble with the law?" The nature of Miller's question startled the jury, but Reynolds knew the wily defense attorney had set up the next line of inquiry brilliantly. Now that he'd gotten the jury to care about the witness, he'd introduce the enemy and make them angry enough to take out their outrage on the prosecution.

"Yes, only once, and it occurred at the end of last year."

Miller finally walked away from the podium and proceeded closer to the jury. "Could you tell us the nature of your problem and what led to it?"

Brandon faced the jury. "I'd been active in leading protests or demonstrations against the men on Professor Matheson's list. I, along with another student, went to Earvin Cooper's home and placed a sign on his front lawn. We wanted to inform his neighbors of the type of man they lived next to. Before I was able to leave, Mr. Cooper and I got into a verbal confrontation. He wrote down my license plate number, so I knew there was a record of my visit. A day or two after the confrontation, Mr. Cooper was murdered."

Miller turned toward his client. "And now Professor Matheson stands accused of that murder."

"Yes."

"Initially, the police assumed you were responsible for the crime, isn't that true?"

"Objection, Your Honor," shouted Reynolds. "Assumes facts not in evidence. Mr. Hamilton was never charged with Mr. Cooper's murder, nor was that the reason for his subsequent arrest."

"Sustained," Tanner ruled. "The jury's instructed to disregard the question."

Miller paused and gave the jury sufficient time to think about the question Tanner had just told them to ignore. "Brandon, why were you arrested?"

"I did something pretty stupid, but at the time it seemed a good idea."

"Isn't that always the case?" Miller studied the jury, but they gave no indication of their feelings. They waited patiently for an explanation.

"Could you tell the jury what you did to cause the police to arrest you?"

"As I said, Mr. Cooper died shortly after our argument. I'd just finished classes and was about to take Thanksgiving break. As I walked to my car in the student parking lot, I noticed two police cars searching the area." He made eye contact with Mrs. Whitney, then shifted to the young, attractive juror who sat next to her. "They stopped and one of the officers pointed at me. Both cars then turned around quickly and headed in my direction. I panicked, got in my car, and tried to get away. They pursued me for a mile or so before I crashed into a hydrant or a signpost. They may have rammed their cars into mine; it happened so fast I wasn't clear on the exact sequence."

"Why did you try to get away from the police?"

"Mr. Miller, as I told you, I simply panicked. I knew from reading the papers and listening to the media there was a lot of pressure to find someone responsible for killing the people on the professor's list. When I saw police heading for me, driving the wrong way down a one-way street and cutting across the lot, I assumed they were pretty hyped and angry. I thought it best to get out of there."

"Did you fear for your safety?"

"I don't know any black man who doesn't fear the police."

Reynolds started to object but knew challenging Brandon's assertion wouldn't go over too well with this jury.

"Brandon, you're obviously a very powerfully built man—a star athlete—and yet you're telling this jury you feared for your safety?"

"It's precisely because of how I look that police feel threatened. Their anxiety about my size and strength places me at particular risk."

"And you've felt this way about police for how long?"

"Since as long as I can remember."

"Did your belief about how the police respond to black men contribute to your behavior on the afternoon in question?"

"The only reason I did what I did was because of those beliefs. I had every intention of reporting to the police, but I planned to do so in a more controlled environment, in the presence of either my parents or legal counsel. As it turned out, I made a foolish mistake that led to a dangerous pursuit. I could've very easily been killed or wound up seriously hurting someone else."

"What happened to you at the end of the police chase?"

"My head struck the windshield or the steering wheel, I'm not sure which. I remember the police screaming at me to put my hands over my head."

"Did you obey their commands?"

"Yes."

"What transpired next?"

Reynolds stood and sought Tanner's attention. "Your Honor, I have to object."

"What grounds?" asked Tanner.

"Relevance. Mr. Hamilton's arrest has nothing to do with these proceedings."

"Mr. Miller, you care to respond?" Tanner's body language appeared to signal support for the objection, although with the judge's girth and his propensity for ruling in favor of the state, it was hard to tell.

"Your Honor, first, the state just moments ago objected to my question suggesting Mr. Hamilton was arrested for murder. But the evidence will show the police acted in a fashion consistent with pursuing and capturing a felony suspect. Second, I intend to establish the nature of the relationship between the witness and Professor Matheson after Mr. Hamilton's arrest, which further reflects my client's true character."

"I'll overrule the objection for now, but I expect you to conclude this portion of the testimony within the next two minutes."

"Your Honor, I expect to be finished with this witness within that time frame."

"Mr. Miller, please restate your question to the witness."

"Thank you, Your Honor. Brandon, could you tell the jury what occurred to you after the car chase ended?"

"I was removed from the front seat of the vehicle, tossed on the ground, and cuffed. A few officers hit or kicked me several times in the back and kidney area. My face was pushed into some broken glass and steaming hot water that leaked from my car's radiator. I tried to lift my head to avoid it."

"Were you successful?"

"For about a second; then I was struck by a police baton. That's all I remember until I woke up in custody."

Miller paused again. Reynolds knew he wanted the jury to envision the assault and picture Brandon lying helplessly on the ground, surrounded by vicious police beating him half to death.

"Were you ever charged with any criminal violations, and if so, what sanctions were imposed?"

"I pled no contest to several traffic violations and had my automobile license suspended for a year. I also agreed to pay restitution for any property damage caused as a result of the police pursuit. In return, charges of resisting arrest and fleeing the police were dropped, and I was placed on three years' probation."

"How long were you in jail?"

"Three of the longest weeks of my life. I'd probably still be there if it weren't for the professor."

"What did Dr. Matheson do to assist in your release?"

"He posted bail and also retained you as my legal counsel."

"Did I do a good job?"

"I hope you do as well for the professor."

"That last comment will be stricken from the record," ordered Tanner. "The witness is reminded he's here to provide answers to the questions posed, not to editorialize or offer his personal best wishes."

"I'm sorry, Your Honor," apologized Brandon.

"I have only a few remaining questions," interjected Miller. "Did Dr. Matheson ever suggest that the men on his list should be murdered?"

"No."

"To your knowledge, did he ever advocate violence against any person on that list?"

"I attended virtually every class he taught on the subject, and I never heard him advocate violence, not once."

"Brandon, were you aware that Professor Matheson mortgaged his home to provide bail for you?"

The question affected Brandon. He lowered his head for a moment and regained his composure. He looked at Matheson. "No," Brandon said softly. "No, I wasn't aware of that, but it shouldn't have surprised me."

"No further questions, Your Honor." Miller sat down and quickly glanced at the jury. Every single juror had his or her attention exactly where Miller wanted it: on his client.

"Mr. Reynolds, your witness," said Tanner.

Reynolds stood but remained at the prosecution table. "Good morning, Mr. Hamilton," he said in a friendly voice.

"Good morning," replied Brandon.

"You have a great deal of admiration and affection for the defendant."

"Yes, sir. I do."

"But, no matter how much you admire or respect or even love an individual, you can never know with absolute certainty whether or not that person committed a crime. Wouldn't you agree?"

"I suppose I would."

"And as you sit here today, you have no way of knowing if the defendant committed this or any other crime, isn't that true?"

"I believe I know the type of person Professor Matheson is, and what he'd do or wouldn't do."

"Really?" Reynolds looked at the jury for a moment. "Did you know yourself well enough to predict you'd ever lead the police on a high-speed pursuit causing thousands of dollars in property damage and endangering the lives of innocent people?"

Brandon lowered his head. "No. I never saw myself as that type of person."

"Did Professor Matheson ever comment about what happened to Earvin Cooper or any other murder victim on his list?"

"No."

"Did he ever express concern or regret that Mr. Cooper was murdered?"

"No."

"Did he ever tell you or students in any of his classes he didn't condone murdering people on his list, and that such activity was wrong and should be discouraged?"

"We discussed why each person was on the list. Once we finished reviewing that, they were never mentioned in class again."

"Were you ever told what to do to Mr. Cooper or others on the list?"

"We wanted to make their lives miserable, but Professor Matheson never had to tell us that. It was something we understood."

"Did you understand Mr. Cooper was supposed to be killed?"

Miller started to rise, but Matheson signaled not to.

"No," answered Brandon. "That was never stated nor implied."

"I have no further questions of this witness." Reynolds walked to the prosecutor's table and sat next to Sinclair.

"Mr. Miller?" asked Tanner. "Do you have any redirect?"

"No, Your Honor."

"Mr. Hamilton, you may step down," Tanner informed the witness.

Brandon left the courtroom with the same grace with which he'd entered, maybe more.

"Mr. Miller, are you ready to call your next witness?" asked Tanner.

Miller stood. "The defense calls Delbert Finney."

Reynolds watched Delbert amble to the witness stand. He wore a pair of baggy pants and a plaid flannel shirt. His quiet nervousness contrasted well with Brandon's confidence. He spoke with a slow country drawl as charming as it was believable. He told the jury about his family and that he'd been the first one to go to college. He described his small town, where everyone knew and trusted each other but pretty much kept to themselves. His eyes brightened and he spoke with more energy when he discussed visiting Dr. Matheson's home, and he choked up when he revealed the books the professor had given him.

"It wasn't a holiday or my birthday or nothin' like that. He just out-and-out gave them to me." He smiled proudly and informed everyone in the court that the volume of poetry "had a genuine soft brown leather cover, and the pages were bound or stamped in gold. I'm not sure of the term, but I can tell you it was the prettiest book I'd ever seen."

Reynolds waited for Tom Sawyer to show up and talk about the professor helping him to paint his fence. He studied the jury and knew they loved this kid, and when Tanner finally asked him if he had any cross, he stood and smiled. "No, Your Honor. But I'd sure like to borrow that volume of poetry from Delbert one day."

The witness grinned, the jury laughed, and Tanner announced a twenty-minute recess.

CHAPTER
54

MILLER ENDED THE day with a witness who combined the best attributes of Brandon and Delbert and had the advantage of immediately being embraced by all the jurors for her beauty and elegance.

"The defense calls Regina Davis," Miller announced proudly.

She wore a conservative dark brown outfit, and as she passed the jurors, she flashed a smile that melted their hearts. She raised her right hand, and Reynolds thought the Statue of Liberty couldn't have made a better impression.

"Ms. Davis, is it all right if I call you by your first name?"

"I would prefer that."

"Thank you. Regina, how long have you known Professor Matheson?"

"Almost five years. Dr. Matheson was the reason I minored in African-American history. I took eight or nine of his courses before my junior year and became his teaching assistant as a senior. When I enrolled in graduate school, I maintained the position."

"Regina, could you evaluate the teaching style or effectiveness of Professor Matheson, particularly as he impacted or influenced his students?"

"He gave us a sense of pride and self-respect. We became more confident because of him, believed more in ourselves and each other." She turned and faced the jury. "I used to have problems looking at people. Making direct eye contact. A lot of the students did. He used to tell us if you can't look at a person eye to eye, you can't face yourself."

"What else did he tell you?"

"That we didn't realize how beautiful we were. But by the end of his class, we'd know."

"Did he ever teach you to hate white people?"

"No."

"Did he ever advocate violence against white people?"

"No."

"When he showed you photos of black victims, did he ever once tell you to seek revenge?"

"No. Never."

"Thank you, Regina." Miller walked to his seat and glanced confidently at Reynolds.

"Mr. Reynolds," barked Tanner. "You have the floor."

"Miss Davis, why did Professor Matheson give his students the names and addresses of those suspected of murdering black people during the Civil Rights Movement?"

"He didn't want us to buy groceries from them."

"He didn't want you to buy groceries?" he asked curiously.

"He used to tell us the Jews traveled all over the world to bring justice to those who murdered their people, but that we were expected to buy groceries from those who murdered our fathers and brothers. He thought that wasn't an honorable use of our time."

The rest of the questioning didn't go any better. Regina remained poised and self-assured without coming across as snobbish or defiant. Reynolds knew these students were painting a portrait of their professor that would be nearly impossible to alter for the jury. Three very different young adults had provided a magnificent representation of the man who'd taught and inspired them. He would have had an easier time convincing twelve nuns to find Mother Teresa guilty of war crimes.

Reynolds ended his cross-examination of Regina, and Tanner promptly adjourned the court for the day. Tomorrow everyone would learn whether Matheson intended to take the stand and testify in his own behalf. Reynolds never doubted he would, which caused him both to desire and dread the upcoming morning.

After Regina's testimony Miller met with his client in the small holding cell in the basement of the courthouse. He once again tried to dissuade him from taking the stand, but to no avail. "The state's proven nothing, and you've got absolutely no reason to take the stand," he pleaded.

Matheson responded calmly. "When a defendant doesn't testify in his own defense, it raises suspicions regarding his innocence."

"The jury is specifically instructed to ignore any such inference."

"I'm not talking about a jury of twelve." Matheson became testier. "I'm concerned about the public. If I don't take the stand, they'll wonder what I have to hide. If I was truly innocent, there'd be no reason for me not to testify."

Miller sat in the chair next to him and leaned close. "If you're concerned about what radio talk show hosts are gonna say, you might as well decorate your cell and plan on stayin', 'cause you won't be leavin' it for a long while." He moved back and studied his recalcitrant client. "That's what you risk by taking the stand. Don't underestimate Reynolds. He's damn good. He's been dealt a weak hand, but don't give him any more cards to play."

Matheson left his chair and moved away from Miller. "This isn't a card game, and the stakes are a lot higher than whether or not I leave here!" he proclaimed angrily.

Miller matched his anger with his own passionate intensity. "This isn't about proving your innocence! You want a public forum to express your views. That's what you've always wanted. Lead actor performing center stage in a trial you've controlled from the very start." He approached Matheson, and the two men stood inches apart. "Well, I don't gamble with the lives of my clients to feed their egos or political ideologies. I don't know if what you've done is right or wrong. I don't even know if you murdered Cooper or anyone else. But my job is to defend you to the best of my ability and prevent the state from frying your arrogant ass in an electric chair that has your name on it. I intend to do that with or without your help."

He started to walk away, but Matheson forcefully placed his hand on his attorney's shoulder. For a moment, Miller feared the man more than he'd ever feared any convicted felon.

"You're to put me on that stand," Matheson said, then removed his hand.

The two men looked at each other in silence before Miller made one last unconvincing effort. "Martin, listen to me, no one on that jury is going to convict you for the murder of Earvin Cooper based on the evidence before them. But throughout this trial we've been dealing with an undercurrent of all those other men on your list who've been murdered. And while nobody has said it, you can bet your life every member of that jury knows not one single other murder has occurred since your arrest. Now if you take that stand, you're going to resurrect all those dead bodies. And a jury is a funny thing. If their gut tells them something different than the evidence, they'll believe their instincts just about every time."

Matheson slowly retreated to his seat. He sat down and spoke without looking at his counsel. "This isn't a request. It's not an option. And from this moment on, it's no longer negotiable. I'm going to testify and I'm going to vindicate myself and my students, and neither you nor anybody else will prevent me from doing that."

Miller shook his head and surrendered. "There are a lot of inmates serving time in prison because they wanted to prove just how innocent they were. There are a lot of guilty ones who are free 'cause they kept their big mouths shut. I don't know which category you belong in, but we're about to find out. I'll notify everyone I've got one last witness to call. I hope he doesn't hurt our case." Miller signaled the guards.

"You only have to ask one or two questions, then get out of the way. This is between Mr. Reynolds and myself. It's time we settled it once and for all."

"Be careful what you ask for—you might get more justice than you can handle."

A guard unlocked the door and entered with another deputy. Miller turned to Matheson. "Your friends are here to give you a ride home. And that's precisely what it could become for you—your permanent home."

Matheson stood and prepared himself for the handcuffs and ankle shackles. Miller watched him until the leg irons were secured, then left.

CHAPTER
55

SINCLAIR AND REYNOLDS spent another late night in the DA's office. She started putting away her files, but Reynolds retrieved a new stack of materials and began going through them.

"I think Matheson could get a lot of votes if he ran for office," Sinclair said. Wearily she grabbed her briefcase and purse.

"He should name me campaign manager," said Reynolds. "I've provided enough assistance."

"You really think he'll take the stand?"

"He's dreaming about it as we speak."

"At least he's getting some sleep. Which is what I intend to do." Sinclair opened the door to leave. "You want my advice, you'll do the same."

"I just need to go over a few things."

"Go home, James. The world will be here waiting for you in the morning."

"To carry its weight on my shoulders, no doubt." He unsealed another box and removed the contents.

Sinclair took a step back into the office, then stopped. "You almost made me feel guilty enough to change my mind and stay."

"You're welcome to take a seat," he offered.

"I said *almost*." She looked at her watch. "See you in six hours."

"Good night, Lauren." He watched her depart, then went back to scanning a set of pathology reports and autopsy documents. Two hours passed before he found himself unintentionally reviewing the same work he'd earlier completed and set aside. He needed to get home, catch a couple of hours' sleep, shower, dress, and face the defendant with some semblance of coherence.

Thoroughly exhausted, he exited the building and made his way through the parking lot. Upon reaching his car, he placed his briefcase on the top of his hood, then fumbled for his keys. It was darker than usual, and he noticed shattered pieces of glass around his vehicle. He checked his headlights, which were fine, then looked up and discovered that one of the lot's overhead lights had been smashed. He returned to the car door and inserted his key into the lock but never had a chance to turn it. He felt a sharp blow to his right kidney; then someone grabbed his head and forced it violently against the automobile's side mirror.

Two men held him while a third pummeled his body and face with heavy punches. They slammed him against the car, and a masked assailant gripped him around the neck. "You get one warnin'," said the voice behind the mask. "This is it. No more questions. No more searchin'.

You wanna know who killed that nigger? Next time we visit, you'll be able to ask him in hell!"

Reynolds made an effort to free himself, but the man yanked him forward by the hair and crushed him with a brutal head butt, then viciously kneed him in the groin. Someone struck him over the head with a hard object. He collapsed to the ground, where they kicked and stomped him until he lost consciousness.

The little boy ran desperately through the darkened woods. He stumbled but wouldn't fall, for he knew if he stopped now, his life would end. He looked ahead and saw a stream glistening in the moonlight. Ghosts couldn't swim, and even if this one did, the boy would drown before he'd ever allow it to take his life. He hurdled a fallen tree and prepared himself to leap beyond a patch of mud, but the fingers finally trapped him within their blood-stained grasp. The boy frantically pounded his tiny hands against the monster's chest, but instead of a beast he saw the frightened face of a beaten black man, who pleaded with him: "Help me! In Jesus' name, please help me!" Then the little boy saw the mob of angry white faces carrying torches and a long knotted rope. They surrounded the man and carried him to a large tree illuminated by a burning cross. Somehow the child overcame his fear and found the courage to rush into the middle of the crowd. "LEAVE HIM ALONE!" he shouted, to the amusement of the mob that had already placed the noose around the black man's neck. He clutched the man's hand, determined to pull him to safety. From the center of the blazing symbol of salvation he saw the swiftly moving blade of an ax slicing the air and striking the man's wrist. He heard the awful sound of crunching bone that left him

*holding the severed limb. The boy screamed in horror
and dropped the bloody fingers that had chased him for
so long. Someone slapped the boy across his cheek,
knocking him to the ground. He looked up to see the black
man swaying a few feet above him. He noticed a sharp
metal knife sparkle underneath a fiery torch. A white
hand thrust the blade into the man's chest. Blood spurted
from the dead man's heart and splattered onto the child's
face. He wiped his eyes and mouth, then stared at the
blood on his hands. He rubbed his palms against his legs,
but the blood remained—if anything, he'd only managed
to spread it. A ghost hadn't chased him after all, but a
man with dark skin similar to his own. The man needed
his help but he'd failed him, brought him farther into the
marsh and closer to his executioners. Jimmie Reynolds
laid his body prone on the cold, damp earth, hoping beyond hope never to see those bloodstained fingers again.
He closed his eyes and shut his mind to what had happened, then pretended to be dead.*

Reynolds woke up in the hospital with Cheryl by his
side. The doctor said there were no broken bones but he'd
be sore for a couple of weeks. He required several
stitches on his forehead from the head butt, and he'd been
given a prescription for pain, which he refused to fill. He
hated medication of any kind, particularly when he
needed to think clearly. He didn't want to delay the trial
but, under the circumstances, would request a day or two.
He'd ask Judge Tanner to inform the jury he was involved in a minor car accident. Given the number of
times his body had struck his vehicle, that would hardly
be a lie.

He filled out a police report while still confined to his

room and demanded to be released. At six years old, he'd spent a week in the hospital to have his appendix removed. While there, he counted seven people who died—one a day for his entire stay. After that experience, he vowed never to return unless as a visitor. Until tonight, the last time he'd been in a hospital was nine years ago, for the birth of his son.

Cheryl drove her husband home, and he lay down on the couch. She sat on the floor next to him and held his hand.

"Help me up, will ya?" he asked.

"I thought you didn't want to go to bed," she said as she carefully assisted him to his feet.

"I don't." He walked with some difficulty and proceeded into the kitchen. He opened one of the cabinets but couldn't reach inside because of the soreness of his ribs.

"What do you want?" Cheryl asked, concerned. He looked away. She retrieved the bottle of bourbon and placed it on the counter. "Is that what you think you need?" she asked disappointedly.

Reynolds didn't answer. He took the bottle and removed the top. He moved to the sink and poured the contents down the drain. She watched the last few drops leave the bottle; then he tossed it into the wastebasket.

She moved closer to him and placed her arm around his. "You told me you were going to keep that forever."

"I thought I'd need it that long. But I don't. Not anymore." He walked gingerly to the breakfast table and sat. Cheryl took the seat across from him.

"It always frightened me when you used to wake up in the middle of the night and reach for that bottle."

"Did you think I was gonna drink it?" he asked.

"No. I guess I was just afraid you couldn't come to me or to anyone else with whatever was troubling you. You needed that thing more than you needed your wife."

"Most of my life I've been afraid of a ghost who I thought was out to hurt me." The corners of his eyes glistened as he spoke softly. "I finally discovered it wasn't a ghost at all, but a man who needed my help. I couldn't give it to him." He found it more difficult to speak. The words constricted his throat as he fought back tears. He looked at Cheryl, and the sight of her tears released his own in a steady stream. "They killed him, Cheryl! Mutilated that man as I held him!" His voice broke with anger and pain. "They hung him right in front of me and put a knife into his heart, and I couldn't do a damn thing about it!"

She held him, and they both wept.

He slept throughout the day and most of the night. Cheryl called Sinclair, who immediately requested a forty-eight-hour delay in the continuation of the trial. Tanner agreed and notified the jury and all the participants of "the unfortunate automobile accident." The judge went on to say: "We're all pleased that Mr. Reynolds wasn't severely injured, and I'm happy to report he'll be able to continue with us in two days. I've been told he'll be a little sore, but that'll make it easier for me to control him. Now, if I could just find a way to do the same with opposing counsel, oh, what a world this would be."

The jurors and courtroom spectators laughed except for Matheson, who studied the jury's reaction and focused on Aubrey Munson, who for some reason needed to take notes.

CHAPTER
56

THE BIG MOMENT had arrived. Reporters, unwilling to risk losing the precious seats that entitled them to a ringside view of the "event," ate sandwiches, shared chips, and guzzled sodas that they had managed to sneak into the courtroom. Politicians and dignitaries had flown in from around the country and tried to use their influence or connections to gain admittance, to no avail. Court spectators chatted in excited anticipation and told jokes to release the tension. It had all the appearances of a championship fight or a superstar rock concert. Even the jurors dressed for the occasion, with new blouses and dresses for the women and freshly pressed jackets and ties for the men. Something special was about to take place, and everyone knew it, especially the two opposing lawyers and the witness who'd just taken the stand.

"State your name for the record," requested the court clerk.

"Martin Samuel Matheson." The professor sat down at the precise moment his attorney asked the first question.

"Dr. Matheson, did you kill Earvin Cooper?"

"I did not."

"Have you killed anyone?"

"No."

Miller walked near the jury box and attempted to make eye contact, but they were all focused on Matheson. "Why did you teach a course on civil rights history focusing on unsolved murders, 'unpunished murderers,' as you called them?"

Matheson turned toward the jury, and immediately several of the women improved their posture. "People sacrificed their lives during a turbulent period in this nation's history." He spoke carefully and clearly. "If we remember them, their blood is in our veins. If we forget them, their blood's on our hands. We've forgotten them, which is why so many young black men find it easy to destroy each other." Matheson looked at Reynolds, who sat motionless at the prosecutor's table. "I tried to teach my students that black life is valuable—that you shouldn't be able to take it without consequence."

Miller glanced at the jury. "I have no further questions."

Tanner placed his hand over his mouth, which had unexpectedly dropped open. The jury shared the judge's shock that the testimony had ended so abruptly.

Miller strode to his table and confidently sat down.

Reporters wrote furiously in their notebooks.

"Mr. Reynolds, it seems as if it's your turn," remarked Judge Tanner. "I assume you wish to take it."

"I do, indeed; thank you, Your Honor." Reynolds's voice echoed inside his own head, and he thought he heard his heart beat rapidly. He rose and wondered if his jacket was rumpled or his shirt collar crooked or if the jury could tell his legs shook. "Good afternoon, Professor Matheson." He wanted to be respectful without appearing friendly. Direct without being hostile. He wasn't sure how he sounded.

"Good afternoon, Mr. Reynolds. I'm sorry about your . . . *accident.*"

The professor's attempt at concern snapped Reynolds back into reality and allowed him to focus on the matter at hand. "Dr. Matheson, how could you be so certain the persons you put on your list were guilty of any crimes?"

Matheson nodded as if approving of the question and eager to answer it. "Based on my research, there were a great many people who deserved to be placed on my list. However, I selected only those where there was irrefutable evidence of guilt, including individuals who'd openly bragged about committing the crimes. Even in those cases I relied on eyewitness identification or information contained in court records."

"In compiling and publicizing your list, you were placing dozens of lives in jeopardy. Did that ever bother you?"

"What might happen to them in the future troubled me far less than what they'd done in the past," Matheson replied matter-of-factly.

"You're aware, are you not, that in the last few years several men involved in some of the most notorious murders committed during the Civil Rights Movement were finally convicted of their crimes?"

"I'm aware of that, with particular emphasis on the word *finally.*"

Reynolds kept his focus and continued the questioning. "Yet you chose to advocate a campaign of personal harassment against the men on your list instead of using the research you uncovered to seek justice in the courts."

"Using the judicial system to penalize criminals three and a half to four decades after they commit their crimes isn't justice, Mr. Reynolds. It's a mockery of justice, and an insult to the victims' families."

"You didn't believe prison sentences would be sufficient." Reynolds moved closer to the jury. "Would that be a fair characterization of your attitude?"

"If your child had been viciously murdered and the person responsible allowed to enjoy his freedom, travel, socialize, lead a full and complete life until he reached the twilight of his years, would you be satisfied using your tax dollars to provide his retirement housing?" Matheson touched his mouth with the tip of his index finger and waited for Reynolds to respond.

"I'm sorry, Professor, this isn't one of your classes where you get to ask the questions. That's my role." Reynolds maintained his cool demeanor. "I take it your answer to my inquiry is no?"

"My answer is a definite no."

"So you felt they needed a more severe form of punishment?"

"I did."

"Something similar to what they allegedly did to their victims."

"That would be impossible to achieve."

Reynolds inched closer to the witness. "You mean you'd never be able to make them suffer enough?"

Matheson directed his reply to the jury. "The crimes they committed were not simply against individuals. They were allowed to terrorize an entire race of people.

Blacks were confronted with incontrovertible evidence their lives didn't matter. That they had absolutely no value."

Pointedly Matheson continued without turning back to face Reynolds. "The victimization of the black community left deep and permanent scars. We see the effects of that psychic damage every day in the way that black youth treat each other. They have no respect because they were never respected. More important, they've come to believe they never deserved to be." He made eye contact with each individual member of the jury. Some nodded their heads, acknowledging they agreed or at least understood.

Reynolds thought about cutting off the lecture but preferred to let Matheson share his philosophies. With luck, he'd say a bit too much.

"If you punish a murderer within a reasonable time after the crime," continued Matheson, "there's a possibility of healing. In a strange sense, it provides an opportunity to recognize and embrace how precious and fragile life is, to gather strength from pain and forge it into a renewed sense of optimism and hope." He folded his hands together and placed them on the edge of the witness stand. "But if that life's taken without the slightest chance of achieving justice, then your view of yourself and the people around you becomes distorted and ultimately abusive to those you love, assuming you're capable of loving at all." He finally looked at Reynolds. "You're correct, Mr. Reynolds. I could never make them suffer enough for their cowardly acts or for the lasting effects their crimes had on a community forced to act cowardly."

"I surmise by your response that I'm likely to have difficulty in getting you to answer a question with a simple yes or no?"

Matheson smiled. "I apologize. When I took the oath, I assumed you wanted me to give as complete and thorough an answer as your question deserved, particularly since you won't accord me the right to ask my own." He smiled more charmingly. "But I do admit my years as a professor have caused me at times to take the longest distance between two points in order to make two more. I'll try to be brief in the future."

"That's quite all right, Dr. Matheson; please take as much time as you need. After all, you're on trial for capital murder, not your teaching style."

"That remains to be seen, but I appreciate your patience." Matheson poured himself a glass of water.

"Why did you use your students to achieve your rather unique brand of justice?"

"I'm not sure I know what you mean by 'use.'"

"Well, let me try and clarify it for you." Reynolds took a step toward the jury. "In your personal crusade to correct past injustices, rather than rely on impressionable students, did you ever make an effort to enlist the support of black leaders?"

Matheson took a sip of water. "Mr. Reynolds, I avoid people who fill in the words *black leader* under the category marked occupation." He placed the glass of water on the ledge in front of him. "I generally find they charge too much and accomplish too little."

"Isn't your father a black leader, Professor Matheson?"

"My father's a minister and a fighter for civil rights. Since you were, until very recently, a member of his church, you're fully aware he's never had any interest in inflating his ego at the expense of the people he tried to help."

"I'm aware of a great many things about your father, but I'm far more interested in having the jury learn more about his son," Reynolds said with the first real sign of hostility.

"They say the apple doesn't fall too far from the tree," replied Matheson.

"They also say the apple was Adam's downfall, and we all know where that obsession led the world." Reynolds spoke with less animosity, but there still existed an edge to his words. "Speaking of obsession, would that describe your behavior in dealing with Earvin Cooper and the other men on your list?"

"I object, Your Honor." Miller stood and addressed the court. "Dr. Matheson is a scholar, but his expertise isn't in the field of psychology."

Tanner turned toward Matheson. "Did you understand the question?"

"As well as its implication," replied Matheson.

"Then you may answer," ruled Tanner.

"Obsession's a disorder which has, happily, never afflicted me." Matheson leaned back and relaxed. "As to my behavior in dealing with Earvin Cooper and the others, that would depend in large part on whether or not they were alive. Since Mr. Cooper is deceased and I'm charged with his murder, I'm not as interested in revealing his guilt as I am in proving my innocence."

"Did you find it odd that you suffered an assault on the same evening Earvin Cooper fought and struggled with his assailant?"

Matheson leaned forward and displayed a slight degree of irritation. "I find a great many things odd, Mr.

Reynolds, including that J. Edgar Hoover's name is plastered all over a building which purportedly represents law and order and justice."

Reynolds glanced at the jury and noticed that Aubrey Munson wasn't too pleased with that remark, but he remained in the clear minority.

"And since you brought up the subject," continued Matheson with a slight shrug of his shoulders, "I also find it odd you sustained so many injuries from just one fender bender. But I'm not a medical doctor, so I'll have to take your word for it."

Reynolds silently counted to five, then ten, then five more. "Since you've indicated you're not a medical doctor, by any chance do you consider yourself God?"

Miller stood. "Your Honor, I object."

"Actually," remarked Tanner, "I'm kinda interested in the answer. Overruled."

"No, Mr. Reynolds, I don't believe I'm God, although in many cultures each individual might be viewed that way. I imagine one could do worse than treat others with the respect and love reserved for a deity."

"Perhaps, but wouldn't we risk worshiping false idols?"

Matheson smiled. "That might not be as bad as it sounds. There was a time when gods weren't nearly so envious. You'd pray to the sun in the morning, a golden calf in the afternoon, and the God Jehovah at night."

"And when did all that change?" Reynolds hoped the more Matheson talked, the greater the chance the jury might see his secret basement.

"With the creation of the Bible," Matheson answered casually. "After the appearance of that great book, the penalty for worshiping multiple gods resulted in floods, pestilence, and other catastrophes." He looked at the jury and smiled warmly. "In that regard, religion isn't terribly different than government—if you challenge their authority you're likely to face disaster."

Reynolds sought to unnerve Matheson, throw him off stride, but it hadn't happened. He glanced at Blaze Hansberry and hoped, if nothing else, the professor's view of more than one god might have offended her. Instead, she appeared to be enamored. He faced Matheson and calmly asked, "Could you tell the jury about Bigger Thomas?"

"Your Honor, we just covered psychology and theology, and now Mr. Reynolds wants to move on to literature. I thought this was a murder trial, not a liberal arts seminar." Miller looked at the jury in feigned bewilderment.

"You have an interesting way of raising objections, Mr. Miller. I'll be sure to record your methods and share them with my law students as glaring examples of what to avoid doing before a judge." Tanner ignored Miller and turned his attention to Reynolds. "Counselor, I assume you have a sustainable reason for your inquiry of the witness?"

"I'll establish it, Your Honor."

"You'll have to. And within the next three questions." Tanner looked down from the bench at Matheson. "You may answer."

The professor addressed Reynolds informally. "Bigger Thomas was a fictional character in a novel written by Richard Wright, called *Native Son*."

"He was a black man who murdered the daughter of his white employer," stated Reynolds.

"He also murdered his own girlfriend, who was

black," interjected Matheson. "That seldom gets as much attention."

"You wrote that Bigger Thomas was a creation of a society that ignores the hatred and bigotry which produce rage."

"That was published about a year ago."

Reynolds retrieved an academic journal from his table and read to the jury. " 'The Bigger Thomas of the future would be neither ignorant nor frightened. Instead, he would be deliberate, methodical. Would seek to maintain honor by overcoming the rules of a system designed to deny him power, self-respect, and justice.' " Reynolds stopped reading and addressed Matheson. "The Bigger Thomas of your article would desire retribution. Condemned as a murderer if he fails. Exalted as a hero if he succeeds." He closed the journal and studied Matheson. "Did I quote you accurately?"

"You've captured the gist of it."

"You believe in revenge, Dr. Matheson?"

"I believe in justice. That you must be willing to pay a price for it."

"Your father devoted a lifetime to teaching nonviolence, did he not?"

"My father is a deeply religious man, as I believe you know. In the tradition of Jesus, he teaches his congregation to love their enemies and forgive them their sins."

"You don't agree with his philosophy?"

"I turn my love inward, and whenever possible I forgive myself. If you can master the art of forgiving yourself, you can accomplish anything."

Several black members of the jury smiled. The rest continued to be riveted to the proceedings.

"Did you spend much time reviewing the photos in your collection?" asked Reynolds.

"It was difficult to study them."

"Did they affect you? Make you angry?"

"We all have the capacity to deaden our pain, become numb when confronted with unrelenting brutality. It didn't take long before the pictures all started to seem the same. Black-and-white photos of death, mutilation."

Reynolds walked in front of the jury and considered Matheson's response with obvious skepticism. "The photos you collected, studied, hung on the walls of your home, and distributed to your students—one day they simply became interchangeable? Is that what you'd like this jury to believe?"

"I have no control over what this jury believes. I answered your question truthfully. The photos over time began to blur together, one example of brutality after another."

Reynolds prepared himself to ask his next question.

"Except for one particular photo," Matheson added teasingly.

Reynolds wondered if he should pursue the matter but knew the jury would be furious if he didn't, or worse, Miller would follow up in redirect. "What was special about that one photo, Professor?"

"It was taken in the aftermath of a church bombing."

"And that made it unusual?"

"It was in color, so naturally it stood out from all the rest. A nine-year-old girl was being carried out of the rubble. She wore a pink-and-white dress with a matching ribbon in her hair. She'd worn gloves, except the bomb had blown away several of the fingers on her left hand, but the upper section of the glove remained intact, covering the thumb and index finger and the rest of her wrist. Her body was twisted in ways made possible only in death." He looked at the jury and spoke so softly that they needed to lean forward to hear him. "Her eyes were open but lifeless. There was a slight hint of makeup on her cheek. She had a gold religious medal around her broken neck. And I saw blood on a mouth that probably had never worn lipstick." He stared at the floor for the first and only time, then spoke sadly. "She looked too innocent ever to have lived."

Matheson's shoulders slumped slightly. "But she *had* lived. With dreams of finishing school, driving a car, making love, one day holding her baby in her arms. All the things a child has a right to expect to do one day." His eyes rose slowly to meet the state's prosecutor. "Yes, Mr. Reynolds"—he sat erect, back straight—"the photos affected me, then and now."

Reynolds looked at the jury, who'd shifted their attention from Matheson to him. He'd stood in front of enough juries, studied enough poker faces to know he'd lost them and had very little time to win them back. He walked closer to them. He attempted to empathize with them and hoped they'd return the favor.

"Did those photos affect you enough to murder the men responsible?"

Miller stood to object, but Matheson placed his hand up to stop him. He sat back down. The professor answered the question very slowly and deliberately, without emotion. "Murder them, their supporters, the people who brought them into this world, and anyone else who'd protect them."

Reynolds had gotten the answer he knew to be true and the one likely to cause the jury to vote not guilty. Just to be sure, Matheson wrapped the verdict in a neat package and set it before the jurors to unseal.

"But fortunately," Matheson said in a lighter tone, "my father taught me there'd be a final justice. One we'll all have to face. They received theirs. This jury will determine mine."

Reynolds continued the cross-examination for another hour, asking questions about Matheson's whereabouts on the night of the crime. At one point he grilled the defendant regarding the alleged men who'd attacked him that night.

"Describe for the jury in detail how that happened."

Matheson responded and sounded convincing.

"Did you fight back?"

The professor joked that he did the best he could, and the jury laughed with him.

"How many of them were there?"

Matheson estimated five or six but wasn't certain.

Reynolds quickened the pace. How old? What did they look like? What did they say? Did anyone see or hear the struggle? Where exactly did it take place? How had he managed to fight them off and escape?

Matheson provided as much detail as he could, starting or ending many answers with "to the best of my recollection."

Reynolds shifted to the fountain pen found at the scene and the discovery of Matheson's blood on the victim. Each of his questions was crisp and logical and established motive and opportunity, and Reynolds knew none of it mattered. When he finished, it didn't surprise him that Miller had no redirect. His client hadn't been impeached by anything he said. Even Tanner appeared a bit embarrassed for Reynolds and addressed him sympathetically with a kindness reserved for attorneys who'd been thoroughly outclassed.

If Reynolds intended to snatch victory from the jaws of defeat, it would come from his closing argument. Despite judges' admonitions, jurors were moved by lawyers' summations. Any remaining chance to gain a verdict of guilty—to make good on the promise he'd made to the black victims about the sanctity of life—rested solely on Reynolds's ability to do with words what he couldn't do with evidence. He'd stand before a jury of twelve men and women and make them see the truth. If he failed, he doubted he'd have the will or desire to address another jury again.

The defense rested its case, as did the state. Tanner adjourned the session, and the reporters rushed out of the courtroom to meet deadlines. The lawyers had one final match to play, and after that the fate of Martin S. Matheson would be in the hands of the jury.

CHAPTER
57

REYNOLDS FLUNG A book across the conference room, striking the wall. Sinclair sat down opposite him at the table. "I hope that wasn't Baldwin," she said. "I hadn't finished reading him."

"The bastard did it! He killed all those people and he's gonna get away with it!" Reynolds placed both hands over his face.

Sinclair looked at him sympathetically. "If that's your closing argument, we're in deep trouble."

"I ought to let Matheson give it for me. He's controlled everything else." He rose from his seat and paced the floor. "I really thought I could get to him. Show the jury what he is."

"You showed them a man capable of murder."

"I showed them a man."

"If you want, I'll handle the first closing. Go over what little evidence hasn't been discredited. Miller can then destroy my argument." She collected her paperwork.

"That'll pave the way for you to give a brilliant, impassioned speech. Matheson will jump up and confess, throwing himself on the mercy of the court." She opened the door and turned to him. "It could happen," she said optimistically, then left the office.

Reynolds removed a .38-caliber pistol from his coat and placed it on the table. After he'd been attacked he decided to take it wherever he went. He'd gotten a license to carry a concealed weapon almost a decade ago. He'd successfully prosecuted two local gang leaders who, after the verdict, ordered their followers to kill him. He never told Cheryl about the threats, nor did he let her know about the gun until she accidentally knocked over his briefcase and it slipped onto the floor. He had offered a few lame excuses, then promised to get rid of it.

He poured himself another cup of coffee and retrieved the book he'd thrown against the wall. He read the title and discovered it was Richard Wright's *Native Son*. He raised it over his head, about to throw it out the window, when he thought better of it. He sat down at the table and placed the book in front of him, strumming its cover several times with his fingers. He suddenly stopped and opened the book. He flipped through the pages and paused occasionally to read notations he'd made in the margins. He closed the book and held it in both hands. After deliberating for about thirty seconds, he took the book and moved to a more comfortable chair. He sat and opened the novel to the first page and began to read.

Monday morning Tanner reviewed numerous procedural matters with the attorneys. Sinclair would conduct the state's initial closing late in the day, and Miller would do his first thing tomorrow. Reynolds would present his final argument in the afternoon, and the judge would issue his instructions to the jury on Thursday. After that, deliberations would commence.

The session got under way at two-thirty, and Sinclair launched into her closing. She covered the salient points, reminding the jury of the key evidence and cautioning them that "no matter how much you may have liked the defendant's students—and I'll admit they were extremely likable—even they couldn't explain the discovery of their professor's pen a few feet away from Earvin Cooper's murdered body." She moved closer to Matheson. "Nor, ladies and gentlemen of the jury, could they rationalize the presence of the defendant's blood underneath the fingernails of his victim."

She debunked the defense's "wild and totally unfounded allegations that a visitor to the police station discovered the pen, then, for reasons better left to the imaginations of science fiction writers, felt compelled to murder someone on the professor's infamous list." Yes, she conceded, the collection and analysis of DNA "requires great care, but if there were mistakes, they'd incorrectly eliminate the professor as a suspect, not deliver the perfect match the laboratory ultimately came back with."

She spent little time with the "inflammatory notion" that any of the evidence existed because police officers "violated their oath to uphold the law and committed a felony act." The idea they'd frame Matheson was not only preposterous, she claimed, "it's also a desperate attempt on the part of defense counsel to smear decent public servants so that a murderer might go free."

Reynolds observed the jury and knew, irrespective of how entertaining and informative Sinclair might be, they were more interested in the main event. They'd come to see the match between Miller and Reynolds, where the prized trophy was at stake. How they'd eventually score that competition would determine Matheson's future and perhaps their own.

Sinclair concluded her argument in the same fashion she'd opened the trial. She displayed the photo of Cooper's slain body and placed it directly next to an enlargement of Matheson's bruised face. "You've had to tolerate a great many gruesome and horrible photographs in this trial," she said regretfully. "I apologize for the discomfort they may have caused. I ask you to look once more at the picture of Martin Matheson's victim." She touched the display board that held Cooper's photo. "And, ladies and gentlemen, how can you be certain that the defendant murdered Earvin Cooper?" She stepped to the second poster and pointed to scratch marks on the side of Matheson's left cheek. "Because in one of his last dying efforts the victim managed to leave behind his fingerprints on the face of his assailant."

She returned to the podium, closed her notebook, and pleaded with the jury: "Earvin Cooper identified his murderer for us. He concealed the clue to his killer in the only safe place he had—underneath the fingernails on his burnt and blistered hands. The blood found there points to one man and only one man. Martin S. Matheson took the life of Earvin Cooper, and because of that, the state implores you to return a verdict of guilty to the charge of first-degree murder." Sinclair thanked the jury and resumed her seat next to Reynolds. A few jurors continued to take notes—most noticeably Aubrey Munson, who'd filled several pages.

Tanner issued his standard instructions to the jury

before dismissing them. The spectators left the court-room, subdued, and milled around the rotunda. Reynolds congratulated Sinclair on the job she'd done, while Miller put an encouraging hand on Matheson's shoulder.

The professor appeared in good spirits and shared a joke with the guards, who waited for him to finish with his lawyer. Reynolds noticed that both guards laughed, which signaled progress, since one was black and the other white. Maybe Matheson had turned over a new leaf and decided to promote racial harmony and reconcilia-tion. That bit of fantasy quickly dissipated when the pro-fessor looked at Reynolds and mouthed the words "good luck."

Matheson turned to leave when suddenly, Earvin Cooper's widow rushed past security and tried to strike him with her purse. She screamed every conceivable pro-fanity until subdued by court deputies. Matheson's guards quickly led him away from the disturbance. Miller followed behind.

Ruth Cooper wept uncontrollably. The deputies dis-cussed whether to take her into custody, when Reynolds intervened on her behalf. Sinclair took the distraught woman aside while Reynolds negotiated with the officers to allow him to handle the matter. They agreed but re-mained in the room to monitor her behavior. Reynolds thanked them, and as he proceeded to join Sinclair, he ob-served Regina standing in the rear of the courtroom. She watched Mrs. Cooper for several moments before finally leaving. Reynolds wondered if that look of concern was compassion for the woman or distress at what had almost happened to the professor. He decided he couldn't be sure of the real motivation driving any of Matheson's stu-dents, particularly this one.

CHAPTER
58

M ILLER FINISHED A peanut butter and jelly sandwich and drank a glass of cold beer. He lay down on his couch and thought about his closing. As always, he'd deliver it without notes. He believed that juries resented lawyers who read to them, and, more important, that they doubted they were telling the truth. He couldn't refer to paperwork while he spoke from his heart. That would be an invitation to observe his planned spontaneity. Jurors liked to cry or feel outraged but not if it was from a manipulative script.

A magician had to perform the same trick every night as if it were new, never allowing the audience to question the existence or power of magic. A lawyer must do the same, convincing the jury it was really the prosecution who was running the shell game. But this time Miller felt he'd engaged in sleight of hand. He'd never been bothered before at the thought his client might be guilty; if the state couldn't prove it, tough luck. After all, he hadn't created the rules; he'd only mastered them.

As he looked back at his career, he remembered less than a handful of cases he regretted taking. This case deviated from the norm. He wanted to be brilliant for reasons that had nothing to do with obtaining his client's acquittal. He felt comfortable that the state hadn't proven its case, although given the passions involved, any verdict was possible. He had a more selfish motive for achieving victory. After having endured rejection from every black organization that had once actively sought his pro bono skills, he now had the delightful opportunity to fling their betrayals back into their smug and hypocritical faces. He'd lived long enough with their arrogance. The struggle had escalated to a level where "no whites need apply," except, of course, when impoverished defendants required representation. Consequently, for the past two decades he'd subsisted on a diet of drug felons and spouse abusers and petty thieves—the remnants of a Civil Rights Movement that had abandoned them in favor of addressing the urgent needs of corporate America.

But now, in a matter of a few weeks, all had changed. He'd landed a case that epitomized the black struggle in all its glory. Professor Martin S. Matheson represented four hundred years of an evolving system of justice forced to come to grips with its own inherent contradictions of greatness and failure. And no one felt more conflicted about the possibility of resolving that dilemma than the lawyer who would soon argue for his client's freedom.

He didn't know how many miles he'd marched, or how much of his money he'd given to losing causes. He didn't want to know how many insults he'd tolerated or death threats he'd ignored. The only thing he wanted to know was whether the sum total of that experience had led him to this moment. Had he suffered so much simply to reach this monumental crossroads, the intersection between his pain and his payback, his idealism and his will to win, no matter the repercussions? When all was said and done, civil rights remained the one thing he'd never deserted despite its having deserted him. Hadn't Earvin Cooper's civil rights been violated, and since when did the horror of lynching depend solely on the color of the victim?

In a show of startling affection, Miranda leaped onto the couch and snuggled next to him. She'd never done that before. Cats, he thought—*such strange creatures.* What would possess her to reach out to him tonight of all nights? Clairvoyance aside, her timing seemed remarkable. *Thank God they don't allow her kind to serve as jurors or IRS officials.* He stroked her fur and she purred, her body rising in sync with the movement of his fingers. He didn't want to admit it, but she'd brought him a moment of peace. This stray cat, who half a dozen years ago moved into his life of her own volition, had been his one true companion. And at his moment of need, his crisis of conscience, a mere animal had gotten him to observe the golden rule. In soothing her, he'd brought himself a bit of temporary comfort.

The phone rang at midnight, and Miranda jumped off his lap and followed him to the corner table. She'd never done that before, either. He lifted the receiver and heard a woman's voice ask, "Is this Todd Miller?" He replied affirmatively and listened to a message that ended with heartfelt condolences. He hung up and returned to the couch but this time didn't lie down. Miranda climbed onto his lap and pushed her back against his side. He placed his hand on her head and massaged her chin. Tears streamed down his face, and yet his expression remained frozen. His father had managed to make him cry once more.

Tanner delayed closing arguments for three days. The weekend would give Miller an additional forty-eight hours to handle the funeral arrangements. He returned to the retirement community and asked permission to enter his father's room. He'd been there for only a few minutes when a nurse's aid entered.

"Mr. Miller?" the black man asked. "I'm Nelson Allen; I was assigned to take care of your father."

"Todd Miller," he said, offering his hand. "It's nice to meet you."

"One of the staff told me you were here. I hope I'm not disturbin' you; I just wanted to stop by and tell you how sorry I am for your loss." Allen looked to be in his late forties and had a large round face divided by a thin mustache. He possessed broad shoulders and thick hands, and Miller wondered what type of hell his father had put this poor guy through.

Miller hesitated, then asked, "Did you know my father well?"

Allen laughed. "Your dad was a handful and then some."

"I trust he didn't make your life too miserable."

"The judge?" Allen exclaimed. "No, no. I enjoyed comin' to work so I could listen to all his stories."

Miller smiled proudly, and his feeling of admiration both surprised and scared him.

"I worked the late afternoon and night shifts, so me and your dad got to be pretty close."

"Really?" The word slipped out of Miller's mouth. Would the surprises ever cease?

"He talked about you a lot until his mind . . ." Allen stopped and looked at Miller with embarrassment. "Until he started havin' trouble rememberin' things."

"Were you with him the night . . ." Now it was Miller's turn to search for the right words. "The night it happened?"

"He died very peacefully, Mr. Miller."

Miller felt enormous gratitude at hearing that.

"I stayed with him almost to the end. I'm not sure he knew I was there or who I was. I said a prayer for him like usual and held his hand to calm him down." Allen became quiet for a moment. He rubbed the side of his face and slowly gazed around the room. "Was your dad always such a restless sleeper?"

Miller thought about it and nodded sadly.

"I sleep like a baby soon as my head hits the pillow."

Miller looked at the empty bed and tried to imagine the position of his father when he died.

"Well, look, I didn't mean to barge in on you; like I said, I just wanted to express my—"

"Mr. Allen, you said my father spoke about me a lot."

"Sure did."

"I'm just curious," Miller said, proceeding awkwardly. "I was wondering, if it's not too much of an imposition . . ."

Allen laughed. "Your daddy used those kind of words all the time. 'If it's not too much of an imposition, could you bring me my bedpan?' 'Could I impose on you to take away this lunch tray?' He always sounded like a judge except for those times we'd talk about you. Then he sounded just like any other father."

Miller took a deep breath and held on to it as long as he could. When he believed he'd managed to control the emotion welling up inside, he released it.

"You must've been very proud of him—him bein' a judge and all."

Miller didn't respond.

"He sure was proud of you."

Miller started on his second deep breath.

"Used to tell everybody 'bout all the cases you'd won. He'd strut up and down the cafeteria and thump the counter to get everyone's attention."

Miller smiled and thought about his father thumping the dining room table to make his point. On occasion he'd just tap his left thigh three times, and the family would wait anxiously for the lecture or a decision or simply permission to commence the Sunday meal.

"He spent the most time explainin' your legal battles against the government. That would get him truly animated. He'd point his fist at anyone who'd listen, and punched the air when he got excited. Then, all of a sudden he'd stop, get completely quiet, like he was embarrassed or disappointed."

"At me?" asked Miller, genuinely afraid of the answer.

"I think at himself."

"Why do you say that?" Miller asked incredulously.

"Just a feelin' I had about him. He told me you were the third generation of lawyers in the family. Then he'd always get real sad. Said you were the only one who . . ." Allen became uneasy.

"I was the only one who what?" Miller's voice cracked.

"The only one who really honored the law the way it was meant to be honored."

Miller's shoulders sank, but his heart soared and then felt as if it would shatter.

"When he started to get worse, with the memory and everything, I'd help him finish his stories about you. Heck, I'd heard 'em so often, I probably could practice law by now." Allen now fought back his emotions. "In the end, I thought I'd see him smile once or twice, but he didn't seem to understand too much. It's a awful thing, that disease, makes a man forget the people he loves most."

Miller stared ahead. "Would you mind very much if I had a few moments alone?"

"You stay as long as you want," Allen said. "If you need help with his things, just let me know." He reached the door and held it open. "Mr. Miller?"

Miller faced him.

"Would it be all right if I attended his service?"

Miller's heart raced, and his legs felt heavy. "I'm sure my father would like that." He watched Allen leave, then sat down in a chair next to the bed and unconsciously tapped his left thigh three times. He'd managed to live much of his adult life refusing to shed any more tears for the man who'd caused him so much pain. Yet since his last meeting with his father he'd cried twice for him. Now he'd do it once more, but this time it would be for himself.

CHAPTER
59

IN AN EFFORT to give Miller sufficient time to handle his family matter, Tanner scheduled the hearing for three o'clock. Miller arrived two hours early and sat in the courtroom alone. He paced back and forth in front of the empty jury box, envisioning where each person sat. He moved to the podium and measured the distance between himself and the judge's bench, then crossed to the prosecutor's table. He counted the steps from one place to the other and mentally choreographed his presentation to make it as seamless as possible. When he felt comfortable with the dry run, he repeated it and made his final adjustments. Then he took his seat and waited for the performance to begin.

He thought about the burial grounds and how lovely they looked. Cemeteries are kept clean for the dead, while the streets are allowed to stay filthy for the living. "Go figure," he mumbled to himself. He laid his father to rest just outside Holly Springs, underneath the proverbial old oak tree on the much sought-after "high bluff overlooking the river's edge." His father had actually acquired several plots many years ago, known simply as the "family grounds." Miller's mother was buried there along with his four grandparents and an uncle. Despite his disinheritance, which he learned his father had revoked in the most recent will, Miller also had a preferred spot on the hill, slightly lower than his father's, of course, but still under the shade and within spiritual spitting distance of the water.

Reynolds attended the funeral accompanied by his wife and children. Mr. Allen brought flowers and cried. The Presbyterian pastor recited a prayer about the power of redemption and asked Miller if he'd like to say a few words over his father's grave. He declined, but not because he maintained any residue of anger. If those feelings hadn't left with the phone call, they'd certainly disappeared by the time he finished meeting with Nelson Allen. Miller's last words to his father had been a one-way conversation to someone hiding behind a wall of shattered memory. But at least that person was alive. He wouldn't speak to his father through the mahogany lid of a coffin, not when the man inside had been so fond of yelling, "Look me in the eyes and say that again. Go 'head, I dare ya!"

Miller smiled at the recollection. Whenever his father got really angry or had one drink too many, the first thing to desert him was the ability to modulate his voice lower than a roar, followed almost immediately by the abandonment of the beginning or ending letters to a third of his words. While they may have been shortened, their pronunciation took considerably longer. When everything else begins to leave, one can always count on southern accents to return, sometimes with a vengeance.

The court's rear doors suddenly opened, and the stampede began. The seats filled within two minutes, and shortly after that, all court personnel were in place. Sinclair arrived and offered condolences to Miller, who thanked her for her thoughtfulness in sending a beautiful wreath of flowers. They shook hands and for the first time in the trial showed no combativeness or hostility.

The jury had been told the second delay was caused by an unexpected judicial appeal that required the judge's immediate attention. Tanner wanted to avoid any sympathetic response to Miller's loss. He'd earlier told both attorneys he hadn't lied this much since he was seven years old and "my daddy took me to the woodshed, had me pull down my trousers, and introduced my behind to his truth-detectin' leather belt."

While he indicated to counsel he was beginning to enjoy his sudden "predilection to fabrication," he'd just as soon not have to devise any new stories for the duration of this trial. They promised to do their best not to create any more delays.

The bailiff called the court to order and announced Tanner's entrance. The judge had a light bounce to his walk and a huge smile on his face. He greeted the jury. "I hope you're as happy to see me as I am to see you."

They signaled agreement, and he took his seat behind the bench with the customary flapping of his long black sleeves. He pressed his hands together in a quick isometric exercise and rotated his head in a full circle, repeating the action in the opposite direction. He removed a freshly sharpened pencil, tested the point, and prepared himself for action.

"I note for the record the defendant is present in court alongside his counsel, and I also observe that both Mr. Reynolds and Ms. Sinclair are in attendance to represent the state. The jury appears ready. Madam court reporter, I see your machine's in place and your paper's filled to capacity." He wiggled his fingers. "Are you limber, or do you need more flex time?"

"Ready, Your Honor." She smiled and sat straight.

"Very well," Tanner said, clearing his throat. "We will now proceed with the closing argument from the defense side. Mr. Miller, you have the floor."

"Thank you, Your Honor." Miller rose and proceeded to the podium. "Thank you, ladies and gentlemen of the jury, for your patience and your attentiveness throughout this trial." He rubbed his palms together, then placed his hands on either side of the lectern.

"Thirty-five years ago, I wouldn't be able to stand in front of a jury that looked like you." Miller pointed to his client. "Dr. Matheson wouldn't be having a trial. The key to his cell would've been secretly slipped to someone hidden in darkness." Miller touched the back of his pony-tail and walked toward the jury box.

"When the morning came, there would've been one more photo taken of one more victim." He rested his hands on the rail in front of Mrs. Whitney and looked at her. "But that form of justice can't happen again. Because you won't let it happen."

Miller crossed to Matheson and put his hand on his shoulder. "The district attorney for this county publicly condemned this man, held him morally responsible for a string of murders even though he admitted Professor Matheson had broken no laws." He walked slowly toward Reynolds. "Perhaps my client did something much worse. He violated custom. Wouldn't remain quiet. Didn't know his place. Insisted on shining a light on our deepest and darkest secrets."

He turned his body so that the jury could observe Reynolds as he gestured toward him. "Thirty-five years ago, Mr. Reynolds wouldn't be sitting at a table like this one. Not as a prosecutor for the people. Times have changed." He looked directly at Reynolds. "We demand more from our system of justice." Miller turned his head toward the jury and spoke solemnly. "We must begin to demand more from each other."

Reynolds watched his adversary cross once again to the jury. He thought about yanking the back of his hair and throwing Miller off stride.

"You can't silence a man because he dares to remind us of things we'd rather forget. You can't convict a man because he wrote some things too frightening for us to read, let alone believe." Miller extended his arms in front of him and raised his palms out toward the courtroom observers. "This isn't thirty-five years ago!" his voice boomed. He waved his hand and pointed an accusatory finger toward the prosecutor's table. His voice rose.

"We need more than speculation and anger and resentment and outrage to take a man's life!" He cradled his hands together and moved them in the direction of the jury. He either offered a precious gift to the twelve men and women before him or else he pleaded for one. "We need proof beyond a reasonable doubt." He walked toward the prosecutor's table and spoke with indignation.

"Not ridiculous probability figures based on a sample of five! Not evidence reported lost at the very police station that now accuses him! Not blood subject to contamination and error! And certainly not wild speculation that a man would slip a size-thirteen boot on a foot that measures nine and one half for the express purpose of committing murder and getting away with it!"

He separated his hands and dropped them to his sides. He moved to his table and stood next to Matheson. This time he spoke more softly and ended on a whisper. "We no longer live in the past." He looked sympathetically at Reynolds. "We can no longer allow the past to live in us." He moved in front of his chair and spoke his final words with absolute conviction. "I ask you to reject the state's case and find Dr. Matheson not guilty." He sat down, and as he lowered his head, the silver braid of hair slipped across his left shoulder and rested near his heart.

Tanner took a breath and expanded his chest. "I hadn't expected counsel to be so brief, but in fairness to everyone, since we started rather late in the day, we'll stay on schedule and adjourn for the evening. When we reconvene tomorrow morning, Mr. Reynolds will conclude with the state's closing arguments. The jury is once again directed to abide by the court's usual admonition regarding discussing this case." He struck the gavel, and the jury quickly filed out.

Matheson left with the deputies, and Miller remained in his seat. Reynolds approached and took the seat next to him. The two adversaries sat together in silence and remained that way until the courtroom cleared. "You remember when I told you about my nightmares?" Reynolds asked.

"The black bogeyman?" Miller inquired without looking at him.

"Turned out he wasn't trying to hurt me at all. Just needed my help."

Miller finally looked at Reynolds. "My friend, if I've

learned anything from my time on earth, it's that the people who need you are also the ones who can hurt you most."

Reynolds gently patted his colleague on the back and left.

Miller remained in his seat and stared at the empty jury box.

CHAPTER
60

REYNOLDS STOOD ALONE in his backyard. A full moon created a sense of calm he hadn't felt in months. In twelve hours he'd face the jury for the last time and try to convince them the man who'd out-dueled him from the witness stand was a murderer. He knelt on his left knee and used his fingers to gently plow the earth in an area of freshly planted flowers. The act of gardening presented a more meaningful alternative to therapy and always resulted in growth.

He preferred working at night. His son had advised him he wouldn't have to see bugs or other "yucky stuff" that way. He also wouldn't have to see the mistakes he'd made until the next morning, which worked out well since he checked progress only during the evening. Just before he placed his other knee into the dirt to double the therapeutic impact, he heard the screen door close and sensed his wife's presence.

"You want me to listen to your closing?" Cheryl asked.

Reynolds shook his head. "I'm not sure I have one."

"You'll come up with something appropriate. You always have."

He stood up from the flowerbed and moved close to her. "I became a prosecutor because I wanted to make the world safe. Put all the bad people away—the ones who terrified little boys while they slept. Now I'm not sure who the monsters are."

"Sometimes they trick us," she said. "That's why they're monsters." She touched his face and moved it toward her. She waited for him to look at her. "What's important is that we always recognize our heroes."

"Sometimes we should fear them most of all." He kissed her gently. "I better get ready for tomorrow."

"You want me to be there with you, at the court?"

"You haven't heard one of my closings in a long time."

"Yes, I have. I just never let you know I was there. This time I'll sit where you can see me."

He smiled and placed his arm around her shoulder. They walked together across the yard and entered their house.

Reynolds proceeded down the hallway and stopped outside his son's bedroom. Christopher heard the knock on his door and quickly shoved his *Playboy* magazine inside his school folder and hid it underneath his pillow.

His father entered. "You still awake? It's late."

"I know, Dad. Just finishing some homework." Christopher crept into bed and pulled the covers over his body. He rested his head on the pillow. "You feelin' okay?"

Reynolds approached his son and sat on the side of the

bed. "A little sore, but I'll live." He rubbed his son on his head. "At least in your fight you got off the first punch."

"Didn't you get to hit any of 'em?"

"No," Reynolds answered dejectedly. "But I must've chased them off while I was unconscious." He winked at his son. "I'm dangerous with my eyes closed."

"Hey, Dad."

"Hey, yourself."

"What's up?" Christopher asked. "You got that look on your face."

"You mean the one with the dark bruises and split lip?"

"No. The one you use when I'm in trouble and you have something serious to tell me. Like when I got a D in science and you said I was gonna miss out on college."

"I never said that."

"I couldn't watch television for two whole weeks! Even people in prison can watch TV."

"What does that tell you?" asked his father.

His son thought for a moment. "They got good grades in science?"

Reynolds gave the boy a strange look. "That's the best you can do?"

"Hey, I'm only a kid and we're havin' an adult conversation."

Reynolds studied his son and searched for the right words. "I got another question for you. This one's important."

"I knew I was in trouble."

"You ready?"

Christopher braced himself and signaled to go ahead.

"You know the difference between justice and revenge?"

Christopher considered the question by staring at the

ceiling. He then offered his best guess. "One's a noun and the other's a verb?"

Reynolds shook his head and gave a bittersweet smile. He put his hand on his son's arm and spoke solemnly. "One's worth your life, the other will destroy it." He looked at his son and studied him. "You understand?"

Christopher gave his dad a puzzled look. "Not really."

Reynolds squeezed his son's arm encouragingly. "You will." He leaned over and kissed him on the cheek. "I love you."

Christopher looked at his father curiously. "I love you, too," he said.

Reynolds walked to the door.

"Dad?"

He turned and faced his son.

"You sure I didn't do something wrong?"

Reynolds shook his head and opened the door. "But get rid of that magazine under your pillow."

Christopher's face turned stone-cold guilty.

Reynolds smiled and said, "Good night."

CHAPTER
61

HARD-EDGED MEDIA professionals shuffled their papers, picked at their fingernails, and anxiously awaited the judge's entrance. Reynolds sat quietly at the table next to Sinclair, who knew enough not to disturb him. The loneliest and most exhilarating moment in the life of any prosecutor had arrived. What would happen next required a combination of legal acumen and intuitive recklessness. Twelve men and women, strangers to each other, would listen to Reynolds ask them to decide the fate of another human being. Most of these people didn't have the power to choose the time they took work breaks. Now they'd determine the life or death of a man they'd never spoken to. And they'd have the courage or audacity to do that based in large part on which lawyer gave the best speech.

Reynolds watched the door crack open and caught a glimpse of the judge's black robe. The bailiff announced Tanner's arrival and commanded everyone to rise. Tanner took his place at the bench and followed the same protocol that hadn't changed much in his thirty-odd years as a judge. But for Reynolds, nothing seemed commonplace anymore—not the room, not the jury, and certainly not Tanner's words.

"Mr. Reynolds, are you ready to begin your closing argument?"

Reynolds stood and held on to the back of his chair. "Yes, Your Honor." He proceeded to the podium and placed his hands on either side. He'd never noticed how long a walk that entailed. The faces of the jury blended into a watercolor painting. He glanced at Miller, then Matheson. He took a look at the Reverend Matheson and for a moment thought he saw him nod his head in acknowledgment. He once again faced the jury and felt relieved they'd come back to life.

"We're taught from an early age that Pharaoh's army drowned in the Red Sea, which caused Moses and his people to give praise." He moved away from the podium and extended his hands to the jury. "And so the cycle continues even today." He walked toward the defense table. "We seek to be delivered from evil. Destroy one enemy only to create another, except this next foe is far more powerful and dangerous. We find temporary safety ultimately at the expense of peace. We call upon a new Moses to step forth, and when he doesn't, we anoint anyone who tells us what we need to hear. We give this leader a different name and greater authority over our lives.

"The Bigger Thomas of today no longer hides in the shadows of submissiveness, concealing his rage with bowed head and a quiet 'yes sir' and 'no sir.'" Reynolds stood in front of the jury railing. "He's no longer frightened by the painful memories of a humiliating past but is fueled by the expectations of a distorted future filled with images of reprisal and retribution." He walked slowly and looked at each individual juror.

"Today's Bigger Thomas wears a tailor-made suit. His hatred is hidden in the language of the articulate. He has all the advantages: a good family, fine education, a respected position in the community, a successful career." His voice sounded reasoned and self-assured. "But somewhere"—his voice suddenly changed and offered a warning alarm—"somehow"—he placed his hands on the railing—"this model of achievement was severely damaged and twisted by an overwhelming desire to return hate for hate, pain for pain, indignity for indignity, and blood for blood."

He removed his hands from the railing and placed them to his side. "What does it cost a society to call a five-year-old child a 'nigger'?" He allowed the word to linger in the air for several unchallenged moments. "What price does that innocent but fragile child pay for our ignorance?" He turned toward Matheson and looked at him along with the jury. "That's the price."

Reynolds moved away from the jury and Matheson, turning his attention to the overflowing crowd of spectators. "For there are people inside and outside this courtroom who in their desperation would embrace or glorify this defendant as a hero, in return for the promise of just once feeling victorious, striking back and getting away with it." He spotted Vanzant, seated in the last row, and looked at him. "Winning no matter the consequence." He returned his attention to the jury. "But there's always a consequence."

He studied the faces of the jury, then bowed his head and sought personal guidance. He looked at Miller, then the judge, and tried to gather his thoughts. He discovered his two children, seated on either side of his wife. He walked in front of the podium and placed his right hand on top of it.

"Justice is often depicted as a woman wearing a blindfold. She doesn't see the race or wealth or status of the victim or the defendant. She searches only for the truth." He shook his head sadly. "There's no revenge in her heart. She takes no enjoyment in the severity of her penalty. There's no celebration for the thing that must be done."

Reynolds carefully approached the jury and spoke proudly. "She is the best of what we hope to be, in responding to the worst of what, too often, we've become." He stopped three feet from the jury box and stood erect with his hands extended toward them, palms facing upward.

"The scales of justice cannot and must not balance one hatred for another." He moved one hand up and the other down, alternating them slowly as he spoke. "Nor dignify one violent act while condemning the source of it. Or ever validate any form of racism, whether it is covered by a white sheet and hood or cloaked in the evil rhetoric of historical justification."

He folded his hands together. "I plead with you, the caretakers of this sacred thing called *justice:* Don't remove her blindfold, for if you do, she will have gained sight at the expense of her soul. And the true victim of that sacrifice . . ." He turned and looked at Reverend Matheson. ". . . will be our children."

Reynolds walked slowly to his chair and sat down. The courtroom remained absolutely silent for several moments. A few throats were cleared, which gave others in the chambers permission to shift in their seats.

Tanner turned toward the jury, half of whom were still looking at Reynolds while the other half were watching Matheson. "We'll take a fifteen-minute break." He thought about it for an instant. "Let's make that thirty minutes. When you return, I'll go over the charges and instruct you as to the law and how to apply it." He panned the jury to ensure he now had their undivided attention.

"After that, we'll go through some procedural and logistical matters. Then, ladies and gentlemen, I'll officially hand the case over to you so that you can select a foreperson and begin your careful deliberations of all the relevant evidence presented to you." He poured a glass of water but delayed drinking it.

"As I told each of you when you were chosen to serve on this case, jury service is an important obligation. You provide a vital function, and without you it's doubtful true justice could be rendered. I commend you for the attention you've paid throughout the proceedings thus far, and I'm certain you'll continue to demonstrate the dedication and seriousness necessary to fulfill your duties." He took a drink of water. "Enjoy your well-deserved respite." Tanner lightly struck his gavel, and the chambers began to clear.

Sinclair patted her colleague on the back, then walked away, as though she knew he needed some personal space.

Reynolds collected his paperwork and returned it to his briefcase. He watched Matheson be led away and made eye contact with Miller, who gave him a respectful and admiring smile.

Regina Davis walked toward him but stopped a few

feet away. Reynolds stood, and they looked at each other until Brandon intervened. Reynolds watched both of them leave and thought about his own children. Not too long ago he would have loved for Angela and Christopher to grow up with the passions and talents of those two graduate students. Now he wasn't sure. He wanted to avoid communicating with anyone, so he sat down and waited for the recess to end.

The jurors returned five minutes early, and Tanner explained basic elements of the statute pertaining to first-degree murder. He reviewed the jury verdict form and articulated the procedures to follow if they wanted portions of the testimony read back, transcripts supplied, or evidence produced. Their first order of business after they found out "where all the good snacks are hidden, is to elect yourself a foreman or forewoman or foreperson or whatever else you wanna call the person who's gonna chair your group, count the votes, and read your decision in open court."

Tanner advised them to select someone "not too opinionated, not too noncommittal, and not someone whose friendship you'll miss." The jury laughed, and Tanner thanked them for their sense of humor and "recognizing my feeble attempts to keep things loose." He went on to reconfirm the importance of their mission and asked them to show each other "patience, understanding, and respect. It wouldn't be a bad idea if you also exhibited wisdom, but objectivity, fairness, and common sense will do quite nicely."

He wished them well and asked the bailiff to escort them to the jury room, a secure site in an undisclosed area of the building. He didn't expect them to conduct any business this late in the day. He preferred they get a good night's rest and meet in the morning. They should decide a convenient time, then inform the bailiff. Tanner adjourned the session and proceeded to his chambers. After Miller and Matheson left with the deputies, the spectators cleared out of the room.

Reynolds remained at the prosecutor's table, and Sinclair placed her hand on his shoulder. "Win or lose, I'm proud to have worked with you, Mr. Reynolds."

"No matter what the jury decides, there'll be no winners in this one," he said.

A deputy approached Reynolds and handed him a note. He opened it and read it. His expression turned pensive.

"Don't tell me it's over already," commented Sinclair.

"I think it's just starting." Reynolds stood and looked at his curious cocounsel. "If I'm not back in ten minutes, secure my bail money."

Sinclair watched him go through the security doors normally reserved for imprisoned defendants. He met with a court deputy, who accompanied him to Matheson's holding cell. Reynolds entered and noticed Matheson sitting alone. "Where's your attorney? I thought he'd be here."

"He's done his job. You've done yours. I wanted to see you alone."

"To confess?"

"I hear it's good for the soul, but no. To clarify."

"I thought you were pretty clear on the witness stand."

"I wasn't speaking of myself." Matheson stood and placed his foot on the chair and hands on his raised knee. "I wanted to correct some assumptions in your eloquent but nonetheless erroneous closing statement."

"I'm your captive guest."

Matheson slowly walked around the table. He moved away from Reynolds and circled back as he spoke. "Every kid grows up thinking his daddy can beat anybody else's daddy. . . . It doesn't matter if it's true. You just want to believe the man who brought you into this world can protect you from it." He'd made it to Reynolds's side of the table and stopped two feet from him. "There aren't many black boys over the age of five who believe that. The really sad thing is, their fathers don't believe it, either."

"You think they believe it now?"

He moved closer and sat on the edge of the table. "It's a start. Why should we be the only people whose heroes know how to pray better than they know how to fight?" He folded his arms across his chest. "Even Jesus used the lash to drive out the moneychangers from the temple, and needless to say, His Father had a legendary temper. Remember those floods?"

Reynolds didn't change expression. "I reread *Native Son* a few nights ago."

Matheson smiled. "It paid off. I liked the way you weaved the new Bigger Thomas into your closing. Very effective."

"I'd like to think so."

"I'm sure you would," responded Matheson.

"I was struck by a particular passage in the book, where Bigger considers the consequence of oppression, the effects that racism had on his life, and what white hate had done to him. He tells his lawyer that 'they kill you before you die.'" Reynolds studied Matheson. "They kill you before you die. . . . It made me pity him all the more."

"Yes," Matheson said softly. "I remember feeling the

same way the first time I read it, many years ago. But it's a funny thing, reacting to injustice. Perhaps Dr. King put it best when he said civil disobedience means you should lovingly accept the consequences." He leaned forward, and both men were inches apart. "James . . . I hope you don't mind me calling you that; we've been through so much together."

"What do you want, *Martin*?" Reynolds had had all that he could or would take.

"In the event this doesn't turn out the way you envisioned, I'm having a little, shall we say, freedom party? I do hope you'll drop by."

All sensation ceased. The confines of this cell should have closed in on Reynolds, yet he felt a huge space separating himself from the man standing directly in front of him. Even though Matheson remained inches away, for some reason Reynolds could barely see him. He had difficulty recognizing anything in the room, even the two guards who entered and announced, "We have to take Dr. Matheson back to the facility."

Matheson patted him on the shoulder, but Reynolds snatched the professor's hand and held it firmly with a look of fierce determination bordering on rage. Matheson didn't resist, nor did he attempt to break free. After a tense moment monitored carefully by the deputies, Reynolds let go and watched him leave.

CHAPTER
62

THE JURY MET in the morning and selected Blaze Hansberry as their foreperson after she'd been nominated by Mrs. Whitney and seconded by both Jefferson Lynch and Faison Sheppard. Aubrey Munson had briefly lobbied for the role but quickly climbed aboard the moving train as soon as the outcome appeared inevitable. They'd spent thirty minutes discussing the case when Octavia Bailey suggested a straw vote. They were about to take it when the bailiff interrupted their proceedings and indicated they should hold tight and do nothing until further advised. He asked Aubrey Munson to accompany him.

"Where you gonna take me?" Munson asked.

"Sir, it would be better if you just came with me. You'll learn soon enough," replied the bailiff.

Munson shrugged and told the group to keep his seat warm and his soda cold. He followed the bailiff to a private elevator that led to the fifth floor. From there the bailiff led him directly to Tanner's chambers. When Munson entered, he saw the judge seated behind his desk, and Miller and Reynolds together on the couch.

"Please have a seat, Mr. Munson," Tanner said with great seriousness, then pointed to a chair.

Munson sat and nervously crossed his legs. "Why y'all lookin' so glum?"

Tanner held up a cassette tape and placed it in a portable player. He pushed the Play button, and Munson heard his own voice spouting off about the Bible and interracial dating and his feeling about Dr. King's holiday. Tanner pushed the Stop button and looked at Munson. "Heard enough?"

"That woman never told me nothin' 'bout bein' recorded," Munson said. "Ain't that against the law?"

"Not in this instance," answered the judge, who was obviously miffed. "But lying under oath is."

"Did you say it was a woman you were speaking to?" asked Reynolds.

"Yeah. Ain't her voice on that thing?"

"Just yours," said the judge with finality.

Munson rubbed his eyes and muttered a profanity. He tried to explain the situation. He was busy at work when he'd gotten the call. The phone connection wasn't all that good. How could they be sure the tape hadn't been altered? "They can do that, you know," he said forcefully. "They splice this and that, add a voice here or there. Hell, now that I think about it, it didn't even sound like me. Play it again, Judge," he implored Tanner. "See if that's me."

Declining the invitation, Tanner dismissed him from the jury, then instructed the bailiff to "kindly remove this man from my sight." After Munson left, the judge indicated he'd call the court to order in an hour. He looked at Miller. "You know, I could see why Mr. Reynolds might want him on the jury, but I was a bit surprised you'd actually select him."

"Your Honor, if it had been up to me, I'd never have done it," confessed Miller, much to the surprise of Reynolds. "My client insisted. That just goes to show that while the professor has been remarkably astute, he's not infallible."

Reynolds had a million divergent thoughts run through his mind, and none of them were particularly comforting.

Tanner reconvened open court and announced that one of the jurors had been stricken from the panel. The clerk randomly selected an alternate from the four available. She chose Lillian Cornfield, a white postal office worker in her forties, who took her place alongside the other eleven members seated in the jury box. Tanner apologized for the inconvenience and indicated they'd have to start over again.

Hardy Wilkins couldn't contain himself. "You mean the whole damn trial?!"

The spectators laughed, and the judge banged his gavel. "No, Mr. Wilkins," Tanner assured. "If that were the case, I would've beaten you to the cussin'."

Wilkins nodded his head in appreciation and relief.

"Fortunately, you didn't spend much more than an hour in total deliberations. You will ignore anything you might've said during that time and begin your discussion anew." Tanner looked at his notes. "I was informed by the bailiff that you elected your foreperson. You will need to have another vote, and you are, of course, free to select that person or any other, including the new addition to your group."

Mrs. Whitney looked at Blaze Hansberry and smiled.

"You are to read nothing positive or negative into the decision to replace one of the members of your panel. I can tell you there are a variety of reasons why that occurs, and believe me—it happens more frequently than you'd imagine." He looked at the jurors. "Any questions?" He waited for a moment. "If not, you know the routine by now. Bailiff, please escort these fine people to their exquisite accommodations."

Reynolds turned to the side and looked at Matheson, but the professor never returned the look.

Tanner adjourned the court.

Reynolds excused himself from Sinclair and hustled to the rotunda, where he managed to catch up with Regina, who'd been present at the hearing. "Ms. Davis," he called out.

She stopped and looked at him.

"Could I ask you a few questions? I won't take much of your time."

"Do you want me to answer under oath?"

Reynolds smiled. "That won't be necessary. I have a feeling you wouldn't know how to lie."

"If that's a compliment, I'll accept it."

"There's an office we can use. It's just down the hall."

She followed him to a small suite of offices partitioned with glass and modular walls. He found a vacant area, and they entered.

"Are you supposed to be talking to me like this?" she asked.

"The trial's over," he explained. "Whatever you say now can't help or hurt the professor."

"I don't believe that, but go ahead and say what you've got to say."

"I was just wondering: How many people did you call for your survey?"

She looked away from him.

"That many?" Reynolds prodded.

"I'm not sure I know what you're talking about." She didn't make eye contact.

"Did you make all the calls yourself or did Professor Matheson divide the assignment?"

"Dr. Matheson encourages his students to work as a team, but then, you've probably discovered that by now on your own."

"Who gave you the names of the jury pool, Regina?" He looked at her and knew she'd never answer. "It had to be someone who worked in the court system."

"Not necessarily," she replied.

He assumed she'd cover for the person or persons involved.

"A great many people support the professor," she told him. "They simply want to see him get a fair trial."

"He had the information on Munson all along, didn't he?" accused Reynolds. "That's why he wanted him on the jury."

"I'm afraid I don't follow."

"He deliberately put Munson on the jury, knowing he'd be challenged as a liar and a racist, and you helped him accomplish that."

"Why would the professor want a racist on the jury? You're not making any sense."

He wondered whether she'd been part of the plan or was used like everyone else. "The first fifteen minutes of jury deliberations reveals an untrustworthy juror moti-

vated by bigotry to convict the professor. It places any
conviction in doubt and reaffirms the community's suspicions of the legal system just the way Matheson intended." Reynolds shook his head as much in disbelief as
in admiration. "I have to hand it to him—he covered all
the bases."

He looked at her for a moment. "Your relationship
with Dr. Matheson . . ." He hesitated and decided he
wouldn't pursue the subject.

"Was it more than student and professor?" Regina
completed the task for him. "I was waiting for you to ask
me that in front of the jury."

"Then I'm glad I didn't," replied Reynolds. "You
made me look foolish enough as it was. I'd hate to think
what you'd have done to me if you already knew the
question."

"The answer is no. Dr. Matheson never took advantage
of me or any other student—although the line of volun-
teers is very long, and I'd be proud to be in it."

Reynolds admired her and didn't care if it showed.
"There are a lot of ways to take advantage of someone,
Regina. The worst ones don't involve touching." He put
the tips of his fingers together and briefly touched his
lips. "Tell me something if you can: If you learned he
murdered any of those people, would you still feel the
same way about him?"

She looked away for a moment and conveyed a troubled expression, then answered, "I'd respect him even
more."

He didn't believe her, but the answer stunned him anyway. "Then I guess I was wrong about you," he said disappointedly. "You really do know how to lie."

Her eyes shifted to the floor.

"At least I hope that's a lie, Regina."

She finally looked at him.

"For your sake as well as mine." Reynolds didn't have the desire or wherewithal to ask her any more questions. Regina left the office.

CHAPTER
63

THE JURY DELIBERATED for less than four hours, then notified the bailiff they were ready to see the judge. Reynolds assumed the worst. Jurors don't make decisions quickly in murder cases unless the defendant's a real scumbag. Long deliberations were impossible to guess; he'd be better off flipping a coin. But when the jury was out for less than half a day, it was a pretty good sign there'd be a vacancy in the state's correctional facilities.

Reynolds glanced around the courtroom, which was more packed than ever. No one wanted to miss the verdict or, for the moment, breathe.

"Madam Forewoman, have you reached a verdict?" Tanner's voice boomed throughout the hushed courtroom.

"We have, Your Honor," stated Blaze Hansberry.

"Please hand your decision to the bailiff."

Hansberry gave a slip of paper to the bailiff, who delivered it to the judge. Tanner glanced at it and showed no emotion. He folded the paper and handed it back to the bailiff. "Before I have the verdict officially announced, I warn the members of this courtroom that I will not tolerate outbursts or demonstrations of any kind." He shifted his attention to each major area of the room and displayed an expression that conveyed he meant business. "Bailiff, please return the verdict form to the jury forewoman."

Blaze Hansberry took the paper, and Reynolds noticed that her hand trembled slightly.

"The defendant will rise and remain standing for the reading of the verdict," ordered Tanner. He looked at the court reporter. "Madam reporter, you may read the charges."

"Case zero, zero, five-three-seven-seven, *the State of Mississippi versus Martin Samuel Matheson*. With regard to count one, murder in the first degree, how say you?"

"We, the jury in the above entitled action, find the defendant, Martin Samuel Matheson . . ." Hansberry paused for a moment and gave Matheson a hint of a smile.

Hundreds of black students and community supporters outside the courthouse erupted in cheers and applause. News cameras and photographers captured their celebration as they jumped up and down, joyously hugging each other. Brandon raised his fist high. Delbert wept openly. Some of the media focused attention on the dozens of white protestors who'd gathered across the street. Most remained quiet, stunned. One man tore up his sign and slammed it to the ground. A mother cursed a black newspaper reporter while her adorable five-year-old son waved a tiny Confederate flag.

Inside the courtroom, Judge Tanner reviewed and

signed paperwork. Sinclair sat quietly next to Reynolds, who had his elbows on the table and his fingers pressed against his lips. While he didn't want to observe the reaction at the defense table, his eyes moved slowly in that direction and spotted Miller with his hand on Matheson's shoulder. Both men had their heads bowed while the Reverend Matheson led a silent prayer. The professor looked up momentarily and made eye contact with Reynolds, then lowered his head again and continued the prayer.

Reynolds stood behind the prosecutor's table and glanced at the members of the jury filing out of their booth, pleased with their verdict and happy the ordeal had ended. He turned and discovered April Reeves sitting in her seat looking at her son. She displayed the expression of a concerned mother, but Reynolds found it impossible to discern the real cause of that concern. He thought it revealed a combination of relief and regret, but he couldn't be certain which dominated her emotions.

Behind her sat Ruth Cooper, staring at the jury. Reynolds had no trouble determining her true feelings. She clenched the bench in front of her tightly with both hands and cried in between her anguished utterances.

He hadn't noticed Vanzant making his way toward him. Once he did, he prepared himself for the worst. Surprisingly, Vanzant extended his hand. Reynolds hesitated, then shook it.

"You did a great job with a weak case," Vanzant said admiringly albeit grudgingly. "Maybe you were right: I brought the charges too soon." The admission crept out uneasily. "But we'll get him next time." Vanzant acknowledged Sinclair with an approving nod. "You both will." Vanzant walked down the aisle and left the courtroom, ignoring the hordes of reporters who surrounded him with questions.

Reynolds felt numb and accepted his condition gratefully. He didn't want to feel anything for at least a week. He didn't trust his emotions at the moment, and it was best they remain dormant and unprovoked. He proceeded to Tanner's chambers, where he'd ask the judge for permission to use the private exit.

CHAPTER
64

REYNOLDS SAT ON his porch and considered everything he could have done differently. He thought about Vanzant's last comment: ". . . we'll get him next time." He wondered if that meant Matheson would face charges on the previous murders based on the collection of future evidence, or if the assurance unwittingly predicted more victims. He didn't believe Matheson would continue with the list. The professor had made his point, and those who were named would forever look over their shoulders and live in the terror they'd once enjoyed causing. Many had already left their homes and moved away, and with the announcement of this verdict, Reynolds knew others would leave as well.

Matheson would have the satisfaction that people throughout the country had embraced his cause and developed their own retaliatory strategies. Soon there'd be lists in every state, with their own unique targets. The professor had won. He'd broken the law in order to mend it and in the process configured a patchwork of justice that had a little bit of something for everyone. That something, contemplated Reynolds, was revenge, and the blanket woven from that desire would smother us all.

Cheryl joined her husband on the porch. "No matter how long you stay out here, the jury's verdict isn't going to change."

"I'm actually thinking about indicting myself, but I can't decide on an appropriate punishment."

"I think you've suffered more than enough."

"I failed them," he said.

"Failed who?"

"Those black victims in the photos. I promised I wouldn't let it happen again. Wouldn't let color decide justice." He took a step away and looked into the darkness of his backyard. "I didn't believe those pictures were real at first. I thought Matheson had altered them. When I showed them to Vanzant, he said maybe some well liquored-up Klansmen committed atrocities, but no way would normal, everyday decent Americans participate in that kind of butchery."

He turned and studied his wife. "Maybe it wasn't race Matheson manipulated, or even our desire for revenge. Maybe it was something as simple as knowing we don't want to believe ordinary people are capable of profound evil. And when it happens, we rally behind a flag or a god or a set of tribal customs to rationalize continuing the madness. After a while we're too busy burying each other to remember who threw the first stone or why."

"We're also capable of extraordinary acts of generosity and decency and love," countered Cheryl. "And eventually, that'll make all the difference. Not in one day or one trial or even one lifetime. But good wins out, James.

You've got to believe that. And you've got to help our children believe it, too." The phone rang. Cheryl looked at her watch. "It's after midnight. Who'd be calling us this late?"

"I'll get it," said Reynolds. "It's probably one of my many fans wanting to offer their congratulations." He reached inside the doorway and grabbed the wall phone. "Hello."

Cheryl watched his face grow increasingly tense.

Reynolds listened to the recognizable voice. "I'm sorry you couldn't make it to my celebration," Matheson said. "I wanted to let you know there are no hard feelings." Reynolds wanted to respond, but the veins in his neck wouldn't allow him.

Matheson continued. "I was recently advised of the nature of your distress. There's no need to thank me, but . . ."

Cheryl touched her husband's arm, but he never looked at her.

"You won't be haunted by nightmares anymore."

Reynolds gripped the phone receiver and stopped breathing until he heard the voice again.

"At least not any from your childhood."

Reynolds's throat finally opened wide enough for him to speak, but by that time Matheson had hung up. He loosened his grip on the phone and listened to the dial tone.

"Honey?" Cheryl said.

His eyes filled with fear and rage.

"James, you're frightening me."

Ignoring the desperate pleas of his wife, he rushed out of his home and raced toward his car. He quickly started the engine and speeded out of the driveway, leaving

Cheryl standing in the middle of the front yard, pleading with him to come back.

Reynolds never thought about the absurdity of his effort. He'd driven all this way, recklessly violating speed limits and racing through traffic signals and stop signs. He didn't know if he'd locate the place this late or, even if he did, how he could be so sure he'd find what he feared most. He slowed down the car and searched aimlessly for the entrance. The moon helped a bit, but every pathway looked the same at night.

He parked the car and decided to follow his instinct. He opened the glove compartment and removed a flashlight. He ran alongside the outer fringes of the state park and headed down one entrance, but stopped after a few yards. The path should have been narrower, with trees spaced apart more evenly. He left the area and returned to the side road.

He remembered that Edwards had pointed to a trail covered by thick brush that he'd pulled back to enter. He grabbed at hedges and branches and anything that moved until he found a spot that seemed familiar, then made his way through the bushes and discovered the trail. As he ran, he heard the night sounds and imagined the fingers chasing behind him. He raced past wild brush and through a thicket of tall grass. Slipping on the moist dew, he fell to the earth, striking his face against dirt and stone. He got up and sprinted as if possessed, flinging his arms to the side, pushing back branches that sliced his hands and ripped his clothing. He gasped for breath and felt his heart pounding. The past reverberated around him, and he saw himself as a child running from the ghost.

He heard a man's voice screaming, *"Help me! In*

Jesus' name, please help me!" He saw the mob and the handheld torches and the long knotted rope and the glistening stream and the ax blade that sparkled and fell brutally beneath the fiery cross. He heard a child's voice yell, *"Leave him alone!"* and through that child's eyes he saw the knife plunge into the dead man's heart. The person who placed it there turned and grinned, posing for his photo at the foot of his victim.

Reynolds lost all feeling in his body as his emotions spiraled through pain and terror. He left the narrow trail, stumbled into a clearing, and saw the silhouette of a man hanging from a gnarled tree a few feet from a burning cross. Against his will he moved closer and watched Gates Beauford twist slowly in the night breeze until he became the corpse of Frank Edwards's father, then changed back into Beauford, with his neck broken and his hand severed and a knife protruding from his heart.

Reynolds collapsed to the ground and pounded the earth with his fists. "No!" he screamed. "Goddamn you, no!" He suddenly became aware of the thick warm liquid underneath his body. He stared at his hands, now stained with the victim's blood. After thirty-five years, it had returned to mark him once again.

CHAPTER
65

MATHESON REMOVED SEVERAL plaques and framed certificates from the wall behind his desk and wrapped them with protective plastic. He placed them carefully in a cardboard box, then took the last row of leather-bound manuscripts from the top shelf of the built-in bookcase and stacked them neatly on the floor. He'd begun putting them into a heavy-duty carton when his office door opened.

"You have a moment?" asked the Reverend Matheson.

"Come on in," replied his son, who continued packing. "I've been invited to give a series of lectures around the country. We can use the fees to help rebuild the church."

The Reverend Matheson hesitated, then moved toward the desk and assisted his son in sealing one of the boxes. "During the time you were in jail, there weren't any murders. You're out less than two days and another man dies."

"Wasn't much of a man," Matheson answered as he tore off a piece of masking tape and ran it across the lid.

The Reverend Matheson stopped helping his son and stepped back to address him. "All my life I've fought against hatred."

"Wasn't much of a fight." Matheson finished with the tape and placed the box against the wall. He wrote some identifying information on a label and pasted it on the side of the cardboard.

"It was a struggle. And we won!"

Matheson placed the top on the Magic Marker and tossed it on the desk. "Those black kids who slaughter each other every day—what did you win for them?"

"Freedom. A chance." The Reverend Matheson never wavered.

"You didn't give them a chance. You gave them a death warrant." Matheson started filling a second box with books. "You sacrificed them on some civil rights altar to conceal your own confusion and cowardice. You begged for acceptance from your enemies and lost the respect of your own children."

Matheson slammed the last set of books into the box and angrily confronted his father. "You had a duty to protect your family, your community, your damn self! But you were so busy wanting to be an American, you forgot what Americans do best. They buy guns and they kick ass. And they never, ever apologize for it."

He took a step back from his father and spoke despondently. "You have any idea what happens to a people who don't believe they're worthy of protection or that their lives matter? All that pain and hurt becomes self-loathing, the loathing turns into rage, and that rage has no choice but to strike out in the only way it can." He moved closer to his father and once again sounded accusatory. "Your pleas for nonviolent resistance made it easier for us to accept our own destruction. And now the murder of black people is not only tolerable, it's justifiable. The really tragic thing is, white folks don't need to brutalize us anymore, because we're doing that to each other." Matheson looked away for a moment, then faced his father and smiled sadly. "It's ironic, isn't it? You wanted us to love our enemy, and we wound up hating ourselves."

He lightly touched his father's shoulder. "Dad," he said, choking back the tears. "Can't you see that once you betray the dead, you've no choice but to condemn the living?"

The Reverend Matheson stared at his son with more than a hint of anger, then moved away, remaining silent for several moments. He regained his composure and turned toward him. "I remember when that man called you 'nigger,'" he said sympathetically. "Remember your face. Remember how the tears just seemed to fill your eyes, frozen, too afraid to come out." The Reverend Matheson closed his eyes briefly. "I was praying to God, 'Don't let those tears fall.' I told myself it was because I didn't want him to have the satisfaction of knowing how much he'd hurt you." He smiled sadly. "But I knew the truth."

He faced his son, speaking firmly. "I knew if so much as one teardrop fell, I would have ripped out that man's throat. Made sure no words ever came out that could ever harm you again." The Reverend Matheson leaned against the side of the desk and confessed to a surprised and attentive son, "If I'd done that, I would have become just like him. He would've succeeded in making me the one thing I knew you and I never were—*niggers*. I wasn't willing to become that. Not for your respect." His voice crackled with emotion. "Not even for your love."

The Reverend Matheson moved from the desk and walked close to his son, speaking in a hushed voice. "I wonder if you realize that man finally succeeded in making you into something you were never born to be." He turned and noticed Reynolds standing at the doorway. The two men looked at each other but exchanged nothing more than eye contact. He walked past Reynolds and left the office. Reynolds slowly approached Matheson, who remained motionless.

"You murdered them all?"

"I thought we settled that in court. I was found not guilty. Isn't the same as innocent, but then, Jesus was the only perfect man, and we both know what happened to him."

"I'm going to bring you to justice," stated Reynolds. "No matter how long it takes."

Matheson nodded agreement. "It took more than thirty years to bring the murderer of Medgar Evers to justice. Almost thirty-nine to convict one of the men who dynamited the Sixteenth Street Baptist Church and murdered four teenaged girls." He moved closer to Reynolds. "Who knows? By that time you might even become man enough to take justice into your own hands."

Reynolds threw a right cross that landed flush on Matheson's jaw, knocking him to the floor. Matheson rubbed the side of his face and looked at Reynolds, who now stood directly over him. "Guess I should've been wearin' one of those slings you told me about," Reynolds said as an afterthought.

The professor rose from the floor. "Felt good, didn't it?" He stood in front of Reynolds. "There's a certain

freedom when you decide you won't take any more—
that you've finally had enough. You gain a genuine sense
of relief, a feeling that perhaps for the first time in your
life, you're really alive." The two men looked at each
other and shared an uncomfortably intimate moment of
mutual understanding. "I imagine that's what Bigger
Thomas must've felt after he killed that woman,"
Matheson said softly. "God have mercy on his soul."

Reynolds walked slowly toward the door. When he
reached to open it, he felt the gun just inside his jacket.
He'd forgotten he brought it. He considered the havoc
Matheson would create, the hatred and violence that
would follow wherever he traveled.

"Did you forget something?" asked Matheson.

Reynolds didn't turn to face the professor. He simply
closed his eyes for a moment and then answered, "Yes."

EPILOGUE

Reynolds walked underneath the brick archway into the sunlight and saw students run toward him. He thought about what Cheryl had said and reluctantly agreed: He had more in common with Matheson than he ever cared to admit. But the thing that made him different also served as his salvation and kept him from crossing a line from which there'd be no return. The students brushed past him and rushed to their classes.

His heart beat rapidly with the realization of how dangerously close he'd gotten to becoming Matheson. Ironically, the same people who condemned the professor would have honored and defended his action, considered him a patriot. They'd never recognize their own hypocrisy, and because of that, Matheson had won a victory to be repeated again and again. Hatred wouldn't end, because it would never be seen as hatred. Someone would always demand a pound of flesh and believe that it was justice rather than revenge.

That was the nature of "an eye for an eye," whether it was white against black, or nation against nation, or the state versus its citizens who for the moment were doomed to be judged by a jury of their peers. He remembered a question Matheson had asked him: What do you call the person who bombs a terrorist? Reynolds now knew the answer to the professor's riddle: a hero.

When he struck Matheson, he had felt a ferociousness he didn't know existed. And yes, he felt an enormous degree of satisfaction. But he also felt something else: an obligation to his children and the world they'd inherit— one he hoped would be free from a vendetta imposed upon it by history. He wouldn't betray Angela's and Christopher's future with violence and hate. He wouldn't lose the ability to touch or be touched by those he loved. Matheson wasn't worth that. Bigger Thomas would not claim his soul, too.

The final hour of one's life couldn't be wasted fighting heroic battles or settling scores. He'd reached that conclusion with an unparalleled degree of moral certainty. It must be devoted to making love or music or writing a poem or holding a child or wiping away the tears of those who mistakenly fear the unknown. The great challenge for him would be finding the courage to live life as if each hour were indeed his last, John Wayne and Miles Davis be damned.

Reynolds descended the steps of the humanities building and stopped at the bottom to observe a campus divided by walkways and magnolia trees and race. He watched groups of blacks and whites move in different directions, oblivious to the conditions that perpetuated their invisibility to each other. He proceeded down the path that would lead him away from the university and closer to a shared fate Matheson had attempted to disavow: In the end, we are all our brother's keeper. And when we deny that, we lose hope and so much more.

For some strange reason Reynolds recalled a hymn composed by Duke Ellington. Perhaps he'd last heard it sung at the Reverend Matheson's church ages ago: *"Lord, dear Lord above, God Almighty, God of love, please look down and see my people through."*

He never felt the tear leave his eye, nor did he notice it fall to the ground to be quickly absorbed by summer's arid earth. This time there'd be no trace that justice had wept—only the burning desire to relinquish the pain.

ACKNOWLEDGMENTS

This has been a long and interesting journey from Harlem to Marina del Rey. There are many people I've met along the way, to whom I owe much.

I offer my grateful appreciation to Rick Horgan, vice president and executive editor, Warner Books, for his support, assistance, and willingness to test his own assumptions.

Many years ago, I chose to attend a small state-supported college rather than accept invitations from a number of more "prestigious" private institutions that wanted me, not for my talent, but for my racial profile. My experience at Framingham State College brought me into contact with some of the most dedicated, idealistic, and decent people I've ever known. I want to thank them for giving me their guidance and the motto "Live to the Truth." I've tried my best to find it and to share it with others, whether they wanted it or not.

To my friends and colleagues in the Massachusetts

State College system and at the California State University, I'll be forever grateful to you for your kindness, support, encouragement, and love. I regret I had to leave education in order to be an educator; perhaps I can return one day.

In the mid-seventies, the students of the Black Artists Union at the Massachusetts College of Art taught me the importance of the artist and, through their sacrifice and courage, inspired me to say "no" when saying "yes" would have been so much easier. To Brenda Walcott, Ricardo Gomes, and the students who never compromised their values or distorted our history, I'm eternally in your debt.

To those actors, directors, artistic staff, and most importantly, audiences, who made each of my plays live— both on and off the stage. Their support has sustained me through the most difficult moments and made it possible for me to enjoy and more fully appreciate the best of times.

At an early age, I discovered and devoured everything James Baldwin ever wrote. I never knew, nor did I expect, to join his honored profession. It was simply enough to follow his vision of how the world might be if we lived with integrity, compassion, and love. I owe him my respect and admiration, and I apologize for taking so long to finally pay the price of the ticket.

To my friends from Natick High, some of whom I've recently rediscovered, thanks for convincing me I could sing, when all I really could do was dance.

To the Los Angeles Black Playwrights and Los Angeles Actors' Theater Playwright's Lab, both no longer in existence—but, for me, never gone—thanks for helping to develop the craft and nurturing the passion.

Lastly, to those who offered love, and allowed me the privilege of loving them back; especially my family, in particular, Raoul, Troy, and Anwar—they're the only heroes I will ever need and the principal reason I have dared to dream.